I0695285

The Eyes Beneath My Father's House

FOR SAM,

AS EVER,

AS ALWAYS.

Acknowledgments

The stories in this collection originally appeared in the Westside Fairytales horror and dark fiction podcast from 2019 to 2020, and are still available in that form online. Due to the maleability of performance — and the late stage edits that accompany any manuscript — some of the stories might be slightly different here than in their audio forms. If that is too great a burden to bear, rest assured that the stories remain free and available wherever you get your podcasts.

Thanks, as always, to Sam, whose wonderful guidance and editing made all the stories as perfect as they are today. And also to Yui Breedlove, who finds the heart of every story and dresses it in ink and color.

Lastly, thank you, patrons and readers, for joining me around the campfire for so many years in your homes, offices, cars, and wherever. You're all terribly, terribly lovely for giving a Cincinnati ne'er-do-well the chance to get all those nasty nightmares off his chest.

Stay Safe Out There,
Tyler

CONTENTS

The Umbrella Man

I won't pretend to understand what happened. What's happening.

It was the summer of 1993 in the South Hills neighborhood of Charleston, West Virginia. If you've never been there, I'll paint the picture for you.

The city lies in the Kanawha River valley, glowing like a puddle of jewels after sundown when you look down from the hundreds of hidden and not-so-hidden overlooks south of the city. That's on the other side of the river, where I lived partway up one of those rocky cliff faces. My house was built on a flat chunk of land blown right out of the limestone maybe 80 years ago, when the rich hilltop family decided they wanted one of those newfangled asphalt roads to wind all the way up to their front porch.

Those were the Compsons, whom you've probably heard of before if you've done even a shallow dive into our state's history. They're still around, of course, but now much diminished and living in normal-sized houses like my own childhood home. A stately, middle-class three-story built on the land the Compsons had to sell piece by piece when their fortunes faded, with off-white siding and green shutters and a wonderful view of the Kanawha River when the wind blew the trees just so.

It's on the cracked grey concrete sidewalk in front of that house that this story begins, with me waiting for my friends on a blue, spring-loaded mountain bike Dad had bought from a second-hand shop. Marley showed up first, because he always did, riding a somehow cheaper-looking and more expensive Schwinn. Then Asshole — the unfortunate nickname of Michael Colon, my oldest friend — and Ricky, both on BMX bikes with oversized pegs on either side of their back tires. We talked for a second and then drove off toward the top of the hill, none of us knowing at the time that we were about to bury ourselves in a shitload of trouble.

The mission was simple: ride up and down the mountains in search of abandoned houses to claim as our own. South Hills is full of them. Foreclosures abandoned by the families that couldn't afford them, slowly going derelict as the woods devoured them. What we wanted was a place to bring girls and smoke pot, maybe even get drunk and listen to music on the weekends.

The golden years of our youth were long behind us, so if you're imagining this as one of those Stephen King boys-on-bikes stories, where we all learn about life and each other, well, strap in, Jack. It ain't like that.

We'd all sort of started hating each other in the early part of our senior year of high school, a persistent feeling that grew in time with the piles of gold and red leaves covering everybody's lawns. Ricky hated all of us because we were going to college, and me, Mike, and Marley hated him because he was always whining about how he wished *his* dad could afford to send him to school. Mike and me hated Marley because, of all of us, he was the one that was going to actually make something of himself in school.

I wanted to write, and I was secretly ashamed of that fact, so I hated the guys because I couldn't share that passion with them. Though I wouldn't understand that about myself until maybe two decades after the events of that cold autumn afternoon.

Mike, lastly, hated us because we'd called him Asshole for going on twelve years.

I thought about the day he got that nickname a fair bit over the years, and even on that cold October day, swerving and pumping my legs and standing tall on my pedals to maneuver around rocks on the path. All of us had only just met. We were six and listening to Ms. White, our teacher, reading off the roll call before we got on the bus. She'd said Mike's name, Michael Colon, and without skipping a beat, Marley had said out loud: "Colon means asshole."

And there you had it. For now and forever, Michael Colon was to be called Asshole.

It wore on him badly, and I can't say that I was some great friend he could always lean on. In fact, we just sort of hung out because we all lived on the same flattened part of the same mountain. Our homes were all within walking distance.

There was no greater purpose to all our friendships than convenience. We overcame no mutual struggles. Hell, we barely had anything in common interest-wise other than doing whatever we could to forget that we lived in Charleston, West Virginia.

Ricky discovered pot in middle school and that became a better glue for our fellowship than any other singular act of kindness or intimacy. He often wondered aloud if we only hung out with him because he had weed. Really his way of saying that it was time for one of us to fork over twenty bucks for pizza.

We rode through the chilly silence of late October, leaves crunching beneath our tires and kicking up in wakes behind us. Ricky led the way, cutting into and through the backyard of a random two-story house on a sharp incline and digging his heel into the dirt to turn. We followed slowly behind him, then opened up in full as we turned out onto a hidden game path that shot straight through the trees.

Then we were on old asphalt in a dead, abandoned neighborhood. Ricky idled, and we pulled up beside him as he pointed out the forms of desolate homes alongside the old street. I looked downhill where the road ended in a patch of thick, high grass covered in leaves. It had been so long since somebody paved it that the forest had simply swallowed the old road up.

"These are all foreclosures," Ricky said. "My dad knows a guy comes up through here to pull all the old copper." He spit and adjusted his sweat-stained camouflage baseball cap. "They're like, thick down here but they get sparse up near the top."

We followed him through the dead neighborhood, the houses more like headstones than what I'd seen in any graveyard. They also seemed less anonymous than the houses in my own neighborhood, as though my mind was trying to see what they'd looked like when they were still occupied. Alive.

This house, with the red siding and blue trim, who had painted it such odd colors just to leave it to rot away alone up here? And the next house down

  THE UMBRELLA MAN

from that, what ever happened to the kids who used to play on the rusted hulk of a swing set rising from the weeds in the backyard?

We eventually came to a sort-of cul-de-sac at the top of the hill. In reality, it was a teardrop-shaped turnaround that also served as the driveway for the largest house in the neighborhood. The place wasn't terribly huge, but it sat in an impressive way that almost seemed intentionally imposing. Not so much a castle, but the derelict manse of some wealthy duke. A menagerie of wood and glass and rusted iron that swayed up over the four of us like a shadow.

Marley was the first to lay his bike in the turnaround and start walking toward the place. He lifted his glasses off his nose and cleaned the skin there with the sleeve of his jacket so they'd stop slipping. Then he turned to Ricky.

"You know *this* fucking place was here?" Marley asked. Ricky shook his head.

"Just that there were houses up here," he said. He looked back at Mike and me like we might have known. We shrugged at him and set our bikes down as well. I put mine in the grass at the center of the turnaround, a scruffy patch of green persisting despite the deepening cold. I gave a second glance to the statue at the center of it, a pewter fat man holding a tarnished copper umbrella.

We walked around inside the house for an hour, together at first, then splitting up when we couldn't all decide on what part to check out next. I ventured toward what I thought would be the attic, where the others didn't want to go because of the thick cobwebs hanging over the stairs. They cleared away easily enough, however, and I found my way to the fifth floor of the place over several minutes.

I found an office of some sort, complete with a nice if not overly large desk pressed against the wall to the left of the stairs. The room was small, the entire fifth floor really being little more than the pinched attic space at the very pointed top of the massive house. Windows opened in all four directions out of the box-shaped office. I could see our bikes through the dusty glass of the window on my right.

I only supposed there was a window in the wall directly opposite me, given the bright corona shining around the bookshelf snugged into the alcove there. I wish the thing still held some books, but it was completely empty, missing a few shelves even.

The desk still had its chair though, and I sat in it, smoothing the dusty surface with my palms and listening to the others creeping through the floors below me. I wondered what it would be like to have an office like this, to have time and such a place to read on my own. The others, mostly Ricky and Asshole, gave me no shortage of shit for reading, and I usually had to keep my books hidden so they wouldn't steal them and draw dicks in the margins or block out sections of text with a marker.

Now that I'm older, I think that was their way of dealing with their own inability to read for any length of time. Asshole had never finished a book in his life. He got through his Honors Literature classes by buying homework off better students — usually me — or occasionally splurging on Cliff's Notes when we didn't have class together.

I looked around the room, taking in the dark corners and the thin divisions between the weather-warped wood paneling on the walls. All the while I tapped my fingers on the desk like it was the keyboard of a typewriter, imagining myself as somebody

     THE UMBRELLA MAN

who *wrote* novels instead of merely *reading* them. I only barely noticed Asshole, Mike I mean, wandering around in the backyard.

He was wearing a dull red hooded sweatshirt that starkly contrasted the patchy brown and green rear lawn. I hadn't seen the back portion of the house yet and was surprised by how big it was. Its borders encircled a clearing maybe the size of my high school football field divided into a series of three concentric, leveled terraces.

The outermost was so large it made up most of the property as a whole. The smallest terrace was covered in weed-spotted river stones and formed a sort of patio in an almost ankh-like shape, being a teardrop that spread into a broad, flat line at the end of the taper. At the center of the teardrop was an empty stone reflecting pool now run riot with moss and mushrooms.

The second terrace was overgrown with weeds and wildflowers, more free-flowing and natural shapes that had replaced what had certainly been a well-manicured garden. An ornate construction, complete with vine-covered arches and a sort of hedge maze, now rendered unsolvable by the overgrowth.

The largest terrace was simply yard, still vast and sharply edged despite the wild things growing in place of the intended lawn. The only deviation from this description was a set of boulders. Blackened, it seemed, as though by ash from a fire. Several fires, probably, to cover their inner sides with so much of the stuff, which stood in stark contrast to the sun-bleached whiteness of their outer sides.

Asshole — Mike — walked through the gardens with his hands out in front of him, picking his way through the foliage. He walked gingerly, which looked odd from five stories up, but I would later discover much of what grew in that garden bore well-hidden and incredibly sharp thorns.

He moved as though in a trance, entrancing me himself as I watched his careful foot-for-foot movement through the second terrace and down a series of hidden stairs to the third. Then he was walking through the much tamer grasses of the bushy lawn and spinning to take in the surroundings. He even cast his eyes up to the fifth floor, and I waved, though he didn't seem to notice. Then he took a sudden and direct path toward the blackened boulders and the space that lay between.

For the life of me I thought I was dreaming. At the time, especially, I did, though given what's happened in the days and years since I've no cause to question what I saw from my perch in that dusty garret.

It was an arm, so impossibly long and thin and jointed I figured it had to be an old stick he was moving out of the way. But that wasn't it at all. It crept from that dark space between the rocks, and its thin fingers intertwined in Mike's. It lifted his arm over his head — at the time I thought he was simply lifting the thing himself — but then a second branching appendage slipped into the light.

Slender fingers — so long and thin I could really see only the motions they made rather than the form of them — traced their way along the contours of Mike's hip and stomach. I saw his face rise gently, as though to give somebody a better look at him, and then the fingers were tracing the lines of his jaw, his lips.

My younger self, mind still competing with the shared realities of the thing being either an arm or an

    THE UMBRELLA MAN

odd branch, tried to formulate some excuse for what I was seeing. The possibilities I arrived at were so banal and stupid — and even oddly jealous — that I won't recount them here.

I watched these branch things touch my friend, pull at him, and eventually lead him into the dark space between the rocks. It was only then that my senses seemed to come back to me, followed almost in time by a terrible thump on the roof over my head. The noise was so severe I ducked instinctively.

The room I turned to when I raised my head no longer seemed the dark and seductively inviting garret. It was simply cramped and dirty and old. And dangerous. Even as I looked around, something slipped past the window facing the front yard to shatter on the ground. A heavy dead branch or something similar.

I glanced one last time out the back window and saw nothing but the stately old yard, as empty and overgrown as the back lot of any cemetery.

Mike was already in the front yard when I came downstairs, chatting idly with Marley about what they'd found on their respective trips through the house. I was already focused on forgetting the odd thing I'd seen happening to Mike, who seemed fine save for a bandage wrapped around his right hand. He seemed more than fine, actually, almost invigorated. He gave me a rakish smile as I walked up to them.

"What'd you find, Ash?" he asked.

I told them about the little garret office on the

fifth floor, having to back up to explain what a garret was once I used the word. Then, of course, having to sit through the usual "then why didn't you just say that" cliché people liked to dump on 17-year-old me when I used my more decadent vocabulary.

It's not something I have to apologize for anymore. By 47 I've all but culled people like that from my life, and those who don't understand the words I use keep their mouths shut for fear of embarrassing themselves in front of me. That might sound harsh, but imagine having to talk like a baby in all your daily conversations, for fear you might offend the fragile egos of the semiliterate.

Marley had searched most of the second and third floor, a series of bedrooms and what he said were a "weird amount of kids' rooms."

"Not like, kids' bedrooms," he said, pushing at his glasses. The noonday sun had us all sweating in our jackets. He took his glasses off to clean the nose pads, squinting blindly around the cul-de-sac as he did so. "More like, playrooms or something? There were drawings on the walls and broken toys and all sorts of weird shit."

"Like?" I asked, but he shrugged and didn't bother to continue. One of Marley's many irritating habits. I turned to Mike. "How about you?" He shrugged.

"Oh, I checked out the kitchen and the rest of the first floor," he said. "Somebody left a whole fuckin' piano in there. Isn't that crazy?" Marley said yes, it was.

"What about the backyard?" I asked. Mike gave me a weird look, coupled with that same odd smile. A shit-eating grin I wasn't accustomed to seeing on his face.

"What about it?" he replied.

"I thought I saw you back there," I said, pointing

up to the fifth floor. "There's windows up there you can see the backyard from."

"In your 'garret'?" Mike asked. He brushed the question off and started talking to Marley again like I hadn't asked it. But before he turned away, his eyes flashed angrily at me. It was a only a second, but I saw it. Like a dog baring its teeth.

It wasn't something completely foreign to Mike. In fact, it was sort of the reason the nickname Asshole had stuck to him for well over a decade. He had a sulky, spoiled streak a mile wide down in the heart of him. I don't know where it came from, but if anything had set the final bridges between us on fire, that was it.

"Check this shit out!" Ricky said, coming up from the side of the building with two big, green bottles in his hands. There were no labels on the things, but even from a distance I could make out the shadows of liquid sloshing around in them. "It's like some fancy fuckin' basement wine."

"Oh yeah?" Mike asked. "How do you know?"

"Because, Asshole, it's on a bunch of racks in the basement," Ricky said, waving the bottles around his head like an idiot. Only I seemed to notice Mike glaring at him.

"Just like in the movies?" Marley asked, smiling with just the corner of his mouth. Ricky gave him a snotty look and then grinned.

"Yer fuckin' right, just like in the movies," he replied. "Lemme see that," Mike said, trying to grab one of the bottles. Ricky looked at him like he was an idiot and swung it outside his reach.

"Hey, Asshole, these aren't for you," he teased.

There was the briefest pause, like when you're about to crash your car, and the whole world stops.

Or maybe like when the static on the ground turns and pulls up into the clouds before a lightning strike, clearing the air just ahead of all that heat and fury snapping down to earth. Then the pause broke and Mike snapped forward, almost like he was falling, and smashed his fist into Ricky's face.

The older boy's nose popped like a tomato and both bottles went flying. One skittered over the pavement unharmed, while the other bounced twice and exploded. The scent of wine and blood mixed into the crisp October air. Marley stepped forward, eyes wide and hands up, while Ricky just lay there.

"I fuckin' hate that name!" Mike yelled at Marley, spinning on him like he was about to catch the next round of knuckles to the face. Marley froze and even stepped back. Of all of us, he was the tallest, with me being the shortest and Ricky and Mike being basically the same height. But he was also the lankiest. Mike had maybe twenty pounds on him and Ricky had a good forty on Mike.

What I'm getting at is there's no way either of us could stop Mike if he lost his shit now, which was a sudden and terrifying revelation. None of us had ever hurt each other like that. We'd always just assumed Ricky could kick everyone's ass and that was that, no reason to find out if it was really the case.

But now Mike had a look in his eyes that froze us in place. He stepped over writhing, half-conscious Ricky and picked up the shard of broken bottle by the neck. The glass descending from his hand glittered, a dozen sharp knives arranged in a circle. Marley stood with his hands up in the air, while I thought of maybe doing something mildly heroic like standing in front of Ricky. Maybe.

"I hate that fuckin' name," Mike said, sniffing the

glass and then, thankfully, tossing it into the grass at the edge of the turnaround.

Things deescalated so quickly after that it was like nothing had happened at all. The only evidence was Ricky's fat nose and the bib of blood on his shirt. I thought he'd be pissed, but it seemed Mike had properly chastised him. They were even joking around with each other by the time we got back on our bikes, though I noticed Mike had stuck the bottle inside *his* jacket.

"This is a pretty cool place," Marley said, and we all agreed, though the fight had clearly ruined whatever good mood might have been there.

"Yeah," Mike said, looking up at the trees and nodding. "You know, we should come back and get some of this wine tomorrow. Maybe bury it somewhere. We could probably put it at your parents' place, right, Ricky?"

"Oh, yeah," Ricky said, generally looking down at the ground in front of his bike and wiping sniffles of bloody snot on his wrist. "That's fine. Probably."

"Cool," Mike said. He was riding in front of us now instead of Ricky. It may have been something only I noticed, though he did occasionally flash that weird smile back at me. "You guys can come, but I think me and Ricky can handle it on our own, right?"

"Yeah, right," Ricky said. The big teenager, the oldest of all of us, looked like he was going to cry. Mike swerved side to side on the broken road. Then he slipped onto the path through the trees and Ricky slid in behind him. And, because I swept my bike in a big arc to look back at the old house, that was the last I ever saw of Ricky. By the time I was finished taking in the dead, ruined neighborhood and back on the trail, he and Mike had already blown free of the woods and were headed back to their respective homes.

Marley called to me before he left, sort of asking me if I'd be okay up here on my own. It was a mildly irritating habit he'd picked up around the time I turned fifteen that I'd never corrected or called him on, though I found it boring at the best of times. I waved him away, and he was gone, tossing out something along the lines of I'll see you tomorrow.

And I don't know why I stuck around looking at that old house, or why I cycled back up to it, driving past the pond of wine and glass. The house was situated so that the sun was at its back at this hour of the day, giving the entire artifice a vignette of shadow that didn't quite reach the cracked wooden siding by the front windows.

I glanced up at the little fifth-floor office, my garret, and saw nothing but the square capped shape of it. From the ground it looked like something that would normally house a bell, though I knew better then of course. But even as I looked, what I had thought was a weathervane or some other such ornament — this curved, inverted pendulum shape on a stick — sunk slowly behind the ridge of the roof until it was gone completely.

Already standing beside my bike instead of on the pedals, I took several steps toward the building, hoping to catch a better angle of what I'd seen where the sun wouldn't leave it in silhouette. Something crunched under my feet and I looked down to see the partial remains of a brass weather vein, badly corroded from decades of exposure and shattered from falling off the house.

I remembered the noise of something thumping against the roof while I stood transfixed by the

          THE UMBRELLA MAN

spectacle of Mike and the branching arms in the yard. Some instinctual mathematics played out in my head and I began moving my body into position on my bike. Slowly, as though not trying to instigate a charge from some unseen predator.

I became suddenly and acutely aware of the silence of the dead neighborhood. In the distance, through the trees, I could hear the rush and rumble of the highway as people commuted home from work. Here, deep in the forest, it could have been the sound of a water-fattened river breaking its banks. It had been some time as well since I last heard the crash of my friends' bikes moving through the woods. I was a short, slender thing and terribly, terribly alone.

Without warning — to myself, as absurd as that sounds — I began to pedal maniacally away from that place. Butt raised in the air like a Tour-de-France racer, I used every fiber of muscle in my legs to push that bike as fucking fast and far from that house as I could, thinking of nothing but what shapeless shadow things might be twining out from between the rocks to wrap my face in their scratchy tendrils.

There was no chase.

I made it home in record time, sweat-soaked and scratched head and shoulders from barreling through the woods, but alive and otherwise uninjured. I soon put the experience out of my head, chalking every odd thing I'd seen up to my viciously over-powerful imagination and what my psychiatrist at the time liked to call "my *desire* to see things that aren't there."

The only thing I couldn't shake was one image from the mad dash away through the teardrop-shaped turnaround. In the tuft of grass there, where there had once been a statue of a fat man holding an umbrella, lay a pile of formless, shattered stone. Ground almost to powder in places, like somebody had been stomping on it.

I soon managed to make myself forget I'd seen that too, or at least I made myself stop fixating on it, and I did my homework and played video games and finished my day like the teenage shut-in I generally tended to be. By the time I went to bed, the events of the day were more to me like something I'd dreamed up than anything that had actually happened.

And by that next afternoon, the police were sitting on the loveseat across from me and my parents, letting me know that my good friend Ricardo Diaz was dead.

Maybe even murdered.

It was the only thing people talked about and then it was something people never talked about at all. By the time Thanksgiving rolled around, Ricky was just one of the names that made it into the first five minutes of a speech at any given event. Thoughts and prayers for the family. Let the authorities know if you have any information. Also, don't forget to donate to the Boosters, if you haven't already.

Joggers had found Ricky at the bottom of a holler the day after we'd gone to that house, about a hundred feet down from a sheer cliff edge. The police told me and my parents that it was lucky they saw him at all, given how thick the foliage was and how far out into the hills they'd decided to run off-trail. Another couple of days and his body might not have been found until spring.

They asked me all sorts of questions about Ricky. Banal things — like when I'd seen him last and who he'd been with — answered honestly. And incredibly personal things — like whether I'd been in relationships with him or any of my other friends — answered begrudgingly.

I'm honestly surprised about how much I cried over the whole thing. By the time they were done and gone, apologizing for the difficulty of the questions before donning coats and heading out into the night, I was an emotional ball shivering myself to pieces inside a hoodie. My parents — good people to this day — offered to talk about it with me, or even to schedule an early visit with my shrink.

I declined on all fronts, choosing instead to cope the way I always did, by smoking pot in the woods behind my house and then curling up with a book in my room. My parents knew about and tolerated my habit, though the talk my dad had with me about drugs shortly after I started smoking was far beyond awkward. Not as bad as the sex talk when I was twelve, but bad.

I started crying again, out there in the tree shadows of the deepening October night. It started because of a terrible, stupid, and selfish thought I had while smoking that I would have to find somewhere else to buy weed. Ricky was dead, after all, and he couldn't be my part-time dealer anymore.

It was an idiotic thing to cry over, I know now as an adult. If anything, I can say the late Ricardo Diaz would have likely found it hilarious that, of all the things I could be upset about regarding his passing, I was worried about my weed connect.

My reaction at the time was to stub out the roach and flick it off the cliff that made up the rear border of my backyard. I watched it fall, a light speck against the slate blackness of the evening waters, and thought again of Ricky despite myself. Perhaps to spite myself. Who knows?

I froze, wiping my face and looking out over the dark expanse of the Kanawha Valley and the city lights flickering off the water. I was seeing something utterly, insanely impossible. I rubbed harder at the tears in my eyes, trying to clear away the blur so I could see better. See the mad spectacle or, better yet, convince myself that I wasn't seeing it at all.

It was a man in flight, hovering several hundred yards over the silent Kanawha. He dangled by one arm from an old-timey umbrella, swept back from the canopy as though his parasol had caught some incredible wind and was now dragging him across the sky. In fact, he hung in silhouette just above the distant horizon, the line of trees on the peaks opposite the river, and so perfectly that it was like somebody had strung a great length of invisible cord over the city. Cord he was sliding down so smoothly and quickly he seemed capable of flight.

And the image, this delusion, would have persisted if I hadn't sobbed right then. An involuntary flexing of the sadness still lingering within me. A noise so soft I could barely have been said to have made it. But *he* heard. The flying man.

His smooth travel halted abruptly, so that he swung around in little circles beneath the canopy of his umbrella as he righted himself. Then — impossibly, incredibly — he turned toward me and began hovering in my direction. Slowly, steadily, sure, but I could see the silhouette of him growing larger. I could even make out some of the details of his clothing: The outmoded three-piece suit festooned with a dozen silver buttons, the gently incurved barrel of his top hat, and the great raincoat flapping behind him in the breeze as he floated toward me.

I told myself I was imagining things, but I ran inside all the same.

As I said before, Ricky's death was old news by late November. It seemed to have been the final nail in the coffin for my group of friends as well. I rarely saw them, on purpose or otherwise, in the crawl of months that continued through winter. There were the occasional brush-ins at the high school, and the awkward phone call or two that went nowhere, but other than that we were now all on our own.

Of the three of us, only Marley seemed to mind much. He wanted to spend time with me, of course, but couldn't work up the gumption to just ask after what he really wanted, so I ignored him. It was too sad otherwise, to see him constantly chickening out of finally making a move. And he wasn't interesting enough for me to pursue on my own. In fact, nobody really was.

I enjoyed being alone, to the degree that anybody does. To this day, I consider social interaction akin to spending time beneath the sun in your bathing suit. For some it's wonderful and warm, and still yet for others it is the only truly enjoyable thing in life. They bathe in it, it is how they glow.

But I? Darling?

I burn. I blister. I peel.

Mike, I was coming to find, was one of the center camp these days. He'd been in the same boat as us for years, not so much a social outcast as a peripheral person, a background character to the various high school dramas. But he'd suddenly amassed a robust group of friends — pretty, smiling people who somehow always looked ready to pose for a Colgate ad.

He'd made a show of coming up to me with a group of them once. The word "accost" isn't correct for how he approached introducing me to his new friends, but it's so fucking close I can't think of anything better. In fact, even in retelling this, I was so irritated by the whole debacle that overstating how much of a dick he was being isn't being unfair to him.

Our interaction went something like this.

Mike comes up to me and puts his hand on the lockers over my shoulder, saying something along the lines of "Hey, beautiful." I am not overstating this. An 18-year-old boy, one of my oldest friends, cornered me and said those words to my face. On purpose. Then, doing what I can only describe as a bad impression of the Fonz, he kicks his thumb over his shoulder, tells me to be cool, and says "let me introduce you to some people."

I might have hit him if I wasn't scared of him now. The last time we'd hung out, more than a month ago, he'd punched Ricky and broken his nose. The next day Ricky had been found dead, and we really hadn't talked much after that. Of the three of us, only I was invited to Ricky's funeral.

The cops had asked a lot of questions about that fight, by the way, though the investigation never really seemed to go anywhere. It, much like everybody's memory of the deceased himself, had faded and stalled and somehow vanished by the turn of the new year. I hadn't forgotten, of course, and given the nature of this retelling I'm sure you understand that I still haven't.

But at the time I didn't believe Mike had anything to do with Ricky's death, though some other people did. Nobody thought he killed him or anything like that, but there was some suspicion that perhaps the fight and its aftermath had stirred some suicidal thoughts in Ricky's heart. No official version of the incident was ever released by the police, however, and to this day the cause of death on Ricky's death certificate simply reads "misadventure."

I did, however, believe Mike was being a complete and absolute fucking dick. And I told him so in a way I was sure would brook no confusion.

"You're being an asshole, Asshole," I said, clutching my books harder against my side and pushing him in the high part of his stomach so it'd hurt. His eyes flashed, that same fiery look he'd given Ricky, but thankfully he didn't punch me in the face. The group of smiling idiots behind him probably stayed his hand as much as anything.

I'd heard he'd been throwing parties at some place in the woods. I figured — much as you probably might — that he was taking his guests to that massive house in the dead neighborhood, but as I'd come to find out, that supposition would prove false. But the throwing of parties was certainly helping him climb the ladder to the point he had his own entourage of fairly popular students. Kids whose accomplishments were regularly called over the loudspeakers each morning. Even Stephanie Kirkpatrick, the glowing blonde gymnast who led our Mock United Nations, stood beside Mike with a dumb look on her face and her fingers tucked in his pocket.

Instead of punching me, Asshole simply smacked

my books to the floor and then walked by without sparing a second glance. Yet again, and not for the last time in this story, earning the ever-loving fuck out of that nickname he so hated.

Even stranger, I noticed he had a tattoo now, on the back of the same hand he'd crudely bandaged at that old house. An odd collection of lines and a curve that reminded me of the shape of the backyard where I'd seen those branching arms reaching out to him.

Marley found me at lunch a week later, looking more strung out than usual. He had a habit of over-doing things, and with the second SAT date of the year rapidly approaching, he was overworking himself.

I set my book down when he started yammering at me, voice low and suspicious. He didn't even bother saying hello, just launched into a conversation he didn't realize he was having with just himself.

"Jesus," I said, putting aside a copy of "Night of the Hunter." "What's your deal?"

He stopped talking and took a breath, slipping his glasses off his face and wiping them clean on the light blue button-up shirt he was wearing.

In a world of torn denim and flannel shirts, Marley bucked the trend by wearing no bottom that couldn't be belted and no top that couldn't be tucked. He wasn't a nerd, per se. In fact, he escaped any perfect designation, being something of an accomplished cross country athlete — though not the best in the school — as well as enjoying a fairly high rank in the student government. He would never attain the illustrious heights of student body president, of course; he was too skittish and utterly lacked the ability to assert himself. But people respected him.

None of those people were sitting at my otherwise empty lunch table this afternoon.

"I keep seeing Ricky," he finally said, hissing the words through his teeth. He ran his fingers through his hair and down his face. "Oh God, it feels good to finally get that out." He smiled at me, an almost colorless gesture. "Thanks."

I didn't point out that after nearly three years of all but hounding me, it was ironic that hallucinating the image of our dead friend was what he was glad "to get out." I took a breath and looked around, but nobody in the lunchroom had heard him. It wouldn't be the worst thing if somebody heard him going on like that, but it was still high school. People were fucking awful, and you couldn't show weakness.

Especially mental weakness.

"What are you talking about?" I asked. He drummed his fingers over the table and then left without saying another word. He was gone so long that I gave up waiting for him and went back to my book. Finally, he returned with a smash of his plastic tray onto the table that made me jump.

I glared. He didn't notice.

I made a mental note to slap him if he mumbled another prom invitation to me in a couple of months, and then set my book down beside the tidy remnants of my lunch. In this case, an apple core and the thin paper baggy my mom packed my sandwiches in. Plastic bags were not allowed at our house.

"I've been seeing Ricky everywhere," he said. His lunch, a reeking menagerie of shapeless fried things, smoked gently on the tray before him. He ate, chewing and swallowing between sentences. This effect I will not commit to paper.

"Everywhere?" I asked.

"In windows, mostly," he said. "But also sometimes in the woods. Just a few trees in, when I'm moving fast or I can't look twice. Like in a car or on the bus, you know?" He gulped down most of the soft drink he'd bought with the meal. Marley's parents were well-compensated medical professionals, and he'd always bought lunch as long as I'd known him. Or brought expensive pre-packed lunches that nobody else but him could afford.

"Have you told your parents?" I asked. He gave me a flat, stupid look.

"Of course not," he said. "They'll send me to a shrink."

"That's sort of what I'm getting at," I told him, returning the same flat, stupid look. I absolutely loathed the conversation I could feel coming, one of Marley's most common, in which he'd ask for advice and then shoot down every suggestion I made so he could work out whatever idiotic plan he'd formulated. I cannot stress enough that this man, this boy, was constantly trying to get me into a relationship. I believe, honestly believe, he was secretly a murderer who planned to get me alone in the back seat of a car somewhere so he could bore me to death.

"I can't go to a shrink, people will think I'm crazy," he said, working on a pile of crinkle fries. Without ketchup, mind you. Without ketchup.

"I go to a shrink," I told him. "Nobody thinks I'm crazy."

"You're bipolar or whatever, it's different," he said, not looking at me. He rattled off my diagnosis in a way that made me want to smack him with the book sitting by my hand. It was a hardcover. It would do damage.

"Not really," I said. "Schizophrenia starts to manifest in the late teens and early twenties." He gave me that same stupid look, but I pushed on. "And if you have PTSD, that can cause delusions, hallucinations, all kinds of things."

"PTSD?"

"Post Traumatic Stress Disorder," I said. "It's a condition you can get from seeing or experiencing something terrible." He just stared. "Like the death of a friend."

I said this last sentence in a leading way, going so far as to circle my hand in the air like, "Hey, catch up, stupid."

"I know you like poring over that psych manual—"

"The DSM III."

"Whatever," he said. "But stop trying to diagnose me with something, okay?"

"I'm trying to help you, you idiot," I said, snatching up my things and standing. He all but spilled his soft drink trying to get me to sit back down. "I'm telling you things that might be causing you to see … what you're seeing, asshole, so that you go and talk to an actual professional. God."

I left and he caught up to me by the trashcans, dumping the remnants of his meal and pleading with me to stop. I would have ignored him and kept walking, but he looked so drawn, so worn out, that I gave him another chance.

"You don't believe me," he said. I rolled my eyes and crossed my arms. The copy of "Night of the Hunter" dangled from my fingers. He shook his head. "You know, of everybody I know, I thought you would believe me. You read all those fucking books. Shit like that always happens in books." He ran his fingers through his hair and knocked his glasses askew. It took a second for him to right them. "I'm fucking cracking up."

"Look," I said, pulling him to the side of the hall. A few people meandered past, wondering at the promises of the summer to come. "You always work yourself too hard. You don't sleep, you drink more coffee than my parents. You're probably just seeing things." I sighed. "It's not the end of the world. Just go talk to somebody."

"Thanks, Ash," he said, laying his hand on my shoulder. Not on the side, but on the top, so that his forefinger was brushing the side of my neck. I stepped back so that his hand fell away, giving him a tight smile. I already knew he wasn't going to take a single word of my advice to heart.

"No problem," I said, leaving him alone by the garbage cans. When he couldn't see my face, I let the polite smile fall away and cursed him under my breath.

I started ignoring Marley altogether after that. Between him and Mike, that meant I was now completely alone almost all the time. That wasn't a big deal as far as I was concerned; I had plenty of other interests to keep me busy. College applications and spending time wrapped up with books in a blanket in my room, mostly.

Marley grew more unhinged until his parents pulled him out of school altogether. By the end, he was embarrassing himself almost every day, screaming at random things and ducking into doorways like he was hiding from someone. He tried to drag me into his mania a few times, slipping odd, barely legible notes into my bag or even replacing my bookmark with them while I was in class.

I caught him once and told him off, ignoring his protests about Ricky slapping his palm against his window while he slept and other such nonsense. Having every eye in the room suddenly turn toward us was wonderful, and getting kicked out of class when he wouldn't shut up was even better. Probably the best part of that day was being lectured by the principal about how I could be a better friend to poor, talented, mad-as-a-loon Marley.

I got the impression that Marley had told him we were an item of some sort, which infuriated me to no end. The principal asked leading questions about my sex life that would be borderline inappropriate even coming from my psychiatrist, much less the head educator of my high school.

Though, I have to say, I think actually the best part of that day was the fifteen minutes I had to spend waiting with Marley in the glass-walled reception area of the principal's office. Most of the time he begged me to listen to him, but he spent the last few minutes with his head tucked between his knees begging Ricky to stop looking at him like that, as well as begging me to see, just *see*, Ricky.

But when I finally looked I saw nothing but clear, clean glass and the first few students emerging from their classrooms after the bell.

I was fully cloaked in that dreamy sort of feeling you get from reading for a long time when I begrudgingly took out the trash for my mom. It was basically my only chore, she had reminded me by calling up the stairs to my room. And, despite how engrossed I was in "Patterns of Silk," I broke my concentration and put on all the warm clothing I could find and went out back to move the cans to the front.

There were three of them, all steel-drum types that clanged and clattered over the pavement as I dragged them from the dark behind our house to the curb. Snow dusted the tops of each can, though thankfully none of them were frozen shut. Even through the thick fabric of my mittens, I could feel the icy steel of the metal handles.

Our neighborhood was most beautiful in the winter. Despite being on top of a mountain, it seemed more like you were in a cave once the thick-trunked oaks and pines covered over with snow. The looping street that led to my house was dark but for the single street light down near the sharpest curve and the dull yellow glow of the other light that lay out of sight uphill. Frost crystals hung in the air, resting like blue diamonds on the coat of golden fog hanging over the street.

I put the second of the trash cans at the top of the street and walked back into the relative dark of my backyard to secure the last can. Charleston glittered in the spaces between the trees, the Kanawha a dusty white line of frost and, thin, icy floes bouncing off the river banks. But there was something else as well.

          THE UMBRELLA MAN

I froze when I saw it, or rather the outline of it, my hand growing cold on the last can's metal handle. A man, or a boy, the black shape of him tucked down amongst the trees. I shifted my head to get a better look, moving as slow as possible and remembering the almost prey-like feel of standing before that odd giant house in the woods. I wished the porch light on the rear of our house was brighter, and almost on cue, it snapped off from lack of motion in the backyard.

With the light gone, the darkness was immense. Cold and heavy. Wavering blue afterimages — shapes made by the missing illumination — clouded my vision. I waved my hand frantically over my head. Nothing.

I kept my eyes on that hole in the trees where I'd seen him.

Him.

My mind wandered frantically over Marley's insane ramblings from the past few weeks. Notes he'd stuffed in my bags and books had said mostly the same few things over and over again, that Ricky was upset with him and had come back from the dead. Maybe he wasn't crazy after all.

I stepped further into the yard, still waving my hand over my head like an idiot. Finally, the light snapped on, nearly blinding me. I put my mitten over my eyes and peered into the trees, but there was nothing there. No man. No ghost of a dead friend. Just the city lights and soft moonlight shading everything a touch lighter.

I dragged the can out front and, even while I was admonishing myself for being a superstitious idiot, I saw him. Not the shape of a boy or man from the spaces between the trees, but the fat man with the umbrella.

I blinked twice, trying to clear my eyes of sleep or exhaustion or whatever ailment was putting this apparition before me. He stood, no, not that, he *floated* in a standing position beneath the streetlight at the far curve of my road. The only house down there belonged to an old woman who'd since been moved out into a nursing home, so there was no chance of anybody seeing this impossibility but me.

Light filled the ground directly beneath his feet, the shadow of him was a hazy disk lying on the ground a yard in front of him. I realized the cold of the trash can handle was burning my skin and I released it, stepping closer to my house as I did so. Just as the umbrella man began to hover toward me, arms high and out to his sides as though to greet an old friend.

The light snapped on behind me again, and I could make out no details of his face, though the color of all his clothing and the umbrella were shades of dull brown. I felt a chill against the back of my neck, almost like a finger, and then I had the sense the umbrella man was putting on his warmest smile for me. It wasn't my own thought, I realized, though it almost felt that way. Instead, it was like a transmission being beamed into my head. A sense of radiant warmth that almost felt like curling up in a blanket beside a space heater on a cold day. Cloying. Deepening.

I wanted to fall into it, to fall and fall and fall.

But there was a smell, too, like burning oil. Sick and chemical, it cleared my head and I snapped out of it, whatever *it* was. The umbrella man froze momentarily in place, standing upright again and fixing the absurd top hat on his head. Then he spun the umbrella with a flourish and pointed it at me, soaring so quickly over the street that the mist parted and spread flat over the ground in little waves.

I ran for my front door and banged loudly on it, shouting for my mother to open it and let me in. I turned back to the fat man and saw his face for the first time, or what amounted to his face. It seemed a mass of putty, into which a handful of eyeballs, a moustache, and a crooked mouth had been smashed into place by somebody with an alien's understanding of human facial anatomy.

His body fluttered behind him with all the noise of a bird on the wing, the subtlest rush of wind over cloth. But then he reached down to the street — I saw something glittering at the tips of his gloved fingers — and traced his path with a flurry of screeching, flying sparks that made me cover my ears.

He was mere yards away when the door opened behind me. I had been leaning on it so hard I fell against my dad and nearly knocked him to the ground. If that hadn't been the case, he surely would have seen the fat man change course and shoot suddenly into the sky.

The umbrella man's putty face made an expression beyond elegant description, a pursing of his non-lips and a recession of the flesh around his eyeballs that I suppose might be surprise. Or, better yet, the sort of warm shock one might display at a surprise party. In the last second before he disappeared out of sight — the noise it made was little more than a slight *poof* — he raised a finger to the pursed lips lying vertically along what might have been his cheekbone.

This is our little secret, that expression said. The threat of breaking that trust was implied by what rested at the end of that gloved finger. A thick, curving steel hook, glittering and untarnished despite its grinding into the blacktop.

I thought that night was over, but of course it wasn't.

I told my parents that I'd seen a man in the trees beside the house, which I suppose wasn't really untrue, and they called the police. Half a dozen officers searched the woods while a severe woman in a masculine suit asked me questions on my parents' couch. These questions took an odd turn as well, though I don't think my parents caught onto it as much as I had.

From what I gathered, this woman had spoken to Marley at some point in the past few weeks. She never said that outright, but she asked me questions that suggested someone close to me had been making complaints about stalkers as well. I made half a joke about a fat man with an umbrella to gauge her reaction, but she remained stony. Then we finished, and she made a quick call to her superiors.

She came back, sat down, and told me Marley was dead. Maybe twenty minutes before I'd gone to take out the trash, he'd climbed the fence behind his house and jumped off the cliff there. His mother had felt the thud of him hitting the ground fifty feet down and then had found the back door hanging ajar. Marley's father had been the one to shine a flashlight down into the gorge, illuminating his son's broken body and the pile of bloody snow and rock where Marley had landed.

It was already looking to be ruled a suicide, the officer said, though there were some mild incongruities that didn't quite make sense.

First was the fact that there didn't seem to be prints leading through Marley's backyard, despite the thick covering of snow. And the second thing — though the police had chalked it up to Marley getting snagged on something on the way down — were the five deep, almost bloodless, punctures in his wrist.

I saw Marley the next morning at the bus stop.

My heart leaped in my chest when I found him leaning against a tree beneath the streetlight where I'd seen the fat man last night. At first, I hoped it was a case of the police making a mistake. That he was alive and just as boring and maladjusted as the last time I'd seen him. Okay, in a word. Fine.

But it only took a second's inspection to realize he was anything but okay. He seemed only partially real, in fact. His skin, his clothing, even his normally green eyes were all a dark shade of grey. There were no gory traces of the wounds that had killed him — broken bones and blood spatter — merely the dark and unnatural colorlessness. I looked down and saw he left no prints in the snow. His feet simply disappeared into it up to the ankle, as though it weren't even there.

I looked around and, satisfied nobody was within earshot, I said hello.

"You killed me," he replied. I crossed my arms and cocked my head to the side.

"Really?" I asked, glaring.

"You didn't listen to me," he said. His voice was as colorless as his body, though he sounded more the bored teenager than the lifeless ghost. "You didn't help. And now I'm dead, Ash. You killed me."

"Fuck you, Marley, you selfish dick," I said, pointing a finger at him. He didn't react. I went to say more, but made sure to look around again before I did. "This is some stupid bullshit. It doesn't make any fucking sense and you know it. Knew it." I threw my hands up. "I don't even know if you're you."

"You killed me, Ash," he repeated. I sighed and shook my head.

"Jesus Christ, fuck you, Marley," I said. Then I turned around and waited for the bus.

~

Ricky showed up around lunch, grey and shadowy and standing like an absolute creeper outside the lunchroom window. He also accused me of having some hand in his death, though I was *completely* clueless as to how that was true. I even tried to grill him on the particulars, but all he ever did was repeat himself.

I can't say what was going on, it made little if any sense at all. Between them and the flying man I took my own advice and went to see my shrink, a nice downtown doctor named Martha Peters who refused to go by anything other than Martha.

Martha and I had a nice chat, we always did, and she listened attentively while I went over the deaths of my friends and the police investigation. I even told her I thought I was seeing Ricky and Marley around, just out of the corner of my eye.

I thought it impudent to mention Marley was,

        THE UMBRELLA MAN

just then, pressed up against the glass of her fourth-floor office window as though he were standing on the ledge outside. He slapped the window with his hand, and, though the glass didn't so much as wiggle, the strike boomed into the room like a mallet on a timpani. The sound was loud enough that it made me flinch.

"Are you okay, Ash?" Martha asked. I smiled at her and nodded.

"Just caught a sneeze," I said.

When I looked to the window again, my breath caught in my chest and I had to ask for a drink of water to get back to rights. There, dawdling about in the distance over Charleston like some mad, fat, male Mary Poppins was my umbrella man. He dangled from his parasol, kicking his legs back and forth below it like he was hanging on for dear life. Then he swung up and over the umbrella so that it was inverted beneath him and he was sitting in the bowl of the canopy.

He doffed his hat to me and I opened my mouth to ask my therapist a question engineered to get her to look out that window without me having to mention *why* I needed her to do so. But he seemed to predict that move and quickly put his finger over his lips. Steel glittered as the umbrella man slowly rotated upside down and then rose up and up and away into the sky, still sitting in the bowl of the umbrella.

I dreamed that night of long, branchy arms crinkle-crackling out of the dark recess behind the old house. I was naked and walking into their embrace, brain fuzzy and eyes only half focused. A fire raged behind me, so hot the skin on my back, butt, and legs hurt. That itchy sort of pain that comes before a real burn.

But it was cool inside the little cave, the alcove where the twitchy arms were leading me. I would be fine there, if I just let go. They would caress me and cool me and let me breathe the deep, wet air. And everything would be fine.

I woke in a sweat, despite it being early February and still only ten degrees. The inside of my room wasn't terribly warm either; my parents preferred to keep the heat off or as low as possible during the winter.

It was around noon on a Saturday, and even the sunlight looked cold. It fell in chilly blue lines across my bedroom. I could hear my mom calling to me from downstairs, saying that I had a visitor. It could only be one person, the only friend I had left.

I'd have preferred to just go back to sleep, but that wasn't in the cards. I yelled down to Mom that I'd be ready in a few minutes and to let *whoever* it was know I wasn't expecting company today. To her credit, she relayed the message loud enough that I could hear, adding that she and Dad were stepping out for brunch. I already knew that, it was more for Mike's benefit to let him know to stay downstairs.

I stripped down and got a shower in the hall bathroom, having to ignore Ricky's stupid, empty eyes ogling me from outside the bathroom window. The hot water felt odd with the mix of temperatures my body was feeling at the moment. That hot, sweaty feeling from when I'd woken up still hadn't faded, and I found myself turning the heat further and further down until the shower was groundwater cold.

I dried off and brushed my teeth and generally took my time getting ready, hoping Mike would get bored and wander off like he usually did. That would save me all the hassle of having to tell him to fuck off, which I would have asked my mom to do if it had been literally any other person on earth. But if I had her get rid of Mike on my behalf, I'd have to have some long talk about it later. There was also the possibility that maybe he knew what was going on, that maybe he was seeing Ricky and Marley lingering around as well. But in my gut I thought that wasn't the case.

I walked back down the hall in my towel, hair flat and drying over my back. I wouldn't have taken the time to wash it any other Saturday, but I was in the mood to grind on Mike and so I had. Despite the relative chilliness inside my house, I was surprised to find my damp hair wasn't making me cold.

I was wondering over the possibilities behind this bizarre internal temperature while walking into my room, when a hand touched my shoulder and I screamed and fell against my closet door. Mike, *Asshole*, stood grinning beside the little white IKEA desk my parents had bought for me in ninth grade. I glared at him and pulled the towel tighter around myself. Then I pointed at the door.

"Get the fuck out, Mike," I said. He sighed and rolled his eyes.

"Want me to wait downstairs?" he asked, flashing me that irritating, rakish smile.

"I mean get the fuck out of my house, Asshole," I said more sternly. He didn't glare, but his body language harshened. He sighed — really he hadn't stopped sighing all throughout that exchange — and then stepped past me. I expected him to close the door when he left, but instead he closed it and didn't leave at all. I felt my body flush with adrenaline, a hot, shaky feeling not unlike the one in the dream I'd woken from.

"We need to talk," he said, turning slowly and leaning against the door.

"Mike, I want you to leave," I said. But he didn't.

Instead, he made a sort of pouty face at me.

"Ash, we need to talk," he said. "About them, mostly." He nodded to my bedroom window, where Ricky and Marley were staring in at us. Well, no, at me. Their eyes made me want to pull the towel even tighter, but it was already strained near to tearing. I took a deep breath, trying to decide what to do next. It was painfully clear that something had gone badly fucking wrong with Mike.

"Whatever," I said. "I need to put on clothes. Can you talk to me from the other side of the door, at least?" He sighed again and gave me a conciliatory smile, then shook his head slowly. I rolled my eyes. "Can you turn around then?"

"Sure," he said, obliging me. Then adding playfully, "I promise not to peek."

I couldn't make Ricky and Marley give me the same consideration. The only consolation to my dignity was that it felt more like being looked at by the plastic eyes of a stuffed animal. There was nothing left of them to react to my nudity, nothing about them that could care or judge. Still, I dressed in a hurry, slipping on the first pair of underwear I could find, my jeans from the day before, and one of my New Order t-shirts. The one from the album with the flowers on the cover.

"Okay," I said, and Mike turned back toward me. I

         THE UMBRELLA MAN

told myself the way he looked at me was just because he was interested in what I was wearing, and nothing else, but of course I'd be wrong. He gestured to the bed. I just glared at him.

"I'll stand," I clarified.

He shrugged and dropped onto my bed, disturbing the pink and purple striped comforter I'd haphazardly thrown into place after waking. I hated the way he leaned back on his hands, chest pushed up, head resting cheek to shoulder while he took me in. And I realized that was what he was doing, *taking me in*, like he was eating me somehow, even just by using his eyes.

"I made a mistake," he said after a long silence. He rubbed his chin with his right hand and I could see that odd tattoo perfectly. It wasn't a tattoo though, I realized. It was straight-edged, like somebody had drawn it in place, but it didn't look like ink on or in the skin. Instead, the colored skin looked like a bad wound that hadn't healed properly, creating an odd and horrific scar.

Just looking at it made me scratch an imaginary itch on the back of my own hand. He saw and held the weird mark up to his own inspection, turning it back to me when he'd finished. I realized the thing wasn't black, but rather a very, very deep purple.

"This is part of … well …" He took a deep breath and sat forward, putting both his hands on his knees. From where I stood, our dead friends hovered equidistantly over his shoulders in the long, slender window above my bed. "You might have noticed things have been … different for me recently."

"You've been a dick, yes," I said, crossing my arms. I hated the way he was talking to me, in that weird and pompous tone. He sounded like a pimp in a bad exploitation movie, one of the ones that isn't as much fun as it is uncomfortable.

"Whatever," he said. "This…" He made a fist with his right hand and tapped it on his knee. "*This* has gotten me to where I need to be in life. Where I've always *deserved* to be." I looked at our two dead friends and then back to him, hoping to hear my parents walking in the door. It didn't happen, of course.

"What are you fucking talking about, Mike?"

"I made a deal," he said. "With Power. A trade, so I could finally realize my full potential." He stood up and walked deeper into the room, staring at my posters now with his back to me. "I was such a pussy. I was afraid of going for what I wanted, of getting rejected. Of being a man."

He turned to me, that same fist clenched again and his face serious.

"So I made a deal," he said, gesturing his hand to the window. "*Them*, for what I wanted." Ricky and Marley stared dull-eyed and stupid at me.

"You what?" I asked, backing toward the door. My dead friends slipped out of sight.

"I traded them," Mike repeated. "The deal was, my best friends for a taste of Power. Real Power. Power like this." He lowered his eyes and I felt heat rising in my chest, a heady, vibrating sort of warmth like I'd never experienced. My face softened. My lips parted. I could barely breathe. All the air was warm cotton holding me afloat.

"Do you like that?" he whispered. He was suddenly very close. His fingers moved up to my cheek and traced the line of my jaw bone. The feeling was electric.

"That's only a fraction of it," he said. His voice was soft. The room felt dark and close now, despite the

    THE UMBRELLA MAN

blue glow of the winter afternoon. I wanted something from him, a voice in my head whispered. I wanted it terribly.

But I also *didn't* want that thing. In fact, that thing disgusted me.

I wanted to move away from him, from the tingle of his skin against mine. Lances of static danced over the fine hairs leading up to my earlobe. Despite myself, I pushed my face into his palm. Or, actually, something else pressed against the side of my head and moved it for me. Something alien and creeping that crawled along the nerves in my spine and head like little fibrous wires. Pulling and shifting. Getting me to where I needed to be, where it told me I *ought* to be.

"If I want something now, I just have to touch somebody," he said. "Just a touch. A handshake, a pat on the back. This." His fingers moved up into my hair. The alien feeling was so profound now it made me sick, but that sickness was like a fishhook sliding up out of a deep, dark river. I grabbed at it, made it mine. I swallowed it all, hook and line and sinker, and felt it ripping me toward the surface.

"I've gotten almost everything I've ever wanted," he said, stepping away from me. The skin contact broke and I could feel myself slipping back down into the muck. He held his arms out to his sides and clenched his fists, grinning like an idiot. "You know how badly I wanted to fuck Steph Kirkpatrick? I *did* it, Ash. I did it so many times I got sick of her and did it with her friends. Her sister even, and she's in college! A college girl!" He laughed and jumped around in a circle, a gesture I was more used to seeing after he'd won a hand in Uno.

I'd like to say I didn't recognize this boy in front

of me, but I did.

I think that's what sickened me the most.

And just like that, I was slipping up out of the muck again.

"I have $200,000 just sitting in my room in my desk," he said now, smiling at me. "I just walked up to people on the street and asked them to give me these little amounts, then more and more until I was walking around downtown Charleston with a stack of bills like this…" He held his hands apart in front of his chest. "…in my backpack. It was so heavy, like, you wouldn't believe."

His arms slapped down to his side.

"But all that? Getting Steph to suck my dick and getting that money and stuff, all of that was kid stuff," he continued. "See, I can do some *crazy* shit here, I think, if I get far enough. 'Cause it's only a touch, see?" He rubbed his fingers over the palm of his left hand. He put a bashful smile on his face.

"I think I could be president, maybe even like, the king of the world if I play my cards right," he said. "But there's one thing I want more than all of that, understand? And that one thing is where I made my mistake." He sighed. "I guess it's one of those Faustian things. The trade was for my best friends, remember? That's what the Crooked Man said he wanted.

"But I've never … considered you a friend, Ash." He smiled at me in a way I'd never seen before, then he got nervous and looked away. Still I remained frozen in place by whatever he'd done to me, that beguiling touch. "I've wanted you since before I wanted girls like I wanted Steph." He chuckled. "It's fun to fuck, and I guess we could do that, but I *want* you, Ash. I really *want* you."

He looked at me as though I was going to say

    THE UMBRELLA MAN

something in response to that, God only knows what he expected. If that was the way he'd felt, it was fucking news to me. We'd only ever just been friends, as far as I'd known. He seemed to take my silence as little more than a symptom of whatever he'd done to me.

"But so does *he*," Mike said, pouting and shrugging. "I'm sure you've seen the fat guy with the umbrella floating around, right? That's not *him*, just what he calls an 'agent.' I guess you might think of him as a debt collector." Mike looked out the window, checking the sky. I knew what for.

"He helped me with Ricky and Marley," Mike said glumly. "All I had to do was take Ricky to the place in the hills. That house, remember?" I did. "Then Marley I had to freeze. That was part of the deal." He shook his head. "Then he said he wanted you, and I had to do it myself, but I didn't want to." He gave me an imploring look.

"When you were taking the trash out that night, I was back by the cans," he said. "You never even saw me 'cause Ricky was down in the woods." He sighed. "I thought if I just went and got it overwith, everything would be fine. But then I touched your neck and … well … the smell of you. I just couldn't do it.

"So I talked to the Crooked Man and he said maybe *you* could make a deal too!" Mike said, grabbing my shoulders over my t-shirt. There was no sudden burst of ugly pleasure. "I don't know for what, exactly, but he said you could make a deal with him and then you could be with me. Wouldn't you like that?" He touched my face and the cottony fugue fell over me again. Behind him, in the window, the fat man with the umbrella floated up into view. His hodgepodge of eyes were twinkling at me.

Mike pressed his mouth to mine and the feeling was unlike anything I'd experienced now or since, though the few heroin addicts I've interviewed during my later work described it to a T. His lips, his transgressing tongue, they were everything in the whole wide world. The pleasure was full-body and intense, so extreme that my muscles were twitching with their inability to handle it.

But at the same time, it was utterly foul. There was a sickness in it, like running milk through a strainer to find a dozen white worms writhing against the mesh. It made me want to vomit, to curl up and die. And that feeling was that fishhook in my guts again, catching deep into the meat of me and dragging me up and up and up.

I punched him, a soft jab with my right hand. Mike jumped and backed away from me, giving the knuckled knot of my fist a second glance before looking into my eyes. The feeling of him going was like having some vital piece of me ripped away, a sensation so visceral I could almost see the thin, vibrating purple cord that connected him to me. I wrenched back and watched it snap.

Then I was human again, *me* again, though my thoughts were muddy from whatever he'd done. I could faintly hear him asking me what the hell I was doing through the fuzz in my ears. Above that, almost painfully clearly, I could hear the umbrella man laughing in the window. The sound of it was like an accordion with a stab wound playing the same sour note over and over.

Mike stepped toward me with that cursed, purple-marked hand of his outstretched and I launched myself at him. It was a Hail Mary effort, the last possible maneuver. I knew that if I missed or didn't hit him hard enough, I'd fall to the floor and he'd put that hand on me again. Then he'd mull my mind, molding it and warping it until it looked no different than the putty face of the umbrella man.

I wrote a story about a retired boxer for a magazine about six years ago. Until then, I'd thought my form that day was wildly ineffective. That what happened when I caught Mike in the face with that mad haymaker had been an absolute fluke. But according to that old pro, what I did is known in the boxing world as the Dempsey Roll. Without getting too deep into the specifics of it, what you should understand is that I hit Mike hard as fuck in his stupid fucking nose.

Mike's head snapped back so far I thought I'd broken his neck. His eyes crossed and closed and a torrent of blood spread over his mouth and chin. For a second, I remembered Ricky, still alive, bleeding just like that in the teardrop roundabout in front of that big old house. And then I landed on my face.

Whatever spell Mike had me under vanished, though I felt like I'd lost a fat chunk of grey matter in the process of vanishing it. It took a monumental effort to get my feet underneath my body, and a good deal more to actually stand on them. But stand I did, wobbling just enough I had to lean against my wall to not fall.

Mike rolled on the ground, cussing at me and crying and clutching his ruined nose.

He'd always handled pain like a little bitch, but now wasn't the time to gloat. My eyes turned toward the window, where I saw the umbrella man make an odd, surprised face and then shoot up out of sight. Mike took advantage of that momentary distraction and grabbed my leg. He tried to push his fingers up underneath my jeans and I swung a kick at him that not only connected, but made me think I'd torn something in my ankle.

Mike curled around his stomach and I fell back on my ass. I got onto my hands and knees and scrambled for the door, opening it and jumping out into the hall just as Mike's hand whipped past my face. I heard the crunch of plaster snapping and Mike howled and cursed at me.

His fingers brushed the back of my neck as my feet hit the first step going down the staircase into the living room. Electric waves of pleasure, those maneuvering alien tendrils, spread out from the contact point and almost made me lose my balance. I did trip, really, but somehow I used the momentum to twist myself up and over the banister, dropping myself to the first floor.

Mike thudded down beside me a second later. I was already running into the kitchen, where I grabbed one of my mom's cast iron skillets off the wall. I turned and threw it at Mike's head, my fingers pointing straight ahead like I'd just hurled a tomahawk at him. The heavy iron pan clipped the front right side of his skull when he failed to dodge all the way, knocking him off balance into the wall. He slid howling to his knees and covered the nasty red mark the blow had left him.

I ran past him without looking back, all but kicking my front door off its hinges and running to the garage. I thanked God my parents never locked the thing, and I threw it open in a single full-body heave. Normally it was something of a struggle for me to get it open, but this time the segmented door hit the back of its track so hard it nearly shut again. It bounced painfully off my forearm as I dragged my bicycle outside and jumped on it.

"Ash!" Mike screamed. I looked back at him and saw blood streaming down his face from where the pan had hit him. Between that and what I'd done to his nose — the blow from the pan seemed to have swelled his right eye shut — his remaining blue eye looked like a life preserver floating in the aftermath of a terrible shipwreck. He was already climbing on his own bike as I took off down the road.

❦

I don't know where I thought I might go; I just wanted to get away. The reality of what he might have done to me, what my oldest friend had *planned* to do to me, was only just then sinking in.

I'm not ashamed to say I was crying. The tears burned my face. Every inch of my skin ached from the winter wind cutting through the thin clothes I'd thrown on in my room, and I made a mental note to put on more sensible escape attire next time my only living friend tried to use his newfound psychic powers to try to rape me.

I actually thought that whole last line out in my head while I was pedaling, and in the midst of all that pain and confusion I began to laugh. I was still laughing when I looked behind me to see Mike gaining rapidly. Much of the blood on his face had dried to a cracking crust in the wind.

More importantly, the umbrella man floated along behind and above him like some twisted kite. He looked at me as he whipped and withered, his parasol ever out in front of him to catch whatever unseen wind drew him toward his purpose. The medley of misappropriated organs in his face shifted and sank and emerged here and there and everywhere else through his putty flesh. I turned and pedaled harder, but there was nowhere to go. The entire downhill slope of the mountain, yes, but I knew I couldn't get away from Mike. *He* hadn't taken off the thick, warm clothing he'd been wearing when he came to my house. *He* wasn't bleeding heat and energy by the second, so that it felt like his head was splitting into pieces.

I crested the last little uphill bit before the big, twisting downhill sprint that was my neighborhood road. In a second, I was at my maximum speed, barely able to keep the bike upright as the tires vibrated violently beneath it. Mike caught up with me, pulling up on my right with his head tucked low against the wind. He was glaring when he reached and grabbed the naked fingers of my right hand.

Warmth, raw heat really, flooded into my numb flesh. I had no will left to fight it, I'm afraid to say. I couldn't bite down on that fishhook again to pull myself up out of the water. So he smiled at me and we floated down that black asphalt river hand in hand for a brief few seconds like the teenage lovers he wanted us to be.

I'm not afraid to admit that I liked that feeling. Even thinking back on it now, all things in context, I can say I experienced something like true happiness in those small moments. I saw us together as he did, hand in hand, and I realized something.

If he hadn't been the way he was. If, instead of keeping whatever secret lusts and wants he felt toward me buried in his heart, he had taken the time to let me know. If he'd possessed the barest bit of courage, I would have given him a chance. If he'd been direct, forward with his feelings, I might have fallen in love with him.

The warmth that flowed out of his fingers tried to spread up my arm, into my heart and mind, but they reached a blockade.

I was too cold, you see. Simply too cold.

"Slow down," Mike said. His words were calm, but his eyes were narrowed. I could hear the umbrella man skating through the wind behind me. "Use your brakes."

"Fuck you, Asshole," I whispered. Then rolled back on my seat and kicked his handlebars, feeling my bike wobble and then disappear from underneath me. Mike's fingers were there and then gone, and for a moment I was floating in space.

And I could see myself as though I were hovering over my own body, a wispy girl of 17 with short, messy boy hair and no bra. My shirt fluttered around my body and my hair around my head. My eyes were soft and hazel, half open. My arms were flailing in a slow motion sort of way, almost like a backstroke. And that little girl I saw, that young woman, reached up to touch the face of the discorporate reflection gazing down at her. And the reflection reached back. And then all was dark.

I woke a few dozen yards down the street, screaming with the first tender movement I could muster. I didn't have to touch myself to know I was bleeding, and badly. My back felt like I'd taken a dozen lashes at the pillory. Nearby, I could hear the steady ratcheting of one of my bike wheels in free spin. When I saw it, the ruin of my bike made me not want to look at my body.

Somehow, I pushed myself to my feet. I felt a jolt in my head that made me almost as sick as it made me dizzy, but I held my ground and took in the scene around me. Just under my feet was a yard of my own skin and scraps of my shirt. I looked down to see the remnants of the t-shirt hanging from my neck like a bib, just barely covering my breasts. I turned my attention to the back of my arm, which looked like burger.

"Shit," I said, or something like that.

The fat man with the umbrella stood in the roadway. He was still and silent, half a dozen eyes arranged in a crescent down the right side of his face. They blinked and shifted and looked in disparate directions, almost as though a few of them were confused how they'd gotten there. I stuck my tongue out at him, because I was too tired to try flipping him off and I didn't know what else to do. His own tongue flipped loose of an opening where a nose should usually be and waggled at me.

Loose flesh around some of his eyes puckered in a sort of smile.

"Ash … Ashley," Mike said. I followed his voice to what was left of him. He lay in a pile against the base of an oak tree sprouting out of the ground maybe two dozen yards up from where I'd come to, just inches from the cliff edge and the glittering white expanse of the river valley. I won't get too into detail, but it was readily apparent he'd never walk again, possibly not live at all. I gave him a piteous look that I don't think he could see, given the condition of his skull.

I did feel bad for him, without the effects of whatever his touch did. Despite the fact that I'd done this to him because of what he'd tried, what he would have done to me, I felt bad for him. I felt terrible for him, in fact. It almost seemed like all this was my fault, for not noticing whatever was growing inside him soon enough to help.

"Is … he near me?" he asked. His voice bubbled and cracked.

"Yeah," I said. The umbrella man swept closer to us.

"Take her," Mike said. "Help me. I'll do anything."

I put my foot on his shoulder and pushed. He simply vanished over the cliff edge, making no noise or sounds of protest. It seemed forever before I heard the soft thud of him hitting the ground. I didn't bother looking over the edge; there was no way on earth I'd be able to keep my balance.

Instead, I looked at the umbrella man. He stood in the air just a couple yards from me, dark and enigmatic and brown. His putty face had assembled itself into a cheap Picasso, mouth and eyes crossways from each other on either side of a crude nose. I raised my arms as high as I could to either side of my body.

What now? that gesture asked.

Its odd mouth smiled at me, and it shrugged. Then it folded its parasol, lowered the point to the ground, and disappeared down into the earth like fog sinking into a warming river. And it was gone.

I spit blood onto the spot where it had disappeared. Then I stumbled to the side of the road, flopped down against Mike's bloody tree, and slept.

I'll spare you the details of my recovery. It was long, painful, and — eventually — full.

The police listened to every detail of my story they needed to hear, all those that made sense anyway. To their credit, they avoided making a big deal out of it.

Perhaps there are people who'd like this part of the story to end with every single iota of the truth of what Mike had done to come out in the public eye. To say the least, what grip he'd had on the people in his circle faded shortly after his death, and all of them had to create their own stories to make sense of the coercions they'd suffered. But there was no public reckoning, no mugshot in the papers, just a quiet sort of whispering that, thankfully, rarely if ever mentioned my name.

Given the state of my house, my body, and the scene Mr. Brian Raynard had come across driving up my neighborhood road to read the electrical meters for the power company, the cops didn't charge me for pushing Mike off the cliff. They knew beyond a shadow of a doubt that I did it. The same lady detective who told me about Ricky went so far as to tell me so. Then she took my hand and squeezed it very, very hard.

Mike got buried and our principal said some nice things about him during the memorial service in the auditorium. Counseling was offered to any students who might have been traumatized by the spate of recent deaths at our school. The principal knew what happened, enough of it to be fairly disgusted even putting Mike Colon's name in his mouth, but the service kept people from talking about what had happened. And, more importantly, from dragging me back into it.

People forgot Mike in time, just like they forgot Marley and Ricky and just like they'd forget each other and me and most everything else about high school in the years to come. The last person who ever brought him up to me never even said his name.

Steph Kirkpatrick found me at graduation, pulling me aside into the bathroom before everybody had to sit down for the diploma ceremony. She said nothing at first, just wrapped her arms around me in a crushing hug that brought my cheek into close contact with her own. It was the first contact like that I'd had with somebody since Mike had touched me in my bedroom.

"I didn't think it would ever stop," she said, simply. Then, "Thank you, Ashley."

We cried, and we parted. I never said another word to her, and last I heard she lived in North Dakota with some guy she married after college.

We don't talk. We don't write.

I wish her the absolute best.

⌐

That summer, while everybody else was shit-faced drunk or coming to terms with the blue collar realities of the rest of their lives, I spent a lot of time in my room. I had nightmares all the time that felt the way Mike's fingers had felt. Good in a bad way, bad in a good way. I hurt myself in ways I'd like to not discuss just so I could feel something that wasn't those feelings.

It sounds worse than it was, just picking at scabs really.

Eventually, I hopped on my bike and rode through the woods with a backpack full of 5W-30 Pennzoil I bought from the gas station. I almost didn't think the dead neighborhood would be there, that it would have been some delusion I cropped up to deal with some other thing in my life. That it had all been bull-shit. And perhaps it had, for all I knew, but it was all still there where I left it.

I walked around inside the big old house for may-be an hour, looking and touching and pouring the motor oil on anything I thought seemed important. Then I left my bike in the vestibule and burned that motherfucker to the ground.

I think that old weather-rotted building would have burned without the extra help I gave it, but the motor oil stench of the fire helped cover up some ug-lier scent that came from the burning wood. Some-thing cloying and familiar, that would go along well with the feeling of being drowned in warm cotton. A scent that might have had me wandering into the conflagration I'd started, just to find the source of it.

But the fishhooks were in the meat of me now, and they'd never let up.

And so I watched the place burn from a respect-able distance, even going so far as to walk around back with my last unused jug of oil. I didn't know what I'd find back there, in the recess where the branching arms had reached out to Mike. A cave of some sort, or some ancient crypt. A great stone-lined hall that led deep into the heart of the mountain be-neath my feet.

But all I found were the remains of an old camp tucked between the boulders there, some junkie's rural getaway. There had been hundreds, even thousands of fires in that little space, but the rocks were solid and the embankment of the higher terrace was smooth and unspoiled stone. The only artifacts there were five old syringes flecked with mud from a recent rainstorm.

The police found me in the teardrop turnaround, sitting with my head tucked against my knees and my arms wrapping all of me I could touch. In the end, the fire I set burned down a building apparently owned by some reclusive descendent of the wealthy Compson family who declined to press charges. The West Virginia Division of Forestry, however, took umbrage with me burning down about two square acres of the woods around the property that caught after the building collapsed.

I was sent to therapy in lieu of prison and spent most of what should have been my freshman year of college in the company of some wonderfully mad folk in Weston. I wrote a book about it that you may or may not have read called "Skull Crickets" that made me bizarrely famous and somewhat wealthy at a very young age.

Decades passed, which saw me become a writer of some note, though "Skull Crickets" remains by and large the only thing people recognize me for. Most of those years I spent living anywhere *but* West Virginia. Namely I lived in California and then Colorado.

I guess I missed the mountains, though the Rockies are cold and lifeless compared to the verdant roll of Appalachia.

And for the most part, this is where the story of the early part of my life ends — the tale of Mike and Ricky and Marley, all dead now nearly twice as long as they ever lived — with me moving into an over-sized and under-furnished mansion of a home in Gun Cotton, West Virginia, with my wife, Darcy.

To save you all the details, a habit I think I should avail myself of more often, my writing was shit and I thought a move could help. All that trouble with Mike seemed distant and unimportant in my later years — I'm almost 50 now — and I thought that moving back to my home state, if not my hometown, might help me start getting the words to flow. And it did, I'm afraid to say.

Afraid to say, that is, because after moving into this dreary old home, buried in the forgotten heart of nowhere, I made an odd discovery. Tucked into a hidden closet in the fifth-floor garret I decided to take as my office, a closet painted over years ago by the nameless former owners, I found an ugly old typewriter.

And with that typewriter I found two things.

The first was an aged, brown umbrella of a familiar design.

And the second was a note written in a jagged, if delicate, hand.

A note signed with a crooked character resembling a moon and stars, which read:

> *A debt paid, for services rendered.*

And, God damn me for being a fool, I actually used the fucking thing.

THE END

TO BE CONTINUED IN: SCARS IN TIME

Best Roses, Manassas, West Virginia

Save for the towers of flame rising in the East, it was an otherwise lovely day.

The neighbors, shoved indoors more by the generic heat of June than by the distant and consumptive flame, shook off their noonday dreams of summer and walked outside. Rationed electricity made for bad air conditioning, so the lot of them lay in the deepest shadows of their great houses, where every wet breath of wind was at least cool by the time it fell across their faces.

"I've won! I've won!" Shelly Masterson called. Her voice was higher, though no less shrill, than the cicada calls that had begun to peter out around noon. Mike Sokolov found the outside of his home first, holding a hand over his brow and squinting across his lawn to where Shelly stood. Of the two of them, he was both older and younger looking, being eighty and looking seventy where Shelly was very much the opposite. She raised a scrawny arm, oversized leather gardening glove dancing about her wrist, and waved to him. He nodded in turn.

"What are you calling out about, Shelly?" he asked, his mole of a wife, Natalya, not quite stepping out onto the deck beside him. She was low and thick-shouldered. Her filthy octagonal seeing glasses caught the sunlight in a sort of matte pall that made her look all the more like some blind, subterranean thing. To the chagrin of her husband, and most anybody who took the time to speak with her, she never cleaned the damn things.

"Look, Michael! I've won!" Shelly yelled again, pointing to the sign beside her with both hands splayed open wide. A practiced gesture for sure. In her heyday of some forty years ago, Shelly had been one of those thin-assed blondes turning boards and revealing prizes on Big-Three television game shows. She had married the West Virginia state senator she'd been caught sleeping with in one of Morgantown's seedier motels, and that had been the end of work for Shelly.

"Big" Ben Masterson, her husband, headed the neighborhood watch but rarely left his house. Mostly out of sheer laziness and a general hatred of his constituency. Which would, in fact, be the lot of us living in this tiny cul-de-sac on the top of Manassas, West Virginia's Indian Hill neighborhood. It was something we didn't let bother us, because, as you should know, that's why we chose to live here,

So things wouldn't bother us.

That's about the time I stepped outside, cracking my joints and looking around the neighborhood. I waved to Mike and Natalya, which caused Natalya to recede into the house like, well, like a mole. She was never a complicated woman. Mike nodded at me and then Shelly raised her hand, stepping partially out into the street to see me better. She was my immediate neighbor, and my house was the first in the southern curve of the cul-de-sac, which ended at the very top of the hill and was entered via a curving, tree-lined road that came up from the west. It would then wind down through a few lesser neighborhoods before ending down near town.

"I've won, Paul!" Shelly said. "Come look!"

"What did you win?" I asked, coming down from my porch just as Natalya poked her mole's face back into the window of their house. The Comely family, Bert and Agatha, had come out onto their front porch as well by now, both shading their eyes with two hands and wearing matching linen track suits. The suits, like the people wearing them, were faded and thin, being of baby-blue fabric with white accents. The Comelys themselves had powder-white hair and dull blue eyes. They were more the color of lab animals than people, but nice otherwise.

"Look! Look! It says, 'Best Roses, Manassas, West Virginia,'" Shelly said. She was all but yelling now, ostensibly talking to me but casting her face about the neighborhood and pointing wildly at the sign. I was close enough to see the lettering now, dark and swirling calligraphy on a board made of three stained cherry panels. The post was a length of galvanized steel pipe fixed to the board with brackets and hammered into the dirt along the front row of Shelly's rose garden. She rested her fingers on it and sighed.

"It's just so … *nice* to get the recognition I deserve," she said to herself.

"They really are wonderful roses," Bert said, his arm wrapped around Agatha's waist. Her arm was similarly wrapped around him.

"Yes, so very wonderful," Agatha said.

"Okay, but according to whom?" The lot of us turned to look across the street at Cap DeMarco, who was standing on his porch. His house was the only other sitting on the throat of the street, directly opposite Shelly's. Despite it being noon on a Sunday, and there really not being anywhere worth going anymore, his hair was slicked back over his head and he was wearing most of a suit. All but the tie, in fact, which meant Cap was pretty much dressed for work.

"The Manassas Gardening Association, I'm sure," Shelly snapped back at him, raising her chin. "Or maybe the Ladies Auxiliary or the Kiwanis or … or even the folks at the Neighborhood Association down at City Hall."

"Or maybe you just put it up yourself," Cap said, leaning over the railing of his porch and sticking his own chin out. The rest of the neighbors let out a collected sigh, including myself. This wasn't unfamiliar territory.

"I. Would. Never," Shelly said, fair skin growing a shade more red. "What an absurd thing to say. And where would I even get something like it from?"

"Where would *anybody* get *anything* from right now?" Cap said, slumping a little and pointing to the fire beyond the back row of houses. We all ignored him. "You probably had your husband make it for you or something."

I laughed at this, despite myself. "Big" Ben Masterson was a lot of things, but a capable craftsman he was not. I'd been called over to my neighbor's house by Shelly on perhaps a dozen errands in the forty some-odd years I'd lived there, almost always to find Ben crammed up underneath a counter half-drowning himself with a pipe he'd managed to crack, or trying to hold up a ceiling he'd all but pulled down over his own fool head.

Shelly gave me a look and I held my hands up.

"I really can't imagine Ben doodling all those fine letters there, Shelly," I said, pointing to the calligraphy. "That's all."

"Besides, Patty Domingo has much better roses anyway," Cap continued despite my interruption. All of us looked back at the Domingo house at the far end of the road. Even with the columns of smoke rising into the sky behind it, the roses there almost glowed with a vibrant, scarlet fury. The grass, however, could use a little work. It seemed like Jon, Patty's husband, hadn't bothered cutting it in a few weeks.

"Patty Domingo doesn't *grow* her own roses," Shelly said, hands resting on her hips defiantly. "She has her brother-in-law Jorge do it for a song with that landscaping company of hers. There's no ... no *honor* in it."

"No honor in this War of Roses?" said Dick Bailey, my neighbor and one of the few people on the street I'd actually consider a friend. "Who should say there is honor in war, but the honorable? And who should be believed in his honor, that is not a winner, for what words may fly from vanquished throats to fall on ears unvanquished? And what pen should find dead hands to make dead thoughts again live?"

"Oh shut up, Dick," Cap said, and Dick flipped him the middle finger in turn. Dick's husband, Jasper, came up beside him and slapped his wrist until he returned the offending digit to his side. His eyes were terribly tired, but he smiled all the same.

"Hello, Cap," Jasper said, waving. "Are we enlivening the neighborhood again today?"

"Look, Jasper," Shelly said, pushing past me to gesture to the sign. "I've won!" He gave the sign a confused glance and then nodded.

"How wonderful for you, Shelly," he said, then louder, for the benefit of Cap. "How absolutely marvelous." Then he smiled at Shelly. "Maybe you should ask that husband of yours to loosen up on the rationing a bit tonight, huh? We could all have a little celebration for you and your, uh, prize-winning roses."

"Maybe!" Shelly said, and this little tableau of our neighborhood could have gone on forever if the wind hadn't shifted right around then, filling the street with smoke. Mike disappeared back into his house in an instant, not having strayed far from the door in the first place. The Comelys turned on their heels and rejoined hands so that they were once again clasped at the waist. In the thickening smoke I thought I saw something brown staining the ankles of their tracksuits, but Dick was slapping me on the back and yelling for me to head inside.

I gave one last look back at Shelly as she worried over her sign — her prize — watching as she brushed the first errant flakes of ash away and then, choking, ran for the door of her house.

It was her damnable beast of a husband that woke me the next day. I was alone when I woke, as I had been for the last decade since Brenda died, but still I groped at the space in my now too-large bed where she should have been. Where she wasn't.

I sighed and got myself out of bed, rubbing my eyes and then my hips when I stood. The sunlight streaming into my bedroom was muddled by the crusting of ash that had come to cover my house in the night. There was the softest haze of smoke, too, though it was much diminished and not enough to cause irritation. It was more of a foul-smelling fog to be honest, but no more bothersome than that.

The banging that had woken me continued, followed now by "Big" Ben Masterson's insistent bellowing. Some accusations of vandalism or the like. I shook my head and went downstairs, picking through the last of my medication for the heart pills that would keep me alive until they ran out and then brushing my teeth with little more than my own spit as water.

"For fuck's sake, what, Ben?" I asked while opening the front door. The noise had continued unabated through the entirety of my diminished morning ritual. Something had finally gotten Ben out of the house and now we all had to suffer, it seemed. I found him, Shelly, and Dick out on the porch. Dick gave me a surreptitious shake of the head when I saw him, the universal sign of "This is just bullshit."

"Where were you between the hours of 10 p.m. and 3 a.m.?" Ben asked without so much as a pleasantry.

"Minding my own fucking business, probably," I snapped back. Ben, being some six-foot-six inches high and still weighing over three hundred pounds at sixty, turned an uglier shade of purple.

"This is *not* a laughing matter, Paul," Ben said, pointing his sausage of a finger at my chest but not going so far as to poke me with it. A smart move on his part, though he might not have known it. "There has been an act of *unthinkable* vandalism in this neighborhood overnight." He pointed to his own front yard, where I could see Shelly's prize for her roses no longer stood. The roses themselves were still there, pink and white and red all over, but not the sign. It lay in the middle of the street, shattered into pieces, a set of three traffic cones with some caution tape surrounding it.

A crime scene, I thought, chuckling to myself.

"*What* is so funny?" Ben asked.

"I'm sorry," I said. "Did somebody break Shelly's sign?"

"*How* did you know that?" Ben said, stepping back and crossing his arms.

"Relax, Columbo," I said, holding up a hand. "I can see it right there." I pointed and everybody followed my finger with their eyes but Dick, who mouthed an "I'm sorry" to me and then shrugged. "Why'd you cover it in crime scene tape?"

"Is it *not* the scene of a crime?" Ben snapped, turning to me. The man had at least six inches and one hundred and fifty pounds on me, but I wasn't muched phased.

"I don't know what happened to the sign," I said. "Do you think I did it? I was sleeping last night and so was everybody else in the neighborhood. There was an ash storm. You'd have to have a pretty decent respirator to go out in it." Ben stared at me, thinking for a long time before finally nodding.

"Like an oxygen tank?" he asked.

"Sure," I said. He nodded and slapped a big hand on my shoulder.

"Then I'm sorry for bothering you," he said, turning and almost immediately screaming for Cap De-Marco to "come outside and show yourself." I blinked and looked to Dick, who opened his mouth, thought twice about whatever he was about to say, and then gestured for me to step back inside my house. He followed me in and closed the door a bit behind him. Ben was already storming across the cul-de-sac toward Cap and Donna's house.

"Somebody broke Shelly's sign," Dick said, not including one of his usual poetic flourishes. The bags under his eyes made him look almost ghoulish in the dim light of my house. The smoke clouds were so close now the sun only shone through the windows in the later part of the day.

"What a travesty," I said, yawning and watching Ben hollering at the closed and quiet front of the De-Marco household. It reminded me of decades before the fire started, when the two of them used to holler at each other that way in public during election season. Now we alone stood in ecclesia for them.

"Do you have any water?" Dick asked, looking around the house. I perked up at this.

"Plenty enough to share, I guess, don't you have any?" I asked.

"Jasper, erm, took a bath last night and now we're low," he said, coughing and pointing to my kitchen. "In here? I'm sorry for rushing you, I just haven't had anything to drink for a while."

I nodded and followed him to my sink, listening to the thrum of the underground pump I'd rigged together sucking up water from the steel cistern buried in my backyard. Dick's hands were shaking as he filled up the glass.

"How is Jasper?" I asked. He took a long drink of water and then filled another glass. His face almost immediately broke out into a sweat and I realized just how thirsty the man had been. He set the glass down after the third and leaned his back against my countertop, sighing.

"He's been pretty down the past few weeks, you know?" he said. "The fires and all the … the smoke. It's been getting to him, but I think he's in a better place now." He nodded and picked up the empty glass. I saw him watching the beads of water slipping down the smooth sides to puddle at the bottom. Then he drank those as well.

"How much water do you have left?" he asked. I smiled.

"Do you really want to know?" I replied. He shook his head, opening his mouth to say something else, but just then Ben's shouting hit a fever pitch. We both looked to my front door and then we were through it and outside, watching with most of the rest of the neighborhood as Ben and Cap circled each other in the street.

"You son of a bitch," Ben said. "You jealous little shit." He was holding the steel sign post in his hand like a club, poking it at Cap's chest between words. Cap just sneered at him, looking as ever like a weasel slipping around the world in stolen skin.

"Fuck *you*, Ben," he said. "Looking for a fucking scapegoat as *usual*. Forty fucking years we spent together at the Capitol and you're still using your one fucking trick. What, we're up here on Indian Hill now and you can't find any goddamn Blacks or immigrants now? Huh? Fuckin' junkies and everybody else, the … the fuckin' welfare queens and the queers are all out there in the fire so all you have left to blame for shit is the last liberal politician in West Virginia?"

"Still here," Dick offered, rolling his eyes at Cap and raising a hand. "And still queer."

"Shut the fuck up," both Cap and Ben said, turning to Dick for just a second before turning back to each other.

"More like you don't have anybody to *hide* behind anymore," Ben said, poking Cap square in the chest this time and knocking the smaller man back a few paces. "Every goddamn election you'd tote out some new fucking hand-out orphan of the universe and *beg* and *plead*. 'Oh, Daddy Government, won't you spare some fucking cheese for these poor what-the-fucks we've forgotten as a society?'" Cap slapped the stick away, but Ben kept pointing it at him, fully red in the face now.

"Then you'd get what you want half the time and fuck if I ever saw you solve a single goddamn problem with all that sympathy," Ben said, spitting on the ground. Shelly came out of her house then, wearing a dress nice enough that I figured it was what she was planning to put on for the now-canceled Best Roses party.

"Stop it!" she shouted, her voice was thin and reedy. The dress had been tailored in a time before rationing, so it hung off old shoulders gone stickish from malnutrition. Still, she retained some of the old senator's wife's vigor and managed to shut up the two old men circling each other in the street. She walked past them and gathered up the pieces of her Best Roses, Manassas, West Virginia sign, tucking them under her arm and returning tearfully to her home. Ben opened his mouth to say something else, but thought better of it, turning to go inside himself.

Bert and Agatha Comely, intertwined and wearing the same powder-blue jumpsuits as the day before, though most certainly more stained now, stopped him. They spoke almost in perfect union, smiling and interlacing their fingers.

"We're sorry, but our rations are running low," they said. "Can we have some more food? We're getting awfully hungry." Ben looked them over, not quite able to conceal his discomfort at talking to them. I didn't blame him; the Comelys had always bothered me as well.

"Shelly…" he started, coughing and clearing his throat. He wasn't the only one; the Sokolovs had barely bothered to leave their porch because of the thickening smoke. If the display in the street hadn't been the only distraction I would likely have had that day, I would have gone inside as well. Given that I only had a few dozen books left — most borrowed from Dick — I figured a good old-fashioned street fight was the best water to stretch the milk, so to say.

"Shelly wanted to come by and say thanks to everybody…" Ben continued. He turned to stare hard at Cap for a second. "*Everybody* … for being so supportive when she won the Best Roses award." Cap rolled his eyes. "She was going to bring out some rations house by house. I guess she's still going to, I don't know." The Comelys shared a look and then turned back to Ben.

"Are you sure *you* wouldn't mind coming out?" they asked. Ben blinked, sucking his teeth for a second.

"Shelly said she'd do it," he replied in a flat voice, before turning and heading inside. The Comelys made as if to protest, but the wind picked up and soon we were all scrambling to get inside our respective homes and out of the smoke. I had to wrap my face in my shirt to get an honest breath it was so bad. Dick tried to say something to me before we broke apart, but I couldn't hear him. This time, with the smoke came the sound of the distant and roaring fires.

Growing. Eating. Devouring everything.

I dreamt of Brenda again that night, and again, as always, woke to the same half-cold and lonely bed. I ran my hand over the smooth covers on her side and then looked out the window to the haze in the street. To the little traffic island in the center of the cul-de-sac and the dead garden in the middle of it.

Some people fear nightmares, but I find dreams to be the most cruel. Only in dreams can I again taste the sweetness of youth and the promise of a long life to come. All the viciousness of existence is ahead of a childish and blithely ignorant me, instead of behind the jaded and bitter old man that I am. In my dream I sat beside my wife in the cul-de-sac, building a fence as she tended her rose garden.

But I awoke without her, as I said, and again to all manner of caterwauling out in the street. I stood and looked down from my window, seeing the scattered dirt across the ash-greyed street and the gathered crowd of my remaining neighbors. Ben again circling his ancient nemesis, and perhaps the only man on the street who might consider Ben his best friend. The Comelys weren't there, and the Sokolovs hadn't made it past their front porch (as usual), but Dick was standing beside the men and urging them to stop. I couldn't hear anything intelligible, but the body language spoke clearly enough. I sighed and went through my morning routine, knowing the fracas would still be there when I finished.

And I was right.

"Tell me what you're *up* to, you bastard!" Ben screamed. Both he and Cap had their hands on the broken sign post this time. Incredibly, Cap's wife Donna was out in the street now, holding her oxygen mask over her face and looking at the odd addition to the grass in her front yard. A portion of the lawn had been dug up and replaced with Shelly's now broken, though still exquisite, roses. But the addition that most caught Donna's eye, I saw, was not the new roses, but the fresh sign planted in the dirt in front of them.

A sign that read, "Best Roses, Manassas, West Virginia."

"Goddammit, why the fuck would I steal your roses and put them in my own front fucking lawn, Ben?" Cap yelled.

"Why the fuck do you do anything ... *anything* you do, you bastard?" Ben screamed back. "Because you're trying to *take* what's *mine*. Hand in my fucking pocket ... your ... goddamn shovel in *my fuckin' yard*." Ben took a step forward then and raised the tip of the broken sign's post, really just a bit of metal pipe as I said before, and I'm not sure if he would have swung at Cap or not. It certainly seemed like he might have, but he froze mid-swing when Cap pulled a pistol out of his waistband and pointed it square between Ben's eyes. Dick gasped.

"My God," he added, stepping back and looking at me. I shrugged.

"Not another step, Ben," Cap said slowly. He

moved his thumb to cock the charging hammer on the back of the gun, but there wasn't one on that model, just smooth black plastic. Maybe only I noticed. "I'll shoot."

"Fuck you will," Ben said. "Where's all your fuckin' anti-Second Amendment talk now, you son of a bitch?"

"Man has the right to defend himself," Cap said, tilting his chin up and holding the gun out in front of him. The weight was too much for his arm and he slowly pulled it back to his hip. The man's confidence had only just outgrown his arm strength, it seemed. Ben snarled at him and swung the pipe without even putting a backswing on the stroke, a simple sort of lacrosse flick aimed right at Cap's wrist.

Cap's eyes widened at the sudden movement and he pulled the trigger, causing the gun to make a single, soft click before the much louder crash and crunch of the pipe hitting his fingers and sending the pistol flying toward Donna. She yelped through the yellowed plastic of her oxygen mask and stepped aside, though the gun had already fallen to the ground a good three feet to her left.

"Got you now!" Ben hollered, swinging the pipe back toward Cap's face like a sword and just barely missing. The next swing missed similarly, as did the third and fourth. Cap rolled and twisted and slipped his way around the cul-de-sac until something, God knows what but it was damn loud, popped in his hip and stood him up so straight he looked freshly electrocuted.

Had he been a younger man, Ben might have closed the mere five or so feet between them in an instant and brained Cap to death right there, but swinging that heavy metal pipe had all but gassed him, so he settled for slumping to his knees and striking Cap across the back. Cap howled and spun perfectly around the axis of his now unbendable right hip, clutching that and not seeming to care much for the fresher wound on his back. As it stood, the only damage I could see was the fat black stripe of dirt the pipe had left on his shirt.

"Damn fine hit, you animal," Mike Sokolov shouted from his porch. I looked up just in time to see him shake his head and disappear back into the house. Ben was resting on his knees, the pipe beneath his hands on the pavement. Cap had forgotten the fight entirely, and was now screaming about his busted hip. Ben remained red-faced and intent on hitting — possibly killing — his neighbor with the pipe.

"You son of a bitch," he muttered between wheezing breaths.

"Cock shit fuck," Cap screamed, only now looking down at Ben and trying to push himself a little farther away with his still-functioning left leg. Ben reared up and smashed the pipe a good ten inches left of Cap's ankle. "Fuck off, you bleeding cunt!"

Just then, Dick grabbed my arm and pointed across the street at Donna. She'd picked up the pistol from the grass and was now leaning over her four-poster walking cane, struggling with feeble arms to cock back the slide. I could see the tracework of her biceps working beneath the liver spots and iridescent blue veins. The black plastic pistol fought her every step of the way, but eventually there was a click and a snap and the gun's return spring kicked the slide forward over the barrel. She nodded with some satisfaction and pointed the thing at Ben, of whom Dick and I were standing just on the other side.

"Fuck!" Dick said, grabbing me just as I started

pulling him. I didn't say anything, just watched as Ben reared up like some great, fat, ancient mixture of Moby Dick and Ahab, the post of the ruined Best Roses sign flashing in the scant light of the midday sun. Then Dick reversed direction and pushed me over onto the ground just as Donna aimed the gun and fired.

The gun outshone "Big" Ben Masterson for just a second as the loudest goddamn thing in Indian Hill. I've heard people say you can't see bullets moving through the air because of the speed, and my scientific mind would beg to agree, but damn if right then I didn't see a black shadow flick off the ground beside Ben and bury itself right in the side of the fat man's belly. Chips of loose asphalt were still clattering over the ground when he fell onto his right side to join Cap in moaning in the middle of the road. Dick and I pushed ourselves up on our elbows to see if Donna would fire another shot, but she just looked at the pistol once and then tossed it away.

"Oh, goddamn bitch motherfucker," Cap said.

"Cock fucking shit monkeys," Ben said.

They went on like that for a while so I won't bore you with more. Dick and I dusted ourselves off and stood, which was harder for me than I like to admit. The tumble had hurt my hip something fierce, bad enough at least that I immediately felt a kinship with Cap as he rolled around on the ground.

"You damn idiots," Donna said, making her way over to her husband and Ben, dragging her oxygen tank along on a cart behind her. She poked Ben and then Cap with her steel, four-poster cane, calling them all sorts of names and admonishing *both* for "making her have to go and shoot that fat idiot in his fat fucking guts."

I took the opportunity to slide past them and re-trieve the pistol. Donna saw me do so and shrugged.

"Better you than anybody else on the street," she said, beginning to wheeze between words. She gave Ben a last pop in the head, not enough so that he even noticed, and bent over Cap to see if he was okay. Dick, being the only person left on the street, attended to Ben, flipping him over on his back and checking out the wound site.

"I wouldn't necessarily agree," I said to Donna, holding the pistol gingerly and then offering it to Dick. He made a disgusted face and wiggled his fingers at it, so I shrugged and tucked it into my waistband after taking out the magazine. I put that in my pocket after thumbing over the little brass nuggets that were the bullets. Odd how much damage such little things could do.

"Where's my goddamn wife?" Ben asked, sobbing. Dick looked up at me and then around at the yard. It was strange she hadn't come out during all that.

"I'm not sure," Dick said.

"I was asking *them!*" Ben shouted, howling in pain with the effort of yelling and clutching the tiny, bloody hole in his shirt. Blood spread there, but it wasn't terrible. Dick had his hand over the wound.

"The hell do you mean, you idiot?" Cap asked. He'd gotten to his feet and was now standing with his weight only gingerly on the right hip. It wasn't broken then, I thought, but something bad had happened.

"She left after the smoke died down last night to come to your house with rations," Ben said through gritted teeth. "To *all* of your houses. She was going to … to apologize for me yelling at y'all yesterday." He sniffed. "She never came back, and then I woke up to her *goddamn roses* in your *goddamn lawn*." Ben sat up and pointed at Cap, who just shook his head.

"She did come by," he said, all the fight now gone out of him. "Said all that, and then left for the Sokolovs' place. That was the last we saw her." Ben opened his mouth, but Cap stopped him by pointing. "I'm not lying, and you damn well know that. You've been calling me on every fucking lie I've ever told for most of our lives, Ben. I know *you* know when I'm telling the truth."

Ben just laid his head back and wept. All of us looked away from him, giving him that, at least, when we couldn't give him much else. But where all our eyes fell was on the smoke and the belching fire just beyond the pale of the valley, where it rose now from the boiling lakes and rivers of Manassas, where it rested or maybe had already died on the distant peaks, glutted on timber that had grown all our lives and in the lives of all those who had come before us. As I watched the somber clouds filling the sky moreso than the sky itself could fill the horizon, I thought perhaps the fire had reached down into the heart of the mountains themselves, creeping through every run and pit down to feed on the coal there, so that the blaze might never die.

"Sokolov," I called to the empty porch of Cap and Donna's neighbors. It lay darkly beneath the front eaves of the house and still darker inside, only the soft orange twinkle of firelight glowing in the glass. Dick and Cap helped Ben to his feet, Dick running off to his house real quick to fetch some bandages and the like. I crossed the cul-de-sac to the Sokolovs' front porch and knocked, waiting a while before trying a second time. Then a third. A fourth.

Nothing.

I held my ear to the door and heard little, save some rhythmic sort of noise. A scratching sound, though it was deep in the house. Then the doorknob clicked and the front door swept open, revealing Mike Sokolov's dark eyes and the barest planes of his face. The interior was terribly dark, so that I expected one could easily lose themselves in the depths of that place, given there were no candles or electricity or any other light sources save the cloud-befouled sky.

"What?" he asked, blocking the door as though I had any chance of seeing inside. I apprised him of the situation and he told me Shelly Masterson had come by, showing me the tin of eaten rations. "Then she left for the Comely house." He wiped his nose, smearing what looked to be dirt across the back of his hand. "When you go there, tell those perverts we can smell the stink of their home when we try to sleep."

Then he shut the door, and I turned around to see my neighbors standing behind me. Cap was walking without support despite his bad leg, and Ben was leaning so hard on Dick that the smaller man seemed about to break at the waist. His face had broken out in a sweat.

"To the Comelys' then, I guess?" I said, and the lot of them shrugged. The cul-de-sac at large was silent, though the fog of smoke rising up the hills below made its own sort of visual noise. The fires still raged of course, but the sound now was as dead to me as the rush of wind through trees was in better times. For better or worse, we often forget the presence of the things most common to us.

Thinking of this, I looked to the dead garden in the heart of the cul-de-sac, and then at nothing at all.

"How's your husband?" Donna asked Dick as we walked. He frowned and then smiled, so subtle a gesture it may not have happened.

"Fine now, I think," Dick said. "Though he's been in a bad way recently, I think he's better. 'The man is perfected.'" I thought he made a sad sort of noise then, but also he was adjusting the great bulk of the sweating, bleeding Ben up onto his shoulder so perhaps it was only that I heard. Donna patted his hand.

"Is that Plath?" she asked.

"Now and forever," he said simply, letting the conversation trail to nothing.

The smell Mike Sokolov had urged me to reprimand the Comelys about was well present when we, well, *I*, ascended the stairs to their front porch.

The Comely family lived in the second-nicest house on the block, only behind the Walther Manor at the head of the cul-de-sac, a divide of quality they would never make up for no matter how many garish and unnecessary additions they slapped onto the sides of their old home. I looked at the Walther Manor just then, before knocking, in an attempt to hide the fact that I was taking a breath ahead of the door opening. It stood as it always had since I'd lived on the street, ominous and tall and dark and yawning empty as a hungry mouth despite being ever closed. There was not a soul on the street who hadn't seen the name "Walther" on one or more of their checks, not a soul still who hadn't funneled or cashed or otherwise fulfilled those debts through the Comely family's bank. But old man Walther hadn't stepped foot in the house or on the cul-de-sac itself since long before the fires started burning. Since long before that first spark out on the coast and the roaring, gushing, tearing rush inward that had devoured, *would* devour, the lot of us.

"Yes?" they asked, startling me so badly I nearly reached for the pistol, an instinct I had thought entirely alien to me until the second it moved my hand. I blinked, I swallowed, and I tried not to breathe. The smell was really quite terrible there, the only explanation coming to mind that their septic system had befouled itself somehow. There had been similar close calls amongst the others in the neighborhood that I'd been called out to fix. The Comelys knew this, and had never been the type to not ask for help whether they deserved it or not, so I figured it must be something else entirely and pushed the smell from my mind.

"We're looking for Shelly Masterson," I said. "She was supposed to have come around here last night with rations. The Sokolovs said…"

"The Sokolovs said what?" the Comelys spat back, their queer, pale eyes narrowing in unison. Their home was far less dark than the Sokolovs', though I could no more see inside it for them both standing in the door, clasped at the waist as always.

"That Shelly had come here after dropping rations at their place," I said, smiling and showing more teeth, perhaps, than necessary. "Is there something *else* they might have said?" They sighed and looked at each other.

"The Sokolovs are nosey," they said. "Not as nosey as the Ashleigh family, thank God." The lot of us looked across the street at the pile of ashes between the Walther Manor and Dick's house. The Ashleighs were both journalists, when they still lived in the cul-de-sac, though God only knows where they might be now. The fire that had burned their home had come before the great blazes now filling the horizon, but it had burned all the same. Now nothing was left save bones.

"In any case, she dropped off her collection of rations and left," the Comelys said. They both gave Ben a pointed look. "She stayed a long while to apologize for your behavior the day previous. We had tea. Then she left." They stepped back and began closing the door. "Check the Domingo residence. Maybe they've seen her." Then the door clicked shut and the Comelys were gone. I sighed and stepped quickly off the porch, glad to be quit of the stink of the place.

"I guess we check the Domingos' place then?" Dick asked. I nodded and our little caravan set off again, a touch deeper into the cul-de-sac.

The Domingo house stood at the farthest end of the cul-de-sac — only the old, abandoned Walther place being any further — so the building itself sat darkly against a backdrop of rolling white-black smoke and fire. The flames were hot enough to feel, though perhaps they always had been, and the lot of us were dabbing our foreheads with shirtsleeves and the like. The light of the fire filled all the spaces in the house in a way that seemed to leave them more lightless than true dark might, shining through the rear windows and falling out the front windows and spilling to pool amongst the flower-burdened branches of Patty Domingo's rose garden.

Really the best in Manassas, West Virginia, if you'd have asked me right then. Despite how overgrown the bushes were, badly trimmed and supporting a few wilted blooms here and there, they were still majestic. The roses were fatter than Shelly Masterson's by a degree; they might even have given my late wife's roses a run for their money, when she was still growing them at least.

Only Donna seemed distracted by them, adjusting herself and her oxygen tank to rest a finger at the bottom of a petal and pushing the rose fully to her face. She pulled aside her mask and breathed deeply from the cup, staying that way for a long moment before coughing a few times and returning her mask. She saw me watching and shrugged and smiled.

"How often do we ever stop to do that?" she asked me. I nodded. Dick was already up on the porch with Ben, setting the man in a porch swing hung from the overhang with steel chains. They groaned, but held. I looked at the man himself, who seemed a bit pale. His eyes wandered over the roses and the yard, but I don't think he was seeing much of what he looked at. His face was blotchy red and flecked with sweat.

"Patty? Jon? You in there?" Dick asked, repeating the words in a yell when he didn't get an answer. Donna sat down beside Ben and rested a hand on his shoulder, which he rested his fingers on in turn. Dick looked at me. "You think we should go in?"

I shrugged. The others remained silent.

"I think we should go in," Dick said finally, turning to the door and patting around the frame. Eventually he came up with a small, copper-colored key that slid right into the lock. He turned it and then opened the door onto a pitch-black foyer.

"How'd you know that was there?" I asked him.

"I'm nosey," was all he said.

Only Cap hobbled into the house along with us, sputtering curses like a bad seal on a steam tank. Dick fumbled around in the dark for a while and then I heard the snap of a flint wheel. Then there was light in the room, fluttering dimly over the walls from a half-burned candle in Dick's hand. I looked at it and then at him.

"There's a few more on the shelf right there," he said. "I've seen them burning here before, but not for a few days. Maybe a week. I thought they'd just … run out or something." He shrugged. The light on his face looked eerie. "Grab yourself one and we'll search the house real quick."

"Search the house?" I asked.

"If they were … I don't know, around? If that was the case, they would have said something to us already."

"Maybe they're sleeping."

"Maybe they're trapped under a mountain of fallen newspapers in the basement, who knows?" He started walking deeper into the house. "I'll check the first floor and you go upstairs."

I nodded and got to it, taking the broad wooden staircase beside the front door up to the second level. Jon Domingo had legitimately ruined his knee slipping down an embankment at the golf course in White Sulfur Springs, so handicap-accessibility hardware seemed to sprout from every surface like some polished steel and plastic parasite. The flame from my candle danced over the well-oiled and maintained oak paneling beside the staircase and also reflected brightly off the dozens of silver screws that had bolted a newer, sturdier handrail to the wall.

The handrail, in fact, started at the base of the

stairs and filled every wall on the second floor, like some broken, alien monorail that glowed just a touch brighter than all the rest of the interiors.

I checked everywhere but found nothing on the second floor. About ten rooms, most cordoned off with weather plastic to keep the heating bill down, and only one showing any sign of habitation. Their bedroom, of course, and the adjoining bathroom.

In this one room, more than any others, the candle wasn't completely necessary. The fires filled the room with orange light that held steady compared to the inconsistent yellow flicker of the candle flame. Its only use here was to penetrate the deepest shadows — in the closet, behind the shower curtain, under the bed. I found only a single, dusty slipper in my searching — lost for how inconvenient it might have been for the Domingos to retrieve it.

I sighed and turned to the windows overlooking their backyard. Their land, as I understood it, likely ran a good ways down through the woods on the back end of the mountain on which our little Indian Hill neighborhood had been built. The yard itself was tidy, mostly plant beds and a few ornamental trees, and then a fence and the thick expanse of old Appalachian forest beyond.

And beyond that, the fire.

It was close now, closer than I ever expected to see it, though I'd known for a while it would come. Perhaps a hundred meters — maybe twice that, I couldn't really tell — the flames rose in a massive column, a wall so wide it obstructed the view of the lower valley behind it. I shook my head and rested my forehead on the glass, which was terribly warm to the touch, and closed my eyes.

We'd known it was coming for a long time. I'd

known better than anybody else, for the most part, though there was little in the way of anything done about it. Oh, people complained and all that. Cap was particularly fond of spouting out his knowledge about the impending collapse, but mostly because Ben's position was that it *wouldn't, couldn't* ever come. The rest of the neighborhood fretted about it in their way, but nobody ever *did* anything. No hard action. No decisive strike. We just sat about and waited. And now it was here.

I opened my eyes and looked down at the yard again, at all of Patty's wonderful plants already starting to brown and wither in their gardens. It was a shame that honest work would all go to rot soon, but what didn't?

Looking down and pondering all that, I noticed something odd. A bit of weirdness in one of the well-coifed bushes just beneath the window. Like a sort of depression, and then again, something else.

I went down the stairs in a hurry, finding Dick just as he was coming up out of the Domingos' basement. Ben and Donna had moved inside and were sitting at the living room table with Cap, sharing drinks from a jug of water the Domingos had left out on the counter.

"There's no food left in here," Ben said, his words a dull whisper. His face was terribly pale now, almost completely white. "They haven't gotten anything to eat from me in a while either."

"Maybe they left?" Dick offered. "I couldn't find anything on this floor *or* in the basement. All the, erm, newspaper piles are still standing straight where Jon left them." He looked at me. "Anything upstairs?"

"No," I started. "But … there's something odd in the back garden. Can you come check it out with me?"

We headed out back and it was immediately obvious something terrible had happened. The bush I had seen was smashed in as though something terribly heavy, a person perhaps, had fallen fully into it. Branches were smashed and snapped clean off in places. Dick bent into the plant and pulled up a single stick covered in old blood. He held it out to me and I took it, then leaned down and held my candle into the shadow of the destruction.

"Jesus," Dick said. I repeat the casual blasphemy, sweeping the candle back and forth to get a better look. Dried, tacky blood filled the space, and even though it was dry, you could still smell it clear as day. I pushed my fingers into the soil and pulled up a reeking lump of dirt, rubbing it between my fingers. We looked around and saw more, streaks dried here and there on the siding of the house and, following the trail further, on the gate leading out of the backyard.

Dick called the others out and showed them what we'd found. Their reactions were mostly indistinguishable from ours, only Donna started crying. Cap wrapped an arm around her, stifling a hiss when the movement aggravated his bad hip. She patted his arm and rubbed her face dry on his shirt.

"Do you think it could be Shelly?" Ben asked. His face was screwed up with worry, but he was keeping it together as best he could.

"I don't think so," I said, pointing back at the bush. "All the broken branches are completely browned. Whatever happened there happened at least a few days ago."

"God, while we were all out having that stupid fucking argument in the street?" Cap said. "What the fuck is going on in this neighborhood? What the fuck could have happened here?"

"I don't know," Dick said, pushing the wooden gate open and stepping into the side yard. "But I'll tell you there's more blood out here, and it leads right to the Comleys' back door."

The air in the Comelys' backyard was barely breathable, full of whatever it was in their house that stank so badly and the choking smoke of the burning hillside below. It was apparent that, no matter what we found, there was little time left to live in the neighborhood.

"Jesus Christ," Dick said, leading the way through a thicket of evergreen bushes that had once been cut into tidy geometric shapes. Between the lack of trimming and the browning effects of the fire, the things looked like balls of rust.

We found our way to where Dick stood alone on the house's rear patio, a sweeping disk that lay flat over the hill behind us. I'd been there before — probably everybody in the neighborhood had at one time or another for parties and the like — though we were never all invited together. The Comleys were like that.

The far end of the disk had crumbled from heat and looked for all the world like a great, grey cookie with a bite out of it. I watched the platform crack, and more slid down into the fire below. The noise of it startled me almost as much as Donna's wheezing scream.

She'd followed Dick through directly, me holding the nasty branches of the bushes aside for her. Ben and Cap were behind me, leaning on each other now that both of them could barely walk. Cap helped Ben against the wall, where the larger man slid down to lie on the concrete, and then stepped up beside his wife. He held a hand to his mouth and then looked away.

It was bones, I saw, and some other human detritus piled into a blue plastic bucket. The kind you could get from any hardware store. Half a skull lay atop the pile of larger bones — all broken neatly in the centers — its black hollow of an eye catching only some of the firelight now bathing all of us. Mixed in with the larger items were other things: torn shreds of clothing and even long, clotted lumps of human hair. I took a breath and picked up the bucket, walking to the edge of the broken patio.

"What are you doing?" Dick asked, the others' eyes repeating the question. I said nothing and looked down into the fire. The heat was terrible. Terrible. I tipped the bones over the edge and watched them disappear without fanfare. The flames didn't care what mixed in with their meal.

"Better that than this bucket," I said, returning to the others. Dick opened his mouth to protest. "Look," I interrupted. "Nobody's coming. Nobody's even left." He swallowed and looked past me to the fire, maybe thinking of his own place in it.

"That was Patty Domingo's shirt in there," Donna said. I turned to her, expecting to see her look at me, or Dick or the others. Maybe down at the ground, I don't know. What she was looking at were the four blue eyes of the Comelys, who stood in the dark entryway of their house, arm in arm. Even as I watched, they stepped back into the darkness, only their eyes remaining to be seen and then not even that.

"This can't stand," Ben said, pushing himself to

his feet. "Where the hell is Shelly?" He was talking, it seemed, to the ground. Blood now covered all of his lower belly and had crept down the interior leg of his pants. His face was drawn. Deflated. Blue bags hung beneath his eyes.

"Goddamnit," he said, almost crying. "Where's my wife?"

With a speed I'd never expected of the man, even in his prime, Ben shoved himself off the wall and turned into the house. Donna gasped and called for him, then for her husband as well when Cap barreled into the house behind the larger man. Then Dick was running into the house and me behind him, pulling Cap's gun from my waistband and shrugging at a confused and, honestly, terrified Donna as I ran inside.

The house was terribly dark and lit only by the ugly orange light of the fire and a smattering of votive candles I knew for sure didn't belong to the Comely family. I picked up one reading Santo Niño de Atocha and Dick grabbed one reading La Virgen de Guadalupe. Of the two, that one I understood the translation for.

We walked deeper into the house, waving the candles around to beat back the darker shadows in the corners. We found nothing interesting, save some plates and a gas grill set up in the kitchen. Five places had been set at the table, and every plate was still dirty with some sort of brown sauce. The worst of the bad smell in the house wasn't here, however. It quite clearly came from the open doorway at the far end of the house leading downstairs. Steady, yellow electric light poured up from down there to shine on the ceiling and the plush Middle Eastern carpets adorning the Comely living room.

Ben huffed over that way, pawing sweat off his

head and mumbling something under his breath. Cap caught up with him, speaking sense to the best of his ability and doing nothing to stop the sweating, bleeding bull of a man from storming toward that doorway. He stopped him right at the edge, however, and Dick and I caught up, both looking down there into the rough shadows at the bottom of the stairs.

"You're almost in no condition to use stairs," Cap said. "Why don't you let the others go down first, huh?" Ben slumped against the wall and shook his head.

"Fine then," he muttered. His voice was barely there anymore, but he continued in a soft whisper. "But I knew them. I knew them. What is all this?"

I had the honor of the first descent, the shitty little plastic gun held out at arm's length in a way I'd only ever seen in movies. The stairs were firm but felt unsteady all the same because of how bad my legs were quaking. Then I was at the bottom, standing on smooth stone and holding my votive candle out underneath the gun.

It was all quite terrible. The Comelys had done a good enough job of corralling the blood off their makeshift butcher's table into a series of mostly full buckets at the foot of the thing. Still, plenty more had dripped from the edges or splattered out against the wall. There was a place to the side of the buckets as well where they had hanged our neighbors before slitting them like pigs. The blood there, the lion's share of it, so to say, had been caught in a big, pink plastic storage box labeled, "CHANUKAH." A collection of ornaments I knew to belong to that holiday lay in an out-of-the-way pile beside the staircase.

What was left of Shelly lay on the butcher table. I could see only her hair; the body itself was on its belly with her face away from me, but that was enough. Her skin had been flayed away piecemeal and hung in strips on a rack against the far wall, where a chugging generator powered the basement lights. Some of the skin remained still, on the hands and feet, the frontward sections of her body, but largely only the deeper flesh remained. Often not even that.

Sections of her thighs and calves were gone, along with both shoulders and all of her ass. I could see the plastic and steel fixtures in her hip where a broken section had been replaced years ago, now laid bare beneath the heartless yellow lamps of this butcher's kitchen. I turned to the others, strewn out along the stairwell, Ben at the topmost step, and tried to tell them not to come downstairs.

Then Bert Comely stabbed Ben in the side of the throat, flitting out of the darkness beyond the electric lights like a specter. His eyes were as simple — as dull — as ever, though slightly wider. Even from down here I could see the tendons on his scrawny wrist flexing as he pushed the knife through the front of Ben's throat, cutting through the trachea, the veins, everything. Blood bubbled out of Ben's mouth and he gave a single, confused look down at the rest of us before turning with a mad ferocity and grabbing Bert by his face.

They tumbled down the stairs together, Bert's eyes full of actual shock now even as he stabbed Ben over and over again in the back and neck. Cap shouted for Donna and pushed her against the side of the stairwell just in time to keep her from getting swept up in the tangle of bloody bodies. He might have dodged as well, had his hip not locked back up at just that moment. I saw the twinge of pain in his eyes as the leg straightened, pushing him directly in front of Ben and Bert at just the wrong moment. The weight of them hit the much scrawnier man and sent him flying down the stairs and toward us.

"Jesus, fuck!" Dick screamed, smashing me out of the way with his arm and nearly knocking the wind clean out of me. I stumbled over something wet and greasy and then slid across the floor with my arms out, shaking, trying to find my balance. It was then that Agatha Comely made her appearance, slipping out from the dark spaces beneath the stairs themselves and rushing me with a carving knife. I smacked her in the face with the gun, which was satisfying if ineffective, given how much of the knife she immediately buried in my guts.

I screamed, nearly lost consciousness, and then started pushing her away from me with the barrel of the gun. Her dull, stupid blue eyes locked on mine, flitting between me and the pile of bodies on the ground. I realized then that neither Donna nor Dick had noticed she'd attacked me. They were focused on Bert, who was now trapped beneath Ben's dead body, still viciously swiping at the two of them while screeching like an addled monkey for his wife to come help him.

"I'll … shoot," I said, pressing the gun into Agatha's eye, trying to hurt her enough to cause some retreat. I was slumped all the way against the wall, hand on hers, trying to keep her from twisting the confounded bit of steel up into my heart.

"Your gun doesn't have a magazine in it," she whispered, smiling at me with bloody teeth. I realized she was right; I hadn't reloaded the thing since Cap and Ben had their stupid little fight this morning. I screamed and pushed harder anyway, pulling the trigger as I did so and surprising myself when Agatha's eye suddenly burned bright white and the back of her head sprayed off with a resounding *pop*. She licked her lips twice, her remaining eye rolling in her head, and then fell off me.

I stared at the gun, which looked almost the same as it had two seconds ago. No magazine, just simple black plastic and a healthy smattering of blood and brain. I dropped it and wrapped a hand around the handle of the knife in my stomach.

"Agatha!" Bert screamed. "Bring me to her! She can't go alone. She's my only sister!" I watched him swipe at Donna with his knife, but the bulk of Ben remained on him, so the gesture was meaningless. His pale blue eyes were fully red now, along with most of his similarly pale blue track suit and almost all of his hair. Donna looked past him at Cap, whose face was slack and blue and set at a terrible angle to both the wall and his body. Ben had landed entirely on him and broken his neck.

"You … MOTHERFUCKERS," Bert screamed. "Oh you, you shits! What have you done? We are going to repopulate the earth!"

Dick gave him one incredibly disgusted look and then turned to find me on the ground. I smiled at him as he knelt down beside me, gingerly touching the knife and then looking around for something to fix the problem with. I pointed to a table of tools the Comelys had used for their … well, their *work* I guess you'd say, and he ran over to it, picking up a pair of pliers. I shook my head and gestured to the left, where the bolt cutters were sitting.

"We are Marked for Yith! Oh, you stupid idiots," Bert was saying. Donna rested her hand on Cap's eyes and shut them. Even though they popped back open a second later, that seemed to do it for her. "Get this fat FUCK off of me so I can kill you. You fucking parasites! Drinking at the breast of society like LEECHES. LEECHES. You took her from me! This fat piece of shit was going to starve us all to death! Did you know that? His wife told us there was only a couple months of food left, but he's still fat. Fat and healthy! Leaving us to starve! The survivors! The Marked!"

Donna cut him off by driving her oxygen tank into the side of his head. I thought she'd let him off at that — it shut him up pretty good — but she wasn't satisfied. She hit him again, and again, until his skull turned lopsided and the skin beside his left eye split and pulled away from the bone. It hung like a used condom over his cheek, the bowl of it filling slowly with blood.

"Jesus, Donna," Dick said, handing me the bolt cutters. I shook my head and pointed to the sliver of metal between the handle of the knife and the much larger portion of steel inside my stomach.

"Cut it off there, bud, okay?" I asked. "We pull it out and I'll just end up bleeding to death right here." He obliged me, and just the slight wiggling of the knife as he got the cutters into place nearly made me puke. The vibration of the steel being cut finished the job, leaving me to apologize for Dick's freshly ruined shoes.

"It's fine," he said, laughing and looking around. He had tears in his eyes that didn't come back when he wiped them away. "It's fine."

"You didn't clear the chamber," Donna said, picking up the gun. She pulled the magazine out of my pocket while Dick bandaged me up with what I realized were tatters of Shelly Masterson's dress. Donna slid the magazine into the chamber and pulled the slide on top of the gun, looking it over. "How do I live in a neighborhood of old men who don't know how fucking guns work?"

She sighed and looked over at her dead husband, pulling a pack of cigarettes and a lighter out of her cardigan. She pulled her oxygen mask aside and lit a cigarette, taking a long pull and then coughing. She stubbed it out after the second drag and tossed the dead butt onto Ben's back. I didn't have the heart to look over at them.

"The fuck am I gonna do now?" she asked herself, looking around the basement. Her eyes settled on something just past Shelly's body. "The hell is that?" She walked in that direction and we followed after Dick managed to pull me up off the floor. I coughed, thinking Donna's cigarette smoke hadn't faded somehow, but when I looked I saw sprinklings of grey ash floating down the stairs.

"The fire," Dick said, and I realized he'd been looking that way too. We exchanged a glance and followed Donna. The fire was on the hill now, probably already eating into the old, abandoned Walther place and the Comelys' house. There was no going back up those stairs now and, soon, there wouldn't be any "there" to go back to. I touched the ridge of knife blade protruding from my stomach and thought that wasn't much of a concern to me anymore.

"Look at this shit," Donna said, and we did. What she'd found was a tunnel cored right into the concrete foundation. It had an odd smoothness to it that kept me from identifying what kind of tool had made the hole, which was strange given my occupation. Dick helped me get closer, and I realized what side of the house the tunnel was sunk into. Then I thought about the plastic storage container filled with blood beneath Bert and Agatha Comelys' slitting station.

The container marked, "CHANUKAH."

"Dick, are … *were* … the Comleys Jewish?" I asked, pointing to the bucket. Both he and Donna looked at it.

"The only Jewish family on the block are the Sokolovs," Dick said. We all looked into the great, black expanse of the tunnel ahead of us, which could lead in only one direction. Toward the Sokolovs' house. There was a sound like scratching deeper inside the tunnel, and Dick held out the votive candle in his hand. It did little to penetrate the dark, painting a swatch of flickering light above the hard angle of yellow dropped onto the rounded floor of the thing by the electric lamps.

"Do you hear that?" Dick asked.

"Yeah," I said.

More scratching then, closer now but still impossible to see. It echoed off the walls just a little bit. I coughed, realizing then that the smoke was now almost filling the basement. I turned my head to see past Dick's shoulder. The stairwell was completely clouded over, so that even Ben, Cap, and Bert's bodies were obscured from view. Inside those white clouds danced the gentle orange of firelight.

"I guess we've only got one way to go," Dick said.

I nodded and looked at Donna. She shrugged, adjusted the dial on her oxygen tank, and then took the first step into the tunnel. It was only then I noticed she'd abandoned her cane to hold the gun at her hip, pointed forward. She moved deeper inside and Dick and I joined her, just before she disappeared into the dark.

The tunnels were blinding only until our eyes adjusted to the votive lights. I insisted on carrying one of the three, despite being mostly dragged by poor Dick, who'd been something of a prop to most everybody in our waning party since this cursed day began. He was a strong man, despite his age and effete occupation as a professor of English, bearing me on without so much as a beleaguered breath. I did my best to hold my own weight, but my limbs — my fingers especially — had lost their dexterity. I could cling, and I could hold a candle, but even that little took all of me.

The tunnel was monstrous in size for an amateur project, nearly five feet in diameter, with a somewhat flattened floor that well accommodated walking. Nothing shored up the sides of the tunnel save the living rock of the West Virginia mountain into which it had been dug, upon which our little neighborhood had been built. We walked a good twenty meters, curving slightly until the yellow lights of the Comely basement and any trace of them vanished completely. I ran my hand along the surface of the stone once or twice, juggling the candle awkwardly to do so, and found no sense of the tools that had dug it.

"There's something up ahead," Donna said. We stopped and, in the sinking silence that followed, heard again that soft scratching. Not so soft now, though still faint, it bounced through the tunnel around us like light from a pebble-broken pond. Somehow sourceless and wavering. I found myself looking over my shoulder as much as forward, searching and failing to find a cause. "Close your ears."

"What?" Dick asked. Then he was screaming and I was blind. Not completely, of course; I saw through the lightning strike still-frames of Donna's gunfire what she'd heard ahead of us. I saw that and only that — the thing — moving with staccato gracelessness toward us and ringed by the darkness of the tunnel itself. Its face stood out in maddening clarity with every pistol crack, which in the small confines of the tunnel was no longer the satisfactory little pop I'd heard outside or even the much louder report that had preceded the death of Agatha Comely at my own hands. No, this was the fire and thunder of God let loose by mortal hands, the Promethean flame given life again in the heart of Hades. I fell to my knees, but did not look away, and I'll tell you what I saw.

In the first cold strike of light, so blinding my eyes could only see a disk of white surrounded by the rainbow coronae of disinformation, at the heart of this was a blackened and feral thing clinging to the roof of the tunnel. I could see nothing of it save the odd humanity remaining in its stretched and broken fingers. The reflective, octagonal blindness of its massive eyes. Then darkness.

With the second shot I saw the thing falling to the ground on thick legs ending in the downturned and clawed feet of some unknown animal. Still too, could I see the ragged wrapping of a dress, all colorless for my blindness, and a wide, flat mouth falling open under the strain of its own incredible weight. Then darkness.

The third shot brought color to my eyes, and I could see now the blackened splits in the fair-colored flesh that had once fully enclosed the thing's face. I could see the feral maw with more clarity now as well, a clumsy thing made by some dishonest huckster of a god — a laughing man with no clarity of thought for form or function. This gaping hole, as dark as the depths of the tunnel itself, was ringed with inward-facing tusks stolen from a half-dozen animals and forced into place through an unthinkable crudeness. Between these teeth flapped slivers of some thin fabric I thought could only be old flesh. Then darkness.

The final shot showed me this thing only a meter from us at best, its mouth fully open and falling so low over its chest it covered the loose and deflated breasts spilling from the rotten old dress. There was some pain in the thing's face now, and through the simple humanity of that expression, I finally realized I was looking at Nancy Sokolov. The little mole of a woman that never left her house.

Then darkness.

🙰

Sound returned slowly, along with pain and a great deal of confusion. Darkness had fallen fully into the tunnel with the last shot. I was lying on my side on the floor, a body on top of me, a chunk of knife in me, and suddenly somebody was slapping my face.

I stopped screaming and realized I could hear again.

"Shut the fuck up, Paul," Donna hissed. She flicked her lighter and I could see again. For a moment I panicked, realizing the body on top of me was Dick, and then sighing with relief when I saw he was fine. He'd jumped on top of me when the thing that had been Nancy Sokolov rushed us. Now he was frantically searching for his votive candle. Donna picked hers up, lit it, and soon enough Dick managed to find his own a short ways down the tunnel.

"Dropped the damn thing when you fired," Dick said sheepishly, holding his hand out for Donna's lighter. She obliged him and shrugged. Her eyes were very tired.

"I dropped mine too," she said. "There's no shame in it."

"I guess not," he said, lighting the candle and handing back the little plastic lighter. Donna looked it over for a long while and then put it back in her cardigan. She held out her own votive, looking over the tunnel while Dick helped me to my feet. The light reflected off half a dozen small pools of blood leading away from us.

"Got the bitch good," Donna said, shaking her head. "The hell is going on here?"

None of us bothered trying to answer.

We kept mostly silent as we made our way through the tunnel, going slowly and making as little noise as we could. It was only a few dozen meters later that we found the branch, a much larger tunnel, nearly ten feet wide, leading down deep into the heart of the mountain. Mike Sokolov lay in a pool of fresh blood by the entrance, hands slack at his sides and his legs sprawled out ahead of him. Donna bent down beside the man, lifting his dead eyes to where we could all see.

"I got him," she said, pointing to holes in his neck and another in the shirt over his stomach. She looked back the way we'd came. "The couple of shots I missed must have bounced all the way down here into him." She shook her head. "Given what we've seen, I can't say I much feel bad about it." She stopped and picked up something on the ground beside him, holding it up where we could all see.

It was a fresh four-pack of baby bottles, still sealed in plastic.

I looked down the larger tunnel, which descended at an impressive grade, and then back the way we'd come, doing a bit of mental math. I pointed down into the somehow deeper dark.

"That would lead beneath the old Walther place, if you kept going," I said, not knowing what that might mean. It was all too insane. But Dick and Donna nodded, Donna taking a step ahead of us and tipping over her votive to drain the wax. Then she set the glass tube on its side and let it roll away down the grade. It bumped and skittered, but maintained a fairly straightforward course. All the way we could see the broad pools of blood the Nancy thing had left behind.

The thing clattered for a long while, casting the orb of its light against the walls, before finally going out. But even still, we could hear the glass casing tap, tap, tapping its way down until it faded beyond hearing. Donna pulled her mask aside and lit a cigarette, coughing into her elbow only a second after the first drag. The gun dangled from her hand when she did this, held as casually as a veteran mother holds her third child.

"I'm gonna go get my candle back," Donna said. We both looked at her. She tossed the baby bottles back into Mike Sokolov's lap.

"Donna, we need to go," Dick said. She looked at him, a severe expression I'd never seen on the woman's face in my life, but a look that all the same seemed more at home there than any she'd ever given. It made me think, knowing what was in my own basement, and having seen inside a few of my neighbors', what things might have lurked inside the foundations of Donna's home. Dick sighed.

"It's not safe down there," he said. "Are you going to be okay?" She chuckled.

"No, but that's not really any of your concern, is it?" She said this and started walking down, steadying herself on the handle of her oxygen tank roller. The pale orange cigarette butt gave off little light, but we watched it all the same until we couldn't see it anymore. Then, having no other real options, the two of us continued on down the smaller of the two tunnels.

We emerged into the Sokolovs' basement, which was full of mostly normal basement stuff. There were also boxes of hand-me-down children's clothes, enough for a dozen kids or more to grow into adulthood and never have to share an outfit. The only out-of-place thing was a tidy little altar built into the deepest wall of the foundation, which bore an odd symbol, like a sun setting over the horizon. When I looked at it, I felt a sort of absence in my skull, as though some thought had once lingered there but was now somehow gone.

Atop the altar lay a flat silver plate and the blackened, half-chewed remnants of a human heart. There were also a few knives and some jeweled nonsense, chalices and the like, but we didn't bother looking them over. Dick tried to find something heavy to put in front of the entrance to the tunnel and, failing that, simply pushed over a few of the heavier-looking boxes. He looked at me, shrugged, and we left.

It's fairly safe to say I wasn't long for this world by the time I again stood above ground. The fire had all but consumed the Walther mansion, which still looked maddeningly whole despite the conflagration surrounding it. This fire had set the Comely place ablaze in a secondary fashion, and that house of cannibals was already falling into itself. I looked across the street to see if Dick's house had been spared, and it had. The burned-out remnants of our former neighbors' home — which lay between the Walther place and Dick's home — had deterred the spread of the fire.

If only for a time.

"Should we warn Jasper?" I said, spitting an unsightly amount of blood onto the front of my shirt. It mixed with the blood from Agatha Comely's shattered skull and I was somehow surprised how indistinguishable the two were. Dick ignored my question and started dragging me toward the end of the street.

"What are you doing?" I asked him.

"We have to leave," he said, his eyes narrowed on the edge of the road.

"What about your husband? What about Jasper?" I asked. He gritted his teeth and said nothing. I started slapping at his hands until he finally stopped. I could barely stand on my own, but I did, bent over at the waist and looking up at him. "We need to go to my shed real quick, okay?" He gave me a quizzical look, his eyes flitting from me, to the fire, to the end of the cul-de-sac, and then back.

"Trust me," I said. And, God bless him, he did.

I had him unlock the door for me. The key was simple, and so was the lock, and once they were clicked off and gone I couldn't really take anything back. Not that I really had much in the way of time to anyway.

"Jesus Christ, Paul," he said, helping me inside. I half expected him to drop me when he saw, but he didn't. He helped me inside to my work bench, where I leaned, dripping blood from my shirt all over a bunch of brand-new, unpainted sign boards. It was no great loss, the much nicer, finished ones were hung neatly to dry on the wall across from where we stood.

All of these read: "Best Roses, Mannassas, West Virginia."

"You made the signs?" Dick asked, looking back at me. The look of shock on his face literally made the entire day worth it. And the week proceeding, really.

I nodded, smiling softly. Laughing a little, even though it hurt.

"Yep," I said.

"And put them out?" he continued.

"And I dug up Shelly's roses and put them across the street," I said. "And I smashed the first Best Roses sign and planted the next one." I grinned. "Gotcha!" I tried to point, but the pain was too much. Dick shook his head.

"Fucking … why?" he asked.

"Boredom," I said, perhaps a bit too quickly. "Loneliness." I sighed. "I made that first one going on fifteen years ago, for Brenda." Dick's expression softened at the mention of my deceased wife's name. "You remember she used to tend that little garden in the middle of the cul-de-sac? That was all just dry dirt before she got here, but she made it beautiful. Folks never even noticed, because she did it for free I guess, and there's not much occasion to notice free things in this life. That is, unless they go away."

I realized I was crying and wiped a tear off my eye.

"Then she died and the garden died," I said. "And nobody noticed. Nobody at all. And it all went back to dirt. To nothing."

"So you, what, pranked all of us?" Dick asked. I nodded.

"Just to pass the time," I said. "Until the real joke started." I pointed out the door to the wall of flame that now hung overtop us, over all the world it seemed. "That's one of mine too, though I played it on myself as much as anything."

"You…" Dick started, looking at the flame.

"Me and everybody else in this neighborhood, you know," I said. "Either through action or inaction, we were all there cupping the first sparks in our hands." I coughed, and this time I didn't stop for a while, though it wasn't the smoke filling my lungs anymore. "Now our baby is too big for us to handle, and he's just gonna go on growing."

Dick sighed and leaned back against the table beside the other Best Roses signs.

"Jasper's dead," he said.

"I know," I told him. When he looked at me, I

added, "I could see it in your eyes. When Brenda died … well. Well. Let's just say it was like looking in a mirror for me."

Dick laughed then, a dry, brittle sound like I'd never heard him make. He covered his mouth and looked away. He was fully crying when he turned back around, furiously rubbing his face as though to scour away the tears. He smiled and cracked all over again, eventually gathering himself and pointing at my stomach.

"And now you're … you're dying too and everybody else," he said, running his fingers into his hair. He seemed on the verge of pulling it all out. Maybe he would, sometime after I could see. Maybe he would. "He … he couldn't take it all. I hate myself so bad for it. He … he did it himself. In the tub. My God." He stumbled around my shed, finally not bothering to keep it together, bleeding all over the place even more than I was. He eventually picked up one of my signs and smashed it. I did my best to keep consciousness, under the circumstances.

"He didn't *trust* me, or … I dunno," Dick continued. "*I. Don't. Know.* And I *never* will, because he checked out on his own." He sucked in a sobbing breath, leaning on the far wall with his hand over his eyes. "He was the beautiful one between us. Me? I'm just the one who talks about stuff he and the other women and men like him make. I'm just an imposter, walking around with giants and feeling giant myself and then he goes … he goes …"

He cried for a while. I would have tried to hold him, but I was in no condition. Nobody was anymore. Everything was over. We were all out of chances.

"It's time to go," I eventually said, pointing to the respirator by the painting station I'd set up. It was nice, too nice for the meager work I'd put it to in these last few weeks. A relic from a time when such things were needed for greater works. "You take that, and go."

"Where?" he asked.

"Anywhere not here," I told him. "This is the only place I know for sure you can't stay." I coughed again then and this time there was no distinguishing between the blood on my shirt that came from me or that came from anybody else. Things have a way of doing that, of coming together in the end despite your expectations. Such it was, and so it goes. "Put it on and start walking."

He nodded and did like I told him, looking for all the world like a spaceman when he was suited up. It would only ever help him with the smoke, not the fire. I'd realized a long time ago, along with all my peers, that there was no help for the gathering flames but distance. Prevention, perhaps, but prevention never seems to help, even when it's helping.

My last request was that he take me to the dead garden in the center of the cul-de-sac. Dick brought along one of the last, best signs I'd made and laid me down in the center of all that dead earth. The fire was so bad now even his house was burning, and the street was bubbling between us and the specter of the Walther mansion, which still seemed to live on in blasphemy inside its flaming shroud.

"Everything he ever wrote was in there," Dick said, placing the sign in my arms and standing to look at his own dying house. "It's all gone now."

"That's fine," I said, grabbing his leg. There was no standing anymore. When he looked down at me, it was hard to see the humanity there behind the black plastic eyes and the tubular exclusion of the mouth. But I knew it was there. I knew it was.

"'There's no beauty we can't find again, if we hunt with honest hearts,'" I recited, patting the ground beside me. The dry earth rose like smoke around my bloody fingers, the dust clinging to what hadn't yet dried. "That's what she told me the first time we brought this little clump of nothing back. She wasn't lying. It worked then."

I gasped, a breath that hurt down to the core of me. The taste of it was dust and blood and smoke and the lingering red scent of pain, but above all that, and beneath it, and inside of it, I smelled the perfume of roses. There, as though it had never left.

"It'll work again," I said. And then I said no more.

My neck was too tired to hold my head, and so both settled to the earth, giving me that perfect view of the sky we are all born to inherit. No matter the smoke and grime, past all that, the great blue and the dusty imperfections of the clouds, sometimes full and grey and black beyond belief, cracking wide and threatening to clean us off this little marble. No matter the clutter and the nonsense, just that sheet of honest firmament rising over all of us, there and there and there forever. Eternal.

Dick knelt down and pressed his palms, still flesh, to the sides of my face and bent his mouth of plastic tubes and wires to my forehead, giving it a last kiss before standing and leaving me to my view of the sky.

I thought of many things as the flames crept forward to devour me, like who might have enjoyed the fifth place at the table at the Comely house, and what a woman with a half-empty oxygen tank, a gun, and a lighter might accomplish in that subterranean hell we'd left behind. But mostly I thought of a beautiful woman you've never met, who never gave up on dry little scraps of earth in the middle of undeserving cul-de-sacs, and who truly, truly, truly deserved the title of Best Roses, Manassas, West Virginia.

THE END

MUD OF THE HEART

FOR JACQUES

I have begun this confession many times, but you must understand that I always began it with this line.

I loved her.

And you must believe me.

I loved her.

I was twenty and some odd years when I came to her home at the end of civilization, a grand and sweeping thing near enough the sea for the smell of salt but too far for those magnetic sunrises which make living on the East Coast worth it. It was still there, of course, the sun. Great and glowing and spreading life over all the world, but her manor sat deeply inland behind a shallow lagoon of cypress and pond scum.

Great catfish dwelled out there beneath the mossy green carpet, and small alligators that enjoyed the brackish waters. It was beautiful, in its own way, as was the owner of this lonely manor in the deepest recesses of the exclusion zone. The light which filtered through the tangled cypress limbs lay gold on the settled waters in the first few hours of the morning, often slipping through competing layers of fog to lay across the wet backs of bullfrogs and the lithe blackness of water snakes flitting bank to bank.

At night the scene dimmed. The fog and shimmer remained, though greatly diminished, so that every speck of moonlight catching in the dewdrops and raindrops and water catchers and pond breaks would float like stars amongst the rising staccato blips of the fireflies.

It was noon when I arrived, bouncing gently along with the thick wheels and suspension of the swamp treader. It is, if you have not seen one, a trailer wagon of sorts I've only ever encountered out here near the end of the world. A mechanical paddle horse drags it through the mud and shallows, and it floats and catches a great deal through all of this. I was almost seasick by the time we arrived. Ill as much from the jostling as from the alligator carcasses stacked like firewood in the cargo portion of the wagon.

"I bet you're surprised someone lives all the way out here," I joked with the otherwise silent and pondering form of the carriageman who'd taken me out on the drive. He'd chewed at the cud in his lips, a sort of shredded tobacco popular out where it's constantly wet, and spit.

"You're saying someone does?" he said. Then he spit and maneuvered around the path to head back to the town where I'd embarked, some ten miles behind us.

I opened my mouth to say something, but decided against it, picking up my valise and my much larger traveling trunk and started toward the house. The mud made dragging the heavy trunk hard going, but only for a few feet. Though the road itself was covered in thickly layered muck, the great treeless courtyard of the manor house was firm. As the trunk scraped along I realized the courtyard was really a stone roundabout that'd become covered over in moss. I was so engrossed with the patterning of the covered stone I didn't notice her looking at me.

Her eyes were startling, as I'd been warned they would be, a glittering, brilliant red that stood in stark contrast with her paper-white skin. She looked almost like a doll standing there in her black-and-blue-patterned dress, steadying hand braced against the wall beside the door. I raised a hand and smiled and she returned the gesture. Then she slipped inside and out of view with almost a flutter.

Again I had opened my mouth to say something and it had stalled in my throat. A sort of rumbling, ratcheting noise croaked out into the courtyard and I looked around, startled to find the noise was just that. A croak.

A great bullfrog sat on the lip of the vine-draped fountain in the center of the courtyard, fat as my fist. As I watched, it hopped onto the head of the tarnished marble rabbit that served as the fountainhead and then out of sight.

❦

Our introductions were polite, but limited. She lived alone and could not speak due to the … terminal nature … of her condition. I will not describe this affliction in detail — it hurts me too much to mention — but I'm sure you'll understand the nature of it given my descriptions of her. She could not write for herself. She could not speak. She could eat, but only soft things and liquids. She could dress herself with some difficulty, but no buttons or zippers or clasps. Her remaining dignities were to bathe and use the restroom unassisted, to walk with a cane, and to read.

I left my things in the lobby of the great house and joined her in the library, a drum of a room two stories tall. We tried to communicate as best we could and ultimately I found that asking her yes and no questions was all the speech left to her.

"You understand who I am? Yes? You expected me?"

Several nods and a soft white hand, fingers extended, patting down the air. *Please, slow down if you could.*

"Ah, sorry," I said, adjusting myself on the old red couch. "Have you been getting on well?"

A shrug and a smile. A slight tilting of the head side to side. *So-so.*

I licked my lips and swallowed.

"Your former nurse, has anybody seen to her?"

A long, sad sigh. Then a slow shake of the head. *No.*

I nodded and laid back against the couch, looking at the ceiling. The isolation of this woman was beyond comprehension. Neither I, nor my hiring agency, nor perhaps anybody, would have known she was out here dying in this swamp if not for the arrival of the letter from her former nurse.

It reads as such.

To Mr. and Mrs. Gretsby Holmes,

It has come to my attention that you are folks of a generous and Godly disposition who run an honest and caring hospice service for the Elderly and Infirm. I am writing not on my own behalf but that of my charge, the Honorable Ms. Hester Withrow of Ebbling Parish in Eastmarch. What you might understand as the Third Exclusion Zone, south of Old Dee Cee.

Without going into great detail, I must admit that I have committed perhaps the greatest sin of a Caretaker, perishing before the death of my charge. I will, in fact, be well and fully dead before this Letter reaches your hands.

It is with that in mind that I have written you today in the Great Hope that you will lend your services to Ms. Withrow. She herself is not long for this world, though longer than I, but also in much more terrible health if you will believe it. She is afflicted with a condition that robs her of much Dignity and that will leave her in a state beyond description if I am no longer here to care for her.

She has no friends or family. Nobody knows she is here save myself and the cruel and stupid peasants of the nearby parish. I do not trust them to tend to her affairs and so I am writing to you for help. I heard of your services through an old friend who is also now gone. Time is very cruel.

(This last sentence was written in a hand that seemed hesitant. The ink had dotted up around where the letters curved.)

I have enclosed my last month's salary along with this letter. Please, please, please, take this money as surety that I am no Con Artist or Prankster. There is just as much and more here that I will never put to use, as I too am bereft of family to whom I might pass on this wealth. Take it as payment for your services.

Please do not allow Ms. Withrow to die in pain and misery. She is a dear, kind heart.

With all due Respect and Honor,

Mrs. Callam Sprattling, CHPLN

My employer, Mrs. Holmes, had put me on the first train out of New Albany headed for the coast after she finished the letter. It should be noted that this is an extremely long way to travel, both for myself and for a letter. And, unlike the letter, I had the benefit of the swamp treader to bring me the ten miles between the manor house and the nearest town. Mrs. Sprattling, full well knowing she was dying of whatever ailment had afflicted her, had walked all ten miles to deposit the letter at the local post office. And then, drawing on some mad reserves of energy, had tramped all the way back here to check on Ms. Withrow one last time.

And so I found this remarkable woman laying deeply past death in her simple twin bed in the servants' quarters of the house. Rot had taken and left her already, leaving little more than a dried and eyeless husk on the yellowed bed sheets. Even though I thought I should be horrified, I was in truth struck speechless by the dignity of the scene.

Service is looked down upon by the young and self-obsessed, seen as little more than kowtowing to the greater figures which you someday secretly hope you will be. And perhaps it is that to some. But to me, standing beside this corpse laying on its common bed, in its common shrouds, its weathered brown hair splayed out on the pillow above it, this dead woman looked no less graceful than any queen. She had perished in a state of such absolute dedication she seemed to me like some demigod, her simple cotton tick more magnificent than a marble bier.

I stooped to wrap and gather her body, lifting it easily and carrying it to the back of the house. Ms. Withrow had thankfully stayed outside the hall, her throatless sobbing following me like the whisper of wind through a keyhole. Our speechless speaking had revealed to me that Mrs. Sprattling had, in fact, built her own coffin in the workshop beside the garden. The woman was sure to have everything in place before her final hour.

I found two boxes in the back: a simple casket, hastily thrown together out of cheap wood clearly taken from apple crates, and a much more ornate (if not somewhat amateurish) thing set beneath a cloth in the corner. This cloth I removed to reveal the whole of the creation, having set the corpse of Mrs. Sprattling to temporary rest amongst the red and purple wildflowers currently devouring the stones of the rear portico.

The coffin beneath was a wonderfully made thing, though not very modern, and inlaid with old pillow stuffing and shreds of silk dresses that made a pattern of sewn rainbows along the interior.

To be buried in a cloud after a rainstorm, I thought, apropos of nothing. Also, apropos of nothing, I dragged this magnificent coffin out of the workshop to lay alongside the form of Mrs. Sprattling. Then I placed her inside it and went to search for a shovel.

When I returned, I found Ms. Withrow sitting beside the coffin, her skirts in a pile over her legs. She saw me and smiled, red eyes almost pink in the sunlight.

She pointed to the coffin and then to herself, shaking her head, and then tapped the space where Mrs. Sprattling's heart might lay and nodded. Then she burst into tears.

          MUD OF THE HEART

I knelt and held her until the crying ebbed and stopped, and then I led her into the house and made her the first true dinner she'd had in a while out of the canned provisions I found stored in the pantry.

I put on my equivalent of work clothes and set to burying Mrs. Sprattling, no mean task given the condition of the ground around the place. My spade buried itself two feet deeper than I thought it might go on a simple push. Then I was pulling buckets of slop out of the way until my body was almost completely slicked with black mud.

I rigged up a pulley system out of stakes and rope laid flat along the ground and maneuvered the coffin in place. It slid down nicely, though I could only dig about three and a half feet down before hitting water. Still, the coffin would be well covered. And, when it was done, I returned to the house to bathe and orchestrate some sort of service for the benefit of Ms. Withrow.

To my surprise, she met me at the door, where I believe she'd been standing for some time as I went through the process of burying her former nurse. And, I'm sure, her only friend for a very long time before the former's death.

She laughed, further to my surprise, and I realized how comical I must look covered head to toe in mud. I told her my intentions of showering and dressing in my best coat and hat, but she simply grabbed my hand and led me slowly to the grave. I may as well have been carried by a breeze, her pull was so gentle and insistent.

There was some more crying and then all ebbed and was done. I placed a simple wooden placard Mrs. Sprattling had engraved with her and her husband's (Carlos) names and dates of birth and death. Her own date of death, bearing the number of the year and the month, but not the day, I finished carving myself with some help from Ms. Withrow. Then we placed the placard and returned to the house.

And so ended my first day at Withrow Manor House.

The schedule of Withrow Manor House is something of a waltz in three parts, all thrumming out that same rhythm in time with the winding of the clock, which, as it so happens, is the first step in the dance.

I wake early, about six, and wind the old thing. Then I prepare a breakfast for Ms. Withrow and I prepare Ms. Withrow for the day.

She is always awake when I enter the room, sitting plaintively with a book in hand or sometimes staring out the window. The latter is always the case when it rains, which is as often as not, because she reads by the natural light of the morning and the clouds make it too dark. It's on these days I bring in a tray to set before her and she asks me to sit with her while she eats. I always acquiesce — it's really no bother — and often I use my younger, stronger eyes to read to her from her place in whatever book she was working on.

Ms. Withrow is, was, *is* a great lover of books and it was my greatest pleasure in her service to have the run of the library. This being part and parcel of the second act of our daily waltz. Partners now in the heightening light and heat of the afternoon, I take Ms. Withrow in hand from her quarters down the stairs to the library or the solar beside the rear gardens.

She sits and reads or otherwise tries to keep her hands busy. They are clumsier, she tells me, than they have ever been. Then she takes me to a large room on the second floor where she keeps her old projects, great blankets and dresses and other textiles she's woven or sewn or stitched or knitted. She points them out to me, all of them save one great piece that hangs catching the light of five great windows at the back of the room. This thing, this tapestry, she pretends as though it's not there. When I ask, she demures, so I don't ask again.

The second two steps of the afternoon are lunch and then a walk around the grounds. She points at parts of the property and tells me their importance and I find it odd the trivial things that can hold such sway over a person's past. In the corner of the east garden lays a small table where her father liked to hold his first conversations with new business partners. And his last conversations.

She tells me he was a kind, but often intemperate man, and he didn't like for his wife and daughter to hear him yelling at people.

In the center of the roundabout is the great rabbit-shaped fountainhead, which she tells me was a gift from an old friend of her father. She smiles at the hunk of white stone, but the smile is sad. I think to ask her more and I don't.

We then move on to the last leg of the day's dance, which begins with supper and ends with bed. But laying between those final steps is the penultimate, in which my lady asks me to attend her to the second floor, and then to leave her and busy myself with something for a few hours.

Though it concerns me to leave her alone for any length of time, I do. My only rules of conduct, imposed on myself *by* myself, are to remain on the first floor and occupy my attentions only with pastimes that require little concentration and make little noise. I must keep an ear out in case of emergency, after all.

Without fail she meets me at the door of her bedroom around 10 p.m., and I assist her as necessary in going to bed and then make my way to the servants' quarters. I pretend not to notice, because I see the way she hides them, the occasional odd dots of blood on the sides of her fingers. The apparent exhaustion in her eyes.

So I shut the door behind her, and thus concludes our daily dance, and it is always an odd thing to be left alone on the dance floor when your partner has taken her leave. It is the finality of it, I think. Standing there in the deepening, echoing shadows of that house and straining my ears for the sound of her clothing and rustling sheets as she climbs into bed. The soft inhalations and exhalations this little exercise necessitates from her worn and infirm body.

They, like the great and empty silence of the hallway, are all as much signs of life as death. I might stand there for hours straining my ears and eyes for more if it weren't so odd. So improper. For there is no family to come to claim this place when it finally finds the last inheriting soul laid to rest in the rear acres. She, my lady, is the last living soul in this property. No, more, she is the last of this property's soul, and with it gone I know not what echoes might come to replace those soft, slow footfalls and the rasp of silk against the faces of the carpeted stairs.

The gentle riffling of pages beneath thumb and finger at the start of the day. The shuffling of feet on cue to meet me at her door at the day's end. They are the poetry of this place, made by and settled inside it, and when they are gone there are no better hands to put ink to the page of this place. It will all end.

It will be a thing for the worms, and as it goes, so shall we in time.

It was on a night such as any other that I heard something else in the halls besides the sounds common to myself and my lady. It was oddly familiar and lingered so that I almost saw the noise moving the dust motes in the air.

I ignored it at first. I'd heard other such bits of mental nonsense since moving here and suffered more than a few share of frights finding my own dark reflection in the mirror of a room where I thought I saw — was *sure* I saw — some lurking figure.

On those nights — as well as this — I carried a simple electric lantern, the Old World sort with a battery that lives forever so long as you keep it out in the sun a while or turn the little crank buried in the base of the thing. I would cast the lantern back and forth like a complete fool, creeping around the house silently so as to not wake Ms. Withrow. Or, honestly, so the embarrassing nature of my late-night detective work would not be revealed to her.

I knew the reaction she would have, of course.

There would be a length of polite laughter as she held a gloved finger to her lips. Then she would assure me that any ghosts in her home were well-invited and welcome to whatever chain-shaking might interest them. Following this joke, she would almost immediately apologize for making fun of me and ask if I'd like some tea.

Most other nights I would have ignored this errant noise as I always did, but it persisted with me even to my room. The sound was such that I found myself looking over my shoulder more than once, half-expecting each time to see some yellow-eyed ghoul in tatty clothing stretching his arms over me in the darkness. As it was, each time I turned I saw nothing but the same dark hallways and slanted beams of starlight creeping in through the house's many windows.

It was raining that night, as well, so the sound worried me more. More than some hellish creature, what if the damn roof had broken or some seam had split in a wall and was pouring water on a priceless antique? Even though Ms. Withrow had expressly told me nothing in the house held much in the way of value to anybody on earth save her, I maintained that everything still holding value in her eyes was then worth its weight in gold to me. As a matter of principle, if nothing else.

I'd told her this once and she'd done her customary laugh before telling me I was a sweet boy and suggesting I find some items I might keep for myself when my service ended. I protested that she should find someone of worth to pass her things on to, to find a museum or something at least, and she'd laughed earnestly. When I further suggested the locals in the closest town might rip the place to piec-

          MUD OF THE HEART

es looking for things of value, she had an even odder reaction.

Ms. Withrow had rested a gloved hand on her chin, rubbing the space beneath her lip with her forefinger as she sometimes did, and then smiled at me. Then she told me, in her wordless way, that if something of that nature were to happen she would be glad for it. The dead bring all they need with them, and all they leave behind has no worth to anybody save those that come across it.

She opined that, perhaps, if this great old building were torn down and reassembled into a hundred little barns and homes and outhouses, those second lives would have all enriched the first in their own small way. I suggested to her that I found the idea of this beautiful place being torn down almost inherently distasteful. She sighed and looked around at the walls and the books and then at me. Then she shrugged and suggested we should mull those thoughts out over some tea.

It was those same thoughts of waste and ruin that brought me slinking up to the second floor in my socks to find out the nature of the odd sound. It wasn't loud and defied any obvious rhythmic pattern. At some moments I lost it to the steady patter of the rain, only to find it again a second later somehow louder and more insistent.

In all honesty, it made sleeping impossible, so I would have had to go inspecting about the second floor anyway.

By the time I passed my lady's room and into the length of the southern wing of the home I began to hear it more clearly. It was almost a smacking sound, a wooden shutter for sure, but the noise was different almost every time. And like I said, arrhythmic, almost searching.

I didn't know what I'd do if I found somebody. I'm not a man of considerable, or even significant, constitution. I feel sometimes the gods determined my profession before I was born and saw fit to provide me only the most necessary body for the task. That is, service and nursing. I could pick up Ms. Withrow, but she was no heavier than a bag of dry grass. A man even my own size would be entirely too much for me to lift.

But I found no burglars, no intruders. My light shone through the room and came to rest on the culprit, a tangle of wet curtain fluttering in and out of a window as the two shutters beat against it. The thickness of the cloth kept them mostly silent until some great buffet of wind would swing them wildly to beat against the shutters and sides of the house like the palm of some giant.

It took a fair deal of wrangling to pull the cloth inside. Mist fell thickly into the room, obscuring the spaces where I tried to place my feet, and I was forced to juggle several old reams of fabric and wooden stitching frames out of the way. Finally, I managed to pull the curtain back inside the house and throw shut the window. The shutter kept banging away, but its noise was much diminished.

I held the cloth in my hand, wondering why my lady had left the window open after an already rainy day. The curtain was, like most of the window dressings in the manor house, made of a base green fabric and laid over with white lace and gold stitching that left the finished product looking more of a rough old bronze. It is a work of craftsmanship I'd never seen in my life and, given its mundane purpose, all the more impressive for the time and care put into it.

I looked up from the curtain to find my lady staring at me from the doorway, only the faintest blues of the burgeoning storm light falling through the window. Electricity crackled and then burst overhead, and I saw to my horror that something had ravaged my lady's face in the night. Deep welts dug into the soft white of her flesh, all of them filled with blood that stood out as black in the weak light.

"Ms. Withrow?" I asked, moving my light up to see her better. Just then the shutter slammed home again, the slats breaking loose and bursting open the window glass. I jumped and turned to see the mist pouring through the new hole as though it were water and the room I stood in a tub. Even as I watched, the lightning broke afresh and a strong gust pulled the curtain out the small hole in the window.

I cursed under my breath and turned my attention back to Ms. Withrow, but my lantern caught only the fluttering trail of her nightdress disappearing into the hallway. I gave another look at the glass but, remembering the condition of my lady's face, promised to see to the mess in the morning.

"Ms. Withrow!" I called after her, moving into the hall. The lightning had gone mad as I walked, stuttering violently now and never quite going out. The result was an electric light show that turned the hall into something of a madhouse. Almost simultaneously light and dark, illumination coming from every conceivable angle, every shadow seemed monstrous, diminutive, here, there, gone, returned, so that I couldn't make sense of the shape of things anymore.

My lady moved ahead of me, her hair rising around her as though the air were water. Electric curled through the writhing strands. She passed her own room and I, stumbling, called out to her again, all but screaming over the thunder rumbling in the walls. It seemed for a moment the entire house would crumble.

A small, soft hand gripped my arm above the elbow. The world seemed to pull itself back into focus as I turned to find my lady's concerned eyes meeting my own. The hallway was dark save my lamp and the soft light of the moon shining through the clouds and into the skylights running the length of the second floor hallway. The red of her eyes was dark enough in the light to seem almost brown.

Are you okay? she asked in her fashion. *What's wrong? You were screaming.*

I stood for a long moment, looking up and down the hallway, mouth ajar. There was nothing out of place, nothing amiss. My lady's hair, laying in loose, clean night braids on the sides of her head, did not jump and dance with curling electricity. In time I said nothing, but she did, leaning her forehead against my chest and touching my arms as they hung limply at their sides.

I did not know the extent to which my pulse was running away with itself until I felt it calm beneath her touch. My own erratic breath, too, lessened so that my head suddenly felt clear. I swallowed and stepped backward, apologizing.

It's fine, she told me, though I could see some concern lingering in her eyes. Concern for me, only for me. She gave me a smile and nodded goodnight before slowly closing her door. I listened for the sound of her finishing her climb into bed, and the low sounds of her breathing, and then I returned to my quarters.

I lay in bed, thinking over what I'd seen, falling asleep despite the distant sound of that infernal thumping coming from my lady's sewing room. The sound of the broken window and the wet rag of curtain slapping the side of the manor house.

The next day, my lady began to die.

Our daily waltz faltered on its second step, and from then on there was no more dancing. I came to her door, opened it, and found my lady's bed empty. Then I saw her feet beyond the edge of the bed, just the bottoms of them, and, running to her, found the woman herself curled on her side on the floor. The look on her face was that of absolute pain, until she saw I'd found her and she favored me with a soft, apologetic smile.

I suppose I've made a fool of myself, she said in her way, and I told her she hadn't before helping her back onto the bed. She sat doubled over for a long while before finally asking me to help her use the restroom. I did, and I thought her no less dignified for doing so.

I carried her everywhere after that, first by letting her loop her arm over my shoulder and then as a child. Her body was light and hot. As I've said before, like a bag of dry grass. Not a terrible thing to be compared to, even if it's not something you yourself might appreciate. Perhaps it is. I don't know.

I did my best to maintain some semblance of our old dance, but she was no longer up to most of it. Food dwindled from three meals a day to just tea in the morning and thin stew at night. Anything else was simply too much.

She still enjoyed the garden, and as we sat out

there, I noticed two things. The first was that the curtain was still hanging out on the side of the house, though it had now dried flat against the bricks. The second was that I couldn't find Mrs. Sprattling's grave marker. I said as much to my lady as we sat for tea in the afternoon on the third day after I had found her on the floor.

It's to be expected, is what she told me, going back to her tea. She saw my confusion and after a moment explained. I had some difficulty comprehending her explanation at first — the weakness had robbed her hands of their spryness, and her expressions were slow — but I came to understand the material of the swamps moved constantly. Anything buried in the mud out there might be sucked under, or moved ten or twenty or a hundred feet down the way, or transported in some other maddening fashion by the next morning. It was just the nature of things.

But the swamp remains, she said, waving a hand out over the gold and green before us. *And that's all that needs be.*

I agreed, even though I felt I might be nodding along to more than she'd simply said, and then excused myself from tea. While there was nothing I could do about the tragically displaced Mrs. Sprattling, I could very well put the upstairs window to rights. Board it up at least.

I told Ms. Withrow that I intended to do just that and she nodded without paying me much attention. She had eyes only for the swamp, with its rising mists and steady, endless music. In truth, I didn't like the thought of her so close to all that danger, the crocodiles and snakes and the like, but she didn't seem to mind it herself. The one time we came close to arguing was when I first mentioned it might not be safe.

          MUD OF THE HEART

So, I left her behind and climbed the stairs to her sewing room. She hadn't had the time or energy for this pastime since she'd fallen by the bed. I could tell it perturbed her some, but she had been more upset by the inability to hold a book for long, so that was the problem we had been addressing in the interim.

The sewing area was a massive room of the sort so cluttered with shelves and stacks of material it actually seemed quite small. Perhaps a dozen half- or mostly finished projects took up the small tables immediately in front of the door, and all the rest of the space was finished items: clothing on figures, fresh curtains to replace any damaged ones in the house that seemed themselves terribly old, if not well-aged, and what seemed to be a hundred blankets and throws and comforters. But what caught my eye most was the great tapestry over the back windows.

I had paid it little mind before — often it was too dark when I tended her in the late hours of the night to see much of it — but now I could see the entirety of the thing. It was a story, stitched into fabric the way one might lay stained glass into a window, almost shining in the afternoon light. The beauty of it took my breath away.

It was the story of a young girl growing up in this house, told in moments I only partially understood. Here, a man sitting at a concrete table and having some ugly conversation with a dark figure. Here, a mother guiding a little girl's hand as she learned her first stitch. Here, a grown woman, a figure of almost complete white with red for eyes, standing over a series of gravestones with her arms out. Here, an equally dark figure with purple eyes holding out a hand and being spurned.

I tried to make sense of it, and all the other images, most of them small things so tiny they could barely cover my thumb. Those I mentioned above were perhaps the only whole scenes larger than a dinner plate, and then even barely. I kept taking them in as I passed the curtain, my eyes barely able to break free of the images.

Then I was at the window and somehow suddenly back in the real world. I pulled the curtain back inside the window and then off the crossbar entirely. The storm had torn the thing to shreds, and what was left was beyond mending. Most of the needlework was gone and the fabric was beginning to stink from mold.

I stopped to look down into the garden and was surprised to see Ms. Withrow standing at the edge of the swamp. She had her arms out to her sides, and a gentle wind was blowing out of the reeds. The smell was fetid, heavy, but not terribly unpleasant. It carried also the dense, full scent of growing things, flowers and fruits and frogs and God knows what else. But life. Rich and terrible life.

I saw then, or thought I saw, the figure of a man amongst the trees at the edge of the water. He stood perhaps a dozen yards from the spot where we'd buried Mrs. Sprattling, his body leaned frontward against the trunk of a cypress so that I could barely make out the shape of him. I wouldn't have seen him, in fact, if Ms. Withrow hadn't been there looking out at him, but even as I watched his motionless form I couldn't tell if I was seeing a man or not. Or anything at all. A second longer staring and I realized it was vines on the side of the tree. A second longer than that, and I saw the face contort in surprise and look up at me, purple eyes shining out of the murk down there like sunlight falling on fresh orchids.

Then Ms. Withrow fell to the ground very suddenly and I was running, running without thinking or caring what I might find, simply running. I was out in the garden in seconds, cradling her thin form and forgetting myself enough in my panic that I was scolding her for being so reckless. She laughed in her rasping way and touched my face, thanking me for being so concerned. I helped her to her feet and then took her back to her seat at the table in the garden.

I returned for her cane, which she had dropped, taking a long second to look out into the swamp. It was there, in all its dangerous glory, much as it had ever been. I stooped over to grab the cane and disturbed a bullfrog that had been resting on the ground beside it. It passed its large, baleful eyes over me and then hopped away toward the water. I stood and my heart caught in my chest for a moment.

In the window above the garden, where I had been standing only moments before, stood a dark man in the shadows. Not dark of skin, but of substance, a thing cut from the whole cloth of the universe to leave nothing but a hole in the fabric. An absence of a thing, or so I thought. A second longer of looking helped me convince myself I was doing nothing more than noticing the motion of the curtain the storm had ruined as the wind blustered through the window glass.

It wasn't until late that night that I shot up in bed, beating the lightswitch on with my hand in a panic, and I remembered I had taken the ruined curtain down and left it in a soggy bundle on one of my lady's work tables.

The final sickness swept in so quickly I felt she'd been stolen from me before she'd even gone. I don't know if I've mentioned this before, but it has been on my mind all the time I've been writing this. Perhaps you might find it odd how much I came to love this woman in such a short time. She was my employer, yes. I was her thrall, surely, to a degree at least, and we had little in the way of months between that first soft meeting and the last hard parting.

She was kind to me, I suppose is the whole of it. Attentive to me even when I was attending to her. She seemed to understand my feelings before I came to know their presence myself, and was always reaching out a hand to help. Perhaps it was some guilt on her part. I was, after all, a young man from a distant place come all the way to watch an old woman die in wasted opulence.

In the city I departed to come to this place, I was nothing. Hardly a man in the eyes of women and men alike. Less of a lover, more of a burden. I am not a happy person, nor a brave one. I prefer darkness to light in a way that perturbs others, though I think myself more of a rabbit in a den than any more nefarious cave dweller.

I think she understood that about me and enjoyed a similar disposition herself. The entirety of her life, she told me, had been lived within the great and sweeping walls of the manor house. She knew from books that others might envy such a grandiose life, but it was not so grandiose by comparison to a man who can see three times as much of the world on his way to buy an apple at the market.

She envied those people. Free out in the world, in a way she knew they would envy her in turn, safe in her great house. But it was merely the way of things, and she was too old to do much about it now. Couldn't at any rate. Though she wouldn't speak to me about it, softly patting my hand and changing the subject when I asked, there was something about this place that held her in thrall to it as much as my occupation did me to her. She had the grounds and the gables and the gardens and not much else. A great lot, and also very little.

And in that way we came to understand each other, and before the terrible last days of her sickness, we spent many hours as introverts do. I would sit reading a few seats away from her. We would share wine or tea or our meals in certain wondrous rooms in the house and simply enjoy each other's company, talking little or not at all. Sometimes I would walk with her from room to room and just explore the confines of this massive prison she'd inherited.

This beginning was pleasant. The end was not.

I gave up on sleeping in my own quarters as my lady's needs were significant and constant toward the end. Together we entered a sleepless dream state of pain and exhaustion, her waking at all hours and sleeping when I wasn't all but forcing her to eat. The sickness she'd come down with was devouring her alive from the inside, starting at her stomach and working its way out. There was nothing to be done.

I am familiar with this disease, as I have said, and to spare you the particulars of the worst of my lady's indignities, I won't share with you its name. I believe I have said this, I may be repeating myself, but I am quite tired.

My only respite was the occasional walk through the halls of the house. I had no sense of the pace of time then, in the last week of my lady's hospice, but it seemed as though the house had fallen in on itself in places. That sections I had walked with her only months ago had collapsed or were now withered and full of detritus falling in through open windows. There were moments where I would have to kneel and clutch my head, pulling it between my knees to regain my composure.

In my delusions, lighting would be wrinkling the blue sky over the open roofs in the distant wings of the house. This flickering blue would fall over my face, catching in my eyes so that I felt the electric burning down into the heart of me. I have heard epileptics give similar accounts of their own conditions, but that particular affliction has never bothered me, then or before or since.

In this glittering, writhing, wrinkling space I would cast about half blind for something to help me to my feet, suddenly worried for my lady's safety. Inevitably I would find her, soaring just above the floor in the hallway, face black with ruin and her white hair curling up around her head. I would raise my hand to her, call to her, but she would never answer. Or I would see that dark man, that thing, peering around some distant corner. His eyes were flat and purple and dull. The color of orchids rotting against the wet bark of a cypress tree.

Then all would return, as though I'd taken a great breath, and I'd hurry back to my lady's side. Usually she'd be in the fit of some dream, only shuddering awake at my touch, sweating and wild-eyed. There was a dwindling supply of morphine in the house I used to quell her worst pains, but it could only ever

     MUD OF THE HEART

do so much. The dose she needed to be free was more than I had the heart to give her.

The day which was the last day found me waking on the thick futon I'd procured from one of the upstairs rooms. My dreams were of the worst sort, seeming almost inseparable from the visions of my waking life. Let me make no small business of how worrisome these delusions were, and how concerned they made me both for myself and my lady, but I had no recourse. In any other circumstance I might have recused myself and found a more suitable candidate, but Ms. Withrow could not survive the travel to town or the wait while I was gone.

I could not even go to town for supplies, which I had done on numerous occasions. Ebbling is a small, ugly town of little note, and nothing happened there worth mentioning to you. People thought I looked odd and that I was even more so for the sort of work I was doing "out there in the swamp." All things I'm fully used to.

I pushed myself to my feet and almost died of a heart attack. My lady was not in her bed, or in the bathroom adjoining the bedroom. I burst into the hall, frantically pulling my clothes into place and calling aloud for her, for what good it might do. She had barely the strength to raise a cup to her mouth, much less knock against something hard to get my attention.

I eventually found her lying delirious in a puddle of her own sweat — an actual puddle mind you, this is how bad the fever had gotten. She had crawled or stumbled, I don't know, into the great and cluttered workroom down the hall. I dropped to my knees and turned her over, sighing with relief when her dazed eyes found mine and she smiled. Her finger raised above her head toward the tapestry, and I followed it to where some dark figure stood entangled with a powder-white woman with red eyes. She touched my face then, and mouthed a single word to me.

Finished.

Seven hours. This is how long I watched her die. After the second, she was no longer sane; the pain was simply too much.

I put her in an ice bath to quell her fever, but the heat of her flesh was so intense it melted the ice and caused a general fog to rise in the bathroom. There was no intimate detail about her I didn't know at this point, but I still did my best to preserve her dignity as I dragged her failing body to and from the tub. By this point, the disease had ravaged her so badly her stomach had receded to lay nearly flat against her spine. Her body hadn't an ounce of spare fat or muscle, though her face seemed fine enough, and her hair was still white and full.

I brought her to the bed to lay her down, not wanting to administer the morphine while she was submerged in water. Knowing, as I do now, that I was already trying to steel myself for braver men's work.

On the seventh hour, holding her hand — it felt like I was touching a fresh kettle — I told her I was sorry. I couldn't do anything else. Her breathing was soft and harsh, like two rough pieces of paper being rubbed together. It made me think of the library and our time we spent there and I began to cry. Delirious with fever, she couldn't raise a hand to my face and laugh and tell me not to worry. She could do nothing but stare unseeing at the ceiling.

I begged her to forgive me. I asked. I begged. I asked. But she could say nothing. I asked her for a sign, to tell me she wanted to be set free of this, clenching her soft hand in my own as I did so. Small beads of blood dripped over my hand from the pinpricks she'd left in her skin fumbling through the last of her work. But from her, there was nothing, save the steady sound and scent of pain and sickness.

I put the first syrette of morphine into her subclavian artery. Then the second. Then the third. Her breathing grew slower. Her body shuddered. She began to cough and then spasm. Then a general blueness settled over her flesh and her muscles stilled, stiffened, went slack. Then she was gone.

There was a final relaxation of her body. I watched the last bit of shine and focus go out of her eyes. The red of them, almost crimson in those last hours, dulled to scarlet, burgundy, and then the clotted color of rust. She was gone.

I wept a great deal, not knowing what to do with myself. Eventually I walked outside as though in a daze, finding the shovel in the woodshed and digging as best I could a suitable grave for my lady. Though what patch of mud is suitable for a life? To what ghastly, cavernous earth could I commend her? To watch her fall into, graceless and slack in death, to be fettered over by worms and centipedes and all manners of dark things?

Forced to choose, I settled on a patch of pinkish flowers by a cypress I thought sturdy enough to keep her body from floating off as did Mrs. Sprattling's. Then I went through the painful process of burying her.

I found a nice frock of sorts I'm sure she'd worn as a younger woman, one of the few things in her closets that still evoked a sense of freedom. It was stitched all over with small, yellow flowers and the occasional image of a rabbit frozen in mid-jump. I cleaned her body and dressed her in this, then worked her hair into something presentable. She had left me no instructions, only given me simple, conciliatory hand-pats when I'd even tried asking her before … well … before.

She was too small for the coffin Mrs. Sprattling had made for herself, though she lay in the space so beatifically it seemed tailor-made. I said a few words, cried, and then nailed the cheap lid shut as best I could. Then I dragged the thing to the mud and lay it beneath, carefully as possible.

I filled the hole with dirt from her feet to her head, cringing at every thump of mud on the uneven and badly-set boards. I cursed myself for not ripping apart every abandoned bit of furniture in the house to make something more suitable for her, but I don't know how I'd have had the strength for the project. Even now I could barely work the shovel I was so distraught.

It was the last shovelful at the head of the cof-

 MUD OF THE HEART

fin that broke me entirely. Heavy with water, the dirt fell onto the face of the coffin and snapped the brittle boards. I watched as the dirt fell inside to stain the white shroud I'd wrapped her in, a section of unused linen from her workshop. Amongst the dirt and the shroud lay a lock of white hair that had spilled free from the wrapping, perhaps while I'd been moving her. I dropped to my knees, hands out and shaking.

I thought of the mud soaking through onto her face, dirtying her hair to a dull brown. I thought more of the dirt, the shards of old wood, falling onto the cloth over her open red eyes. Those beautiful eyes, which had looked on me in friendship a thousand times, now committed to the grave. To worms and centipedes and pill bugs, to dirt-crawlers that would rend them to pieces as though they had no value at all. As though they had meant nothing to the world. To me. To me. To me!

To me, the man who had let this woman die. Who was no doctor, no fixer of broken things, who allowed a perfect and beautiful woman to go mad with pain and sickness and finally kill her because he was so beyond his depth.

It was my fault! Me!

I stretched out my fingers to the spot where the mud had caved in the casket. How was I so sure she was dead? I was so incompetent, she looked so alive! I needed to dig her back up, to pull her out of that filth. She was no mere worm food. She was the most kind and understanding person I'd ever known. I couldn't do this to her!

I screamed and dug my hand into the mound of raised earth over the head of the casket, dragging it over the opening in the ground fistful by fistful until the space beneath me was flat and I was lying over it and sobbing like a child. My stomach was thick with steel. I was dying. I would die with her and damn the burial. I would give myself to the ravens.

A bullfrog croaked beside my filth-streaked face and I opened my eyes to look at it. It stared back at me for a long moment and then hopped off to wherever, content in its own existence. Not knowing what to do with myself, I stripped naked in the kitchen and washed myself and my dirty clothes in the sink using the hottest water the boilers would provide.

I awoke in my own quarters, still partially drunk off the brandy I'd stolen from my lady's larders. They were near to empty now, save for liquor and some dry ingredients that would last all eternity if eternity ever came.

The inside of my room was yellow with lamplight, but the hall outside my door flickered with the mad blue of the mental lightning storms of my delusions. I stepped out into that maelstrom, where the light moved on the walls like water and nothing had shape or sense. I saw something on the upstairs landing and sprinted the length of the library to the stairs, screaming her name.

I found her, this image of my lady, floating in her mad way in the hall. Her face lay in tatters over the bone. Only a single eye remained, still dully red despite the causal deflations of death. I held my hands out to her and begged her forgiveness.

"I am sorry," I sobbed at the apparition. "I had no better choice. You were in such pain, I … I didn't want to see you hurt like that." She said nothing, merely floated back and out of sight, coloring the walls with her passing. I chased after her, but she moved all the faster for my efforts, and soon I was on my knees in front of a wall, screaming and beating my fists against it alone in the dark.

Then I felt a presence behind me and turned to see him, the dark man, peering as was his way from the door of my lady's room. I screamed to him.

"Don't you dare! Not there! Never there!" Then I sprinted the length of the hall and into the room, not caring if he'd grow teeth and claws and rip me to pieces. I was beyond fear, or so I thought. I turned and saw him in front of me, close now, so that his mad, sunken eyes and slack, pale face were just before me. I screamed, startled, and stepped back only to stumble over something.

There was a thump, and then utter blackness.

I saw her sinking into the mud. At the far end of the garden. Her legs slipped beneath first, up to her ankles, and then the rest of her. She gave me that casual smile as though nothing in all the world was wrong. Even as she grew deeper, as the skin of her face moldered and stiffened, as the carrion bugs devoured the very flesh from her bones, she smiled. I ran, hand out, but I could not reach her.

The mud had her. The mud had her.

I awoke to a headache worse than any hangover. The morning light — I knew it was morning from the angle it came into my lady's bedroom — hurt not just my eyes but my brain. I clutched my pounding head and pulled away a hand covered in tacky, mostly dried blood. Looking up, I saw myself reflected in my lady's dressing mirror, a youth of nearly twenty-six, bedraggled from misery and face covered half in blood from falling and striking my fool head on my lady's nightstand.

My eyes were deeply bloodshot, an almost hilariously ugly answer to the radiant crimson of my lady's eyes. Great purple bags lay beneath them. My clothes were muddy and torn at the shoulder, an injury of which I don't recall the cause.

Then I remembered my dream, her smiling and sinking into the ground. Sobbing, I made my way out into the garden, picking around for the shovel and searching for the cypress beside which I'd buried her. I could only think of her down there, dirty and uncared for, alone in the mud.

I struck the mud with the shovel and began to dig. I found nothing, so I tried in another spot. Then another. Then another. It wasn't until an hour later, when my hands were so raw I could no longer hold the shovel and was digging with just the sides of my palms, moving thin amounts of earth aside, that I remembered my lady's comments about how the earth moves in this place. How Mrs. Sprattling's grave was gone to the swamps. And now I knew hers would be too.

I felt again that presence, that awful presence, and turned to see *him* staring down at me from my lady's work room. That dark figure, face all but concealed by shadow, staring down at me from the second-floor window. I snatched up the shovel in my bloody hands, fully intent on staving in the bastard's head with it, and rushed into the house. Again the halls were filled with that flickering light, but it was much diminished now, so that it felt more like a film on reality than a new reality wholly substituted for the one in which I existed.

This thin delusion persisted with me into my lady's work room. The figure wasn't there, as I believe now I knew before I even started into the house. Still I flailed about for him, getting mud and blood on all my lady's fine new silks and denims and linens, all those unrolled bolts of fabric she'd never put needle to. Eventually I stood in the window where he had looked out and saw myself down there, or at least a memory of myself, standing beside Ms. Withrow and looking out into the swamp.

It really was beautiful, the swamp, though perhaps you have to be a connoisseur of sorts to truly appreciate it. Then, when I'd stood beside her, I could think only of the dangers of the place. But now she was a part of it, truly within it and beyond where I or anybody else could reach her. It was a place where she was truly happy, a home beyond the home she'd been bound to.

A heaven only she understood, but a heaven nonetheless.

I dropped my bloody spade and sank into the corner, fully cloaked in my grief and wondering even what right I had to linger alone in this woman's home and mourn her. For all the closeness I felt, I was still a short-time interloper in a long life. It only took a single look at this mural on her wall to understand that. The story of her life played out in fine tapestry stitching.

As I looked closer, I saw many things I had not before. The version of my lady I had seen in my hallway delusions was represented here, and there, and there again, always spectral and distant. Often this thing would be found by that dark figure, who once spoke with my lady's father beside the concrete table in the garden. I saw him many times in the work, and then I saw myself.

In the end, her diminished abilities didn't allow her to work so well with the thread as at her height. The last years of her life mirrored the earliest in the lack of complexity, though the developed talents were heartbreakingly apparent. There was frustration in the tightness of the stitching, the angular and then sometimes crooked bits of patchwork placed here and there as cover-up.

The last entry in the quilt was flecked over with bits of blood, and I remembered the times I had found her at work in here and her fingers red with pin pricks. She'd forced herself through the last of it, and the final image was this:

The man, the dark figure, intertwined with the electric white figure, both of them twisted together until they were merged irrevocably, becoming a grey and new thing with the familiar features of a rabbit.

I sat and looked at this image for a long time, and the single, crooked word stitched into the fabric beneath. It was, in fact, the only word of any sort on the grand tapestry, and I still think on it at times. Should I tell you it? Perhaps not. Perhaps some things are, even though they might not seem it, quite private.

I stood after a long while and got myself together, cleaning up with the last of the house's hot water before turning off the boilers. I attended to the last matters of Ms. Withrow's estate, ensuring the windows and the like were closed as tightly as they could be and washing all the dishes. When everything was in place, beds made and all that, I collected the entirety of my earnings and the sums required be paid to the Holmes Company as part of my hiring.

I am an avid reader, as I have said, and I would like to say there was some great final confrontation. That perhaps I, through ingenuity or attention to detail, or through the strength of my convictions, set some great fault to rights. I cannot say any of that happened, though I did find I do not have the stomach for hospice work. I am a soft-hearted sort, and this occupation will certainly kill me if I keep at it.

I do not know the true meaning of Ms. Withrow's tapestry, or the life that played out on it. Despite the love I felt for my lady, I cannot pretend to truly know her, though I believe I had some idea. I think my part in her story was to be a handrail of sorts to the next stage of something I cannot understand, for better or worse, and I believe I accomplished that. I must believe it or I will simply drive myself mad.

I am now far removed from Ms. Withrow's estate, which has, like the woman herself, passed into the hands of the swamp. If you wish to come find me and make me answer for any of what transpired there, I am living in Cincinnatus and have included my address in this letter.

I do not believe I am insane, though you may disagree.

Thank you for your time, and for employing me these last three years in the service of the Holmes Company. Mrs. Holmes, I cannot express how much the opportunity meant to me. Hopefully I might rely on your good reference as I try to find a more fitting occupation.

In parting, I would like to leave you with an experience of Withrow Manor House I had upon leaving.

I had locked the front door and then hidden the key beneath one of the large rocks bordering the turnaround. Even then, the great fountainhead there had already become so overrun with vines it was unrecognizable. Much of the house was now so covered in green I could not make out where it ended and the swamp began. But as I stood, I felt something quite remarkable.

Utter peace.

It was as though it was shared with me, slipped into my hand like a note at a party. The feeling was intense enough I almost swooned from it, but I stood somehow, swaying like one of the great cypress trees in a windstorm. I caught no sight of untoward apparitions, no dark figures slinking about in the distance, but I did hear the rush and tumble of small creatures in the bushes just beyond the cobblestones.

I stood there for a long while and listened to the swamp. It was truly beautiful. And I think I understood her love for it as well in that moment. Then I heard the croak of a bullfrog, and looked down to see one the size of my fist standing on my foot. He looked at me, and I at him.

Then he bounded off in his own direction, and I in mine.

Yours truly,

Amos Huntley

THE END

Oh, Heaven

Upon mine eyes are coins, but they keep slipping off.

Nothing I can do to keep them on, to keep myself from rolling back across the planks, away from the sweet, cold water and the light. Oh, that blinding light.

On earth, as it is in Heaven, Otaheiti.

⌐

It's his fault, of course. That bloody madman, Christian. It was he who led us out into the dark, who turned us against the captain, who pulled us sure as a crosswind until we were floating in these doldrums.

I say we, but it is just I. Maybach, an Able Seaman

of no great accomplishment, but many, many years upon the foredecks and in the masts of ships.

I set sail on the Golden Fist shortly before the hurricanes came to those blighted sugar islands south of the New World. I had tired of traveling with human cargo and so took work as a hand on a ship headed in the opposite direction of those tired, dark faces. The lot of them would ever be half-dead with exhaustion and jaundice or fat with scurvy and bleeding even when they weren't cut. Those eyes, so flat and white and miserable, God that I'd never looked into them.

We didn't take on Christian in truth until we off-loaded in Djibouti, spice and rum and cotton and sundry other goods from the Keys that packed hulls still rank with the sweat of human misery. Captain Luxly, a lifetime man with the Company who'd done time as a pirate hunter under the Cook, strode up on decks with enough swagger to set us all rocking.

And with him, Christian Vetter. First mate. Protégé.

Luxly got to work straightaway, and even though many of us were on furlough or leave, the few remaining were held responsible for the condition of the ship. Within hours we were holystoning and washing every bulkhead and deck until the Golden Fist actually seemed its namesake. Weren't long before the lads took to saying that Luxly had shoved the Golden Fist right up our asses.

Still, it weren't a big ado then, just another brassy twat letting the lads know who the new boss was. Brass is like that, and I will say, they got to be. Otherwise things start getting out of hand. There are only two ways to tie a knot, they say, tight and right. Anything else and you're asking to get fucked. Man like that's gotta be a right, tight fist in the ass to get anything done. Just the nature of things.

Captain stayed ashore with his wife while we were overhauling the ship, but he left Christian behind. Christian were a queer sort, even then. Before everything. The man perched when he rested, like an albatross. He hadn't more flesh on him than a half-starved alleycat, but he sat fatly on things. Barrels, cross-ropes, banisters, it didn't matter. The man would pull himself up on them, just a little bit higher than you, and tuck his feet and legs up under his ass.

You'd come up the stairs and find him at the top, staring down at you with his mouth not quite matching his eyes. He'd fix you a smile and return the greeting of the day when you offered it to him. Then he'd flit off, going wherever the fucking wind blew him and bothering somebody else.

That's how I found him that last night before we shoved off. I'd been given the duty to relay the count — sailors, cargo, and the like — to the captain's quarters before he tucked in for the night. Luxly sat behind his desk in his quarters, mulling over a natty-looking map done up in characters I'd never seen before. I'd never learned my letters by any stretch, but traveling around as much as I did I could tell most characters apart at least by language.

The Arabs had their swooping, looping lines of curls. The Chinese had their little boxes and houses that went upways and downways on paper like chicken-scratch pillars. The Russians' nonsense looked like the Greeks' nonsense, and most everything else that was European looked like those enough I got 'em confused sometimes, but this was something new entirely.

The letters were completely black, and connected. They looked like rose bush switches to me, in honest, or maybe the shadows of them on the paper. Luxly seemed to be having his own bit of trouble working over the characters. He barely paid me attention as I rattled off the counts and he jotted them down in the book.

I myself was distracted by the other man in the room, Christian, though I didn't know him well at the time. He was a pale sort with dull, coin-gold eyes, dressed in dandy finery that always seemed a little too nice for being shipboard. As it was, his generally blue-black clothing was badly worn around the wrists and stained through on the white collars. Even his curly hair seemed oily and limp and brittle.

Christian was perched up on the piano Luxly had ordered brought aboard. A fucking sight that had been, Luxly's hen of a wife clucking after that thing every bloody fucking inch as we took it aboard. It was a pretty, flat, black piece of work the carpenters had toiled over carefully so it'd stay in place. Luxly proudly boasted there were only ten or so in the world like it.

If Luxly's wife was a hen, he was a rooster. The man had stick legs and a barrel chest that complemented his assless strutting. Though he claimed to have been a sailing man since birth, he had hands softer than kitten pussy and a dead-fish handshake. But we only knew that because he shook every man's hand when we got aboard that last day before shoving off. My mate, Lamplighter, reckoned it was on account of how much glad-handing the man did. Said it smoothed him like a holystone, them round rocks we used to sand the decks.

Still, it was well enough that he shook our hands in the first place. His sort rarely deigned to look men like me and Lamplighter in the eyes, much less actually reach out and touch us. Maybe to cuff an ear or the like, but never to show a man you saw him as that. As a man. Little good it did him in the end though, shame to say.

We shoved off and that was that, cool blue and green oceans all the way down south. Did a great deal of pirate watching passing France and especially around the shoulder of Africa. Not much we could do if we'd have seen them either. The Golden Fist was a slow tub if there ever was one, and twice as sluggish as the slowest pirate cutter. Moreover, we hadn't a single Marine aboard. Maybe a handful of the men could wield a knife or an ax well enough, but that'd do little against an accompaniment of men with flintlocks and cutlasses and the like.

Captain Luxly pushed us hard through them straights, near halving the time we'd expected to make down to the horn of Africa. I'll not waste your time with the technicals of it, but understand the man was a true master of the seas. He'd sit afore decks with Christian, pointing this way and that with his soft little hands and giving out directions like none the helmsmen and navigator had ever heard. They'd been through those waters a dozen times more than most of us and they grumbled at what they called "uppity new blood." But their complaints lost their wind as the Golden Fist found its own, again and again, slipping into currents and tailwinds them on the helm had never seen a once, despite their traveling.

That was the first of the troubles right there. One of the ship's helmsmen, a flat-nosed Moor, raised a stink about traveling through a shallows near Djibouti. He said he'd traveled those waters more times than possibly any man living on earth. Maybe he was right, though I doubt it. He had a habit of drinking and running off at the mouth to the crew belowdecks. The boys would get him riled up for sport, and I think that gave his heart a poisonous sort of bravery.

We were three slow, unsteady days traveling through the shadows when the helmsman lost his tongue in front of the captain. Aleph, his name was, was on edge from days of gripping the helm like a vice, guiding the Golden Fist between shoals littered with broken wood and rigging from other ships. The sand there was black as well, tarred dark from a rotten, stinking algae that had bloomed and died in the past weeks. Every slight rub against the high sandbars shook the ship.

"Steady now," was all Captain Luxly had said. Simple enough, but poor Aleph had heard that uselessness come from Luxly's face a dozen times in the past hour or so. He said it every time we sounded bottom with the hull of the ship. If you've never sailed, it's about the most frightening thing you can feel, aside from it outright rolling or breaking out from underneath you. It's like every plank and seam is shuddering, threatening to pop loose. It gets in your teeth, in your bones.

"We'd not be dealing with this if you'd just gone 'round these shoals," Aleph said, releasing the helm

     OH, HEAVEN

and rounding on Captain Luxly hard enough to make the man start. The currents took the rudder and the ship threatened to turn. In a single motion, Christian leapt down from the rear banister and lashed the Moor across his back with a ninetails I'd never seen him hold, much less use. Aleph fell out of the way, and Captain Luxly calmly stepped up to the helm, setting the course right and not saying a thing until he asked Christian to stop whipping Aleph. The man had all but shredded the poor helmsman down to the bone.

I had seen all this from a few paces away, set as I was to cleaning the decks thereabouts. The black algae — more some nefarious mold, we were learning — had begun growing up the bulkheads of the ship. It was foul and thin and slimy, impossible to clean without sanding the deck down to fresh wood. It stank as well, like a corpse pit, and any man not busy with the sailing of the Fist was always being called on for cleaning duties. Aleph lay in a pile of our sandings and scrapings as it were, barely moving, his blood making a nasty mush of the wood and mold. Other men on the cleaning detail worked around him, some casting mean glances at him for bleeding on the freshly cleaned parts. But nobody dared look at Luxly, for fear of Christian's cat.

The mood on the ship grew cold after that. Luxly's earlier affability was soon forgotten, and all talk became complaints of the ship's morale. Men grumbled their way from task to task, but even that little bit of freedom seemed curtailed by Christian's constant presence. The queer man roamed the ship like a specter, an imp, somehow always just up and out of sight wherever you were.

I found him hovering over me once during watch. I was posted on the starboard banister, shining a lamp down over the rolling black beneath the ship. Big water is most frightening at night. In the day it shines the light of heaven back at itself, a mirror over all the earth that God may look down and admire himself in. But that light don't go far down into that cold darkness.

You can see this at night, like I was then, when you're shining a lamp down at the surface. You see just how far the ocean will truly tolerate the light. It sits in a layer on the surface, like a pocket of oil. The deeper waters though, they hold illumination in contempt. You see, they neither need nor want it. And the surface serves that darkness by shining God's own glory back into His face. Blinding Him, so he can't see what horrors lay down there, just beneath the waves.

I snapped up from my reverie and turned to see two glowing, golden eyes burning in the dark above me. Christian sat perched atop the foremast spreader. In the Caribbean, there are fat-bottomed spiders that slide down on strings and drop their nets on prey, instead of just waiting for the tug of their web. That's what he reminded me of, sitting up there and just watching me.

He said nothing when I spotted him, though I shone the projecting lantern straight onto his face. The most he did was clear a scratchy throat and itch at some rash spreading up his left arm. I grew uncomfortable, watching him watching me, and turned around without saying anything. It would normally be polite to hail the first mate, but I didn't want to make a noise, for fear it might set him off somehow.

Despite Christian's queerness, he was popular with the rest of the crew. There were about forty of us in total, all sailors of some stripe and age, and he knew how to speak to us in our own tongue. People forget that — the high classes — that we don't all speak the same. It's like setting port in a strange land, better to stick with your own if you can't blend in, but Christian could blend.

I kept away from him for my own reasons, having always preferred to take my leisure in solitude. The others diced with him, and occasionally tried their hands at cards, though that was good as giving money away to the man. He had the devil's luck, they said, though I expect he made his own.

He drank too, and preferred the company of some of the roundabout types amongst the younger members of the crew. He'd snuggle them up in the first mate's quarters, and they'd walk around like new made brides the next few days. You ate better if you warmed better beds than your own, though some turned their noses up at that sort of thing. Thought it no better than whoring, or perhaps only slightly.

The captain kept hard on us through the Indian Ocean, where we made a show of firing our four ancient canons at would-be pirates and hoping they didn't notice our terrible lack of practice. More pirates — French in Arab ships, by the captain's speculation — tailed us through the heart of the Indian.

They were smaller ships, maneuverable and capable of getting close in bad wind or intercepting off-shore, but the Golden Fist made its money in the straight-aways, and they fell away over the course of days.

It seems like little, but the experience frayed the nerves. Word got around belowdecks of the horrible treatment of men taken by pirates in these waters. A story spread of a man branded and hobbled, chained to an oar to row from port to port until he took his own life by splintering the haft beside his chains and driving it into his throat.

A high-class man like the captain would be treated handsomely and then ransomed back to the Company for a tidy sum, everybody knew. So his taking chances in pirate waters to cut a few short weeks off the journey sat ill with the entire crew. And, if he heard the acidic mumblings in the corners of his ship, he gave no indication of concern save for pushing us harder. That was always his answer to the question: hard work and harder work still to keep men honest.

"The captain has little respect for us lower-class folk," was the grumbling heard most often. Aleph, who remained stiff till his dying day from the striping Christian had given him, complained that we hadn't need of any captain to run the ship. Talk turned lightly mutinous before we reached the straights of Indonesia, the Timor Sea, and then the islands of the Pacific.

We saw less and less of Christian at this time. The man had secreted himself away in his quarters, taken badly with some sort of illness. The captain elevated Lamplighter of all people to Christian's place, having decided my friend was a capable and honest man. The authority changed Lamplighter over the course of days, warping his earnest affability into sullen, rough distrust of his former shipmates.

"You've no idea the strain of dealing with you fools," he said to me once, after I'd complained of his new behaviors. "No idea at all." This caused a row between us that never healed, and only grew worse. Christian's illness had upset the delicate balance of ship life in a way nobody could have predicted, except perhaps Christian, I expect.

Without Lamplighter, I had nobody else to vent my complaints to on the ship. And so, I started venting them to everybody who would listen. The other men divided into two camps: those who couldn't tolerate the sight of me and those who clung to my every word. Who'd sneak over to my bunk to listen as I voided my spiritual bowels of complaints of treatment, class, and respect.

My reputation as a rabble-rouser grew on the ship until it caught the captain's ears. I was on my nightly watch, staring down in the roiling murk, when Captain Luxly himself came to visit me. His face was a vision of barely concealed anger and worry, and he pushed my shoulder roughly to get my attention. Then he lambasted me about my queer behavior and my carousing with the crew. I listened politely and gave him a greeting fitting his station, formal and clipped, which met with another concerned look. Then he shook his head and took leave.

Days later we reached Otaheiti. That chunk of gold set in the blue expanse of the Pacific. We breathed a sigh of relief across the entire ship that felt like a knife sliding back into its sheath. Even the captain smiled and laughed when the lookout spotted land. We had arrived more than two months ahead of time, and so had at least a month in port before leaving with our cargo for the return trip.

I supervised most of the offloading, though I remember little of it. It seemed every man had his head craned just over his shoulder as he bent to his work. Eyes shifted from boxes and barrels to the lithe brown bodies of the local women and the hutted drinkeries and smoke dens where we'd spend our hard-earned coin. The offloading ended shortly after dark, and I even saw Christian slink out of his quarters and down into the dockside alleys.

Oh Heaven, Otaheiti. Nights and days carousing with beautiful men and women, drowning in drink and song.

Oh Heaven, Otaheiti. Where sweat mixes with rum and the soft ocean salts debride away the stench of life.

Oh Heaven, Otaheiti. Denied and taken from us, when we were only just learning to love you properly.

It was Captain Luxly who dragged the lot of us back aboard the next month, sending the constabulary into every nook and cranny on the island until he checked off every name on the manifest. Only one didn't make it back aboard, on account of he'd been hanged the day after we'd landed for cutting off a native girl's nose when she'd insulted him. The captain gave that man's lay to the girl's family in recompense, though by all rights it should have been divided back out into the crew's take. Another slight against us, though he didn't know.

Another slight.

Christian crept back aboard with the setting sun, coughing badly and giving the watch a start. He didn't bother with the gangplank, but instead went hand over hand up the mooring line like a cat. Rumors spread that he'd gone after the services of some island witch doctor to cure the rash on his arm. Anybody the man passed smelled the rot in his skin, so like that black algae bloom off the coast of Africa.

His quarters reeked of it, and even when I couldn't see him, I could smell the stench as though it clung to me.

Heavy hearts cast off those lines that tied the Golden Fist to the shores of Otaheiti. Luxly addressed the men that first night, the placid ocean beneath us like a bale of deadening cotton. The stillness of the night belied our speed, the movement of the ship detectable only in the intangible creak and shiver of the wood and rigging.

From his speech, it was apparent he thought our escapades in Otaheiti had burned away the malaise gripping the ship before it reached port. In fact, the opposite was true. If anybody had trusted him enough to say, he would have known it.

We had tasted freedom there, in Otaheiti, a truer and more honest freedom than London had ever shown us. We had stretched legs we never knew we had, had felt blood pumping in veins long thirsty for heat. Many of us had become iron, red hot and needing a true, pure oil for the quench.

Not another four months in crucible.

Luxly ended his speech on a sour note, trailing off as though another thought had entered his head. Perhaps he had expected a more favorable reaction. Christian watched him from his perch beside the ladder well, yellow eyes catching the sparse lantern light with feverish wetness. He plucked at his rotting arm. The lesions there had bled through the linen shirt sleeve, and black dandruff fell from the cuff to gather on his stained blue trousers. He looked at me and I averted my eyes.

⌐

The mood on the ship soured quickly over the next week. Lamplighter, face stretched from the worries of his new position, seemed almost green from stress. Back talk and belligerence had become daily on the ship, and he had employed one of the bilge boys to take up his duty with the lash. His own arm had tired after the third or fourth day.

I kept counsel at nights. The men gathered around my hammock now formed a sort of wall for our secret meeting space. They seemed a mass of uniform black, dotted throughout with sets of eyes. We would tell the concerned others, the men whose loyalties to Luxly had never wavered, that we were rolling dice to avoid suspicion.

There we talked about many things. How we would run the Golden Fist if it were ours and not Captain Luxly's. How every man would rate a fair share of the lay and how we'd replace the lash with civility and direct conversation.

But most often we talked of Otaheiti, that golden paradise. We shared stories of rum and women, and our plans for when we returned. How we would conquer one of those islands for ourselves, then dismount the cannons and build a fort.

Our own Heaven. A Paradise. Otaheiti.

Lamplighter found me on my watch on a night soon after. A storm had broken the sky in the far distance, lightning thrashing the open sea with all the wrath of God. But here, so far away, the sea remained placid. The only hint of the storm was the sweet smell of rain on the wind, mixed with the ever present salt.

"You are a fool," Lamplighter told me.

"You are a bootlick," I told him in return. We argued like that for a while, Lamplighter threatening to have me striped, to have me hanged for my little meetings with the disaffected crew. I warned him in turn that a man wouldn't waste time with threats if he had the spine to carry through with them. He told me the captain planned to put me off the boat in Australia, chained and headed for the gibbet as a mutineer. I told him it was too dark to mount a search for a man overboard at this time of night, and that, anyway, nobody would probably hear if somebody fell off the ship.

Lamplighter blanched and called me a fool again, then stormed off into the ship. I turned back to the dark water, watching the film of green light skating over the oily blackness below. I pretended that I didn't see Christian perched up in the rigging again, eyes catching the light like stolen coins.

He found me the next day, when I was alone in my hammock after the night watch. He sat on the crossbeam that held our scant hammocks, twisted up into the curve of the bulkhead to do so. I watched with suspicion as his queer eyes played over me, looking for Heaven only knows what. When the silence had dragged on so that I thought I might scream to break it, he spoke.

"They'll put you off today, if you and the others don't take the ship," he said. His voice was slow and oily. The corruption on his arm had spread to his chin, and the blackish rash had taken on red and purple veining. I could not tell if those veins belonged to his flesh, or the creeping rot slowly devouring him.

"Why are you telling me this?" I asked him, not daring to move. In the stillness amidships, in the sulking darkness, his gaze felt like that of a large cat. He would devour me if I moved too quickly, moved at all. He scratched at the lesions on his arm. The shirt there lay in shreds.

"Don't you miss her, Otaheiti?" he asked.

"Yes," I said quickly, as though reciting a catechism. Even in this monster's mouth that name sounded so beautiful. Every syllable rang. Four of them in sequence, two beats, an accent, and another beat, music built into the word itself.

Otaheiti.

"Then go back to her," he said. His eyes flashed. The black dandruff fell from his face to settle on my bedroll. It disgusted me, but I dared not brush it away, dared not move at all. "Take the ship today. He'll have guessed your play by tomorrow."

So I acted, moving quickly through the lower decks and gathering the men I could. Some of the rest I could count on remained above decks, but by the time we had armed ourselves with hatchets and muskets from the powder keg, we numbered 24.

Our mutiny was a quiet affair. We walked above decks and stood like fools until one of the ship's lieutenants, a man named Fry, demanded to know what we were doing. Christian took his perch on the banister and so left it to me, of all people, to take charge of this fool thing. I demanded to see the captain, thinking I'd be abandoned by my men and hanged on the spot.

Luxly blanched at my platoon of mutineers. Knowledge of what was happening hadn't yet spread to the rest of the crew, and a dozen or so deckhands still milled about in the rigging overhead, seeing to the ship. Luxly's face turned red with anger, but he never so much as raised his voice. Instead, he commanded Lamplighter to have me surrender my weapon.

My friend approached with the bilge boy in tow.

"What have you done, you fool?" he asked. "Surrender, before there's any bloodshed." An honest request. I wish to this day I had honored it, had turned over my rifle and walked quickly and quietly to my noose.

Instead, I swung the gaff I'd brought as a weapon at his head. He ducked, but the barb caught the bilge boy in the cheek and dropped him to the deck. The boy clutched his face and howled, blood seeping through his fingers. The men behind me shouted, and our mutiny began in earnest. In minutes, and with no blood spilled by any hand but mine, it ended.

Captain Luxly stood resolute beside an aft banister with the rest of his loyal men, most of them officers and warrant officers. Useless plotters and planners that did no real work about the ship. He stayed calm and suggested we surrender, keeping at it until Aleph held a bayonet to his throat.

In the end, we set him and 18 others to sail on a lifeboat with enough provisions to get them to Australia. Luxly endeavored to remain captain until the very last, promising amnesty to the lot of us, save myself, if we returned the ship to his control. I felt my mutineers sway even as they pictured the nooses around their necks, a promise surely to be kept should Pursuers ever find us.

The thought of being betrayed by my own mutineers before my mutiny had finished rankled me. Then I felt Christian's eyes on me. They glittered up in the mizzenmast. They shone like steel left too long in the coals.

Lamplighter stepped forward to give some impassioned plea for sanity. He raised his hands to the side, standing in front of the captain and begging us to think rationally. I felt the tide shift against me and struck without thinking, burying my gaff in his chest, pushing it through his heart and into Captain Luxly's shoulder.

Both of them fell back into the lifeboat amidst cries of shock and outrage. The loyal men gave me looks of contempt like none I'd ever known. Those hateful eyes watched me as Aleph and the others lowered them to the sea. All those eyes save Lamplighter's, whose blank gaze looked only on the sky.

Little time was spent turning the ship around toward Otaheiti. It was with cries of "Otaheiti!" and "To Otaheiti!" that we raised sail and curved the Golden Fist into the waves. Only Christian looked back to the horizon, where Captain Luxly and his loyal men sailed with a dead Lamplighter.

The sun sank beneath the waves between us and our Heaven, Otaheiti.

We drank the captain's store of rum over the next two days, and lost a man to a fall on the third. I do not know his name now, and didn't then. We had allowed the captain to leave with the ship's register, having no need of it ourselves and not wanting such damning evidence aboard our ship anyway. The man had fallen from the foremast while tending to the Jacob's ladder. It had caught his throat on the way down, snapping his neck before he ever touched the deck. We put him overboard wrapped in sailcloth, though nobody knew what words to say over his body.

Work became much harder with the crew reduced by near half. Our nightly watches were ever half-asleep, and theft became an issue when the food stores grew low. I spent many nights with Christian, listening to his tales of what he'd gotten up to in the mountains of Otaheiti. He told me stories of golden temples and an old man who could make you immortal by carving a third eye into your forehead with cold iron.

Days passed, maybe weeks, and we did not reach

Otaheiti. Aleph came to me first, nervous and wring-
ing his hands. His fingers seemed long from the way
hunger wasted them. He said there was a man, named
Tav, among the rest who was suspected of stealing
food. All the men blamed him at least, but nobody
could find him. He said the mood on the ship was
getting bad.

Discipline had slipped or disappeared completely, and men had to be asked many times to do the
slightest thing. Ropes swung wild on the deck during
even the smallest storm. Worst of all, the creeping
black mold had slipped beyond the gunwales and
now sat on the deck, treacherously slippery in places
and reeking at all times of old, cold sewage.

Christian sat atop Captain Luxly's piano. The
corruption had spread across his chest so that even
his blue vest had soaked through with juice from
the weeping sores. He cracked his teeth, and Aleph
looked around the room. Then back at me. I grumbled about something — I can't remember what —
then I told him to bring everybody above decks for
a count.

We found the number at only 18, though I
thought I'd seen shadows of men in the rigging above.
The other men had grown nervous since the mutiny. Their eyes roamed over every stretch of the horizon for signs of Pursuers, when they were not keeping watch on their fellow hands. Hunger gnawed at
them, and thirst would come soon; we'd exhausted
nearly half the water barrels somehow.

I tried to make a brave show of leadership, storming up and down the rows and demanding Tav show
himself. I asked if anybody knew him, and most remained quiet. The few who did speak said they knew
that was the name of the man who'd been stealing the

                    OH, HEAVEN

food. An argument broke out and soon a man was left bloodied and alone near the base of the foremast, a knife sticking out of his stomach.

It took little for all aboard to agree that this man was Tav, so we strung him up by the spreader, despite him being near dead already from the stabbing. His dying body twitched and kicked and stilled.

We pulled him down and tossed him overboard, not bothering with words or sailcloth. A scrim of the black sludge seemed to cling around the sadly floating body as it faded into the waves and, finally, disappeared.

At Christian's urging I opened the coffers and divided the ship's remaining coin amongst the surviving mutineers. They made a show of being happy about it, but coin is little comfort when there's no spending it, and so the mood grew sour again. I began to feel eyes on me everywhere, and the men no longer sought me out to hear my stories of Otaheiti and the times we'd have there. Spotting land, I think, was the only thing that kept a knife from my back.

Three islands, each nearly as small as the ship itself, sat in a broad network of shoals in the water off portside. As many men grumbled about it not being Otaheiti as did celebrate any sight of land at all. With the lifeboat gone, we had no way to reach shore without grounding the boat. A sure suicide, if Captain Luxly had reached land and set Pursuers on us.

Two men volunteered to swim to shore, glad to be quit of the boat in any case. They leapt off the Golden Fist to cheers and shouts, waving from the water before paddling into the island. We watched a crowd of natives gather on the beach, coming up from huts hidden in the brush. In seconds they had filled the two men with spears and set canoes in the water to come for the ship herself.

On my orders, the remaining mutineers set up the cannons and fired at the natives. Only one shot hit, that I could see, blasting a canoe and the men inside to splinters. The other canoes retreated back to the island, where the natives gathered up our dead shipmates and dragged their bodies into the brush. God only knows why.

I had the men shell the island until the guns overheated and the splintered palm trees burst into flame. Then we sailed on.

I saw less and less of the men over the next few days. When I did, all I heard were stories of the elusive Tav, who'd squirreled himself away somewhere in the hold with a hoard of jerky and biscuits and limes. Or who'd learned to turn himself into mist with the help of some Otaheiti witch doctor, and was simply throwing the food into the sea to punish us for mutiny and murder.

Some days only Aleph would appear when I called the men up for a count. Other times maybe five or six would show. No matter what the hour, however, the ship always stayed in the wind, cruising along on a calm, dark sea. At any time of day you could hear men in the rigging, at the banisters, shifting the sails and tying the lines and keeping the Golden Fist moving.

You just couldn't look at them. Not long, anyway.

Lingering any sort of time on deck could make you sick from the smell of the creeping mold. It grew in thick patches now, fat little pads like loamy earth that were not slippery, but smelled all the more foul than the normal scrims of black.

My most pressing need came to be trying to find Tav so I could kill him and save my ship, and finding Christian. The man had disappeared somehow, but I knew he was still around. The black dandruff from his hideous rash lingered over all the ship's interior, sometimes filling the air between decks. It gave me grim thoughts of Captain Luxly and how the ship had once sparkled under his command.

A stink had built up belowdecks, where I never went anymore. The other mutineers now frightened and disgusted me. They slunk around in the shadows, drawn and grey, stretched thin from starvation. Aleph had taken to slinking around down there, picking up shares of the coin the men who disappeared left behind.

I finally found him slumped against the bulkhead.

Madness had reddened his eyes. His bloated gut slumped over his belt, skin splitting down over his belly button from distension. Bags of gold coins sat around him on the deck, and as I watched, he took a handful and put them in his mouth. Then he took a mouthful of saltwater from a bucket at his left hand and swallowed them.

He saw me and smiled. His teeth had all fallen out or gone black.

"What are you doing?" I asked him, prying another handful of gold out of his fist before he could put them in his mouth.

"Going to Otaheiti, Captain," he said with a laugh.

"Where are the other men?" I asked, and he shrugged.

"Look to the rigging," he laughed. "They'll not have me though. I'm for Otaheiti." He scraped a coin off the deck and raised it to his lips, but burped a bloody chunk of something into his palm instead. Gold coins shone amongst shreds of skin and other horrors. His eyes rolled toward me.

"On to Heaven," he whispered. "To Otaheiti."

I ran to my quarters, hoping to find Christian to ask for his help. I found him sitting on the top of the bookshelf, crushed into the tiny space between it and the ceiling. His head twisted nearly upside-down underneath his shoulders. Black fungus and thick red veins covered his face. His tongue lolled out over his nose, reaching his eye.

I thought him dead until he blinked and rolled his body back into a normal alignment, slimming himself like a cat until he was free of the space. I thought to ask him something, but my voice caught in my throat as he rolled along the ceiling, pressed there by some unseen force. His arms smacked hard against the planks with each turn. Face up against the ceiling, his back contorted violently so that his eyes could meet mine. His arms coiled back and forth over his body like snakes.

I screamed and ran from the room. Nothing remained of Aleph but a few bags of gold coins on the deck and some blood. I do not know if he threw himself overboard, but he was gone. Shadows flew overhead in the rotten sails, though my mind ached for me to look up at them.

I ran through the ship then, frantically searching for any sign of life other than myself. Even the elusive Tav, if I could find him, I would savor as company. But there was nothing, not a soul in all the ship save myself. Myself and perhaps Christian, though his foul dandruff seemed to cover every surface now. It even stuck to my clothes and face, turning my skin dark as Aleph's had been, darker even.

Months pass. I have not eaten. I have not drank. Hunger and thirst burn in me and yet I do not die. Overhead the shadows swing in the masts, which are rotted and gone now, yet still seem to flutter overhead. The sun does not shine through them, because there is no sun. Here, in these doldrums, it is always twilight.

I have thrown myself overboard, I have hanged myself, but always I awake again into this feverish, flickering nightmare.

I can sleep, here and there, but I remain tired.

Every time I dream of Otaheiti, a golden paradise. I dream the beach is underneath my feet. I have jumped free of this nightmare and swam to shore. There are lights on in the distance. Lights that shine on supple brown skin and endless feasts of flesh and liquor and all the sweet things between. And I can smell it. I can taste it. I can almost feel it, like warm breath on my neck.

Then the ship rolls over a wave and I am again awake, the stench of this carrion vessel in my nose and the rot slowly eating away at me. So slowly. So that I think it may never finish me. So I wait here and try to sleep and dream of Otaheiti.

I place coins on my eyes and beg for rest, but this ship is my own and only. There is no Charon to ferry me from this place. My money is no good.

I have felt the gentle touch of shallows beneath this vessel. They shake the Golden Fist, but they cannot destroy it. There are fluttering things in the endless dark overhead. Alien birds of an unknown shore. My crew of mutinous shadows dance in the rigging, preparing for us to land, even as the mold grows thicker over me. Grows into me. Pulls me into the ship.

Further from the light. Further from Heaven.
From Heaven. Otaheiti.

THE END

Ojos Oscuros

When I was a child, I lived in an agave field.

We lived in the highlands, east of Guadalajara, where the ground is low and flat and brown. It stretches to the horizon in all directions, until all you can see is the rocky dirt and the sky and the agave. You have never seen agave, because I brought myself to America long before you were born, but it is nothing special to look at.

The leaves are long, thick, flat, and barbed at the edges like saw blades. They grow taller than a child, sometimes as tall as a man, spiny things that erupt from the earth in slow motion over a decade, longer even, before they are harvested.

We lived amongst these formidable things in a shack my father's father had built as a hideaway during one of the revolutions. It doesn't matter which, only that he came to hide on this land and, in so doing, passed the destiny of our insignificant brood into the hands of Don Martino and his family, the Martinez Clan. Don Martino died in my father's thirtieth year, and passed control of the land, the agave, and our lives into the hand of his son, Don Javier "Bello" Martinez.

The entirety of that family were criminals. Their patriarch, Don Martino, robbed stage coaches and trains in Texas before escaping American justice to return to his "ancestral" homeland. In truth, Martino was nothing more than a peasant, like I was growing up, born a bastard to some nameless woman in Guadalajara. He adopted the surname of Martinez in the old way to pass a sort of legitimacy down to his children, which all of them squandered in time.

Except one of his granddaughters. But I will tell you her story much later.

I tell you all of this because you do not know what it is to be a peasant. You know poor, you understand impoverished. Your mother has told me you have aspirations to help the poor and indigent of this nation, people who look like you and who, by that logic, you think you have some brotherhood with.

I will not dissuade you from this. It's not my place, and, anyway, I believe it's as good a way to pass the years as any. Better than most, in fact.

But what you must know is that you have no understanding of what it is to be a peasant.

To be a peasant is to be below. To be beneath. There is always the understanding that there are real people, the people who wear fresh clothing and go where they please, and those people are above you. And so you may think, at least the animals are beneath me, but you would be wrong. Because every well-bred horse and dog is above you. And so you might think, well, at least the plants growing from beneath my own dirty feet are beneath me.

And you would be wrong, because still there is

the agave.

I walked with my father through the rows of agave the day this story begins, truly begins, listening as he pointed out plants to me one after another and told me what was happening the year and day they were planted.

"This one," he said, "was planted when President Carranza had Zapata assassinated. You can see in the color and the size that it's ready to be harvested. Eight to twelve years, Abella, then they're ready." He held out his hand and I handed him the coa, what you might think to call a hoe if you'd never seen it used, though there's really no English word for the thing. Imagine a spear, but instead of a point, the blade is a flat disk just *this* much smaller than a dinner plate. The disk is kept sharp along the forward edge, and it's with this tool we harvested the agave.

Father worked the great plant out of the ground, wedging it up and cutting away the roots that lay beneath the soil. Then he chopped the long sawblade arms away one-by-one, until all that was left of the thing was a great, round ball. The piña, most jimadores call this, because it looks like a pineapple. But my father, he called this part el Corazon. The Heart.

"I think you are strong enough for the harvest, eh Abella?" he said, turning to me and handing over the coa. His hands were broad and flat, and very rough, though my father himself was not a large man. He wore a faded burlap patch over his right eye where a bullet had smashed into his cheek as a young man.

The traces of a crude eyeball I had drawn there with chalk years earlier still lingered.

"Yes, Papa," I said, taking the coa from him. I had followed him through the fields for years, watching him work and carrying water and occasionally dragging the agave hearts to our little wagon for loading. I had held this crude, sharp tool a thousand times before, but only now did I feel the weight of it. It was by this thing, and by sweat of my father's labor, that our family ate.

He saw in my eyes that I understood the responsibility he was passing to me, and smiled. His remaining eye was very dark, though it twinkled brightly in the shadows beneath the ruinous weaving of his sombrero. Beneath that he had the same thick mustache that most men found fashionable at the time, though he grew his wide at the sides to cover the scars of his ruined cheek. Other than that, he wore the simple cotton trousers and linen shirts afforded us by the kindness of the Martinez Clan, whose land we worked by the mercy and grace of God.

Oh, and he wore a crucifix, which was more dangerous in those times than you might ever imagine.

I worked for the next hour or so in the fields, straining my child's body to its limits to show my father my value as a worker. I fell into a rhythm, chopping the agaves down to the hearts as he carried them to the wagon. All the while he sang songs I knew half the words to, and I would try to sing along with him. Before the sun began to set, we had maybe thirteen hearts packed between the worn wood slats of the wagon. They were so heavy that our mule, Grovier, stamped in consternation with every weighty thump.

Father lifted the water jug from Grovier's side satchel and set it atop one of the hearts as I fitted the back door of the wagon into place. He stretched his arms, rubbed his back, and then took off his sweat-stained shirt and laid it out across the sidewalls of the cart to dry a bit. I followed suit on the other side of the wagon, relishing the feel of the sun wicking the sweat off my shoulders. I set my own straw hat, a child's hat now almost too small for me, atop one of the hearts and chuckled to myself at the thought of a little piña man going into town wearing such a thing.

My father laughed himself and turned around to see what I was going on about. He had been standing with his back to me, so I could see the lines of purple scar traveling left to right over his spine. He made a noise I would have laughed at when he saw me, if it hadn't scared me so badly. A sort of gasp choked off as he inhaled the bit of water he'd been drinking. He turned back around quickly and waved a hand blindly behind him. At me.

"Abella," he said. "For the love of God, put your shirt back on, girl." He cast his eye to the ground and I stood dumbfounded for a moment. The sun no longer felt so good, but hot and oppressive instead. I looked down at myself and saw the two small lumps of flesh that had only just started pushing out of my chest. In the deep brown of my skin, you could never see the blush that suffused me, but I felt that hot creep of blood crawling just beneath the surface of me from head to toe.

I grabbed the shirt and pulled it on quickly, wrapping my familiar old work shirt tightly across my chest like a shawl. The agave stood vigil around us, the knife shapes of their silhouettes slashing at the last tangerine hints of the sun. My shirt was thin and wet and smelled of dirt and sweat and agave sap.

I didn't dare turn around until the soft scent of tobacco smoke filled the air.

My father, still not looking at me, stood beside Grovier with his hand on the mule's neck. The stubborn animal stamped and tossed baleful looks back in my direction, but otherwise remained quiet. The polished crescent beneath the rim of the coa shone orange from where my father had rested it atop the pile. Not knowing what else to do, I stepped up beside my father and we quietly returned home.

That night I sat outside our little home, that pile of mismatched wood my father had done his best to keep from falling over all these years, and I watched the moon. I had forsaken the simple pants and shirt I almost always wore for some of my mother's old clothes, a simple brown dress and blouse with an orange woolen poncho. It was the time of year when the heat of the day gave way to terrible cold at night, and like my own wet workshirt earlier that day, I pulled the poncho tight around myself and tried to become small and unnoticeable.

The clothes *were* warm, but uncomfortable. My mother was no larger or smaller than me at that age, but they were not clothes I was comfortable in. They felt impractical and fragile, as though anything might ruin them at any time. The fit was such that I felt I was drowning in the clothes, rather than wearing them. Even then, I thought perhaps that was preferable to the odd look my father had given me.

I had given honest effort to speaking with my mother about the odd exchange while Father was up at the Martinez Clan's palatial hacienda dropping off the agave hearts, but it was a waste of my time. My mother, God bless her heart, was a stupid and cowardly woman, the sort who loathed to think and loathed even more any who tried to make her think.

She realized fairly quickly that some tension had built between my father and me during our work in the field once we returned. Her matronly reaction had been to busy herself with the washing and cooking at the back of the house — unnecessary chores, of course, but welcome distractions. I had tried to make myself useful to my father, but he had shrugged me off, sparing me only one worried glance before giving the cart a once-over and heading up to the hacienda.

For years I had followed along with him after a harvest. I liked walking through the high gates and over the well-swept orange and brown tiles that led to the tequila distillery at the back of the property. Serious men lounged here and there throughout the place, and beautiful women who were always caked in makeup and perfume and smelled and looked like roses. They would always smile at me and sometimes the men would offer me cigarettes, though I had taken to turning them down after the first — and last — time I tried smoking.

But this night my father left me behind. Behind with my mother, who spoke little and thought less, who stirred at pots of rice and pots of laundry and did nothing of note save pass as a shadow through the small spaces of our house. I tried to speak with her several times, as I said, and the last was met with a simple revelation.

"Perhaps you have something to do outside," she suggested, stopping in her stirring and moping for just a moment. Like Father earlier that day, she didn't deign to look directly at me, simply tilted her head slightly in my direction. At best I saw the faintest brown crescent of her eye, and then I was outside.

And I sat out there for a long while, curled up in the folds of my mother's old dress and listening to the night. Flying things and creeping things, coyotes howling somewhere in the hills to the west, all of them mixed with the steady rush of the wind through the broad leaves of the agaves, which twitched to the gentle rhythm of the desert air. But beneath all these things — at the time I thought the noise was only in my mind — another sound stood in cacophonous opposition to nature.

Chuckling, is what it was. Not laughing. Chuckling. As if at some sick joke.

I thought at first it was my mother, but the sound was too mad for such a boring woman to make, and too masculine anyway. It was the voice of perhaps a young man, the sort who was just a touch older than me, and always getting into trouble.

Most incredibly, I realized, it was coming from beneath my family's little house.

I turned so fast I stumbled over my skirts and tumbled over myself and ended upside down and staring into the darkness under the house. The space there was a simple crawlspace, filled with little more than dirt and a few odd, rusting farm implements Father had either only a rare use for, or no use at all. But in that space of twisted shadow I saw something that caught my heart in my throat.

The moon was very bright that night, and full, and the soft grey light that found its way beneath my house caught in the wet blackness of two large eyes. The eyes of no animal on this earth, though in that moment I thought my throat was in immediate danger of being torn out by a ranging mountain lion. Then it laughed at me.

"You look like a fool," it said. I remained still. Like a fool, I had laid on my stomach to see better under the house, and now I was in no position to push myself away and run. As if sensing this, it spoke again. "No need, little darling." And a little paw — like that of a cat, though attached to an appendage seemingly devoid of bones — slipped from the very edge of the shadow and laid over my wrist. It was simultaneously warm and chill, like the bottom of a hot pan filled with ice, and covered in fine black hair. Like a kitten's hair, almost.

"Please, don't hurt me," I said to it. In those times, in that land of arid flatness, old superstitions still held in the hearts of the people. None matched perfectly with what I was seeing, with what I was speaking to in the shadows beneath my family's home, but still that feeling remained. A sort of grandness in the heart, like falling off a great cliff. The knowledge that you are suddenly face to face with legend. With the arcane. That you are in conversation with something beyond your own little self.

"No," it said. Its teeth, tiny and sharp and black, caught the moonlight sometimes as it spoke, but otherwise remained invisible. The creature spoke a soft, lisping, and very old sort of Spanish. And it was *Spanish*, from the old continent, the tongue of the conquistadors, not the weathered dialect you might call Mexicano.

"I would not hurt you for a million reasons, little dear one," it said. "You are safe when you speak to me."

"Why?" I asked him, for it seemed to me this thing was male. And even in this retelling I think, perhaps, it would be rude for me to refer to him otherwise.

"Because I see the strings," he said. "My mother taught me how a long time ago." His paw slid under my wrist, the two black claws at the end of it scratching gently at the soft flesh on the underside of my arm, making the cloth there feel worthless and immaterial. The pads of his fingers rested in my palm for the briefest second, and then were gone back into the shadows.

"The strings touch every part of this land," he continued. "They dangle from the leaves of the agaves here and stretch into your home. They are wrapped like cord around the throats of your father and mother. They hang like nooses over the arches of the hacienda on the hill." He chuckled. "But they don't touch you."

"I don't know what you're talking about," I told him.

"You do," he replied. "But not just now. Like I said, I *see* the strings, and I see you having this conversation now and remembering it years after and thinking long and hard on it years after that. I see you as all sorts of things, sitting around and thinking about my words. A doctor. A criminal. A mother."

"A doctor?" I blurted. An image had formed in my mind with such clarity it stole my breath. It was me, an old woman, standing over a plastic bed covered in white sheets where a man with a missing arm was sweating out a terrible fever. I didn't even know what "plastic" was, but there it was in my mind, as sudden and sharp as a knife to the heart. I found I was holding my breath and exhaled.

"So that is what you'd like to be, eh?" he said. I looked into the eyes of this terrible little thing beneath my house and nodded, terrified, my own eyes nearly as wide as his. Like the tide sweeping back out to sea, I felt the other memories, held by the women I might become, filling my mind. One was a mother, embittered by the world and as frightened and thoughtless as my own mother. The other was a violent, sneering woman, face more badly scarred and worn than my father's.

But both of these thoughts were merely that, thoughts. Memories. Smudged windows obscuring the true image in the far distance. Me, an old woman, standing beside that strange and alien bed. Through these other, filthy versions of myself I saw my true and real future. I saw myself reading papers — in *English* of all things — attached to a board and resting my hand on the man's head.

The man smiled and slept.

"You are going to die here, in this place," the thing said. His eyes were full of mirth despite the sentence he imposed upon me.

"Why do you say that?" I asked. A spell had broken that I didn't even realize I'd been under. The visions of my future no longer seemed so real, so possible. So sure.

"Because I see the strings," he said. The statement was simple. Matter-of-fact. "You will be, at best, the criminal. At worst, the mother." His teeth shone again as he smiled. They were black and viciously curved, though I could see little else of him but the occasional tuft of hair. "But I can help."

"How?"

"Trade," he said. "Fair trade." Three paws flitted to the air in front of my face, all at the ends of wriggling black arms. Five claws shone in the moonlight, two on each hand save one that remained retracted. "You

OJOS OSCUROS

are a peasant now, a farmer, despite the lofty heights of your future. So I will trade you for harvest."

"Harvest?" I asked. And he smiled.

"Five hearts," he replied. "Not of the agaves, you understand." I opened my mouth to speak and his wriggling arms wrapped around my wrist, dragging me deep into the shadows beneath the house. The air was cool and the dirt cooler, so that it felt like the great icebox in the hacienda. His body was an almost unbearable pressure on my chest, but it warmed me as the invisible parts of him wrapped tightly around me.

I found the back of my own hand hovering just inches from my face. The brown of my skin almost glowed in the faint moonlight compared to the jet blackness of the creature resting on top of me. His teeth were more evident now, and I saw there were enough of them — long and sharp as they were — to tear a pig's head from its shoulder with a single bite if the mood struck. I thought to beg, but remained quiet.

"Five hearts," he said, softly. "The strings don't touch you, but they should, you understand? Something has conspired to shuffle you loose, to steal your destiny." He chuckled. "But I am a hungry Diosito, and perhaps they didn't know I was watching you. That their little machinations spun such chaos into the threads that their deception has been writ large across reality."

"I don't know what you mean," I said, tears welling in my eyes. I thought my chest would break under the weight of him. His words smelled like blood and ripped meat.

"You *will*," he whispered. "But to get to that point, I will have to unweave you. Five is the price, delivered in time. On credit, as they say." His claw found the back of my hand and cut deep into the flesh. "The Patron." Blood shone bright, brighter than anything in that dark space. It dripped onto my face, onto the corners of my lips.

"The Matron," he continued, cutting me again and again with each name. "The Lover. The Stranger. The Fool."

My own blood covered my face by the time he finished, so that I could barely open my eyes for how it burned them. The smell was overpowering.

"Do you accept?" he asked.

"Yes," I whispered, and he pressed my own palm to my face, smearing the blood from my forehead to my chin.

"Then it's done," he said with a last, long chuckle. "When you are ready to pay, call my name. Look into the darkness and whisper, *Sombrero*."

His face moved closer and closer to mine, until I could feel his fur sticking to the gore on my cheeks. Then he licked me with a tongue longer and thicker than my forearm. Roughly, like a mother cat cleaning a kitten. The flesh of the organ was hard as Grovier's thighs under a load and dappled with knobs like a pickle. The motion was so harsh it pulled my mouth and eyelids open several times.

Then it was over, and he was gone. The pressure of him vanished without noise, and I crawled from beneath the house in a panic, taking several shaking steps without ever looking away from that shadowy space.

This is how I came to nearly knock over my father, who cursed loudly and jumped when I slammed into him. He wrapped his hands around my arms and looked into my eyes. His own were painfully bloodshot and sick with worry, but about something other than me.

"What is it, Abella?" he asked. I looked behind me and then again at him. A man stepped out of the shadows and into the light coming from inside our house, a man I knew from some degree by my trips to the hacienda, though I could not place his name. His eyes were tight and tipped up with a laugh that seemed chained deep in his throat, strapped down just ever before the point of bursting. Our eyes met for the briefest second and I saw him grind his teeth, if only just a bit, biting down on that errant bit of joy to keep it controlled.

"Abella," my father said, repeating himself. He leaned forward so that I would see his eye again. The faintest touch of candlelight caught like a spark, but it otherwise remained dark. The faintly painted blue eye on the burlap covering the empty socket sat in shadow as well. I looked back and forth between both, not knowing what to say, what words might answer the question and not leave me looking mad or addled.

"A snake," I told him. "I saw it go beneath the house." My father looked past me and the familiar man looked at me, those teeth crunching gently against each other. The light from the windows pooled over his face, dancing mad and orange though the sky itself was green and deeply darkening over his shoulder. His eyebrows were thick and stood like mounds over the deep brown plains of his otherwise flat and angular face, giving me the impression of an unfinished charcoal drawing.

"Time for that later," the man said, and by his voice I knew him. He was Paolo, the son of the Hacendado, Don Martino. Their voices were perfect imitations of one another, differentiated only by age, the slight cracking of the gently rolled Rs. "I want to meet your family. They are *my* family as well, after all."

My father gave one last look to the space beneath the house and then joined our somber procession inside.

There is little to say of the dinner and drinks that followed. Paolo Martinez poured mezcal down his throat as though he were trying to quench a fire, or perhaps start one, and my father kept up with him out of politeness. My mother and I retreated to her room and sat awkwardly as they passed stories between one another, most of which Paolo happened to be the hero of to some degree.

Hero is a generous term here; *protagonist* is probably more accurate. The man was a drunk and a gambler and a proud murderer of other men in duels. He had a passion for starting fights on others' behalfs and then finishing them, only to swallow whomever he'd helped with the debt of the action.

He considered all of this as a sort of philanthropy, to hear him tell it, the *Noblesse Oblige* of the Mexican ruling class. But any simple child — even as I was then — could see he was little more than a chest-beating thug who enforced his father's whims on the people of the countryside. These self-absorbed stories existed only to be challenged, so that he might have a reason to slap the handle of the pistol he carried around in a black leather holster on his hip.

Because at the true depths of this man, he was no hero or villain or any such thing.

     OJOS OSCUROS

No.

He was simply a boy who'd never been told "no," who had never found a fruit too forbidden to savor. Who had grown into a man living at the very edge of sanity, ever waiting for any reason to slip down into the black waters below.

He stayed with us through the night, falling asleep in the communal room where I made my bed. I found him there with dawn light seeping over him, painting his face orange where the floorboard behind him remained dark and almost green from wear. I made to quietly pick my work clothes off the ground and his eyes snapped open suddenly, his hand whipping out to latch onto my arm. For a moment, I was reminded of that dark creature in the space beneath my house, the little animal with which I'd made a deal I barely understood.

The back of my hand was twisted up to my face again in that moment, though it was Paolo Martinez's angry eyes on the other side of it, and not the large, smiling eyes of the one who called himself "Sombrero." My hand was clean and uninjured, though I'd gone to bed the night before cradling the nasty cuts, hiding them in my skirts.

"Never sneak up on me," he said, tapping his incisors together twice. *Click click.* This was followed by a slow grind of his teeth throughout his mouth, the way another man might stroke his beard while thinking.

"I'm sorry," I said.

"No, you're not," he replied. "You're lucky." He pushed my hand back at me and then laid back down as though I were not there at all. "Now let me sleep."

I obeyed him and got to work outside, taking care of Grovier's morning necessities and harnessing him to the cart. Mother came outside as well after a minute to tend to her own chores. We worked in silence, waiting for Father to show, though he never did. It seemed Paolo's mezcal had done him in for the day.

It was not the sort of tequila they made from our agaves. That was cheap stuff, for farmers and Americans. In fact, most of what they made at the hacienda was headed for America before it touched the inside of a bottle. Don Martino's family sold it at four times its worth to American bootleggers in Texas, who would in turn inflate the stuff on its way further north.

"Look at this," Paolo said, stepping out of our house. "Women hard at work." He smiled at me, tipping the flat brim of his hat to just overtop his eyes. His jaw worked back and forth. "I like that."

"Thank you, Don Martinez," my mother said reflexively, stopping her work for just a second to nod at him. He smiled. I said something in kind and went back to Grovier, petting the back of his neck and hoping my father would come outside so we could leave for the fields. So I could leave this man.

"Oh, a coa," he said, picking my father's tool from the back of our cart and waving it around his head like an idiot. "I've never really seen one up close before. No reason to. But I heard they cut through the agave like butter." He smiled at me and his face opened up over that grin. His *eyes* opened up, for just a second, so that I couldn't help but see deep down into the core of him. I felt myself tightening my clothes around my chest the way I had the day before, stepping back toward Grovier.

Then he lashed out with the coa, swinging it down in an arc I was sure would catch Grovier in the neck. I would have jumped in front of the sweet, stupid animal if I'd have had the time, but thankfully I was still frozen in place by that hideous look on Paolo's face. Grovier whined as the coa struck home.

But it didn't strike Grovier. Instead, I heard a steady, harsh rattling and the noise of gravel scattering away from the impact. I looked down to see the head and first twenty odd centimeters of a rattlesnake wriggling madly away from the rest of its body. The head of the coa sat half-buried in the ground, blood from the snake streaking the dull silver disk in a perfect red stripe.

"I guess it works on snakes, as well," Paolo said. The laugh he'd been biting down on all the day before cracked his throat open wide. It chilled me to the bone. When he laughed, it was like there was somebody squeezing something out of his chest, pumping it open and closed like a bellows. His eyes widened nearly as far as his mouth, and his head swiveled to me. Then it was over. Done. Gone.

I looked to my mother and saw she'd frozen in place. Her fingers shivered over the flatbreads she'd been laying out to cook in the stone oven behind the house. I turned back to Grovier as the poor, stupid thing started stamping and squalling. It had only just begun to understand the presence of the snake. The noise of the snake's rattle, still going despite the decapitation, was driving him into a fit.

"Look at him go," Paolo said, poking at the rattlesnake with the now bloody coa. The thing was flipping over itself and making feeble attempts to strike.

The rest of its body had coiled into a perfect, circular pile as though the head might soon rejoin the rest. Or perhaps, as though it had never left.

"Please, just finish it," I whispered despite myself. Paolo gave me a look so condescending it made me blush, and then struck the snake again just behind the skull. It stopped struggling and Paolo flicked it away toward the house. Then he spread out his arms and nodded his head slightly. "You're welcome."

Several awkward minutes passed with Paolo inserting himself into our daily lives, asking foolish questions and being purposefully in the way. Then a stagecoach pulled onto the road alongside our house, coming down from the hacienda. Paolo stretched his arms and walked to it, setting his hands behind his head. A man and a young woman stepped out onto the ground.

The man was Paolo's father, Don Javier "Bello" Martinez, the acting head of the Martinez family. The young woman was Paolo's little sister, Maria. She frowned at her brother and then looked us over and waved. She was perhaps my age, a touch older even, but tremendously beautiful and well-educated and all the things that separated her from people like my family and the dirt we lived on. I waved back.

My hand curled, wilted even, when Paulo looked back at me and waved himself, thinking my hand was raised to him. For the third time I felt myself wrapping my chest tighter in my sad old work clothes, a feeling I was beginning to hate. Then all of them were back on the carriage and bouncing away down the road. Heading for some social engagement in Guadalajara, if I had to guess.

I plucked my father's coa off the ground and cleaned the blood from the blade by rubbing it in the dirt. My father still hadn't woken by the time I had sharpened the thing again, still hadn't woken by the time mother had all but finished collecting the trash to burn in the pit behind the house.

Perhaps her screaming woke him, though, when she picked up the severed rattlesnake head and the thing flipped in her hands and bit her on the wrist. I wouldn't know, I had eyes only for my mother, and the insane dead thing gnawing mindlessly into the soft flesh of her arm. Its eyes were fully grey, and clouded over, but even as I watched it pumped slow death into my mother.

Even as I watched, it ended the life I'd always known.

Though, if I'd have paid more attention, I'd maybe have seen the dark eyes glittering in the shadows beneath my family's home.

She didn't die right away — that came later — but death set in her bones sure as any strong thing roots in fertile ground. My mother's body had always been fertile ground for death. Even in my old age I believe that's all she'd been given to from birth, some small amount of suffering and then death.

The short months after the bite saw her lose the arm to infection, even though she survived the venom. Then she lay in the back room of our house and stank and rotted and never died. Father would lay with her in some attempt at normalcy, or perhaps because he knew no other option. Perhaps still it was to keep her from sleepwalking, which she did with some regularity, wandering blank-eyed through the kitchen and even outside to tend to chores as though her missing hand weren't missing. Dabbing fever sweat away with her stump.

Father believed that better doctors could help her, out in the city, but they were far beyond our means to afford. He would go to Guadalajara and to the missions in the countryside in his free time, begging for help to save his wife. Of the hundreds he talked to, only two ever humored him and visited Mother. The first, a country doctor, looked her over and then hugged Father for a long moment. They drank together after for a long while and then the man left, and Father spent the rest of the week cursing his name and sobbing at Mother's bedside.

The second man came at the recommendation of Don Bello, an expensive city doctor who smiled a lot and smelled like cigarettes and wet flowers. He was tall and thin and spoke with a painfully American accent that convinced Father he could cure death itself with the right amount of money. Perhaps even that's what he said, because soon my father was trying everything under the sun to scrounge together dollars.

I won't waste your time with the details of these mild endeavors; they were stupid and ill-advised. And, ultimately, every one of them to the last was completely futile. Even the one that worked.

Father began to leave me alone in the fields in the fourth month after the bite, mostly because he stopped coming home for days or weeks at a time. He would leave with Paolo Martinez in one of the little touring cars that people had begun driving around then. He would come home tired and drunk sometimes, and one time mistook me for my mother.

He stopped me in the doorway and held me against himself in a way that wasn't … inappropriate, though it was too forward for a father to hold his daughter that way. His big hands pressed my face into the cigar and liquor stink of his shirt. He had begun wearing a pistol on his belt as well, and that dug into my hip painfully. I tried to push him away, but it didn't work.

Nothing happened, save that he wept on me like a child. He called me by my mother's name and kissed my forehead, gently, and then slumped back against the wall behind him and fell into a sweating, sobbing heap.

A few days later he was dead.

There was little in the way of a funeral. Paolo and Maria Martinez came by the house with their father and a bloody little slip of burlap. My father's cheap eyepatch, the blue eye there flecked with dry burgundy droplets. Don Martinez handed it to me with a somber expression, and then his daughter wrapped me in a hug.

"Thank you so much for the sacrifice your father made for our family," she said to me, pressing her pink, perfect lips to my cheek. I'd never been kissed by somebody that beautiful, and so it came as a bit of a shock. She stepped away and Paolo took her place, teeth grinding so hard the sound was just slightly louder than the sweep of desert air blowing through the agaves.

"I'll be around to take care of you, now that your father's gone," he whispered in my ear before pressing his lips to my cheek. And I'd never been kissed by somebody that terrible before, and so it came as something of a shock. Paolo's sister saw how the kiss lingered and a sad look came over her face. She turned quickly and hopped into a carriage, her father glaring at his son and calling for him to follow.

Then they left, just as they had the day of the bite, hopping onto their little carriage and bouncing away up the road without a care in the world. But not all of them, no, Paolo stayed behind to "look after me." Just as he promised he would.

✦

We stood beside my dying mother's bed and then he sat beside her. Paolo's fingers slipped beneath her head and tilted it up to the light, rocking it back and forth. He shook his head and set her skull back into the concavity it had worn in the pillow. Sweat glistened on his hand, and he wiped it off on the chest of her nightshirt.

Then he looked at me.

"She's dying," he said.

"She's already dead," I said back to him, turning to leave. He grabbed my arm.

"Your father said her name before he died," Paolo said. His words were like oil in the humid quiet of the room. The only light came from a gas lantern he'd set beside the bed, an amenity we'd rarely used in my father's lifetime. His face was mad and orange beside my mother's, which was pale and green and grey and all but bloodless. They made my stomach turn, those swirling, mixing colors. It felt like the hissing gas flame was sucking all the oxygen out of the room, making all the shapes dance and warp out of shape.

Paolo's teeth cracked and ground behind his lips. His mustache was coal-black and slicked into position with some sort of pomade I could see caked up around the edges of his lips. Some of the hairs were stained off color from cigarette and cigar smoke, which even now colored his breath and made me want to vomit.

He reached up and twined his fingers through my hair.

"He said, 'Take care of Abella and Carlita,'" Paolo recited, his eyes dancing over my face. His grip tightened and he pulled me closer. "He said, 'Carlita is sick. But your father knows a doctor that can make my wife better. Please.'" He leaned in. "'Please Paolo, take care of my family.'" His other hand came up to rest on my hip, his fingers splaying up the small of my back. He pulled me closer.

My mother's eyes fluttered beneath the lids like they had since the amputation, since the doctor had put her under and cut her arm off and finished what the snake started. Well, almost finished. Before her, clouding all the right of my vision, was the face of a man I barely knew. Paolo. The man with the tight eyes and insane, sudden laughter. His teeth cracked left to right. *Snik crunch. Crack.*

I said nothing. I didn't know what to say.

"I'm going to take care of you," he said. I was now close enough to see the shape of my own face highlighted in his eyes. "And your mother of course. But you? I like you. I think you hate me, and I like that. Father said you're too young, but you're a jimadora, aren't you? Twelve years, you know, that's almost *too* old to harvest an agave, isn't it?" He pressed his mouth and that black, reeking mustache to my lips and I bit him. I wasn't even planning to, it just happened.

He slapped me, kicked me, and slapped me some more. He started laughing as he did it, that same terrible laugh from when he'd beheaded the snake. It ended abruptly and he dragged me to my feet. I stood, shaking and meeting his gaze as evenly as I could. I watched him pull the laughter back into himself, button it up and lock it back in his throat. His teeth clicked a few times.

"Don't you want to take care of your mother?" he said. He finished the sentence with a little hiccup of a chuckle. "She'll die without a doctor. A good one, like only a man like me can afford."

"She's already dead," I said, glaring at him. He cocked an eyebrow and pulled that mad laughter even deeper into himself. Then he grabbed my mother's throat and squeezed. The reaction was slow, but after a moment she began to cough and wheeze. Her hands slapped feebly at his wrist. He released her.

"No, she's not," he said. His hand moved lower and he grabbed her breast beneath the tatty blanket that covered her. It had been a happy thing in its past, brilliantly green and yellow and red, but time and mother's sickness had greyed the woven cord. Now it looked no cheerier than a child's funerary shroud.

Mother moaned and tried to shrug away, her eyes opening and looking at me. They found the shape of her daughter in that room and gazed balefully. There was a cry for help in there, I'm sure, but I steeled myself against it. I had eyes only for Paolo.

"Let me get some of you and I won't take any of her," he said. "She still works the way a woman needs to." He let my mother go and bent over me. Though he wasn't a tall man, short by American standards, he still towered over me at twelve. "But I want that sweet, ripe *piña,* understand? I want you, my sharp little agave." He touched my chin and I could do nothing but glare.

"Please leave, Don Martinez," I told him. "There is nothing for you here."

He let go of my chin and slapped my cheek, but lightly. The sensation wasn't too painful, in truth, but it sent an electric chill down my spine that sickened me. The room stank of him and my dying mother. Perhaps my own terrified sweat as well, though above all else was the smell of him, of this man. This creature. This thing.

"Everything on *earth* is for me," he said. Then he left, calling back over his shoulder to me. "My father expects his agaves, *jimadora.*"

I stepped outside when I was sure he'd left, when I was positive he wouldn't snatch me by my hair and throw me to the ground outside my family's home. But out in the cool night air there was only the agaves and the sky and Grovier's steady, gentle breaths as he slept in his tiny stable. I walked to the side of the house and sat before the shadows beneath it, and I said his name.

"Sombrero," I called.

"Yes," he said. There was no motion before he spoke, nothing to suggest he'd been anywhere but there since the night I'd spoken to him.

"Are you real?" I asked.

"Possibly," he replied. His eyes opened and I saw them shining in the moonlight. "What is and isn't real in this world sits on either side of a faint line. It grows fainter every year. Perhaps soon it will go entirely." I took a breath and pulled my father's eye patch from my pocket. I held it to my chest and squeezed it in my hand. Though it was little more than burlap and chalk, I felt as though I held his entire body, his entire life in my hands. I cried, despite myself, and Sombrero said nothing.

"This," I said in time, holding out my father's eye patch. The creature's little two-clawed hands snaked from the shadows and wrapped carefully around the bloodstained burlap. He tugged at it and I felt the pull throughout my body. Then he pulled harder and the fabric scratched my hands and was gone, along with something deep at the core of me. I felt a trickling coldness in my chest.

"I accept," he said. Any trace of a chuckle was gone. "Though you've paid in different currency than I expected, the rate of exchange is even." His mouth opened and I saw the sad flap of burlap disappear between his black teeth. And then it was gone.

I hissed as something burned into the back of my hand, and, looking down, I saw one of the vicious rents Sombrero had left reopened in my skin. It bled freely into the dirt, a single, straight line from my wrist to center knuckle. I licked the blood away without thinking and saw the cut had already sealed itself, though an ugly purple scar remained.

I stood.

"Four more," Sombrero said. I nodded, and went inside to Mother.

She lay in a pool of her own sweat, eyes barely open, skin so grey she looked like a filthy white woman. I sat at her bedside, feeling a clarity I hadn't known before just then. I saw her, still beautiful despite the sickness, though just as dull and uninspired all the same. She would never be useful to me or herself ever again.

"Mother, can you hear me?" I asked. She nodded slowly. "Can you walk?" She shook her head. It was my turn to nod. "I need to take you outside. I will carry you, but it may not be comfortable." She nodded again and tried to speak, though her words were little more than a rasp. I understood her on her second try.

"Where is your father?" she asked. And then again. "Where is he?"

"Let's go find him," I said.

I carried her outside on my back, the blanket trailing along behind her as we went. She was so tangled in the thing I didn't bother trying to work her free of it, and it kicked up a small cloud of dust that lingered in the night air. That same dust speckled her grey cheeks as I laid her beside the house.

Her hand caressed my neck for just a second before I let go of her, her untrimmed nails scratching at the skin. *Not so deeply yet*, I thought, grabbing my father's coa from beside the house and standing next to her. She was looking at me, her eyes misted with confusion and fever. The silver crescent of the coa hung just over my shoulder, shining down on her like a second moon.

"Close your eyes, Mother," I told her. And she did.

I was not as strong as my father then, as a child,

when I killed my mother in the dirt and shadows beside our house in the agave fields. But I had worked with him for years by then, and my muscles, my hands, were trained as well as any young jimador. My father could have struck through to the earth below in a single, well-placed strike. It took me two, though my hand slipped on that second blow and I fell sobbing over my shivering, rasping mother.

I turned to her face and held it in my hands. Her own hands, forgetting the fatigue of her illness, rose to the sky. She worked her fingers open and shut, clutching at something only she could see. She tried to speak as well, despite the blood bubbling out of her throat.

"He is there, Mama," I said to her. "Go. Go to him quickly." I could not bear to see the madness in her eyes, the fading color as death gently suckled the life out of her bones. I put my head against her chest and kept it there, listening to the rhythm of her heart grow harder, louder, and then emptier and softer until there was no rhythm at all, simply the last soft beat of a loose drumhead.

Her arms, which had flown up beside my head in her death throes, fell over my back with a soft thud. I would like to think it was her last embrace of a sullen and thankless daughter, but they fell as they did because my arms were beneath her still, and positioned so that my hands cradled her face.

Even knowing that, I let myself pretend for a long moment.

The moment ended and I stood, looking to the shadows. I found my father's coa and opened my mother's chest with it, calling for Sombrero after I finished. This butchery took more effort than the killing, and I fell on my bottom when I was done. Blood soaked the earth around me, thickening the dirt to a tacky mud that stank of copper and death. Slender arms crept from beneath the house and disappeared inside my mother's chest.

Then they pulled her heart into the shadows, and were gone.

⌐

Paolo found me amongst the agave a few days later.

I don't know where he went in that time, or what he did, and don't and never will care. But he found me all the same, walking through the field of green daggers with a damp cloth pressed to his forehead and a cadre of his men at his heels. All of them I had seen at one point or another in the past, often in the halls of the hacienda or by the tequila plant behind it. They dressed too dark for the thickening summer heat, and all of them wore guns in ornate holsters.

"Don Paolo," I said as they approached, wrapping my arms around the coa, my coa, and resting the way I'd seen my father do a thousand times before. It was noon and I'd already filled half the wagon with piñas. Sweat soaked my clothing head to toe, making my shirt cling to me. In maybe half an hour I would have dropped it entirely, as I had been doing in the days since my mother's death, working bare-chested in the mid-afternoon sun and letting it wick the moisture from my shoulders.

"Abella," he said, stopping a few meters away with his hands on his hips. His fingertips brushed the tooled black leather on the holsters slung south of his waist like he were some sort of cowboy. The guns themselves were shining chrome and pearl things too reflective to look at in the daylight. "Where is your mother?" He chuckled, and his laughter flowed into the men around him like poison. He raised his hands to his sides. "I brought my friends around to see her. Wish her well … see if we couldn't find a way to raise those … *funds* she needed for the doctor."

"My mother is gone," I said plainly, smiling warmly at him. I bent to pick one of the severed agave leaves off the ground and then pulled out my father's old work knife to strip a few sections away. The coa remained in the crook of my arm. I placed the strip of agave in my mouth and chewed. It was terribly bitter.

"Gone?" Paolo asked. His eyes lowered. "Gone where?"

"Gone," I replied. "Where all things go." I smiled at him around the thick slice of agave in my mouth and swallowed the bitter juice. Some of the swagger had gone out of his men. They looked around the agave field.

"She's dead?" he asked. "She died?" For a moment, the laughter swelling a knot in his throat faded. It made him seem empty. I nodded. Now the men began to grumble. A few even looked bored, tossing glances back to the relative cool of the hacienda. But Paolo had eyes only for me. I could see him working things over, a new play, a new plan. But he couldn't see as I had begun to see.

"What do you want with my mother anyway?" I asked, letting the coa slip down to my side and walking up to him. His teeth gritted side to side as I stopped just out of arm's reach and pulled the strip of agave out of my mouth. "You know, agave gets bitter, if you let it grow too long. It gets bitter." I put the half-

OJOS OSCUROS

chewed strip of agave in his mouth, slowly, tracing his teeth with it until he bit down. "But if you harvest it at just the right time, it's very sweet, isn't it?"

Paolo's insane eyes widened, and he raised a hand to touch me, but I stepped just out of his reach and touched his chest with the blade of the coa.

"I have work to do, Don Paolo," I said, turning and going back to my cart. Grovier threw baleful glances at the assembled men as I stripped off my shirt and got back to work. I never looked at them myself, but I heard Paolo cursing one of them that decided to whistle at the sight of my naked back. Then they left, the sound of their boots crunching over the dirt fading into the steady dull rush of the wind amongst the agaves.

And I set myself to my work, the long, arduous, and patience-testing process of bringing the agave to harvest. I remembered again the bitter taste, and swallowed.

🐛

Paolo came to me that night and I gave myself to him. It was rough and awkward and terrible, but eventually it ended. I had not grown up around other girls, other people really, save for my mother and father. There were no preconceptions in my mind about what to expect from sex. All I knew about my body was that my father was afraid of it, and that Paolo desired it terribly.

What I knew about the act itself was that Paolo expected it to hurt me to some degree, that it might remove some part of me and transfer it to him. He saw it as some theft he expected me to be the victim of, and that I was such a foolish and simple thing I liked to be robbed in this way.

I let him believe that because it suited my purposes. In truth, the feel of him was little more than a chore I got used to. Working in the fields hurt worse, and demanded more of me than laying with him in my mother's bed. He would get rough as well — slapping my body and pulling my hair — but I had cut myself a dozen times and weathered a thousand blisters out there amongst the agave. My threshold for pain — my endurance — was far beyond his cruel and boyish ministrations.

When he was done — after he fell overtop me gasping and cursing — he would talk to me about himself. We would lay in a pile of sweaty sheets on my dead parents' bed and he would tell me about his family and their business. Men he had killed and intimidated, family members his father didn't trust. He would tell me the iniquities and weaknesses of himself, his father, and his sister, though he would often say little about her. When he did, it would be in hushed and reverent tones.

In the mornings I would wake and go to the fields, working as I always did, strengthening myself in that field of knives. He would remain at home in my parents' bed, still stinking from what we'd done the night before, and I would cleanse myself with sweat and sunlight. Then I would return at night and the process would repeat — he'd fuck me and gasp and curse and then talk.

This routine was broken only twice before it ended entirely.

The first interruption was at the beginning of the second month, a few weeks after I celebrated my thirteenth birthday by pretending it never happened at all. I slipped my way out from beneath his arm and readied myself for the day, eating and drinking coffee and dressing. I was harnessing Grovier when a terrible nausea struck me and I had to rush to the side of the house to vomit. Waves of sickness came over me throughout the day, and I had to stop working several times to rest myself in the shade.

That night I was too unwell to roll with Paolo the way he liked. I was sullen and bloated. He pawed at my body and fulfilled his little needs anyway, and after we finished he gave me a long and cold look.

Usually, after he finished with me, that sickening click-clack of his grinding teeth, the trapped laughter, it would fade. He would be like a normal human man — for all the pros and cons of that diagnosis — at least for a few hours. But this night he just stared at my body, looked me over and up and down, eventually settling on some consensus with himself. Then he dressed and left without a word.

It was a couple months before I saw him again, even though I was up at the hacienda nearly every day. When I'd first started sleeping with him, he'd sometimes ambush me after I dropped off the day's piñas, groping me in the storage room and following me back to my parents' dismal home like an excited dog. But he would never try to actually go all the way while on the grounds of his family home, nor would he carry on in the usual loud and grotesque manner about what he planned to do to me.

In those intervening months, I would walk through a hacienda so empty it seemed like a ghost town. I knew from the way the few people I spoke with reacted to me that Paolo had laid some sort of hex on me to keep others away. There was only one person on the grounds who would dare to speak to me in that odd, lonely time.

The only way to describe her appearance was that she fluttered out of the house. That daughter of the Martinez Clan, Maria, came dressed in flowing white silk that complemented her dark hair and soft features well. Her brother told me I was beautiful, which I suppose was true because of the way he acted toward me, but next to this girl I was a creature of dirt. I dipped my head to her.

"Doña Maria," I said respectfully, continuing to lead Grovier out of the hacienda. The girl put her hand on my arm and I stopped. She put her fingertips on my chin and moved my face to hers. We had the same dark brown eyes, though hers seemed so large and doe-like because of her light complexion. I was brown as old wood from working in the harsh sunlight all the time, my skin rough from the wind.

"I am so sorry," she said to me. She pulled me in for a hug I never expected, and I pushed away reflexively to keep her fine white clothes from getting dirty. She held onto me anyway and I felt her stomach against mine. It was just as swollen as mine had grown, more so even, so that I understood why she was wearing so much clothing in the near dead of

     OJOS OSCUROS

summer. My own stomach had only just started to show.

"He …" she started, resting her forehead against my chin so that I could have kissed it if I wanted to. I half expect that might have been her desire, but the moment passed and she buried her face in my neck. I saw one of the men who worked the agave kilns looking down the hill at us. Maria was sobbing. "If it wasn't me it was going to be somebody else. And even that wasn't enough for him."

"Doña Maria," I said. "People are watching. Please." She stiffened and sniffed and backed away, comporting herself as best she could. Tears fell over her cheeks with all the simple beauty of a raindrop slipping down the side of an agave leaf. I plucked one off her skin and dried it on my dirty shirt. Then I nodded to her and tugged Grovier to get him moving again.

"I am going away soon," she called after me. "If you ever need anything from me, anything. Please, just let me know."

I stopped and turned back to her, Grovier halting and grumbling beside me. He bumped my leg with his snout and snorted, eager to get home. I tapped his backside and turned to Maria Martinez, now my sister of sorts, and smiled.

"I will, Doña Maria," I said, nodding my head. "Thank you, I will."

Paolo returned to me just days later, and we resumed as though nothing happened, though he was drunk nearly every day. The stink of alcohol on him reminded me of my father near the end. My memory of him in this time is the stench of mezcal and his grunting, grinning face painted orange by the gas flame. His face, hanging over me and smothering my mouth and scratching my neck with his little beard hairs.

It was a month still until he finally brought up the incident with his sister. We were both naked on the bed, his eyes wide and staring into the darkness beyond the window. The gas flame danced as always and behind him were the dense blue interior shadows of my dead parents' home. My stomach was beyond hiding, beyond ignoring, and his eyes stole to the swell of flesh over my hips. He traced his fingers over it.

"This is mine," he said. "Any other girl I'd have an excuse for, but you've been mine and only mine as well." The tight laughter in his throat hiccupped out, making his whole body jerk. "I know you talked to my sister."

"I did," I said.

"I have people all over this land that tell me everything," he said.

"And I'd have no reason to lie to you even if you didn't," I told him, stretching my legs and pulling the covers over my hips to keep warm. Cold wind blew through the window despite the summer heat. A promise of rain.

"She is going to leave me," he whispered. His jaw clicked and his eyes returned to the window. "Father is sending her to America to have the baby. Some boarding school for unmarried pregnant girls." His fist clenched. "He's taking her away from me."

"Does he know?" I asked. Paolo shrugged.

"Family is family," he replied. "Father will have a grandchild, and that's all that matters. If my sister needs a husband, he'll invent one for her." He turned and smacked the bed. "But her? Her and her child? They're *mine*." The same hand crept over the mattress to my body and squeezed what could be squeezed. "*This* is mine. And *this*. And *this*."

He had me again and then dressed himself. He took a long second adjusting the flat brimmed black hat he liked to wear, staring again out the window.

"She's leaving tomorrow night," he said without looking at me. "I'm going to drive her to the train." He sighed. "Father doesn't want me to see her before she goes, but I've told the driver to bring her here. That man is *my* man, and he'll do what I say." And then, to himself. "Perhaps a last taste of her, as well." He nodded.

"And what're you going to do all day?" I asked. "Linger around my house?"

"If I want," he said, turning to me. He belched a laugh. "Maybe I'll have some from both my ladies tomorrow, how about that?" I shrugged.

"It doesn't matter to me," I told him. I was already thinking about other things. He walked to the window and rested his hands on the sill. His thumbs drubbed against the wood incessantly. Impatiently.

"I'm going to keep you, though," he said, nodding again to himself. Then he turned. "I have places in the country up north where you can go. Other houses. I can't have a son with some *jimadora*, but if Father can invent a husband for my sister, then I'll invent myself a wife." I turned on my side, letting my hand rest on the swell of my belly. His eyes were hideous as they looked me over.

"I'll be rich, then?" I asked. He nodded. "And

I'll live in a big house, with servants, and I'll never have to work the fields?" He nodded again, smiling this time, though his teeth cracked some as his jaw shifted. "But what if I grow old? Won't you get sick of me?" His smile faded, but he snorted up a laugh all the same. Then he came over to me and caressed my cheek. His hands were soft, like his sister's.

"You'll never grow old, jimadorita," he said. His hand moved slowly over my face until his palm lay over my throat. He squeezed. "Not ever."

I woke and worked the next day, though I never ventured into the fields. Grovier stood beside me as I grew filthier and filthier. He stamped as the clouds rolled in, anticipating the coming storm. By the time the sun was setting, when Paolo rode up with his little cadre of foot soldiers, I was streaked head to toe with dirt. The thick sort of clay you get covered in when you dig deep.

I watched them ride away from my place behind the house and then stepped into the light where he could see me, completely naked and slightly swollen with pregnancy, covered in clay like some ancient native priestess. He stopped when he saw me and I brushed a hand over myself.

"Look," I said to him. "I'm filthy."

He took me into the agave and I enjoyed him for the first and only time we were together, returning his savagery blow for blow. He was as naked and filthy as me when we finished, and I stood overtop him.

"I can't let my sister see me like this," he said.

"No, and she won't," I said. "Let me get something to fix you up with." He lay back, smiling, with his hands behind his head. I thought it odd he didn't scream when I severed his foot with the coa. There was a short, yelping laugh and then something like a howl. He clutched the leg above the cut, where his ruined flesh still clung together in strips beneath the bone. Blood spread amongst the agaves.

"You fucking bitch," he said, or something like that. He tried to swipe at me with one of his arms and I sidestepped and brought the coa down into the flesh at the joint of his right shoulder. The noise of the cut was no different than when I cut the leaves from the agave, save the odd, stuttering laughs coming from Paolo's throat.

Another strike and the arm was off and laying in the blood and mud by Paolo's ass. He flipped forward and began crawling back toward my dead family's house, to where I'd stripped off his clothes and where his guns lay safe and useless in their holsters. With an arm and most of a leg gone, he could do little more than slither his way over the ground. I watched him go, more concerned about Grovier whining in his tiny stable. I knew what he was thinking, watching Paolo crawl like that.

"Snakes make him nervous," I told Paolo. The man was laughing maniacally now, reminding me of the time he beat me at my mother's bedside. I stepped up beside him and raised the coa. "But, like you said, I guess this works on snakes as well."

I buried the coa in the back of his neck and his body stuttered and died, though he didn't stop laughing. In fact, it only got louder. His chin lay flat on the ground now, his throat stretched but yet to be severed. Blood covered his teeth and lips, and shot in little streamers out onto the ground in front of him.

One last strike finished the job, and then I went to work, cutting him down to the piña. To the corazon. For this one I didn't need Sombrero's wandering arms, I pulled Paolo's steaming heart out of his chest myself. I held it in my hands and knelt beside my dead family's home and called to the creature that lived in the shadows there. His eyes opened, he took the offering, and he ate.

The skin on the back of my hand split and bled tracks through the mud and clay.

🐾

I put the rest of Paolo into the deep, slender hole I'd dug beside Grovier's pen and kicked some of the dirt over him. The last I saw of the man was his mouth and eyes filling with earth, still open in a last, mad laugh. His throat was finally unbuttoned, for what good it did him, and the skin of his face as dull grey-green as the rest of the mud around him.

I heard a coach pull up and I went into the agaves, letting them hide me. I heard a short argument, then a man's heavy footsteps followed by the small feet of a girl dropping down out of a carriage. She yelled after him, but his footsteps receded all the same. The storm threatened to break overhead. The last small traces of the sun had fled. I knelt — naked and streaked with blood and clay — amongst the agaves.

Maria looked beautiful, as always, dressed in white lace and high black riding boots with a little red flower in her hair. She looked young, too, younger even than her real age of fourteen. A child with child. A mother still in need of mothering. I stood and walked to where she could see me and the coa — my coa — glimmering in the little light remaining to the day.

"Who are you?" she asked when she saw me. Her eyes went wide with fear. She looked absolutely piti- ful, adorable even. Like a lamb given to God. I raised my hands and the coa to my sides.

"I am the dirt," I said. "And the agaves. I am what your family eats to live." She backed against the wall of my house, her hands clutched in front of her chest.

"Abella?" she asked. "Is that you?"

"Yes," I replied, moving ever closer. In the grow- ing dark she could see only me and the agaves, the whites of my eyes shining amidst all the blackness of what I'd done that day. The grime slicking my body head to toe.

The storm cracked and showered us with rain. I raised my open eyes to the sky and let it fall cool and hard on my face and shoulders. Maria merely flinched.

"Where's my brother?" she asked.

"I killed him," I said.

"Why?" she asked, and I struck her in the throat with the coa. Her beautiful lamb's eyes widened in shock and pain. Rain slicked her hair to her face and the little red flower fell free to the ground. Her hands found the sharpened disk of the blade and she rent her fingers along the edges, trying to pull it free of her throat. I pushed harder, sending the blade all the way to her spine and pushing her body against the wall of my house. Her hands found the shaft of the coa and gave one last tug. Then she died, slumping down into the mud at my feet.

I stripped her naked before butchering her, pushing the ruined dress down into the hole overtop her brother. She lay naked and dead on the ground where I'd butchered my own mother, in much the same place. Her body was beautiful in its ruin, her breasts were full and her stomach broad with the pregnancy. I stared down at that swollen lump for a long while, touching my own stomach and thinking on the fate of my child's half-sibling.

Then I cut open Doña Maria's chest and fed her heart to Sombrero.

Two fresh lines of blood had joined the others on the back of my hand. The rush of killing the siblings, Maria and Paolo, had dulled the pain of the other-worldly cuts when they came. I only noticed them after, when they were nearly totally clean and all that remained were the nasty purple scars. There were four in a line now, all traveling from one knuckle of my hand to the wrist, a spot saved for the fifth along my thumb bone.

This mark is called *The Hand of Sticks* when it is finished, but mine wasn't yet. That was a long time off, though on the night when I murdered those two I thought Maria's unborn child would count as the fifth. But, for whatever reason, it didn't.

I walked naked in the rain — having buried Maria and Paolo and pushed the rest of the dirt over them — and let the falling water wash me clean. I dug through some of Maria's luggage and brought it into my house, then took some of her soap outside to finish cleaning my body and hair.

Before I went inside, I walked to Grovier and cut him free of his harness, leaving a pile of hay and agave leaves for him to eat when I was gone. I tried to go, but I found I almost couldn't leave the poor, stupid thing. I wrapped my arms around his big, wet face and crushed it against my chest, relishing the scratch of his fur against my skin and crying despite myself. He was, after all, the only real family I had left.

I dressed in Maria's clothing inside my house, taking care not to get it dirty. To her credit, the girl had packed an assortment of clothing that wasn't an idiotic, virginal white. I put on a pair of her dark riding pants, a matching blouse, and found a complementary dark jacket and gloves and boots. I cleaned my feet with the sheets from my dead parents' bed, the mud there being the only thing the storm couldn't wash away, and put on the boots and left.

I stole Maria's carriage and drove myself to the train station in Guadalajara, not knowing in the least what would happen when I got there. The storm had died down while I dressed, until it was little more than a fine mist and the distant thunderclaps and splitting bursts of lightning. I rode toward town and gave the first trustworthy man I saw a few hundred pesos to take me to the train station on the tickets I dug out of Maria's purse. He didn't ask any questions, and, after he got me there, he jumped down from the driver's seat and disappeared without a word.

A concierge was waiting for Maria on the platform, and when I told him that, yes, *I* was Doña Maria Martinez, he smiled and bowed and showed me to the train. I had worn one of Maria's dark, wide-brimmed hats low over my eyes, favoring him with a shy, coquettish smile and touching the swell of belly showing through my clothes. I suppose the rumor of Don Bello's pregnant daughter was well enough known in Guadalajara that I didn't bear much of a second look. With her father's reputation, the impudence of a second glance may have been more risk than anybody thought worthwhile.

So I boarded the train as Maria Martinez, wearing the woman's clothes and wondering behind which of the dark, distant hills I had buried her.

I gave birth to your mother in America about six months later. I told people at the boarding school to call me Abella, because the growing notoriety of the Martinez crime family in Guadalajara made it somewhat unsafe to be Maria Martinez.

I named your mother Raquel, and she was beautiful. I sent pictures of her to her grandfather in Mexico, who wrote me letters and promised to visit just as soon as he quelled the violence with the neighboring gangs. He would complain how Paolo had disappeared with some whore jimadora who lived on their land, leaving him in a bad situation. Paolo had been in control of the family's army of killers and assassins before he vanished, and hadn't left an effective chain of command in his place.

He also apologized to me for my brother's "iniquities" but promised he would do everything in his power to ensure nobody ever knew the truth of what had happened. He said I would be returned to Mexico someday and married to a respectable man, and my daughter would be legitimized as part of that.

I wrote him constantly, thanking him and keeping up with the family gossip, all of which I knew from the nights I spent talking with Paolo. I told him about my studies and how I was learning to speak English and I joked that one day my daughter could be the American president because she was born here. He didn't appreciate that as much, but generally the man treated me like the daughter he didn't know he'd lost.

In two years, I went from knowing almost no mathematics and absolutely no English to being at the top of most of my classes. You might find that extraordinary, because I was an absolute bumpkin and no-account before going there, but you must understand: These girls who had become my peers were weak-willed pink things from soft families. Me? I was a woman who, at thirteen, had fucked and murdered my way off an agave farm in Jalisco to a posh boarding school in America. I did all this while carrying a child and never, not *once*, missing a harvest.

My palms were so calloused they made the other girls nervous when I shook their hands. When the headmistresses tried to scold me for breaking some norm I had no time for, I would fix them with a stare that chilled them to the bone. When a man from the State of Texas came and told me they'd take my child, your mother, my first and only daughter, from me when her grandfather was arrested, I slapped that man so hard he had to spit the fake, gold tooth I knocked free into his hand.

Yes, my grandson, in two years I learned to speak the language of the Americas as fluently as I spoke

Spanish. In three more years, I'd learned nearly as much Latin, as well as every bone, muscle, and artery in the human body.

Three years after that, when I was cutting into my first body on an anatomy table in the State of Massachusetts, I thought for the first time almost since that night of when I butchered Maria and Paolo. I said a silent prayer in thanks to them, just as I said little prayers to the agaves sometimes with your great-grandfather. Those plants are sacred, you understand, and have been since long before that land was called Jalisco or Mexico or anything at all. They are difficult to cultivate, difficult to cut and harvest, but this harvesting is the lifeblood of the jimador. Just as I harvested those agave, I harvested Maria, Paolo, my mother, and my father.

❦

But, of course, you are wondering what became of the fifth mark? How did I get it?

I had pondered for a long, long time at what I had traded to Sombrero, and what I had gotten in turn. He asked for five sacrifices, "The Matron, The Patron, The Stranger, The Lover, and the Fool." For a long while I had confused myself as to whom I'd given to him.

❦

Twelve years after I left my home in Jalisco, I returned. Your great-grandfather had surrendered to the other crime syndicates in the region just years after I left. It was a gentle transition, all things considered. Don Bello was a relic of the bootlegger days, ill-equipped to handle the banal cruelties of what was to come. They let him keep his tequila business and so he did, though it turned a middling profit and his house remained in decline until his death.

But the wars were over, and the daughter he believed he'd never lost was now about to be a practicing doctor in America. His little granddaughter was twelve and speaking with a hilariously bad American accent when she spoke to him over the phone. He believed my voice had simply changed as I finally matured into a woman.

There were no soldiers on the property anymore, and we drove to the hacienda in a touring car with a convertible top. The agave fields remained, ageless and blue beneath an azure sky. Only the foundations of my dead parents' home remained, though most of Grovier's pen still stood. I wept as I thought of the poor, wonderful animal and where he might have gone after I left. The driver attempted to comfort "Doña Maria Martinez" by handing me a handkerchief. I declined, and smiled.

Your great-grandfather was happy to see your mother, unbelievably so, though he didn't much recognize the woman with her. I declined to introduce myself and instead went to the hacienda's kitchen to make drinks, leaving little Raquel to bounce on her grandfather's knee. He was in tears.

But, as I said, I went to the kitchen. The staff there wasn't a quarter of what it was when I was a dirty little jimadora dropping off piñas. Still, there was a woman who gladly brought me a bottle of the house tequila.

I tasted it and found it no different than when I'd left. I realized that one or two of the last agaves I'd ever planted were probably in that bottle. A fitting ending, all things considered.

I filled two glasses, poisoned one of them, and brought it back to Don Bello. Again he had no idea who I was, to the point that he asked where Maria was.

"You really don't recognize me?" I asked, taking off my hat and setting it on the table beside our drinks. I asked one of the house attendants to take my daughter on a tour of the grounds. Don Bello gave me a confused smile.

"Are you not an *au pair?*" he asked. I laughed and crossed my legs, leaning back in the easy chair. We sat on the north patio of the hacienda, which provided a view of the grounds I had never seen before. The remains of my dead family's house were less than a collection of shadows in the distance, and all around us was agave and the Mexican countryside. I could even see jimadores working, which made cold swirl in the core of my chest.

"No, that's my daughter," I said. "Isn't she beautiful? She has her father's eyes, unfortunately, but at least she doesn't have his smile. Or, God forbid, his laugh." Don Bello gave me a cold look, but realization dawned slowly over his face.

"You … *Abella?* The *jimadora?*" He held his hands up in front of his face and looked at his palms. Then he looked over his shoulder. "Is … is this some sort of joke? Is … is my son with you? Is Paolo with you?" He was nearly in tears. "What is going on?"

"Paolo is dead," I told him. "I'm sorry to say, but so is Maria." He blinked. "Both of them died … *almost* together twelve years ago. The woman whose room and board you paid for? Whose schooling you paid for? That was me. I killed Maria and took her place." His face had gone pale. "But the girl is your granddaughter. Paolo forced me into a relationship and we had a child together. Her. She's the one you've been speaking to on the phone. She's the one who has told you she loves you and has called you grandpa all these years."

"Goddamn you," he whispered, his eyes wide. He knew by the set of my face I wasn't joking. This was no scam, no game. This was the world I had made for all of us to live in, the dirty little jimadora his boy liked to fuck on the sly. "I'll have you killed. Arrested." I laughed in his face and took a sip of the tequila. It tasted like home.

"No you won't," I said. "You'll ruin her life, and she's all you have left. Don't think I'm being cruel, forcing your hand like this, it's just the way things are." I sighed. "I'm a doctor, and your granddaughter is going to live a life of luxury and success. She can be anything she wants in this life, and I gave that to her." I lowered my eyes at him.

"Maria? That little girl couldn't stand up to her own brother," I continued. "My girl is the daughter of the woman who sits before you. The woman who can look into the eyes of Don Bello Martinez and *laugh*." I pushed the glass I'd filled for him across the table and he looked at it. He seemed very old.

"You being alive is in the way of my daughter being happy, though," I told him. "Your family can't be trusted with things like this, and these last threads need to be tied off." I pointed to the glass. "It's poisoned. You'll go quickly, painlessly. It'll be the easiest death I've ever given somebody." He glared. "But like anything in this life, it's a choice." I glared back at him. "With consequences, as well, for not taking it."

I raised my glass to him and downed it. He watched me with a sick expression.

"Spend the day with your granddaughter," I said. "But just the day." I stood and left him alone in his great, empty house. "You've earned that, at least."

⚓

Your mother was heartbroken when they found her grandfather cold in bed the next morning. She would tell me, still tells me sometimes, that one day she spent with him was the most fun of her life. They went to the zoo in Guadalajara and he took her around the tequila factory. I spent the day walking through the agaves, remembering a time when the leaves weren't so rough on my fingers.

I found something in the dirt beside the house that I'd long since forgotten, though I don't know how that's possible. It was rusted and dull, but I found the sharpening stick in the ruins of the shed and sat on the old foundations and honed the crescent to a point. I even managed to knock off most of the rust.

When I finished, it shone like a crescent moon in the sunlight.

⚓

It took just a few hundred pesos of bribery to get the mortician to leave me alone with your grandfather's body. I wore gloves and a mask and apron for this one, but the process was just the same. His chest sprung open as I cut into it, the sad old flesh parting to reveal the ribs and the heart beneath. I thought that, even if the bribe didn't take, no man on earth would investigate why Don Bello Martinez's daughter cut his heart out of his chest the night before his funeral.

Your mother cried at the small service, and so did I for that matter. It was a somber and very private affair. I didn't want to bother with the sparse extended family that might recognize me as someone other than Maria, though my passport and every living document I owned proved I was.

When all was done, I sold the hacienda and the tequila business and all the land and property in Don Bello's name. I have turned my back on Mexico forever, even if you have not, despite your never having been there. The United States government might believe that moment came when I finished naturalizing myself, but that would be terribly inaccurate.

I returned to my dead family's home one last time, carrying Don Bello's heart wrapped in parchment like a butcher's steak. Your mother and the driver stayed well out by the road, beyond where they could see what I was doing.

I knelt beside the shadows and called for Sombrero, and he came.

"It's been a long time," he said with a chuckle.

"Very," I said, holding out the heart. He held up a hand.

"What's a few seconds between old friends, eh?" he said. His eyes were large and his teeth were deeply black, though none of it was so frightening to me as the first time I saw him. "You've accomplished quite a lot, little girl."

"I know," I told him.

"Oh, but do you?" he asked, chuckling. "Where once there stood a small girl, free of tethers, now stands a woman with a thousand cords twisted in a single fist. Where I saw three fibers, three lives, three possibilities, now is a great cable made of all the original paths. You, little girl, are a creature who kills maybes. You have slain your other selves and bound them to you, creating Order."

He slipped the heart of Don Bello Martinez, last owner of these lands and fields, from my hands and held it in his own. In one of his other hands, he lifted a fistful of dust and showed both of them to me. Then he ate the heart and let the dust fall.

"Which is more honest?" he asked me, after he finished chewing. I felt the sharp pain of the last cut scoring the flesh of my hand. His dark eyes narrowed. "There are many other possibilities we've undone. Choices that can never be made now, because of the pact you made. Worlds have ended. Universes have disappeared."

"And?" I asked. He cackled so loudly I thought my daughter might hear; the sound penetrated the earth and my bones and shook the agaves.

"And..." he repeated. "Goodbye, Abella. *Jimadorita*. Doctor. Mother. Criminal." He smiled one last time. "Keep an eye on your shadow, and see that it stays lonely." Then his eyes disappeared and a score of rattlesnakes rushed out of the shadows between the old foundations, which seemed not so deep as I thought. Though it may have been my imagination, one of the rattlesnakes lacked a head, but moved anyway.

This story has no true end, because it's yours now, grandson — the story of why we became Americans — though I don't believe being an American is all that important in the end. But, the story of how I killed my family to make my family ends like this.

I stood alone amongst the agaves. They grew thick and tall where I grew up, sprouting from the ground like clusters of knives bigger than a child and as tall as some adults.

I closed my eyes and listened to the sound of the wind, straining to hear the steady picking of somebody cutting away the leaves, searching for the heart.

I thought of the pact I'd made with Sombrero, which you might believe is a silly name, if you didn't know the original Spanish doesn't mean "hat," but rather, "Shadower."

I wondered at what he'd asked me for, and who fulfilled the rolls of The Matron, The Patron, The Fool, The Stranger, and The Lover. And I wonder what I traded in stead, when I gave over my father's eye patch instead of a human heart.

But in the end I decided that none of it mattered.

Death and Pain are merely the wages of life, which bought me the most beautiful girl on earth. A girl who looks like every person who had to die to create her and to secure her future.

I thought of those things, and more, and in time I knelt before the agaves and washed away the blood on the back of my hand with the dirt of those sacred fields.

Then I turned my back on them, and I left.

THE END

Within As Without

Heat radiated off the great jagged hills of asphalt still jutting from the river. What remained of the bridge lay like strips of rotten flesh over the water, clinging to rusty supports standing in silhouette like the ribs of some great, gutted beast. The city beyond wore the crust of life borne by any dead thing. Structural frames lay at rest as blackened bones amongst the crush of fresh green.

Braxton Fujima let himself rest for the first time in days, sucking on a plastic button and hoping the water below would test drinkable. It likely would. It almost always did. What warnings passed among the other soldiers before the blasts had almost all turned out to be false. The water was clean. The soil was healthy.

Nature had reclaimed all the lost territory it could find. Birds flocked through skies a deeper blue than Fujima had ever known. The orange clouds of the

City had receded as the pollution dampers fell offline, as the lights went out one by one. It seemed as though the world was trying to forget its odd human experiment.

Fujima filled his canteens when the tester on his wrist compact blinked out a bright green "OK." No radiation. No parasites. No detectable poisons. He drank deeply of one canteen and let himself relish the feel of the fresh water inside his body. He'd never known thirst like this before the war ended. It was deep inside every cell of his body, a chronic dehydration that had made itself companion to the almost endless hunger. Hunger made him think of the deer he'd killed two weeks before.

It had taken him four days to eat most of it. He'd dried some, doing a half-assed but serviceable enough job. The remnants were wrapped up in plastic scraps in his pack. He'd learned how to do the drying from a survival guide he'd scavenged from a library, along with an abridged MERCK manual and two novels he hadn't had the time to open yet. He could only read in the day, and daylight was for walking.

He rediscovered the tracks he'd been following for the last few weeks on the other side of the bridge. Crossing it was easier than he'd expected. It looked completely unsafe, but a natural bridge of silt and driftwood had formed in the wreckage, concealed somewhat by the moving water. The other party's footprints were fresh and partially filled, along with the occasional muddy handprints from somebody falling and then righting themselves.

The tracks were painfully obvious. Fujima crouched low and slid his rifle from his shoulder to scan the opposite bank for an ambush. He found only trees, and the deep, abiding silence of the new forest.

Prints by his feet suggested there were only ten or so left in the party. They'd camped here for the night, leaving their fire to die on its own.

Animals had pawed through the ash, looking for the source of the scent left by the molten fat that had dripped into the firepit. It had rained two days prior, a short summer shower that came in around noon, but the ashes were dry and still warm in places. They had one morning's worth of a lead on him, maybe two. Fujima scanned the edges of the encampment and saw the stake holes he knew he'd find. There were only five now, down from ten when he'd started.

He cursed under his breath, thinking of what had made the grease beneath the fire. His stomach rumbled. He sat and gnawed a hard strip of venison. He chewed it like tobacco, savoring it to stave off the hunger pains. The fat he'd built up gorging on the deer had all but disappeared. He was leaner than he'd ever been in his life, and something had been coming alive in him in the months since he'd set out on this hunt. A sort of coldness in his skull, a heat in his neck when he held his rifle that he'd never felt before.

When he looked at the world, he saw it. Every minute detail, every slight motion.

Something stirred in the trees ahead of him, opposite the river and far left of where the party's tracks led into the ruined city. There was so little motion that he believed he'd seen none at all, but his rifle was up and cracking fire toward the subtle shifting before he could think. Something screamed, an inhuman noise that froze Fujima in place. Foliage crunched and crashed, and he saw the entire top of a tree shake.

He ran, shuttling himself through the jungle gym of rusted beams and old steel wires embedded in the natural silt footbridge. The other party had

     WITHIN AS WITHOUT

rifles. Maybe they could use them and maybe they couldn't, but they wouldn't need to be good shots if they caught him in this bottleneck. Whatever he'd hit didn't sound human, but shot-up humans rarely sounded like themselves.

Nothing he could hear followed him as he rushed through streets so choked with weeds they could rightly be called meadows. Worn boots made little noise on the pavement, but he stepped lightly anyway, trying not to brush the thick-leaved vines hanging low from the eves of the closest building. He stopped, looking down the street, a long stretch of open area with few safe places to hide. Without thinking he ducked into the building, feet crunching over pebbles of broken glass.

He pushed himself into the shadows and entwined his body to give the rifle a resting spot on his knee. His eyes were as coldly reflective as the rifle scope, the glass on the ground. The weather-worn shards in the window. He waited, unblinking.

It passed the door a second later, lithe and long, a shadow against the bright daylight. Powerful shoulders moved it almost soundlessly over the same pavement he'd been standing on seconds before. Then it was gone.

Too many tracks to follow, Fujima thought. The rifle was in his shoulder and pointed at the door, but there was nothing to shoot. The thing had gone.

He waited another hour until leaving the cramped reception area where he'd taken refuge. There was still time to move, but not much. There was nowhere to run if the thing came back, and nothing that quiet and big ate vegetables to live. But if the other party turned back on their own tracks, he didn't have the firepower to hold them all off in a small space like this.

So he walked.

Carefully at first, his heart beating hard in his chest. He cursed at himself to be calm, knowing a hard-beating heart meant burning calories. He'd have to eat the rest of the jerky tonight if he expected not to be dizzy and plagued by headaches the next day. He could feel the earliest signs of them already. The only positive thought was that large predators meant large game. Somewhere in this sepulcher there was something to eat.

Plenty of blood dotted the pavement where the thing had passed. Fujima couldn't imagine how badly hurt the creature might be, if it was still silent after losing so much blood. He followed the tracks with his eyes and then his mind, making a mental note of the way they curved away into the buildings. The thing had taken a heading away from both Fujima and the obvious tracks of the other party. His path lay to the east, and the thing's to the north, it seemed.

"'Take yourself far from me, wandering soul,'" Fujima sang under his breath to the thing. Along that path lay a honeycomb city of broken windows and black, hidden places. The sunlight wasn't strong enough to break those shadows. The old snatch of song stayed with Fujima often these days. He sang the rest quietly. "'The light out here is fading. The place where you lived in my heart is cold.'" There was nobody to sing the accompanying verse, and he left the spot empty.

          WITHIN AS WITHOUT

He sang the rest anyway, watching a light mist roll off the tops of the buildings as the sun began to set.

He camped on the third floor of what might once have been an office building, the dull and cubicle-filled sort he might have worked in if it weren't for the war. Several floors were missing from the northern half of the structure, as though somebody had carved a chunk out of it with a giant ice cream scoop. He recognized burns from an old explosion where the weather hadn't worn them away and thought this floor might have made a perfect sniper's nest.

He'd chosen the building for the vantage it gave him over the central boulevard, where he'd found fresh tracks in the thick forest of ankle-high mushrooms. There were old tracks there as well, worn spaces from multiple trips. If there was a larger encampment, he was getting close, which wasn't good. The party he'd been tracking could be taken care of with planning, but all that went out the window if he ran into another dozen armed men.

But that was a problem for tomorrow. Night held its own dangers.

He fiddled with the screen on his wrist until it activated the simple utility light. That and the water tester were the only things of any real use anymore. The digital compass worked only sometimes. The GPS and communications suite had gone out before the war had even ended.

If he ever ran across another soldier out here, the device would prove his identity. If, *when*, he died, it would send out a signal marking his location until the little radioactive isotope that powered it died. The half-life on the battery was something like 50 years, though he hadn't gotten a new battery in it since before the comms and the GPS died. He didn't bother with the math on how long his little arm-mounted grave might continue sending out its lonely SOS. He'd long since turned off the notifications about just such signals in his vicinity. It was too depressing.

He used the light to work strips of piss-poor deer leather into wonky snare traps that would pull damaged parts of the office down if tripped. Possibly they'd just break, but the office was still full of loud things to tumble over: Old cans and rusted hulks of computer towers, staplers and desks and drawers. He figured this place had been evacuated early, maybe even near the beginning of the fighting. If he had a map, or any real idea where he'd wandered to after getting the final order from his captain, he'd know instantly.

There had been a lot of southward marching since he'd left the 109th near Syracuse. Some of the sub-cities he'd passed through still had their own neighborhood identities, names he recognized from news reports and movies when he was a kid. But after a while, after the rot set in, there was nothing more than the same old street names here and there — Vine, Main, Martin Luther King Jr., Washington, North, South, 14th. Arteries and veins running through organs that no longer had any purpose. Empty avenues of blackened blood coursing through a bloated corpse.

This is what everybody had called the City.

Capital C.

Nobody knew the proper name of the City when it was alive, and nobody cared now that it was no more. The sub-cities, the neighborhoods, they had names. Community identities after a fashion. But the City itself was a heartless tangle of brick and steel that left behind no mourners.

Fujima woke to the sound of dragging steel. The noises were tentative, cautious. Dark had settled in full and deep, though no night was truly dark now that the City was gone. Unless there were clouds, the stars formed a band of light across the sky so blazingly brilliant it still stunned him they'd never been visible in his younger life.

Blue-grey light filled the inside of the building, making a charcoal etching of the interior. Shapes grew and shifted from what he knew they were. His brain demanded he turn on the utility light, but he kept it off, letting the sound move closer.

The black of the darkest shadows seemed to pulse and roll as his eyes tried to focus, as his brain strained to make sense of them. He saw faces in the black, human and blank-eyed, that shifted and faded and became more familiar shapes. Two computer screens on the far side of the room had become a set of square glasses on the face of a ghost just inches in front of him. His mind made a clawed hand from the cracks in a window, a raising gun from the subtle shift in a strand of leather beside his cheek.

Fujima almost didn't believe he saw the eyes when they opened. There was no color to them, aside from the faintest tinge of blue, a cousin to the starlight falling on the abandoned office equipment around him.

They grew larger, to the size of the palms of his hands. His heart beat against his ribcage. Sweat rolled down his face. The thing in front of him breathed and Fujima brought the rifle to bear on it, slowly.

It was a simple, bolt-action .308 with a telescopic sight. A single round to fire at this range, if something charged him, then he would have only an 18-inch bayonet and his own body. There was a sound of dragging steel again, soft, and then the sudden crash of something massive and metallic striking the ground.

The thing didn't scream this time; it didn't make a sound at all. It was simply gone, the weight of its passing felt only in the stiff current of cold air rushing to fill the void it had left. In half a second, Fujima heard the sound of a hunk of metal smashing into stone, and then nothing but the ring of that, echoing again and again into the empty night.

Fujima woke with a start into a grey morning. Birds were his alarm clock now, and the first of them started singing when the morning dew boiled off where it had settled. He begrudgingly chewed the last of his jerky, washing it down with most of his water reserves. He assured himself not for the last time that where there was green, there was water, and that where there were predators, there was prey.

A survey of his campsite told him the story of the previous night. A filing cabinet he'd attached nothing at all to had fallen over beside his bedroll, just in front of the door to the closet where he'd slept. He found the snare that *did* catch three floors down by the front door. The maybe five-kilo computer terminal he'd tied the leather to had disintegrated after impacting the wall beside the door. The snare itself was gone entirely.

Half a day of walking took him through the bowl-shaped remains of a college campus, where the founding fathers sat in a tight circle of moss amidst rows of long-empty concrete benches. Bronze had run to black, so that he could barely make out their features. The plaque on the marble plinth had rusted off and fallen face-down on the ground. He wasn't interested in reading it.

Fujima tightened his grip on the gunstock when he found the remnants of his quarry's encampment. Crude butchery remained of a middle-aged man, his body opened from calf to neck along his backside. The worthwhile meat there — Fujima could see even from what was left of him that he was terribly thin and unhealthy — had been stripped away and cooked on the nearby fire. He touched the coals.

Warm. Still smoldering in places.

No stake holes marked the ground at this encampment, and he wondered if the remaining prisoners were simply too weak to try to run. His own stomach grumbled, and he felt the first nasty, sweaty rush of endorphins as his body started eating itself. A tentative queasiness settled over him and he steadied himself against a marble pillar that held up the steel awning over the campsite. A nearby sign named this place as the "Adelaide Stephenson Reading Garden."

He found the apple trees a short while later, as if by providence. The walk that preceded their discovery passed in the sort of haze he knew meant the first early roots of starvation were draining him. His vision swam and fell back into focus, and his legs worked more by memory than intention. The first apple nearly smacked him in the head.

He'd walked into the grove while just tracking on instinct. His quarry had once moved softly, taking care to keep their traces to a minimum. This other party's former pursuers had likely given up the ghost long before Fujima had stumbled across their trail. Much like these trees, he had discovered them on accident. But he had heard the screaming, and then he'd seen the tattoo.

Fujima's mouth watered when his fingers brushed the skin of the apple. It was the hard-skinned green kind, though when he took it the thing felt marshmallow soft. He bit deep into it and nearly passed out from the pain of vomiting. It was utterly rancid, so rotten the insides of the skin were nearly liquid.

Fujima felt his breath catch in his chest and looked at the space between his hands. The grass here was short in wide patches. It slipped out of focus and then burst into a series of grid-shaped colors, alternating ripples of sight and sound.

"Oh. Shit." Fujima heard himself say. Something squalled in the distance and he pushed himself to his feet. The ground felt blue beneath him, tight as

     WITHIN AS WITHOUT

a drumhead and reverberating with the deeper motions of the earth below. Bark on the trees shifted and split into a million rolling scales, all glittering gold and red like a roulette wheel. There was a louder noise and Fujima moved toward it.

The air parted around him like a curtain, rolling in and out as waves of barely audible orange and purple. There was a taste to it like copper that filled his nose and forced its way up into the space behind his eyes.

He found a place in the grove of apple trees where the grass was matted down with blood, thick and black as pudding. A deer lay dying in the clearing, hooves flailing beneath a torn body. It had run a long way before falling there, finally dropping when its intestines caught in a pile of stray branches beneath a dead apple tree. Fujima fell on the deer as though he were a rock dropped from a great height, a mindless thing devoid of purpose, devoid of anything but its own self and the heartless physics of momentum. He crashed upon the deer like a wave, tearing at it with his bare teeth.

Fujima woke in the clearing. Deep night had come and was on him fully, so that again all he could see were the faintest traces of blue. Odd shapes made worse by the clinging effects of the poisoned apple on his mind. But before him he saw again the eyes of the thing that had found him in the ruined building. They hung over the shapeless carcass of the deer, over the sound of thick teeth tearing muscle.

The space around them was a rolling miasma of black and green and blue stripes, all falling over and through each other like cards in the hands of a cheating gambler. Low, throaty growling came from the thing, and then from Fujima himself. He realized he had crawled onto his hands and feet, raising his back like a wolf. The thing seemed not to care, ignoring him and going back to its meal.

Fujima woke to singing birds. Blood had dried to a tacky scum over his face and hands, and he was terribly thirsty, but his stomach was full. He could still hear the faintest apple-poison ringing in his ears. It was a dull, deep note that lived at the tails of its own tone. A sound just shy of silence.

What remained of the deer lay in the grass beside him. The grass itself had risen in the night, no longer pressed down by death and those that fed on the dying. Fujima could feel a sore spot in his gums where he'd lost a tooth, probably from pulling at the raw meat with just his bare teeth. What remained of the meat — and little remained — were colorless scraps of connective tissue and red smears of tripe.

Its bones rose amongst the emerging grasses, so clean in places they glowed. Lines of red ants had already found the corpse and were polishing away what remained. Birds darted in and picked at bits of hair and what thin facial flesh hadn't been eaten.

What they left would go to the ground, forgotten amongst this grove of poisoned apples. Fujima cleaned his face and hands with some of his remaining water, naked to his waist and steaming slightly in the growing summer heat. He drank the rest and stood, finding the road, the tracks, and his quarry soon after.

Five men remained of the larger party he'd been tracking. He could only imagine where the others had gone; there was no indication they were hidden away in the foliage growing through the sidewalks. Nor could they be in the buildings beside the road. From a distance of maybe 500 meters he scanned the windows and every other dark place beside the people. There was nothing.

He watched them walk the last of the prisoners, a woman and two children, several paces ahead of them. The woman's steps were hesitant and weak, her arms and legs a shade shy of skeletal. The children seemed much better, probably they didn't have such bad calorie deficiencies given the same rations. Their little faces scanned the buildings with wide eyes, looking for something they'd been told to be afraid of.

Fujima let them travel out of sight, waiting for at least twenty minutes before moving, expecting any rear ambush they'd set up would get tired of waiting and leave their hides to catch up with the group.

Nothing.

He pushed himself to his feet and moved down the road, taking each step carefully. The buildings here were ancient, but well-built. Uneven bricks paved the road beneath his feet, overgrown with moss so thick it drank the noise of every footstep.

He caught the men's shadows moving up a wall in a pass ahead and found a building that would look in that direction. He quickened his pace, running long and low over the street until he was climbing through the pitch black floors using his utility light. He could hear some screaming from the people, desperate men barking orders at somebody, each other perhaps. The woman screamed something back at them.

They were clearing out a tiny space between two buildings on the opposite side of the street and down some from where Fujima had set up. The men were scrawny, heavily bearded, and sported old plague sores around their eyes and mouths. The women and children had clean skin, as far as he could see. Fujima dropped his pack in front of the window and took aim.

The source of the argument was plainly clear. The men were selecting which of the children they were going to butcher, and the woman wasn't happy with either choice. If they had brought the corpse in the university garden, the meat at least, they'd have had a few more days of food. The wastefulness was un-characteristic, Fujima thought. Then he saw the men drive a stake between the cobbles. They tied the child to the stake and then set up a hide in the cleared area.

Bait, Fujima thought. Now he knew where the rest of the men had gone. He thought of the eyes in the dark the past two nights. The long stretch of open street leading into this sub-city. The body left to rot in the sun, only half eaten. He moved his sight over the leg of the man staking down the child. The little girl was dirt-streaked and half-dazed from fear, maltreat-ment, and malnutrition. Fujima pulled the trigger.

Blood misted the cobbles behind the man, and

his ruined femur collapsed under the strain of his weight. He dropped the automatic rifle he'd been carrying on the ground and grabbed his leg, screaming. The other men began firing blindly into the building, nothing coming close to Fujima. He left his rifle perched on the bag and lay back on the floor, watching the occasional stray round knock chunks off the ceiling.

The gunfire slowed and he heard the men screaming to each other, clips and phrases about covering this or watching that. He pulled a thin fiber-optic cord from the device on his wrist and bent it so it could see over the rim of the window. A grainy image of the men cowering in their hide filled the screen. One of them crawled toward the wounded man with a determined look on his face.

Fujima rose, shouldered the rifle, and fired a round through the left eye of one of the men in the hide. His face turned to red dust and scraps of bone that flew into the open mouth of the man behind him. That one fell down below where Fujima could see. He racked another round and shot the crawling man, who had stopped moving forward on his belly to scan the buildings with his rifle. Fujima hit him in the heart, and the man's body deflated slowly until he looked like he was sleeping with his rifle as a pillow. The woman screamed.

Fujima turned the scope in time to see one of the two remaining men dart from the hide and snatch the boy off the ground. Rifle in hand, he sprinted off down the road past where Fujima could see. Fujima sighed, stood, and shouldered his pack and his rifle. It took him several minutes to descend the building.

He approached the place where he'd killed the men, rifle raised, cutting the alley into thin slices his eye ate step by careful step. The man with the shot leg was still dying. The girl he'd staked to the ground by her wrists sat patiently with her hands behind her back, waiting for whatever was going to happen to just be overwith. She looked at Fujima, and he put a finger to his lips.

"Danny," the man on the ground yelled, trying to crawl closer to his gun. His face had gone slack and ashen, but his lungs worked well enough. He turned toward Fujima and opened his mouth to scream. Fujima clucked his tongue and planted his boot on the man's chest. The man's next words were little more than a hiccup. His hands slapped at Fujima's pants leg as Fujima pushed his foot up and down, pumping the blood through the man's chest and out through his leg. He didn't make another sound. The girl watched with cold, sad eyes as the man died.

"Jalen?" called a man from inside the hide. "Jalen. Is it out there? What the hell is going on? Jalen?" The woman fell into sight and onto the cobbles, yelping when the bricks scraped her hands raw. Fujima brought the sight to his eye slowly, and when the last man — Danny, he figured — stepped out, he shot him through the temple. It was a better — and faster — death than maybe he deserved.

Fujima looked over the woman and child. Her eyes did the same, catching on the screen on his wrist, then taking a hard second look at his equipment.

"Are you with the military?" she asked. She had her hands up in front of her, but she was edging closer to the girl on her knees.

"There is no military," Fujima replied. He pointed at the girl. "Is she yours?" The woman shook her head.

"Her mother died before we crossed the river,"

the woman said. The little girl began to sob. "I'm a friend of the family. We were headed for —" Fujima raised a hand.

"I know where you're from," he said. "Don't care where you're going." He walked past both of them scanning the streets ahead for the last man. He'd seen enough through the scope alone to know *that* was the one with the tattoo. "Take what you can off the dead ones and go west. There's folk past the mountains taking in strays."

She maybe said something else — he didn't stay behind to listen — but after a while he could hear her and the girl falling in behind him. They stayed at a distance, feet softer on the stones than even his. Fujima's breath caught in his chest.

The buildings fell away after a turn in the road and he found himself staring at the ocean. A breeze caught him in the face and he could smell the salt of it. The last man, the one with the tattoo, was screaming on the beach. The boy hung limp from his arms — not dead, but probably unconscious. A clean, heartless sort of feeling washed away the months of stress and starvation.

Fujima approached the last man slowly.

He was yelling at somebody who wasn't there, another party that was supposed to meet him. He said he was on time. He said it wasn't fair. Fujima looked over the beach and saw nothing that suggested anybody had been here for months, maybe years. The way sand kept its secrets, perhaps nobody had ever been here at all.

They were a dozen paces apart when the man finally realized how close he'd gotten, spinning around and trying to get his rifle up to shoot at Fujima. Fujima didn't even aim, just shot the man from the hip.

The bullet passed within an inch of the boy's swinging head and punched a hole beside the man's throat. Chunks of vertebrae and skin spilled onto the sand. The man dropped like a brick. The woman screamed and ran past Fujima, snatching the boy up with both hands. She said his name and caressed his face, trying to wake him.

"Who?" the man gasped. Fujima meant to answer him, but a cold, ugly chill rolled up his spine. He turned back to the piles of reeds growing at the edge of the sandbar, from where he'd come. The thing that had been hunting him — them — emerged. It strode casually, its massive forepaws carrying it forward in regal silence. In the interceding years since somebody had freed it from its last cage, it had eaten luxuriously.

"Tiger," the girl said, pointing at the big cat. Its head seemed nearly half the size of Fujima's entire torso, a lithe box of orange and black muscle and teeth, marred only by an ugly wound channel running through its nose and up the front of its skull. The bullet Fujima had fired had nearly killed it, but it would not die. Not this thing. This thing would never die. It bared its teeth and growled, a deep, soft sound.

Fujima lowered his rifle and drew his knife. He stepped backward and over the bleeding man. The woman and children breathed as quietly as they could, but both he and the animal could hear the bone-deepness of their panic. The tiger darted forward and Fujima rose to his feet, screaming and waving the knife. The beast stopped, licking its lips and pacing back and forth over the sand.

Fujima kept his eyes on it, kneeling and taking the man's arm up in his hands. He dropped his gaze only long enough to find the tattoo, then he sliced the printed skin away and stepped back, holding the scrap of flesh in his hand. The tiger stepped forward, sniffed the dying man, and then grabbed his head in its jaws. The man moaned and then was gone into the reeds. In the last second before he disappeared, Fujima saw the eyes of two smaller tigers — kittens — glaring at him from the shadows.

The exchange ended and he found himself alone on the beach. The woman and children had run at some point, and he could see the specks of them moving north. Perhaps they'd wise up when the terror faded and turn west like he'd told them. He'd come from the north, and there was nothing there anybody wanted to find.

More buildings. More cold. More death. Black sickness in what dared to live.

He sat on the beach, listening to the bones of the City howling as the ocean-borne wind blew through them. He found a lighter in his pack and burned the strip of skin with the feather tattoo, watching it turn and twist and burst into purple sparks and smoke. He tossed it onto the wet sand and watched it finish burning.

It wasn't the last, of course, but it was one closer to being finished. Another small footstep closer to the true end of the war, the last drop in a rainstorm of blood that had fallen over the country. He rubbed his own arm, wondering what color he might burn if somebody stripped *his* skin someday.

A thought for a more complex time, he figured. These days were simple.

He lay out on the sand, using his pack as a pillow. In the morning, birds would wake him, as they always did now, and he would continue to pick his way through the bones of the City. Like the ants who finished the remains of the deer, he would find the scraps of flesh that still clung to this dead beast, and he would polish them away.

He would render this place empty again, or free — at least — of what had damned it. Consigned to an eternity of unblemished shining. Dead beyond death.

Within as without.

He parted his lips and sang for the tiger, hoping it could hear.

THE END

     WITHIN AS WITHOUT

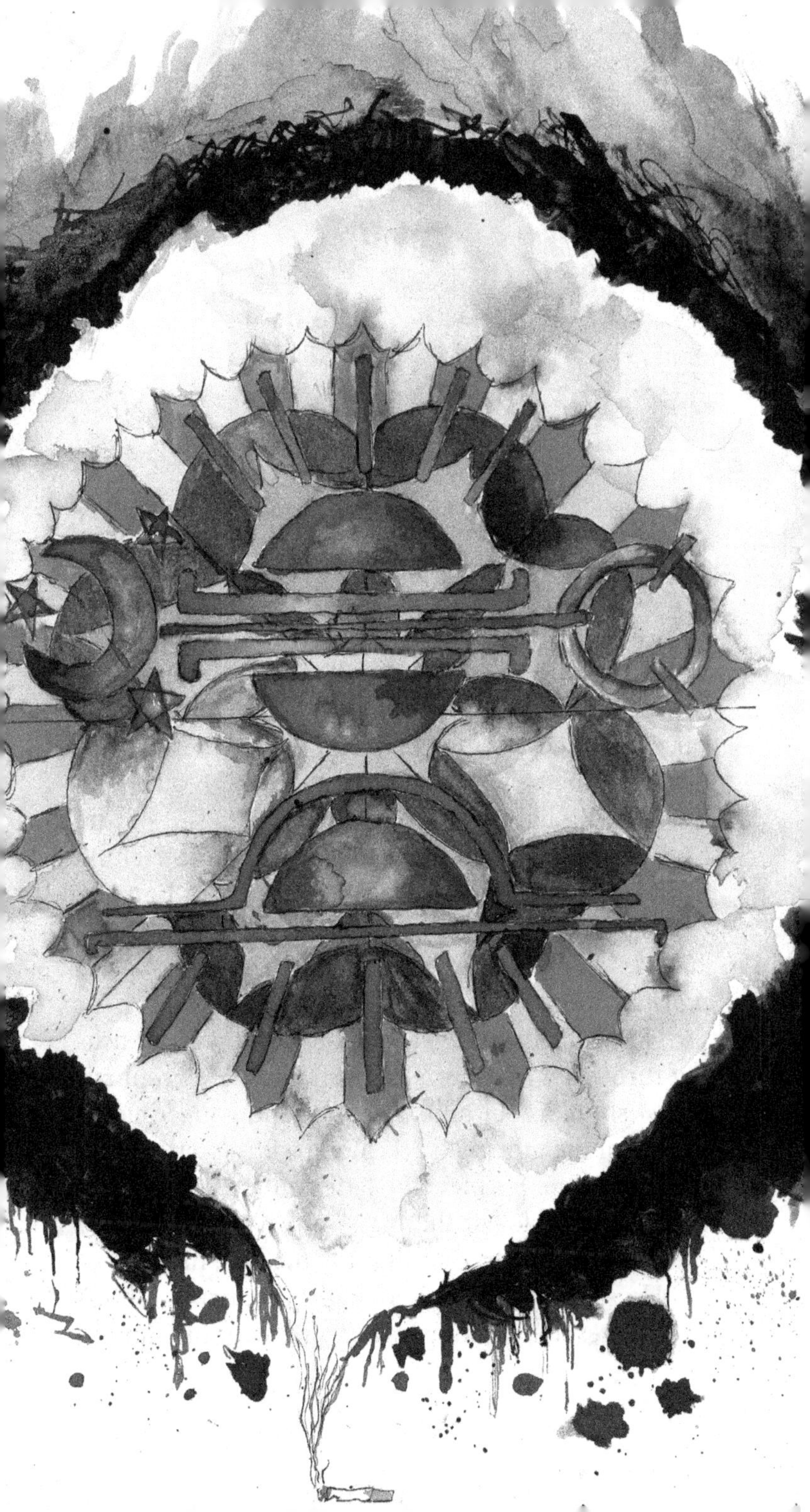

THE MOVE

"Gentlemen, we had to call him out of retirement," Bookie said in a deep voice, slapping Marlow on the back as Dawes walked up the hill from his car. "Our need was too great. This great American nation couldn't be left to suffer without him, our hero, our guiding light. Dawes Freely." Bookie slid off the back of the truck bed and made a loud, screeching noise and pretended he was playing guitar. In a terrible approximation of a hair metal vocalist, he sang, *"Dawes Freely. The only man to answer our call this morning."*

"Jesus fucking Christ, Bookie," Marlow said, fishing through a Marlboro Red soft pack. He eventually just shook it out onto the worn and gouged floorboards of the moving truck, along with a scattering of loose tobacco. He blew the latter out onto the dusty, cobbled-brick lot of the massive driveway. "Do you ever. I mean, really, *ever* shut the fuck up, man?"

He said all this with a laugh, producing a book of matches and flicking one aflame with his thumbnail. It was probably the only reason he even carried matches in the first place. The man exuded a sort of practiced cool that was oddly common amongst blue-collar workers up here in Portland, as though working at a moving company was a stop on the way somewhere else. Marlow was lithe and athletically built, with dark skin and a movie star's rumbling voice. He seemed like a good fit for almost anything *other* than pushing old mattresses and flea-riddled wardrobes up into the guts of an old box truck.

Bookie wasn't much different, though his looks were nothing to brag about. The light orange "Miracle '75 Moving" T-shirt he wore fit tightly over a chest that had stayed birdy even after five years as a grunt in this line of work. He had an unruly mop of dirty blond hair that looked somehow perpetually filthy, as though he'd just run a handful of Vaseline into it. It stuck out at random angles and fell down around the old '50s-style coke-bottle glasses he'd worn since high school and refused to replace.

Dawes himself had short-cropped, almost white blond hair and faded blue eyes that proved a fair match to the denim jacket he'd worn to work that day. He had the ropey muscularity one picked up working dive bars and cleanup crews and every other sort of physical labor job a guy could get wandering up the West Coast from California. He smiled, showing a front tooth chipped crossways from a bar fight gone wrong in his late twenties. Bookie dragged him into a back-slapping hug.

"Where the hell have you been?" he asked. "It's been like a year since you picked up hours with good old Miracle '75." Bookie pulled open Dawes' jacket and feigned a shocked expression when he saw the plain white muscle shirt underneath. "And look at this, Marlow. Out of uniform!" Dawes laughed and pushed him away, pulling a pack of cigarettes free of his jacket and lighting one.

"Lost most of my clothes about a year ago," he said, grinning around the cigarette. He inhaled and puffed out a big cloud of smoke that hung in the chill autumn air with the cigarette staying clamped between his teeth. "Girl I was with then got sick of me and threw my stuff out on the lawn. We were living in Old Town, and, wouldn't you know it, none of it was there when I finally got back." Marlow laughed. "Seriously. I saw a doper like three days later wearing my Doc Martens."

"He did you a favor," Marlow said with a chuckle. "I remember those boots."

"I *liked* those boots," Dawes laughed. "I was stuck in my no-slips from this restaurant job for like two weeks until I could afford something new."

"Sounds like you had it coming," Bookie said. "What'd you do?"

"I told my side girl I was leaving my girlfriend to be with her, you know? Just couldn't live without her," Dawes said. "Turns out I'd forgotten which one I was talking to, and basically confessed to my girl I was running out on her." All three of them laughed and Bookie shook his head.

"You're full of shit, Dawes," he said. "But that's why I like you."

"I aim to please."

"Hey, you layabouts," called a voice from up the driveway. Dawes shielded his eyes with his hand and found Demarkus Winters bounding down the winding stairway to the drive. The man was a clean hundred pounds overweight, but at seven feet tall that didn't amount to much more than a pot belly.

A cauldron belly, more like, Bookie had once said, striving as ever to show off the advanced vocabulary that had netted him this cushy moving job. It was Demarkus who'd given Graham McAliffe the nickname Bookie five years ago when he'd tried to sound smart by naming the plots of all the titles on a bookshelf they were tasked with moving. Bookie enjoyed the nickname immensely. It was a story, he liked to say, he would one day tell when he was a famous author.

He'd threatened Dawes and Marlow and the other men at the company with one day quitting Miracle '75 to write the Great American Novel, but so far hadn't.

"Well shit, Dawes *did* show up," Demarkus said. He trundled over to Dawes and shook his hand, pulling him in for a hug the way a wrecking ball might pull down a building. Dawes let out a puff of air when the big man slapped him on the back. "Oh, look at this. You do some time, little man? Don't appreciate prison tattoos on my crew." He pointed at the feather tattoo on the back of Dawes' wrist. Dawes turned his hand over to look at the ink. It had already faded some in the last year.

"This?" Dawes asked, laughing. "Just a … bad decision I made. My record's clean as a whistle, big man, you know that."

"Clean as a whistle then, alright, alright," Demarkus said. He turned to the others. "Okay, boys, take a knee. I'm going to get right down to it because we got a whole *shit. Load. Of. Work. To-day.*" Dawes and the others reluctantly took a knee. Demarkus wouldn't start talking until they did, a holdover from his days as a lineman for the Seattle Seahawks. His career had been cut short by a host of injuries he'd sustained in a plane crash in 1975. Surviving that had been the "miracle" that let him start this moving company.

A thin, tall man with mushroomy skin stepped up just a few feet behind Demarkus. Dawes was startled to realize he'd been standing there the entire time, hands clasped demurely at his waist. He wore a simple black suit with a pale purple tie and a white shirt. Odd metal cufflinks glittered at his wrists, a stylized sort of eye or setting sun set in gold and black. Expensive, to say the least.

Grit in the driveway dug into Dawes' knee and he shifted uncomfortably. The movement drew the thin man's eye, which crawled over Dawes and then the other movers. The man's irises were a stunning, almost fake-looking mix of purple and gold, though maybe it was a trick of the sun shining on them. His face was drawn and pale, stubbled lightly around his chin and cheeks. The mustache over his lip seemed a touch overgrown, as though it were normally trimmed thin. His eyes were puffy, like he was about to fall out from exhaustion.

"This is Shelby Goldstein, Esq., of Walther, Dunbarton, and Loeb," Demarkus said, giving everybody a stern look, like they were about to take the field in the biggest game of their life. "His client, a miss Hirishiko Ami, passed just last week and her next of kin are relocating her old possessions for the estate sale. There is a *lot* of stuff inside this house, boys, and *'We gonna mooove it alllll.'*" Demarkus couldn't help but sneak the company slogan into any conversation it might even half fit inside.

"Now, Mr. Goldstein has labeled Ms. Ami's possessions—"

"Mrs. Hirishiko," Goldstein interrupted. The man's voice was cloying and silky, the soft voice of suggestions and deals made behind closed doors. Demarkus gave him a confused look, not so much that he didn't understand *why* he'd been interrupted, rather than he *could* be interrupted. Goldstein explained anyway. "Mrs. Hirishiko is a dual citizen of Japan and the United States, and spent her life in America doing her best to live up to the proud heritage of her ancestors. As such, her name is given surname first." He paused and looked over the movers, favoring them with a thin smile. "Additionally, she was married in 1935. Thus, *Mrs.* Hirishiko."

"Okay," Demarkus said, turning back to his men. "*Mrs. Hirishiko* has a lot of expensive things being moved with priority to places all over the city for storage and auction. We gonna treat every item like it was our own baby, understand? And, Mr. Goldstein has been kind enough to label items with colored stickers so we know which ones go first. ROY-G-BIV. In that order, just like the rainbow. Any questions?"

Bookie raised his hand.

"No? Good," Demarkus said, turning to Goldstein. Bookie sighed and dropped his hand, standing with the others. "Lead on, Mr. Goldstein."

Dawes got a better look at the house as they climbed the steep drive and then the seemingly steeper staircase leading to the front door. Castellations soared over the brocade of the old growth trees. Over his shoulder, to the east, Mt. Hood sat behind a thin blue veil of ozone. Portland lay somewhere between him and that great mountain, in a valley obscured by the thick tree cover to the southeast.

Mt. St. Helens lay to the northeast, also obscured, though he could still see the tracework of smoke guttering from its mouth into the sky. It had been five years since the eruption, and curious geologists from across the globe were still visiting in droves to figure out why the thing was still sputtering long after it should have gone dormant. People in town — normally a sunny bunch despite the rain — had started talking about Mt. Hood "getting hot like Helen" in hushed voices.

"How the fuck are we supposed to carry shit up and down this fucking thing?" Bookie grumbled. The stairs under their feet were surprisingly economical compared to the grandness of the house hanging over them. They were simple molded concrete, and not very wide, snaking uphill at nearly 45 degrees. A black-painted steel pipe handrail ran most of the length of the stairs, disappearing in places where time had rusted away the brackets holding it in place. Beside the stairs grew a forest of shin-high weeds and uncut grass. He couldn't see any bugs dancing amongst those blades, but he could hear them singing all around. The steady buzzsaw humming of deep summer, despite it being November.

"It's temporary," Demarkus said. "This is just a like, fact-finding tour for y'all, so you can see what needs goin' where before we start. Hideo, who got here *early* unlike you layabouts, is already inside organizing stuff. There's a lot of … *stuff* in there." Dawes felt the hitch when Demarkus kept himself from saying "shit" and chuckled. "It's hard to get to the garage, where we'll be backing up into to take the rest of the loads. So we're going to take some of the larger items down this here staircase."

Marlow sighed and Bookie cursed under his breath. Dawes looked down the landing behind them. A few two-man carries down that slope would be most of the day's effort expended. The thought vanished from his mind when he saw the house.

"Holy shit," Marlow said. "How the fuck they *get* this all the way up here?"

The front of the building soared into the sky. It made Dawes feel small and unimportant, the way national monuments sometimes did. This place had power, a purpose. It was built by important people for important reasons, and he was just an ant that had to crawl up through the cracks.

He couldn't quite place the style. It screamed old European in his mind, though what part of Europe he couldn't decide. A colonnaded portico led into the entrance closest to them, away from which sprawled stonework cut in mad spirals and fractal patterns that somehow formed themselves into the square façade of a Tudor castle. But around and over that flew buttresses and an assortment of different towers, tubes and drums and bulbous Russian minarets. They seemed colored a multitude of browns, greys, and whites, but on closer inspection, Dawes saw the entire building seemed made of the exact same brown stone. The appearance of different colors was caused by a trick of the patterns carved into the surface.

"This thing is fucking full to the brim, boys," Demarkus said in a low voice as Goldstein stepped away from them to unlock the door. "I'm not going to say what we're getting paid to do this, but it's a daily rate, and it's high. And between you boys and me, it's going to take us months to empty this place. Maybe a year."

"That mean more money for us?" Marlow asked.

"Yes, sir," Demarkus said. His and everybody else's eyes wandered the face of the mansion, the *castle*, before them. Dawes particularly looked from window to window. All of them were flat, singular panels of glass save for a massive rose window of purple and red that glowed like an eye in the center of the building. He expected it would hang over the main hall.

Probably looks amazing when the sun's rising, he thought.

Something caught his eye, a touch of movement in a high window that tickled a primal part of his mind. *Eyes,* it said, and *face.* But when he focused on that spot, there was nothing more than the watery glitter of the warped old glass in the noonday sun. The wind, which never stopped this high in the mountains, picked up and blew leaves and shreds of grass and sticks across the wide marble patio. Some of this debris caught in the errant fronds of weeds growing between the slabs. Bookie cleared his throat and spoke.

"*Lo, did the Gates of Heaven rise before me,*" he quoted in a purposefully eerie voice. "*And I saw the mad Black Scrawl upon their faces. And I heard in their squealing hinges the voices of the betrayed. And I felt on their bars the chill of ages. And I saw in the great expanse beyond, a Nothing beyond Nothing. The empty promise. The last lie of God.*" Marlow slapped him in the back of the head.

"Quoting fuckin' Common Ledes?" he snapped. "Creepy motherfucker. How many times your momma drop you?" Bookie laughed.

"So many," he said, running a hand through his crazy hair. "And come on, look at this place. How could you *not* quote Common Ledes?" He waved a hand at the building, and then snapped a finger and turned to Marlow. "And how do *you* know Common Ledes?"

"Please," Marlow said. "You can't watch a horror movie these days without somebody quoting that weak shit and raising the dead or bringing back Charles Manson's ghost. It's always that same five fucking lines too. 'Gates of Heaven' my ass." Dawes hadn't appreciated the recitation much either, but he didn't say so.

"Welcome to the Hirishiko residence, gentlemen," Goldstein said, pushing the massive double doors open wide and then gesturing for them to step inside.

◆

"This place is fucking haunted," Bookie said, looking up at the ceiling. Between the rose window and the dozens of recessed skylights, the place was fairly well lit. The impression Dawes got was that they'd just walked inside a thicker part of the woods around the property. Wind blowing from the depths of the house brought a musty, almost hot-smelling odor into the hall. It rose and died over and over. It made Dawes feel like he was in the mouth of some huge thing, feeling it breathe.

"You believe in ghosts, Mr. McAliffe?" Goldstein asked, turning and raising an appraising eye at the movers. Dawes thought again of having stepped into the woods as Goldstein moved closer to them, the patchwork shadows left by the skylights dancing up and over his face. His eyes glittered and dulled, an almost calming sort of strobe, like a mouse might see in the face of a snake.

"No," Bookie said, still looking around the ceiling. "But I like ghost stories. I bet a place like this has a few." He snapped out of his reverie and looked at Goldstein. "Hey, how do you know my name?"

"I told him," Demarkus said. The movers looked at their boss and he shrugged. "Had to run a background check on the firm, isn't that what you said?"

"Yes," Goldstein replied. "There are valuables here of extreme worth. We can't entrust just anybody with this job." He gave Dawes a long look. "You though, I believe you're Mr. Freely?" Goldstein touched his fingertips together, his hands resting in a V below his belt.

"Yeah," Dawes said, facing the man and crossing his arms.

"Mr. Winters added you at the last minute," Goldstein said, giving Demarkus a glance. "You don't mind us … snooping around in your past?" He smiled in a way the situation didn't call for. Dawes looked at his own feet and then smiled, raising his eyes back to the glittering black orbs in the twilight.

"Go for it," he said. "I'd be interested to see what you find." He cleared his throat and looked around the massive, empty hall. "If anything."

"Yes," Goldstein said. "Anyway, if you'll follow me. There's little time to waste."

⬥

What followed was a tour of the first floor of the north wing. Dawes had never been inside a home like this in his life. Any building, really. The hall leading through the heart of the wing was tiled in ornate black and white checks. The walls along the hall and in much of the rooms were paneled mahogany, all carved in the same style as the façade of the house. Dawes found his fingers tracing the odd curves more than once. The pattern beneath his fingertips felt almost like code.

The hallways grew more cluttered the farther they got from the main hall. Stacks of boxes, old crates even, were piled up near to the ceiling in places. Amongst all of these were odd bits of furniture. Ornate bookshelves, spinning globes with the names of the continents and countries all in Arabic script, couches stacked on top of other couches and all draped with yellowed dropcloths.

Cobwebs grew thick in the spaces between everything. They seemed to Dawes like a sort of ethereal grey mist, a material shadow of some strange thing that had fallen from the walls to rest over all this forgotten history like a shroud. He ran a hand through a net of the stuff and found it surprisingly tough. It clumped over his hand and he had to shake himself free. The great shadowy network of web puckered and pitched and stretched out into the depths of the hallways beyond where he could see.

In the depths of the building, they heard something thump.

"Oh dear," Goldstein said. Dawes saw him touch a slender hand to his face at the front of their little pack. "I hope that wasn't another collapse in the basement."

"This place has a basement too?" Marlow asked. He was walking with his head much lower than it needed to be, slapping at the cobwebs every time one stuck to his hair. Despite his best efforts, the tight black curls were steadily turning grey.

"Two basements, in fact," Goldstein replied, flicking his fingers through the air. "One beneath either wing. The south wing's basement suffered a terrible collapse during the Mt. St. Helens explosion, I'm afraid. I've been told we lost something like 10,000 bottles of wine in that incident. Most of that area was wine storage. There were a few dozen barrels of bourbon lost too, some of them more than a hundred years old."

"Maybe a few of them are still around," Bookie muttered, looking back over his shoulder toward the south wing. He caught Dawes looking and winked.

"I wouldn't try to find out, if I were you, Mr. McAliffe," Goldstein said. "That entire side of the mansion is terribly unstable now, and completely off limits." The party passed a heavy wooden door with iron bandings set into a flourished archway, and Goldstein pointed. A line of red plastic was fastened over the front of the door with neat strips of duct tape. "Just as with any area where you see this red marking." Goldstein stopped walking in front of a door filled with soft blue light. Dawes hadn't really even realized how dark it had gotten this deep in the halls. Without the lady of the house around, he figured, there was no reason to keep paying the electric bill.

"Oh, hey, Hideo!" Bookie shouted. His voice was loud enough to make Marlow duck. The man was an easy startle. Dawes looked past Bookie into the room, where Hideo, the last member of the crew, was organizing old crates full of irregularly colored glasses. He gave a sharp wave and went back to work.

"Nice of you to show up, Book," he said, pulling a red sticker off a roll and mushing it into place with his thumb. It didn't want to stick to the old wood, and

Hideo eventually got sick of dicking with the thing and jammed the sticker between the slats on the side of the crate. He held his hands up to the sky, looking at nobody. "And now this room is done. I'm taking my lunch break."

"Log your minutes," Demarkus said.

"Log your fucking dick," Hideo muttered, storming past them into the dark hallway. He was wearing the high-visibility vest they were all supposed to wear on job sites, and Dawes could see it bobbing in the darkness long after Hideo's outline had faded. There was a loud thump, and the vest disappeared.

"Bleeding fuck nugget," Hideo shouted. His voice was softened by the distance. Dawes saw the orange glow rise up out of the dark and laughed.

"Be careful down there, Hideo," Dawes yelled after him.

"Suck a fart out of my ass, you fucking blister!" Hideo shouted back. Then the vest really was gone. Dawes looked that way a second longer.

The hallways curve, he thought. *That's why it's so fucking dark in here.*

"Your employee has quite a mouth on him," Goldstein said to Demarkus, voice sharp with displeasure. Demarkus shrugged.

"If I could do something about it, I already would have," he replied.

Goldstein liked to slip in and out of the house's deep shadows as they worked. He gave long, irritating lectures about being careful and constant, stern reminders of how fragile and expensive and important every last bauble was to the estate. Dawes had heard the same shit a million times as a mover, though in his experience it was only rich fucks that ever stretched the speeches out that long. Middle-class people would try to be cool most of the move, until you touched the one thing they cared about, then they broke out into a sweat until it was bundled and buried in the van.

Poor people cared more than the rich people about every last thing, though that was usually because they didn't have all that much. If you broke the table, they were out a table fucking indefinitely. Or they'd just have to make do using a fucked up, broken ass table. Put phonebooks under the legs. Embarrass the kids' friends.

Dawes remembered one middle-aged Black lady, the wife of a naval petty officer overseeing a move from just south of Portland down to Corpus Christi. He'd risked a tricky move with a chest of drawers and she'd just cleared her throat.

"No you ain't," she said, shifting the child on her hip and staring at him.

Dawes chuckled at the memory.

"What the fuck are you laughing about?" Hideo asked.

It was the third day of work now, and they were getting used to the job. Given the obnoxious route they had to take to get out of the house, they'd been slowed to just one room per day. They'd cleared the hallway first, and those cobwebs had given them a monster of a time. So had Goldstein, slipping in and out of sight to point and worry over every last thing.

But eventually, they'd cleared the hall. It had taken something like three truckloads to finish it, the rough equivalent of an entire single-family home.

 THE MOVE

Dawes had ridden along on a few of the offload trips, which were thankfully handled by a separate crew at the storage warehouse everything seemed to be going to. They all wore grey jumpsuits with Grady Shipping emblazoned on the back.

"Hey, man," Dawes asked one of them. "Where is all this going?" The guy just shrugged and kicked out the bottom of the dolly, dragging a stack of book-laden crates into the airplane hangar-sized doors.

"This is a fucking kitchen," Hideo said, leaning into what they found out seconds later was a heavy, six-foot-wide claw-footed bookshelf. It could have been used for anything; the shelves themselves were inch-thick slabs of stained oak, all of them at least two feet deep. They could have held stacks of gold without bending. As such, they just held books. So, Dawes figured, they were bookshelves.

"Are you sure?" Dawes asked. He dialed up the Coleman gas lanterns Demarkus had bought them in a bid to better navigate the house. The deeper they went into the north wing, the darker the rooms got. Windows in any given room would be filled with stacks of old books and newspapers with Chinese characters. One room even had plastic-wrapped wholesale boxes of Pez candy pellets and dispensers packed so tightly into a window frame they had to use a pry bar to loosen them.

"Fucking why?" Hideo had said, face streaming with sweat. The work wasn't that exhausting; the house just got hotter the deeper they got into it. It wasn't the dry heat of a furnace or radiator, but a raw, wet sort of hotness. Like being in a greenhouse a few minutes after the sprinklers have stopped running. It stuck to you, in a way, and the odd, breathy blowing up the corridors never seemed to stop.

"Look, right there," Hideo said, back in the maybe kitchen. Dawes followed his finger until he saw too. "It's a stovetop under all that. What are those, bindles of silk or something?" Dawes *could* see it, the black tracework of burner covers and corners of polished steel poking out here and there beneath maybe 80 neatly stacked rolls of expensive-looking fabric. The kind you might see in a Middle Eastern bazaar.

Two hours of digging — Goldstein materialized in that time and passed out the stickers, naming what needed to go where and how to color-code it — revealed a fully set up kitchen, complete with stainless steel prep tables, two stoves, a flatiron range, and a chest of drawers filled with boxes of industrial kitchen knives.

The entire thing had been set up like people were about to come in and pull a full day shift in a four-star restaurant. The only things missing were gas hookups, the parts for which Dawes found in an oily box under the prep table. He couldn't wait to announce the ridiculous find to Hideo. Dawes had been passing the time every day by getting the man riled up so he could hear him complain about every little thing. But Hideo was quiet now, standing with arms crossed and looking down at the table.

"Hey, what's up, man?" Dawes asked, heading over to see what he was looking at. He had to bat away more than a few dangling sheets of web that were only just low enough for someone his height to have to deal with. Hideo was a good four inches shorter than him and walked under most of the stuff without ever even noticing it. Hideo unfolded one of his arms and pointed at the table.

"Check this out," he said. There was a sticker on the corner of the table, one of the kind they'd been putting on everything. A fine layer of dust lay over the tiny violet disk. Dawes realized the sticker was old, ancient even. Even back here in the dark, the color had faded some, and the corners were starting to peel up of their own accord. He put a finger on it and pushed. The glue, decayed from years of sticking to the stainless steel, gave way, leaving a grimy smear on the silvery metal.

"Lady Hirishiko has always been one for extensive organization," Goldstein said just over Dawes' shoulder. Dawes jumped.

"Oh fuck," Hideo shouted, turning to Goldstein. "What the fuck, man? You just sneaking up on people? God … damnit." He put his knuckle in his mouth and turned around to pace.

"My apologies," Goldstein said with a smile. He pointed to the sticker. "She liked her systems. A methodical woman. Repetitive. Dedicated." He put his pale forefinger on the sticker and slid it off the edge of the table. He held the tiny piece of paper up in front of his nose and then crumpled it and dropped it in his pocket. "That would have been the wrong color anyway. This item should be coded blue."

"Sure, boss," Dawes said. "No problem." They had been repeating the color scheme every couple of days. ROY-G-BIV. The guys at the storage hangar hadn't seemed to pay the color scheme much attention, and Dawes couldn't see a pattern to it. If anything, the rationale behind it was risky, sometimes outright dangerous from a moving perspective. Heavy things went on the truck in the wrong order, fragile items were put in compromising situations. It didn't make a lick of sense, but any deviation would summon Goldstein like a vengeful, irritating spirit.

He favored the movers with one of his smiles and then left the room. Dawes watched him fade into the darkness in the hall, watching for the exact moment he disappeared.

They cleared the first floor. No matter how much furniture they removed, however, the cobwebs never seemed to abate. If anything, they accumulated more freely, sometimes collapsing into makeshift screens in the hallway. They broke apart with the first touch, but they'd cling to Dawes for hours, sometimes until he finally scrubbed them away in the shower after work.

They worked on the second floor now, which had all the problems of the first floor compounded by a broad spiral staircase that led from level to level. The pro to this was that the staircase, located behind the massive iron-belted wooden door in the hall, was near the smoking lounge where they'd found the makeshift kitchen. That room, for whatever reason, bordered the house's garage.

Garage wasn't really the correct word either. *Carriage house* is what came to mind when Dawes stepped inside the place. It was packed as full as the rest of the house. There was even a dry-rotted saddle buried beneath a stack of newspapers from West Virginia of all places. The *Charleston Independent-Star.*

Some of them were absurdly old, and simply read *The Charleston Independent* across the masthead.

Once cleared, they'd backed the old Miracle '75 box truck right up to the massive double doors. Those swung open on fat-barreled black hinges coated in a thick, grey-black grease. The doors were so heavy they needed the support of stubby iron wheels, which ran along rusted steel guide tracks recessed into the cobbles. The doors were wide and high enough to accommodate the back of the truck, which made loading a breeze compared to the winding staircase in front of the house.

The only bad thing about this new arrangement was the staircase *inside* the house they now had to contend with. It wasn't steep or cramped, but the stairs themselves were trapezoidal, thinning as they got close to the pin of the screw-shaped staircase.

Backing down the things while carrying anything that blocked your view of your feet was a complete fucking nightmare. And many of the larger objects — six king-size redwood bed frames without mattresses for instance — had to be carried just so or they'd catch on the wall or the pin.

What Dawes hated most was the passage to the lower floor, though he hadn't shared that with the other guys. The spiral staircase went up and down, down to the basement according to Goldstein. The breathy heat in the place seemed to come from down there, and the sticky, sweaty feeling was at its worst near that descending staircase. The red tape that had formerly blocked the door now hung there at the head of the stairs, affixed again by neat strips of tape.

"This place is creepy as hell," Marlow said, shifting his footing to get a better grip on the iron table they were carrying. The thing was only three feet tall and weighed at least 150 pounds. It was ugly, blocky, and made totally out of metal. It looked like something that would get dropped on a cartoon cat's head. Marlow set it on the steps and sat down himself, wiping his forehead.

"I got to tell you something, man," he said. His face was calm but his eyes were worried. Puffy bags lay underneath them. "I think I'm going to take my payout early on this one and go."

"Yeah?"

"Yeah," Marlow said. He shook his head. "This stuff is weird. That fucking Goldstein is weird." Dawes looked up the staircase, sure the guy would appear behind Marlow like a boogeyman. He noticed Marlow doing the same, only downstairs. "I've been having dreams, man, like every night. I'm stuck in this place and I don't have a lantern. It's hot. There's a woman just ahead of me, in the dark like, so I can only barely see her." He swallowed. Dawes said nothing. The moment felt crisp.

Somehow breakable.

"I feel like I'm running after that, only I'm just standing there, looking at her," he continued. "But I'm also running at the same time, and I've got to focus on that, on running, or I'll just be in the hallway. And she's getting closer. In the hallway and … and while I'm running." He shook his head. "Man, I'm sorry for telling you all this."

"Nah, get it off your chest, dude," Dawes said. The breathy wind blew around them. Marlow chuckled, an uncomfortable noise, and nodded without looking at Dawes.

"Well," he said, tapping his thumb on his blue jeans. "Well. I run until I get to these fucking stairs. And there's this … purplish light bobbing away down the steps ahead of me. I figure it's somebody. Anybody. And at least it isn't dark where the light is." He paused on a thought, clearly wanting to say more but deciding against it.

"Anyway," he said. "I'm not the kind of guy has dreams like that. 'Specially not every goddamn night. It's probably just nerves or something. I dunno. I'm getting old. Anyway, I'm going to talk to Demarkus when we're done moving this thing."

They finished lugging the uncomfortable hunk of iron out to the truck, and Dawes rode up the lift with it alone. Marlow gave him half a smile and waved, then walked back inside the house. He seemed relieved. Excited almost.

Demarkus caught up with Dawes later, while he was helping Bookie maneuver an old baby crib with moving steel sides down the stairs. The retention pegs on the heavy sidings kept loosing themselves as the men walked, dropping the metal crossbars and nearly snapping all their fingers off at the second knuckle.

"Hey," Demarkus said. "You seen Marlow? I told him to stick around to the end of the day at least. It's a fucking two-mile walk down this mountain and I'm his ride."

"He give you notice?" Dawes asked. Demarkus nodded, looking sad.

"Marlow quit, huh?" Bookie said. It wasn't surprise so much as the question of a possibility. Almost like Bookie was saying, "Maybe I could too."

"Yeah," Demarkus said. "Said this place gave him the creeps and he wanted to be gone." He looked at the walls, with their mad interlacing scrollwork. "Can't really say I blame him. But damn he left me in the lurch."

Bookie and Dawes said nothing. A moment

passed and Demarkus wandered back up the stairs to see to whatever Hideo was doing. Bookie and Dawes got the thing downstairs and into the hallway, where they set it down to let their hands rest. Bookie leaned on the side of the crib, looking down at the stained, stripped mattress attached to the bedsprings by cloth tie-offs. He saw something in that thin, pitiful sleeping pad that made him shake and bow his head.

Dawes turned back to the stairs and his breath caught in his chest. There was really nothing wrong; it was just that the tape holding the red band blocking the basement stairs had come loose. The strip of thin red plastic was fluttering over the stairs, tangled in a wad of errant, fallen cobwebs.

Dawes picked the strip up and pressed the tape against the wall hard, holding it there a while before stepping back and making sure it stayed in place. He made an effort not to look down into the shadows of the winding basement staircase.

And succeeded, to a degree.

Dawes had his own dream that night. Portland, the valley around it, and all the mountains beyond were bare and dead. He was standing naked on the concrete dais in front of the house, watching Mt. Hood erupt. The exploding caldera had ripped the mountain in two. The very air was on fire. Poisonous.

A black thing pushed its hand out of the molten flames. The uppermost tip of its misshapen head — larger even than the mountain — crowned, knocking loose slabs of stone larger than city blocks. Dawes caught a glimpse of a single, great, purple eyeball. Then the thing cracked open its mouth and sunk back inside the mountain.

All the land heaved and shuddered and buckled and fell into that maw.

Fell into a nothing more absolute than the Word of God.

Dawes snapped awake. The feather tattoo on the back of his wrist itched terribly, worse even than it had in the first few weeks after he'd gotten it. He'd scratched the skin around it raw. Somebody was talking to him.

"Dude, seriously," Bookie said, kicking the bottom of his foot again. "We thought you'd quit. How long have you been sleeping here?" Dawes yawned and looked around. The room was filled with a vapory light that fell through the tall, ornate windows covering its oblong western wall. It was a hidden sort of third floor they'd been made to clear out, a lonely room with almost nothing in it.

The windows, five of them, were all emblazoned with fractal scrollwork that occasionally formed into shapes. But in the center of each window was a symbol on its own, cordoned off from the scrollwork by a meridian of untouched blue glass.

There was a hand-shaped symbol on the left-most window.

A Hand of Sticks, Dawes thought. The words came to him like they'd been spoken into his head. The same happened with the other symbols. The next window over, second from the middle on the left, bore a crescent moon and stars.

A Starred Crescent, the voice in his mind said.

At the far right, a stylized sort of eye or setting sun. He remembered it from Goldstein's metal cufflinks.

A Blind Horizon, he thought.

To the left of that, the least complex symbol, a circle with three intersecting lines at each third. Of all of them, it seemed the most like the patterned scrollwork.

A Lined Circle, he thought.

The centermost window, larger than the others so that its borders touched the floor and ceiling, held the most uniform symbol. A black disk separated by three lines running through its center. The top and bottom lines curved upward and downward slightly at the ends, respectively.

A Divided Sun, he thought.

"Dude, what the fuck," Bookie said. His eyes were baggy, and almost purple from exhaustion. "Are you stoned?" He chuckled, which seemed like it took some effort on his part. "Hey, can I get some?"

"No, I'm just beat, man," Dawes said. The chair he'd fallen asleep in was an ornate, heavy thing made of some dark wood he couldn't place. Ebony or something like it. The cushion was ancient and weird-smelling, but thick as a twin-size mattress and about ten times more comfortable. "What time is it?"

"About quitting time," Bookie said. He looked around the odd, empty room and grumbled to himself. "Maybe for-fucking-ever."

"You thinking about bailing on this job too?"

"Yeah, man," he replied. "Or at least juicing Demarkus for double what I'm being paid." He sniffed.

"Nah, actually, fuck that. I think Marlow had the right idea." He sighed. "This is, like, the only room in this place that has some fucking light coming into it, you know? I'm sick of how dark it is. And these … fucking cobwebs." He waved a hand around, but there were none in this room. Bookie seemed to notice this and slowly lowered his arm.

"What is the fucking deal with this house, dude?"

"I don't know," Dawes said, itching his tattoo again. "But I know I'll be glad to be fucking quit of this place."

"Quit of this place," Bookie parroted. "Look at you."

Dawes rolled his eyes, stood, and stretched.

"Fuck off, Bookie," he said. "You're not the only one of us apes with a library card." Bookie laughed and Dawes grabbed a side of the big chair. "Now help me carry this cumbersome piece of shit downstairs before Demarkus docks my pay."

The garage was empty. Dawes set the chair down and looked at Bookie.

"Did we send out a load?" he asked. "Thought the truck was only like half full." Bookie just shrugged and dropped down into the chair. A whiff of something hot, a brief chemical reek tinged the air. Dawes rubbed his eyes.

"Jeez, no wonder you fell asleep in this thing," he said, crossing his legs and putting his hands behind his head. "You just let me know if you see Demarkus coming." Dawes flicked him behind the ear and Bookie started up, rubbing the side of his head. He gave Dawes an ugly look.

"Dude," he said. "What the fuck?"

"You don't have a weird feeling right now?" Dawes asked. Bookie said nothing, which was all he had to say. He cast his eyes to the empty spot in the garage where the truck should be. Hideo walked in the door behind them.

"Hey," he said. "You guys seen Demarkus?" He paused. "Where's the van?"

"What the hell are you doing here?" Dawes asked. Bookie jumped out of the chair, looking around the empty room. The chemical smell grew worse.

"Following you guys," Hideo said. "I've been hunting you all over the fucking house, you dickhead."

"What?" Dawes asked. "We thought you and Demarkus were taking a load out to the hangar. The van's gone." He pointed and Hideo followed his finger. "And what do you mean 'following us around'? We've been hauling this heavy fucking chair down from upstairs at like a foot per second."

"Fuck off," Hideo said. "I spent half my break following one of you dickheads around this gloomy fucking shithole. You know that's why you're all supposed to be wearing these stupid fucking things, right?" He pointed to his orange high-vis vest.

"It couldn't have been us," Bookie said. "I was wandering around upstairs like thirty minutes ago looking for this turd." He pointed at Dawes. "He was sleeping in that weird room that's sort of hidden over the main hallway." Hideo gave Dawes an ugly look and Dawes rolled his eyes.

"So who were you following? Demarkus?" he asked. "How could you not catch up with him? He moves like shit sliding down a toilet bowl."

"Again, Dawes, where does this come from?" Bookie said, laughing. "That was beautiful, man. Are you trying to show me up?"

"Shut the fuck up, Bookie," Hideo said. "Maybe it was that fucking spook, Goldstein. This is the only haunted house I've ever been inside where the ghosts hire you to move them the fuck out." Wind gusted inside the carriage house, carrying a thickly chemical smell that made them all gag. It tinged the air grey.

"Oh, what the fuck?" Bookie said, ducking down and gagging. They all figured out what the smell was at the same time, but Bookie said it first. "Is something burning?"

None of them had heard it, which was something of a miracle in and of itself, though Dawes remembered a rumble passing through the floor after Bookie had woken him. Walking outside, they saw a column of smoke rising thick and dark from the two full hundred-gallon diesel tanks that powered the Miracle '75 box truck. The rest of the conflagration was a poisonous mixture of ancient, stained wood and various plastic appliances loaded into the bed. Even from three hundred feet up, they could see the tangled limbs of shattered furniture burning around the impact site.

"Shit, was Demarkus in there?" Hideo said.

"If he was, we are going to have a hard time getting paid over this job," Bookie said. Dawes looked back at the house, the only one of them to do so, and thought he saw the shape of something in one of the closest windows. A pale face with long black hair, which might have just been the shape of the old curtains brushing the glass.

"There's a phone inside, in the south wing," Hideo said.

"You've been in there?" Dawes asked.

"I've been stealing all kinds of shit from over there," Hideo said with a shrug. "There's weird little gold statues and shit. Otherwise I would have quit this weird fucking job day one."

"Dude, fuck that," Bookie said. "Let's just … walk the fuck down the mountain."

"We need to call the police before the whole fucking mountain goes up," Hideo said, pointing down at the flames. They had already spread into the trees the box truck had smashed to pieces when it tumbled off the mountain. The truck itself seemed to be on the verge of going out, but everything else was crisping brown at the edges and starting to smolder. It had been a dry year.

"That's pretty noble of you," Bookie said. "I'm fucking leaving. Good luck, guys."

"Wait," Dawes said. He couldn't exactly explain why he thought it was a bad idea to walk down the hill alone, but he tried anyway. "I think you should stick with us, man. What if … what if that spreads super fast and you get caught in it?"

"Figure this out on your own," Hideo said, walking back to the house. Dawes tried to stop him too, but Bookie started talking.

"I'll take that chance," he said. "And fuck ever going back in there again. Fuck even trying to get paid on this mess." He put his fingers on his temples. "What the fuck is going on right now? How long have we even been working here? I think my girlfriend broke up with me because all I've been doing is sleeping, I've been so tired, and I spend most of that time flopping around and making noises. I feel like … like I've already seen this fucking fire too."

Bookie looked at Dawes and Dawes found himself wordless. He didn't even know where to start. A bad chill was running laps up and down his spine. He looked back down at the rising column of smoke. He'd seen the same thing in his dreams, but much larger. Smoke choking the entire sky. In his dream though, the smoke had shattered against the blue and split into the shapes of a billion birds on the wing. They had swooped down over the land, spreading across the country.

He touched the feather tattoo on his wrist. It itched badly, burned almost.

"I'm going back inside," Dawes said. He sighed. "I think you're right, but we can't leave Hideo up here alone." Bookie looked at Dawes and then at the access road leading back down the mountain. "Just … stick around out here and wait for us, okay?" Bookie nodded without looking back at him.

Dawes walked through the garage back into the house. Hideo had lit up a cigarette on the way inside; he could smell the smoke trapped in the cobwebs. The faint light of the lantern he brought with him into the house moved through the webs and the smoke. The shifting patterns made Dawes feel like he wasn't moving in the direction his feet were taking him, and he had to focus on the shadows on the floor ahead to get his mind to understand where he was going.

Those shadows suddenly grew long in front of him, stretching forward through the hall so far they touched the very end of the curving walls. Somebody was coming up behind him. Dawes turned around and yelled when he saw two glowing orange eyes bobbing through the darkness. The eyes yelled back at him, spinning back into the dark. Dawes' heart leapt in his chest, and then he caught his breath.

"Goddamnit, Bookie," he said. "What the fuck?" The glowing orange eyes were nothing more than the reflection of his lantern in Bookie's glasses. Bookie had his own lantern stretched out into the hall behind them. That's what had sent Dawes' shadow flying out ahead of him.

"Jesus, what's back there?" Bookie asked.

"Nothing, you idiot," Dawes said. "You just scared the shit out of me." Bookie stiffened and turned back around.

"Sorry," he said. "It was too quiet out there. Too weird." He smiled, even though his heart didn't seem all the way in it. "I figured I'd come in here with you after all." Dawes opened his mouth to say something when they heard a loud thump down the hallway. The cobwebs around them shuddered and seemed all at once to pull in one direction. Dawes and Bookie both followed the odd motion with their eyes to the end of the hallway, where they saw Hideo's orange hi-vis vest in the darkness. The cherry of a lit cigarette glowed on the floor. Even at this distance, Dawes could make out the smoke curling upward.

"Hideo?" Dawes called. "Hey, man, what's up?" The vest moved away, slipping quietly past the curve in the hallway. "Fuck."

"Fuck," Bookie agreed. "Hey, Hideo!" They moved toward the lit cigarette laying on the ground. "Cigarette like that on these nice floors," he called after Hideo. "It'll probably leave a stain, burning against the wood." The smoke amongst the cobwebs seemed thicker than anything such a little cigarette could produce. One of the hot breaths billowed up from the basement and everything shifted. The smoke over their heads had thickened to a mist. Still, they could see the cigarette glowing through the fuzz.

Dawes picked it up and dropped it just as fast.

"Fuck," he said.

"What?" Bookie asked. His voice was shaking, at the edge of panic. Dawes pointed at the thing and Bookie saw. "Oh fuck."

"Yeah," Dawes said, now keeping his eyes strictly down the hallway. Almost all of the cigarette butt was soggy with blood. Some had gotten on Dawes' fingers and he hurriedly wiped them on his work jacket. "Hid-Hideo? You okay, man?" He held the lantern up to spread the light out farther, though the thickening mist pushed it back. More blood glittered on the ground in front of them, a smattering of thick dots the size of quarters. Two of them had been smeared into foot-long streaks by something. Dawes swallowed.

"What the fuck," Bookie said.

"You look behind us," Dawes said. He heard Bookie turn around, and saw the shift of shadow as the other lantern spun with him.

"What do you think's back there?" Bookie asked.

"Nothing," Dawes said. "Nothing's back there. Just make sure it stays that way, yeah?" Bookie mumbled an affirmative and they started walking, Bookie keeping ever in contact with Dawes, reaching back to touch his hip, his elbow, anything to keep himself from falling behind. The blood disappeared further down the hall, and for a moment Dawes held out hope that Hideo might be okay.

He knew that wasn't even remotely possible when he found the puddles further down. Blood covered the wooden floor from wall to wall over a stretch of about three feet. Further out, the stuff had splattered into errant constellations. Splashes caused by a heavy pour from the source, Dawes knew.

"Don't fall," he said to Bookie, not bothering to clarify. A second later he heard Bookie's feet splashing through the gore, and the man himself cursing softly under his breath. The mist had grown so thick it felt almost like the building was on fire. He could only see fifteen feet or so in front of his face. Hideo's orange hi-vis vest bloomed in the haze ahead in an almost radioactive-looking corona.

"Hideo," Dawes said. He could see the man's arms and legs now, hanging straight down by his sides. His head slumped over his chest like a moping child. The sound of something dripping came from that direction. The orange glow of the vest slipped away into the mist and Dawes heard something else, an almost inaudible clicking noise. And a brushing sound, like a hand running over rough fabric.

Dawes stepped closer.

The vest pulled away rapidly and Dawes picked up his pace. Hideo floated into the dark without moving. His legs remained still and straight as he moved deeper into the hall. Dawes took off in a run, and still the vest remained out of reach. Bookie yelled and Dawes heard his feet pounding on the floor behind him.

There was a brief moment, as they reached the end of the hallway, where Dawes thought he saw Hideo look back at them. What he knew happened — what he could say he definitively saw — was Hideo spinning rapidly in the square opening of the hallway. His arms fluttered out to his sides, and then he vanished. Most all of Hideo's body remained steeped

    THE MOVE

in shadow, but Dawes' lantern lit upon his face, and in that brief second he saw something that made him stop in his tracks.

He couldn't be sure, of course. It was too quick. There wasn't enough light. But still, the image of that brief slice of time remained burned against the back of his eyes like the afterimage of a lightning strike.

Hideo's face had been slashed into tatters, that was clear, but there was something else about it. He should have been able to see the man's eyes, but there were only black hollows where those would have been. The flesh, the bone even, around the sockets was scored inches deep. And his mouth. It had hung far too low, the cheeks gouged away to show the faintest glimmers of white bone where the jaw muscles had been sliced through. It had looked almost like a slack-jawed grin.

"Hideo!" Bookie shouted. The clicking noise was more obvious in the main hall. Light still shone in through the windows here, though it was sparse and none seemed to touch the high corners of the ceiling. "Hideo, man, what's up? What's up, buddy? You in here? You okay?" Bookie stepped past Dawes and swung his lantern in wide circles. The glow seemed to fill the mist, rather than be stopped by it.

Dawes looked up and saw the faint glow of orange swooping back and forth down from the ceiling. He slapped Bookie and pointed. Bookie shut up without saying another word, as transfixed as Dawes by what they were seeing. The vest floated down until Dawes reached out and it landed softly on his hand. Other than a spray of blood across the back, and a long, thin cut amongst that mess, the vest was fine. Dawes looked up at the ceiling and felt something drip onto his face.

He didn't have to see it to know it would be red.

"Jesus fuck," Bookie shouted, turning and running for the front door. Dawes ran after him and grabbed his collar just in time, wrenching him back so hard he heard the man's teeth chatter. Bookie nearly lost his footing just as something broad and dark skittered through the falling curtains of cobweb over the front doors. Dawes saw a series of misshapen legs silhouetted against the glow from outside, and then nothing.

There was a moment of brilliance before Bookie's lantern shattered against the wall; Dawes didn't even realize he'd thrown it at first. The lantern soared through the room like a displaced star, an orb of golden light marking its passage through the mist until it burst over the stones in a sudden, sputtering eruption of flame. Some seal broke in the natural gas canister on the bottom of the lantern and ignited, belching light and curling tongues of smokeless fire across the wall.

The explosion seared another image into Dawes' eyes — he was only dimly aware that he was running now, Bookie close behind him again — of a long-haired woman holding onto the wall. Her eyes were black and wide, bearing the confused and heartless expression of a predator, her mouth limp and soft and full at the bottom of her face. But there was something else. A distortion beside her left eye, in the shadows beyond where the fire had reached. Something he could not see.

They ran headlong into the south wing of the mansion. This hallway curved as well, hooking to the left as they ran, obscuring their vision with mists and cobwebs. Dawes could hear Bookie shouting something about not leaving him behind, and questions about where they were going. He could barely hear the man over the sound of his own heart and the panicked rush of blood in his temples. The mind pulling in every ounce of information from the air and trying to make sense of it.

All the while, his tattoo burned. Hot now, almost to the touch. It felt like a million mosquito bites all centered on the same place. He ignored it and kept his feet moving, traveling by sense and instinct. Bookie had stopped complaining, but he could still hear him behind him. He almost didn't want to look back, seeing an image in his mind of Bookie floating along in the half-lit mists, black sockets where his eyes had been clawed out. His mouth hanging open in an idiot's too-wide grin.

Dawes took the stairs to the basement. They curved only once around the central pin before descending at a straight, downward angle into the earth. The mists grew so thick they blinded him, and then he was running down a set of stairs suspended by nothing in an infinite black void. Bookie was screaming for him to run faster, and so he did, taking the stairs two at a time until he was again buried in mist.

The stairs curved suddenly and violently left and Dawes struck the wall hard with his right arm. The glass housing around the lantern shattered, spilling shards over the finely detailed carvings on the stone stairs. It stayed lit, however, and they kept moving. A few turns around the pin and they burst into an almost familiar hallway. Dawes held his lamp up and could barely see past the clutter of furniture in the hall.

"I know all this shit," Bookie said between breaths. "It's all the stuff we moved before we moved it. There is no fucking doubt." He howled and fell to his knees, pressing the palm of his hand over his left eye. "Oh fuck, it hurts so bad. I've been here before, I *knew* this would happen. Ahh! Dawes, help! It fucking hurts."

Dawes pulled Bookie to his feet. Tears of blood seeped through the cornea around his iris. The entire sclera had gone red, and his nose was bleeding. Dawes was fine, save for the infernal burning in his wrist. He shook Bookie gently, casting the light around them. Every small move pushed air against the exposed gas-catchers now, making the light frail and inconsistent. It seemed to almost buckle under the weight of his movement. The mists grew thicker.

"Fuck. Can you move?" Dawes asked. Bookie nodded and spit a mouthful of pink froth onto the ground. Dawes threw the man's arm over his shoulders and ran for the stairs. For the briefest of seconds, he almost laughed at how lucky he was that it wasn't Demarkus he was carrying.

"I died here like eighty times already," Bookie said in a muted, sloppy voice. "Duck."

Dawes did so without thinking and saw something thick and furred with needle-like black hairs whip out of the mist. It clawed the stone where Bookie's throat would have been. Something smelled faintly like burning flesh.

Down was the only way they could go, and so they did, toward what Dawes thought would be the basement. The humid, breathy feeling washed over him and for a moment the color of the walls drained away, and Dawes could see the entirety of the mansion. A series of interconnecting and confounding fractal hallways and stairs and chases and runs curving in crystal elegance through an infinitely small void. Something like a black marble he could see resting in the palm of his own hand, as he watched himself scurry through it like a weevil through the intricate vertices inside a loaf of risen bread.

Then they were in the hall again, but it was hardly a hallway at all now. The walls that remained were stripped bare to the stone by weather and time. Trees and vines wove their way through the lonely skeleton exposure had left of the place. And yet still the mists lingered, and the ever-present cobwebs, and Dawes felt as if this corpse of a house was no less full and alive than the one he knew. This state was no diminishment, no reduction, but the well and true whole of the thing.

The main hall they emerged into was almost completely bereft of manmade artifice, and yet still the tracework of the building Dawes had known remained fully intact. Trees rose where the columns had stood, and fissured rock had risen from the ground to make stairs. Even the complicated rose window over the front doors was in place, made by a complex twisting of vines and leaves through which the sun shone to cast a bizarre shadow over them as they stood.

"I never wrote any books," Bookie said. "I wasted all my time. Fuck." Dawes hauled him up and nearly puked when he saw the man's face. His left eye had fully ruptured, leaving a trail of blood and scraps of eye tissue laying over his cheek. "I should never have taken this job. Now all the roads end here. Somewhere in here."

"Bookie," Dawes said, but the man said nothing. He grew steadily heavier as the strength left him and Dawes had to lay him on the carpet of dead leaves covering the uneven stone floor. His breathing softened, then faded altogether. Dawes looked at him and then around the great hall. His eyes stopped on the far staircase.

"What the fuck?" he whispered. Goldstein lay on the stones there, draped almost, like a towel left to dry. His black eyes were empty and unfocused, but he looked no less alive than he ever did. Dawes jumped when the body twitched, and then watched as it flexed itself into a sitting position and looked at him. Cobwebs trailed from the shoulders and neck to join the greater network along the walls.

"Hello, Dawson," he said. Dawes took in the room.

"I don't go by that anymore," he replied, looking down at the lantern. One of the gas catchers had been damaged and was barely glowing. The other seemed like it wanted to give up too. A single shard of glass remained in the housing, which Dawes pulled free. He had to hold it at a weird angle to keep from cutting his hand.

"What are you going to do with that?" Goldstein asked, an amused smile cutting across his face. "It's not much, if you're planning to fight for your life."

"I know," Dawes said. "But I've had less before." He stepped onto Goldstein's chest, which didn't move an inch under his foot. It seemed, in fact, that he was stepping on little more than clothing and some sort of rudimentary skeleton. A wooden cage somebody had draped cloth over.

"We looked into you," Goldstein said as Dawes gathered a handful of corded web from the floor. This was whiter, thicker, and coarser than the stuff dangling from the ceilings. He started cutting into it. "You fell in with the Corsicans after they broke that door in the Nevada desert, correct? They didn't give you much of a choice whether to join after that, did they?" One of the cords snapped and Goldstein's head fell slack against the stones. He kept talking all the same.

"How about that?" Dawes said, watching the severed web shrivel. "And, no, they didn't." He kept at the cords, but Goldstein didn't seem to mind.

"Why don't you jump in with us?" Goldstein said. "The Conscription of Walther and Dunbarton would be glad to have you. Even Blackwell might make you an offer. You could do very well with a mentorship like that."

"Pass," Dawes said, almost through the last fibers. Goldstein's mouth and face had stopped moving now, but the voice still boiled up from somewhere in his chest.

"Your loss," he said, then something hit Dawes like a ton of bricks, tossing him against the wall. The lantern housing split and a gout of flame spit from its new throat onto the old trees beside the landing. The bark caught easily. The thing standing over Dawes, poised to strike, reared back and covered its face. It skittered back on a mismatched set of six legs and he finally got a good look at it.

To Dawes, it looked like a four-legged spider had tried to force itself into an under-sized woman suit and split the fabric in several places. The woman, naked and of east Asian descent, gazed at Dawes with hungry, stupid eyes. Her mouth hung slightly open, in an almost pout, but split hideously at the left corner where the spider's wriggling mouth parts emerged. A single black fang protruded from her cheekbone.

"Come get a taste, you fucking bitch," Dawes said, barely able to speak. "Come on." The thing had easily broken a couple of his ribs with that first hit. He could taste blood in his mouth as well. The woman part of the thing had eyes only for him, but the spider's face kept nervously turning the shared neck to the fire quickly spreading into the cobwebs.

She had been incredibly beautiful once, that was apparent even now. Her face was rounded and pale, looking almost carved from some soft, white stone. What remained of her body was still eye-catching too, though the limbs on her right side were jutted out at nightmarishly painful angles to accommodate the spider thing.

She charged, closing the distance in a second, urging her other half around the fire and barreling fangs-first into Dawes. He took the hit readily, jamming the shard of glass into the human half's neck so hard it shattered, cutting him badly as well. The other hand he buried in the spider's mouth on instinct, fully expecting it to be snatched off at the elbow with one nasty bite. Instead, it burst into flame.

Neon green fire belched from the spider's shared gullet, washing up Dawes' arm and singeing the flesh of his shoulder. The woman side frantically struggled with the glass in her throat. A blackish ichor bubbled out of her mouth, and her previously stupid eyes were now turned in worry. The entire body of the thing reared back, dragging Dawes down the stairs at an odd angle so quickly he heard several loud pops in the bones of his arm. The pain from the fire was so intense he barely noticed.

A second later, an ocean of endorphins washed over him, pushing his consciousness all the way to the rear of his brain. He was only dimly aware of the electrical green flame burning his right arm to cinders. Instead, he noticed the ghosts of dozens, hundreds of copies of the same scene rolling across the floor toward the front door.

At every space in the room were more of the same spider lady, all of them dragging him across the floor.

All of them trailing columns of smoke and green fire. In some, Goldstein was hitching and jerking after him, or trying to pull the flaming arm out of the spider. In a few, Dawes could see he was plainly dead. His head gone, or his torso all that remained of him. In others, he wasn't there at all, only the stump of his blackening arm jutting out of the thing's mouth.

That was the scene he saw a second later, when his arm snapped off just above the elbow. The sound it gave when it finally broke was something akin to crumbling, and flecks of ash fell to the ground and over Dawes, lighting on his face and chest. As he watched, all the hundreds and millions and thousands and dozens of copies of the creature coalesced into a single space, overlapping and then becoming one. It burst through the front door and finally collapsed, green fire erupting through the soft spots of its body until all of it was engulfed in flame.

Dawes lay on the floor, watching the ceiling shimmer in and out of focus with the reality he was inside of at the moment. Sometimes there was no ceiling, sometimes there was. Sometimes, half-invisible feet stepped through his face as people in strange animalistic masks stepped in time to music he couldn't hear. The ground began shaking in every reality he could see, and then it hitched once underneath him with such force he went momentarily airborne.

Then there was only the one ceiling over his head. Pain slipped back into his mind and he screamed, rolling onto his side and clutching the stump of his arm to his chest. Squeezing it didn't make it feel any better, and the remnants were almost too hot to touch.

Gentle, firm hands pushed him down against the floor. He felt a pressure in his chest, just below his collarbone, and a syrupy sort of sweetness flooded his body. A face came into view, a woman he'd become well acquainted with in the years since they'd found him scumming up and down the West Coast after Nevada.

"Hi, Abella," he said.

"Hello, Dawson," she said in her light Mexican accent. "Your arm's gone." He nodded slowly, not bothering to look. "You need another one?" He almost said "Yes," thinking she was talking about his missing limb. Then she held a second morphine ampoule so he could see and he shook his head.

"I have enough bad habits," he said. She shrugged and nodded, and then she and a man he'd never met before helped him to his feet. A dozen men and woman surged past them, all wearing fairly nondescript work clothes and carrying submachine guns. They spread out into the house, flashlights gliding over the intricate scrollwork in the walls. Dawes stopped and leaned into Abella.

"Tell them to stay off the stairs," he said. She nodded to the other man holding up Dawes and he darted off to relay the order. "That's the transition point. I have no idea how it works though. Everything happened so fast…"

"It's fine," Abella said. "You did your best."

"The other guys," he whispered, shaking his head. "It was bad."

"I know," Abella said. "Just breathe. You did more than we could have ever asked of you. You can rest now."

She led him outside to a rock where he could sit and watch the others as they took control of the property. In the distance, on the other side of Portland, smoke and fire rained down the side of Mt. Hood. Some of the faster flows had already reached the city, and he could see a few buildings slipping sideways on their foundations and sinking into the conflagration.

"Nothing you can do about that," Abella said. She had brought back a medical kit bag and opened it beside him. She treated and bandaged the stump as they spoke. It had already begun leaking blood and some foul, yellow jelly from the wound.

"That's a lot of pain," Dawes said to himself. "I know people down there." He thought of the story he'd told the guys on that first day. It had all been bullshit except one part: He did have a girlfriend, and she lived down there.

"It will all be worth it though, you'll see," Abella said.

Eventually, she left to see to the interior of the mansion. Dawes sat in silence for a long time. After Bookie's body was brought out on a sheeted stretcher. After the glowing orange and black cloud of death had fully covered Portland. Even after the ambulance had come to pick him up. He sat there and looked over what he'd done, what he'd caused, and found himself unable to think of a single thing to say.

It was an old voice that finally broke his reverie. He turned to see an aged woman in a crisp, grey suit standing beside him. She too looked out over the destruction, her eyes cool and quiet to any emotion.

"I'm sorry," Dawes said. The drugs slurred his words. "What did you say?" She looked at him, raising her eyebrows in surprise as though she hadn't noticed him. When she spoke, her words were colored with some unplaceable Slavic accent.

"So it begins," she replied, repeating herself, nothing more. She laid a hand on his shoulder, then stepped past the ruined circular altar in front of the house. He watched her stand in silhouette against the dull glow of Portland as it burned to the ground, and seeing the way the feather tattoo on her hand seemed to glow in the firelight, he knew she was right.

THE END

THE MOVE

Dog Star

Mikosh sat back against the dinted steel walls of the freight elevator, watching asteroids burn odd shapes into the infinite black surrounding the local star.

At this distance, the shielding on the farm bay windows was at something approaching 99 percent tint, though the ionized crystal seemed as clear as simple silicate glass. He waved his hand in front of his visor, watching the light radiation fractalize in the errant fibers on the stitching in his glove. The effect was akin to watching fire creep up the side of a log in slow motion, a phenomenon so alien to the human eye it was almost impossible for his mind to make sense of.

Kaid watched him playing with his hands from the other side of the elevator, hood down and his rebreather mask tucked under his arm. He took a long inhale off the cigarette he'd lit at the top of the silo and finished it, flicking out the errant tobacco and stowing the butt in his suit. Mikosh's hand waving gained renewed purpose as the cloud of smoke reached his eyes and nose.

"You gotta smoke that shit in the elevator *every* time?" Mikosh complained, not bothering to look at Kaid. Kaid didn't respond, just looked balefully out the window, yawning and bringing up the day's work order.

"We've got three fucking rows to do today," he said, handing the paper to Mikosh. The recycled fibers crinkled loudly, but the paper was so light against his glove Mikosh felt like he wasn't holding anything at all. "I can't *wait* for this goddamn rotation to end." Mikosh looked over the numbers and then down at the rows in question. They spread out beneath the great bay windows for miles, looking like grey dust pits. Thick wads of dryer lint basking in the alien blue sun.

"Three," Mikosh whispered under his breath, handing Kaid the crumpled work order. He already felt tired. Kaid folded the little paper carefully and tucked it away in his suit, considering whether he had time for another cigarette and then deciding against it. "What are you doing when you rotate back?"

"There's this ramen place I've been meaning to check out," Kaid said, looking at Mikosh. Kaid was a tall, slender man with almost perfectly nut brown skin that darkened to near black around his dark green eyes. The man's color seemed to jive just right with the red, tan-trimmed uniforms they wore down in the harvesting bays. Mikosh — himself an odd jumble of pale skin tones and garishly colored hair and eyes — thought his uniform made him look like a fast-food worker. Which, coincidentally, he had been before taking this assignment and the roughly 10 percent pay raise it entailed.

"You like ramen?" Mikosh asked, stepping forward to look out the window at a downward angle.

The grey fields were rushing closer and then gone with a whoosh of air as they passed into the service hub at the heart of the silo.

"Everybody likes ramen, Mikosh," Kaid said, standing and cracking his neck in time with the pneumatic hiss of the elevator docking in station. The doors cracked and Mikosh followed Kaid into the service hub. Silver, diamond-plate floor spread to the walls in every direction, demarcated here and there by orange and red and blue lines that sequestered off areas for certain workers and equipment.

For most of the operational year of the station, this deck would be packed to the brim with laborers and technicians and heavy equipment operators milling about their respective areas and shit-talking over the coffee percolators in the cafeteria segment. Today, the place was empty save for Kaid, Mikosh, and the moderate fog of dust that always floated in from the harvesting rows. It hung in conical yellow clouds below every overhead light, making the Administration deck look like the universe's worst dance club.

They wandered over to the assignment desk and swiped the keycards fastened into the wrists of their suits over the reader. Normally, the desk would be manned by a few dozen of the Administration staff, typically young college grads training to work in the accounting sectors "upstairs." "Upstairs" being any and all places too high up the hub elevators for scrubs like Mikosh to visit.

He'd be down here on the Administration deck until he died or found an easier job off station that somehow also paid better. As a matter of course, he preferred to fail upwards whenever possible, though he usually only ever managed to succeed sideways. Picking up a new title, new responsibilities, and no

     DOG STAR

additional money.

"Rows Two, Four, and Eighteen," Kaid said when the duty admin turned on her screen and smiled at them. She was probably twenty-two, blue eyed and sporting skin as orange as a tangerine, a keratin-phil-ia that meant she grew up on a defunct class two station. She cleared her throat at Kaid's impatience, but said nothing, tapping out their assignments in quick succession. A second later, two plastic cards popped out of the terminal. Kaid took his first.

"Two *and* Four," he muttered, giving the woman a look. "Thanks." Mikosh looked at his own card, con-firming he only had to work Row Eighteen. Normally Kaid got the cushier assignment, being his superior by several years, but not today.

"Row Eighteen," Mikosh confirmed. He looked at the girl on the other side of the monitor. Even if she was twenty-five, she was still ten years younger than him. A sad thought he didn't mean to have, but that came anyway.

He smiled and thanked her, really meaning it, un-like Kaid.

The woman from Admin — Velona, he'd learned her name was — gave them the standard safety brief-ing and the daily company update. Daily was a gen-erous term, the station revolution time on this as-signment was something like 75 hours. According to Velona, Blackwell Corporation stocks were doing fan-fucking-tastic and it was just a matter of time be-fore everybody finally got those cost of living adjustments they'd been hinting at since before Mikosh had been hired.

"Fat fucking chance," Kaid said as they left assignment for outfitting. "I'll be dead as a doornail before they finally pay me what I'm worth." He gave Mikosh a look. "They'd have to dock you three rotations to get your pay down to what you deserve." Mikosh glared at him, hopping awkwardly on one foot to pull his boots on.

"Is that why you've been pocketing lumps of catalyst?" Mikosh asked. Kaid froze for just a moment, the top locking strap of his boot still in his hand. Then he continued dressing as though nothing had happened.

"I don't know what you're talking about," Kaid said. "And maybe you don't either." He walked past Mikosh and got into the transport car, leaving without another word. Mikosh finished dressing in silence.

Mikosh's transport — an orange and tan box shooting along one of the twenty or so magnetic tracks encircling the station's hub elevator — had a bad habit of rattling. He felt like he had to hold the cupped plastic seat under his legs and stare at the ground to keep from getting sick. Other workers — more valuable workers — might use the larger, multitrack units that glided like melting butter. Mikosh got to ride in Transport, Human, Number 23, which felt like going down the side of a mountain sliding on a single, broken roller skate.

"Worker Mikosh?" his intercom blurted. He found the transmit button by slapping against the thin wall of the carrier until he heard a click. Velona's face flitted up onto the screen opposite him. He smiled, though she wouldn't be able to see his face through the heavy, double-barreled respirator covering his mouth and nose. It took a few stiff nods for her to see he was listening to her. She smiled and looked down at a sheaf of paper in her hands.

"I've already appraised Worker Kaid of this, but it seems the network-wide intercom is disabled during these skeleton shifts," she started, flipping to wherever she needed to be in the stack of papers. "Okay, it seems that Sol Azul 22, the local star, has begun pulsing at irregular intervals. Station X11 noticed and announced the phenomena about twenty minutes ago, pinging off Stations X12 and X15 to relay the message to us."

Mikosh looked out at "Sol Azul 22," the radiant blue dwarf around which this mining expedition revolved. The thing was several millions of miles away, but still loomed outside the bay windows like a great, pale eye. He'd seen dozens of stars up close in his lifetime, but this one made him and most everybody else uncomfortable. A byproduct of the stellar body's odd light emissions was the operative rumor around the station. In all honesty, he felt like it was looking at him sometimes.

"Administration has been informed of the phenomena and preliminary calculations suggest this pulse will be an *invaluable* source of growth radiation," Velona continued. Mikosh turned back to her and saw her eyes steadily tracking the words on the page as she read. "Thus, it's imperative that the skeleton crews finish their work on the double, as the bay windows will be reducing to zero tinting for several seconds to maximize absorption. Additionally, there is an increased possibility of asteroid movement toward the station. Solar winds are expected to reach velocities sufficient to breach magnetic shielding, though catastrophic impacts are … are unlikely." Velona took a breath. "Oh my." She looked up at Mikosh.

"They just added that," she said. "I'll have to rebrief Worker Kaid." She scanned the paper again and then set it down. "That's it for the briefing, Worker Mikosh. Good luck out there, and don't forget to keep track of shelter points in case of impact. Do you have any questions?" Mikosh shook his head. The asteroid impact news was a little unsettling, but hardly rare. If anything, he just wished he'd had time to pack additional protective equipment.

—

Mikosh rode the rest of the way in relative silence, eventually growing accustomed to the transport's incessant rattling. In just under an hour, he had swooped out to the far end of the station's central ring, where Row Eighteen curved up to a narrow point in the distance. The point was, of course, an optical illusion caused by being so damn far away. Five kilometers, in fact.

At two kilometers, the rows split off from each other, forming what an outside observer might think looked like a great, glittering metal flower adrift in space. The administration, transport, housing, and other general sectors were spaced out along the central hub in the center of the bloom. A sort of pistil, to overextend the metaphor. And along all the rows, thick, endless fields of formless grey fluff.

Mikosh jumped down off the transport and swiped his work card over the locker at the end of the platform. The equipment was universal and would be returned at the end of the shift — a pack and the requisite tools to do his job. He opened the metal and canvas bag and shifted through the contents, checking boxes on the machine as he ensured everything was in place.

Radiation meters, large-field and small-field, to check for pre-exposure rocks in the rows. Extractors. Emergency cocoons for three. Collection bags for any odd samples. Analogue communications equipment. Flares. Everything was in place. He hit the final check and jumped on the utility sled that would take him out into the center of the row, equipping the large field radiation meter and scanning the fluff.

This was the part and parcel of his occupation with Blackwell Energy Management, a subsidiary of the Blackwell Corporation. The grey fluff, catalyst, would absorb tremendous amounts of radiation from the solar pulses and crystalize into novel materials. Those would be collected and refined by more qualified people than Mikosh using machines he could barely understand. His only purpose was to ride the sled and check for pre-exposure crystallization in the rows and collect whatever had started growing so it wouldn't ruin the entire harvest.

Any idiot could do it, which is why Mikosh had the job. But most idiots were too smart to ride around hip-deep in phenomenal astral radiation catalyst for little more salary than a manager at Cosmo Burger, so he also had job security. So long as he wasn't caught stealing the catalyst — like Kaid was bound to be eventually; nobody got away with it — he'd have the job until he died.

The large-field radiation meter pinged and he homed in on the location of the wad of pre-exposure flickering green on the screen. He worked the controls on the sled, slowing to a near stop as he tried to get close enough to the anomaly that he wouldn't have to spend too much time on his feet. Eventually, the large-field meter overloaded and he had to pull out the small-field. He was close.

Mikosh stopped the sled and kicked down the metal folding ladder, taking his time getting down into the row itself. The catalyst was about knee deep and kicked up fine particles of dust that occluded his goggles and tinged his uniform grey. Without his respirator on, even the tiniest motes could cause symptoms ranging from paralytic pneumonia and blindness to delirium and hallucinations.

Catalyst exposure varied from person to person, and even from star to star. He'd heard some stellar bodies turned the catalyst carcinogenic or mutagenic, and even rumors that it could cure baldness. People who lived off station were willing to pay a pretty price for a decent dose of catalyst; they'd take it like any other drug and fuck it if they ended up with a third lung growing out of their neck, which was why Kaid was risking his job and up to ten years in prison smuggling it off station.

None of that was Mikosh's business, though, he thought as he pawed through the dust with the long steel arm of the extractor. He preferred not to bother with up-jumping and cons and reporting on fellow workers to get ahead. No, he liked late nights playing video games and take-out and porno. The occasional prostitute. Everything else was a giant pain in the ass, or a heartbreak waiting to happen.

He found the gently glowing lump of blue crystal in a pack of catalyst just a few meters away from his sled, grabbing at it cautiously with the extractor and then dumping it unceremoniously into the waste bag when he determined it to be inert. If it weren't, it would destabilize the second it touched the metal and pop like a balloon, eating away the last foot or so of steel. If it were his hand that touched it, then the hand and the arm would go instead. But these crystals were, for whatever reason, inert. So he just had to pick them out of the pile and tuck them into the plastic disposal bags. Nothing to it.

He wandered through the row, following signal after signal on the radiation meter and picking out what crystals he found. The sled followed him along the track, synced to keep up with a transmitter welded into the plastic of his rebreather. Half a dozen bags hung from it by the end of the first hour of work, twice that many by lunch time three hours after that. The rows weren't badly irradiated, it seemed, so he'd probably have a pretty easy day ahead of him.

Mikosh pushed himself onto the platform and pressed the call button for the disposal sled. He was nearly half the distance to the far wall of the station now, and it took a few minutes before he could feel the waste carrier vibrating along the magnetic carry rail. It arrived and he hopped down into the bucket, pulling a plastic sheet over the top of it and removing his rebreather to eat lunch. Steam from the instant ramen left beads of condensation on the plastic.

He ate quietly, listening to the little sounds of the space station, the hums and clicks and the occasional deep, almost inaudible vibration of the greater support structure adjusting as it heated and cooled during rotation. In the rows, the dense clouds of catalyst filling the seed beds devoured any errant sound. He'd gotten somewhat used to the unnatural quiet in the last few years, but it always unnerved him. It was too deep, almost substantial. He would work himself into a trance, removing crystals and refilling the beds and then pause for a breather only to notice the hollow depths of the silence around him. There would be nothing but his breath and the steady thrum of his pulse in his temple.

He'd learned to make a sort of fort out of the disposal sleds watching a coworker do the same thing in his first year of rotations. Inside the metal and plastic sled, his every movement carried an echo. His boots scraped against the floor when he adjusted his position. He could hear his clothing shifting and settling while he worked his way through whatever he'd brought to eat.

Even this tiny bit of noise was almost like music to him. In all his life before taking this job, he'd never suspected he'd ever need a daily break from silence. He wondered if stoic, criminally-minded Kaid took breaks in the disposal sled and figured the man probably didn't. Despite his inclinations, Kaid was one of the most effective workers on station. He probably didn't even *take* breaks, which maybe was the reason he'd been getting away with catalyst trafficking for so long.

Mikosh realized he couldn't hear all of a sudden, feeling a dense pressure in his chest followed by a crunch louder than anything he had ever heard in his life. His mind pictured somebody dropping a cube of hard metal into a bin full of old beer bottles. It was sudden and incredible, a sound so harsh that he felt it in his teeth. He thought it *was* his teeth, at least for a moment. The sheer force of the noise was so incredible his mind momentarily lost connection with itself.

It was almost like going blind.

Then he was flying — floating really — up out of the plastic bucket of the disposal sled and into the air. For a moment he was floating in perfect zero gravity. At least, that's what it felt like, but he knew that wasn't the case. Not *knew*, really, *understood.* The most primal, rear parts of his brain *understood* he'd been thrown into the air.

There had been another sound, immediately after the crunch. Something like a thump that had rolled through the complicated network of steel plating and supports that made up the rows to toss Mikosh into the air like a doll. An impact so immense it had caused the supple steel to roll like an ocean in a storm.

Mikosh's cup of ramen floated into the space just in front of his face, the remaining noodles writhing like confused worms. Beneath him, catalyst had floated out of the seed beds in long, perfect lines. Ahead of him, a great, orange flower was blooming in the distance. He could see for miles at this height, and as the front ends of his brain re-engaged, he realized he was looking at a cloud of catalyst blowing away from a heavy impact. Above this swirling, growing ball of dust, a great, flat shadow was flying over the bay windows. A sealant curtain, unfurling to cover a hole something had punched into the station.

Mikosh's stomach lurched as he reached the height of his arc. The cloud of orange was growing faster than his mind could process. He could see veins of blue lightning tearing through the excited particles along its surface as the grey dust catalyzed the radiation from the blue local star. He saw his respirator floating just within arm's reach as the grey fluff on the ground shot up past him. His fingers brushed it and caught in the elastic headband.

Then the great ball of dust from the impact hit him full in the face and he was soaring backward through the air, fighting against the blinding maelstrom to pull down his mask. Dust thickened on his teeth. He felt the plastic rim of the mask settle around his mouth over dirty skin. A wave of panic shot through him as he realized just how much he might have breathed in, but then his body struck something flat and hard and bounced and twirled madly through the air, and everything went dark.

He came to while coughing, breathing in rough, haggard, and uneven intervals, but breathing all the same. He'd been conscious, though dazed, for some time. Mindful enough at least to pull himself to his knees and begin his mask-clearing drill.

He was supposed to be exhaling all the air in his lungs to clear the inside of the mask of pollutants, which coughing did quite effectively, but he was having a hard time breathing in the air he needed to stay conscious through the rebreather's tight filtration mechanism. His eyes watered badly. He was basically blind and choking to death on the small, panicked breaths he could manage.

     DOG STAR

Calm down, you fucking idiot, Mikosh told himself. *Calm the fuck down.* He coughed out a lungful and held the exhale for a single, impossible second. *You're not dead, so you're breathing. Stop freaking the fuck out.* He inhaled, long and steady. He'd gotten halfway through the breath when he started coughing again, though not so wildly out of control as a second ago. Pain started to leak in through the panic of suffocation, a steady bleed up through the numbness.

His work suit had hardened to near-immobility in places. He could tell one of his ankles, his right ankle, was completely frozen in place. The same was true of the better part of his left arm, which hung at an odd, straight angle down from his shoulder. The coughing had unlocked his hips and upper legs, as well as most of his torso. If the emergency stiffening had relaxed that much, then at least five minutes or so had passed since he'd skipped across the rows like a stone.

Mikosh squinted into the dust around him. His goggles had been ripped off his head at some point before he came to. He could see nothing but the steady wave and ripple of the settling dust cloud. Something slipped in his mind, and he saw reality tearing slightly in the dust. It was a great white rip like a door that split and widened and grew and then disappeared.

He tried to wipe his eyes but only managed to smear sweat-soaked grime across his face. He knelt down, hissing when the locked-up ankle screamed under his weight. Barely able to breathe anyway, he held his breath and worked his hand around the ankle until he found the little node that would keep it fully locked and braced, and pressed it. He yelped when he felt the crush of the support material inflate fully against his ankle. It hurt, but a hell of a lot less than when he'd put his weight on the thing.

Mikosh slapped around at the catalyst, hoping to God he wouldn't accidentally hit a non-inert crystal buried in the fluff. There was absolutely no noise as he did this. With the amount of dust in the air, the row was even more silent than normal. Eventually, he hit the low steel wall of the seed bed separator and shifted to crouch down alongside it. He tried to make some sense of where he was in the thick dust and found the hazy blue disk of the local star in the fuzz of the cloud.

Mikosh may as well have been adrift in the cosmos himself, floating loose in an errant cloud of hydrogen crystals that never managed to collapse into the millennial furnace now spilling its light through the dust. There was no sense of the physical world around him. There was the ground, but that was merely a fixation point. A meaningless spot devoid of any context inside the greater universe. But he knew that if he turned his back on the blue dwarf, he could find his way back to the center of the station. When he did turn, he saw his own shadow suspended in the motes.

He began to walk, feeling the same crawling sensation as when he'd seen the white tear in the fabric of reality. That impossible thing. He ran his fingers over the miniscule air cartridge screwed in near the mouth of the rebreather, wondering how much oxygen he had left. Wondering if he'd be one of those statistics they talked about during orientation, one of those immortal examples of poor preparation and failure to follow safety standards. He could actually see them talking about him.

"That fucking idiot, they found him wandering

around naked by the bay windows, whispering to the glass."

"Who the fuck takes their rebreather off?"

"I'm not going to take my rebreather off," Mikosh told them. The two new workers were standing in a hallway up near the Administration deck where all the debriefings were done, casually leaning against a wall and sipping coffee. One of them looked at Mikosh and shook his head.

"Who the fuck are you talking to?" he asked.

Mikosh stopped walking for a second, the fingers inside his right glove tensing and untensing. He could hear nothing but his own breathing in the mask. He swallowed, and the noise was like a sink draining. He started coughing and the force of it brought him to his knees. The floor of the Administration hallway was superimposed over the thick covering of catalyst, but it faded as he watched.

He could hear a slight buzzing now in his left ear. He brought his hand up to the side of his head and realized he was touching his own hair. He'd put down his hood — which served as a helmet when the hardening factor kicked in — during his short lunch. He'd flown through the air without a scrap of protection on his head. It was an absolute fucking miracle he hadn't been brained to death by a wall during the mad, rolling flight.

The noise came from the earpiece set into the rebreather. The sides of the mask were long flanges that came up alongside the ears before splitting into the elastic bands that actually held the thing in place. The buzzing was a woman's voice, so faint he could barely hear it. Velona. He pawed at the controls on the side of the mask until he could hear her fully.

"Worker Mikosh, this is Administration," she

said. Her voice was haggard and dull. Worried. She'd been at this for a while. "Please respond if you can hear me."

"I can hear you … Administration," Mikosh said between coughs. The woman sighed with relief. She sounded on the verge of crying. The channel to his earpiece remained open once somebody from Administration activated the connection. Mikosh realized she might have been listening to him mutter to himself like a crazy person for a good several minutes now.

"Oh, thank God," she said with a sigh. "Are you okay?"

"Not really," Mikosh replied, barely able to keep the pain out of his voice. "Something happened down here. I think … I don't know what I think. There was an explosion, maybe even a hole in one of the bay windows." He stopped talking to cough, a slight clearing of the throat that ended with him curled over his knees and struggling to breathe. "I was thrown, and my rebreather … came loose. I think I inhaled some catalyst." He paused. Her breathing was steady on the other end of the line. It laid a counter beat to his own labored breaths. "I'm seeing things."

Velona cursed under her breath. He could almost see her holding the microphone away from her face and looking around her office as she tried to think of something to say. Then he *could* see her, blue eyes worriedly searching the muted patterns of her prefabricated desktop. She wore the standard black and white suit of the administrative rank and file. Only the red shirt cuffs on her wrists — the color everybody on their shift wore somewhere on their person — broke up the monotony of drab colors. She took a breath and scanned the hundreds of other desks in the office, all empty, where she might have been able to ask for help if this shift wasn't so barebones.

"Mikosh," she said, but her tone didn't match her face. "*Mikosh*," she repeated, and he snapped out of it. She'd been talking to him, trying to get his attention for a while now, he knew. Her voice sounded mildly impatient, but it carried an edge of deep concern. Like she was speaking to a terminal cancer patient. Or a deranged person.

"Sorry," Mikosh said. "I'm … just, go on."

Discordant thoughts in his mind popped back into place, resetting his history from front to back until he had the full picture. It had been roughly ten minutes since "the incident" as Velona had taken to calling whatever it was that had happened. He'd managed to continue the conversation while simultaneously having a vivid hallucination of her sitting in the office.

The hallucination felt real to him, too. More so than the conversation he'd actually had. Those defragmented and reset memories had a watery quality to them, almost like their existence was the suggestion of an untrustworthy stranger. But the more he held on to them, the more real they seemed.

"I need you to repeat that, Mikosh," Velona said. He'd tripped out again, but he heard his mouth saying the things she wanted to hear. It felt like he was hearing them for the first time as well.

"I need to head to Row Two to check on Kaid," Mikosh said, to himself as much as to Velona. He started to envision himself, his internal self, walking alongside him through the fluff. This version of him didn't touch the waking world. The dust in the air passed through him in an orange haze. His eyes met Mikosh's.

"You're going to check on Kaid and get him to Medical with you if possible," the man said. He wasn't really Mikosh, Mikosh realized. This man was trimmer around the middle and had *all* of his hair. Every last bit. And though he was a redhead, his hair wasn't the pale sort of orange that plagued Mikosh's scalp. His hair was like curling ringlets of liquid fire. Dark red, almost like blood.

"You need to hit the closest emergency eye wash before you get into the transport," the man said, pointing ahead down the line. Mikosh followed his finger to where he was pointing. He could almost see a rising black space in front of him demarcating the edge of the row, the place where the steel dipped down about three meters from the massive disk-shaped platform around the central hub. The light from the local star penetrated the cloud enough here to catch in the scratches and whorls worn and machined into the steel.

Pulling himself out of the seedbed was harder than he expected. His left arm, now appreciably numb, still hadn't unlocked. If he had to guess, it was broken and the suit wouldn't unlock the makeshift splint until he was in the medical bay. That meant he had to pull himself up the access ladder one-handed until he could finally roll out of the row and onto the central hub decking.

He was able to rest for only a moment until a terrible cough built in his chest. It started low, rising quickly to a crescendo that left him red-faced and breathless, curled over his knees and wheezing. He tried to stop but couldn't. He could even hear Velona in his ear, trying to tell him to just slow down and breathe.

Mikosh pulled himself to his feet and crawled for

the eyewash station he knew was somewhere near the restroom facilities spread throughout the work decks by the rows. Squinting through the thick, painful covering of dust, he managed to find the orange lines and arrows showing the way to the station. He could taste the dust still clinging to his teeth. It was like a mud he didn't dare swallow.

Velona was all but yelling something he couldn't hear into his earpiece when he reached the station. He ripped off the rebreather and fell into the booth, slapping the activation paddles and letting gallons of fresh, filtered water spray into his open eyes. Then he pulled the full chemical wash handle and felt the waterfall crash of fresh water over his head and shoulders.

The booth was closed off from the rows, and though it wasn't airtight, the water effectively knocked all the dust out of the air. Mikosh took in a great long breath that tasted sweeter than honey. Then he collapsed to his knees and coughed little congealed chunks of snot and dust onto the ground. He coughed until his face tingled and he felt on the verge of vomiting.

"You need to put your rebreather on, Mikosh," Velona said in his ear. He nodded and agreed, trying to push himself to his feet and failing. The bottom of the booth was a steel grating covered in little nubs for traction. Terribly uncomfortable, but very effective for draining a swimming pool's worth of water. Mikosh ran his finger over the divisions between the holes and tried to catch his breath.

Something passed in front of the booth and he froze. The feeling was sudden and electric — primal. Mikosh was painfully aware of how much louder the booth was than the rows outside. Despite the eyewash, he was still nearly blind, but he could make out the writhing, irregular shadows superimposed on the translucent door of the booth. He wiped his eyes twice, quickly, squinting to see what it was.

"Don't move, Mikosh," Velona said. "I don't know what you're looking at, but you shouldn't move. Just … stay still."

"I'm not fucking moving," Mikosh said. The shape outside the booth wavered like four people walking in unison, blending into a lone silhouette with arms that moved like slow fire.

"Don't talk either," Velona said. "Stay absolutely quiet." Mikosh nodded and said nothing, watching the shape speed up and then slip out of sight. It faded, really, the shadows disintegrated into the pale blue light of the local star. For not the first time, Mikosh felt like that great burning thing was an eye. An eye focused on him.

"I think it's gone," Mikosh said, tilting his ear in wait for Velona's reply, for her to give him the okay to leave the stall. The man with the blood red hair — the better version of Mikosh — looked down at him from the corner of the booth.

"Who are you talking to?" he asked. Mikosh touched his face and realized he wasn't wearing the rebreather anymore. Velona couldn't be talking to him. She did anyway.

"Just put the rebreather back on, okay?" she said. "Then you can sort things out."

Mikosh took a breath and then slowly opened the stall door. Almost immediately, unsettled dust from the catalyst blown up by the explosion filled the space. By the time he had the rebreather settled on his face again, his eyes were already starting to burn. He didn't even bother trying to wipe them. They were better than they had been in the first place, and even if he tried, his wet skin and uniform had acquired a thick, grey coating of catalyst.

If he fell into a seedbed right then, they'd never find him. He'd be scorched into nonexistence by the bay windows when they dropped the tinting, reducing him to, at best, a microscopic carbon imperfection in one of the crystals the irradiating process would produce. He looked to the great blue eye, the local star, and shivered thinking of how it would look growing brighter and brighter as the tinting dropped.

Beneath that odd, pale sun, the dust had fallen to a reasonable level over the seedbeds, though the content in the air was still far above safe levels. The thickest cloud lay just a few meters over the lowest part of the rows, creating an orange-brown fog that cut off just below his knees. This low-lying mist swirled and bucked when he walked through it like water at low tide.

In the distance — almost three kilometers into the bed he'd been tending when the day had gone completely tits up — something shifted under the fog. He tried to get a better view of the now rippling cloud and saw the faint glint of his sled beside the row divider. Clean metal shined beside that as well, where the disposal sled's bucket had been ripped sheer off the magnetic railing couplings.

Again something moved out in that sea of low, grey fog, and it caused Mikosh to pause. He raised a finger to his ear and tapped twice, pausing before asking Velona a question he thought might make him sound crazy.

"Hey, Velona," he started. The fog had stilled, but some instinctual, internal thing made him sure he could see errant motion amongst the gently rolling clouds of dust. He kept an eye on that area, watching the shadows dance between the cresting waves of fog. Maybe something was whipping around in there, but then again maybe it was just the wind.

"Yes?" she asked. Her voiced echoed, both her and the real her talking to Mikosh at the same time. Overlapping. He clenched his eyes shut, risking the loss of sight to make himself focus. Not that it could really help much.

"Is there … any chance Kaid came to check on me in Row 23?" Mikosh asked. There was a long silence.

"No, it's not possible," Velona said. "It could happen, but it's very unlikely. Why do you ask? What do you see? Or, I guess, what makes you ask that?"

Mikosh pressed his hands against his head in frustration. Despite himself, he began to cough. It wasn't so bad this time, the coughing, but it still doubled him over.

"I thought I saw something … moving out by my sled," Mikosh said. "A couple kilometers out. Where I was when the explosion or … whatever happened."

"A couple kilometers?" Velona repeated. The two voices synced slowly and then merged into one. The discordance faded, and Mikosh sighed with relief. Maybe she thought it was just relief from the coughing; she didn't comment on it. "That's … extremely far in that dust cloud, Mikosh." He heard her fiddling with something. Camera controls.

"I have the infrared, everything up where you are and I can barely see you," she continued. "The overseers' cameras can pick up anything down there during normal work hours, but this dust has fucked everything sideways." He heard her pause for a second when she realized she'd cursed on official company comms. Everything *was* recorded for quality assurance, after all.

"Anyway, Mikosh, I can't see anything moving down there but you, and only barely and only because I know where you are," she said. "Are you … sure — *really* sure — that you can even see that far right now? I can see your sled and there's nothing moving over there that I can see from up here. And, as far as I know, Kaid is still in the vicinity of Row Three. He …" She took a long breath, considering how to phrase whatever she was trying to say.

"His rebreather isn't functioning as a telecoms device right now," she eventually said. "I can't get any readings off it as of a few minutes after the explosion." Another long pause. "Mikosh. Goddamnit. Mikosh, you and I are probably alone on the station right now if Kaid's dead. Or crazy and wandering around lost in the rows."

"What?" Mikosh asked. The man with the blood red hair stepped into view and waved his hand in front of Mikosh's face, then pointed at a spot half-way between the sled and where they, where *Mikosh alone,* stood on the central hub deck. Mikosh stifled a cough and watched as something dark broke the surface of the dust cloud and then vanished, leaving a pool of eddying, shifting fog in its wake.

"What was that, you think?" the better Mikosh asked. Mikosh started walking quickly for the transport he'd ridden out to Row Eighteen. He found it right where he left it, though it looked somehow more sinister, resting in the darkness under a lift shed with the dusty rays of the blue star shining on it. Velona had kept talking the entire time, though he could barely process what she'd said.

"The entire station has been evacuated already," she said. "Whatever caused that explosion hit the

Row Three bay window so hard it completely ruined its functionality. That screen is for the rare micro meteorite that punches through the magnetic atmosphere around the station, but the hole that object left is about eight meters in diameter." She cursed. "That polymer is rated for weapons-grade barrages. Admin One thinks the stellar pulse we were going to capture later today … *pre-fired* or something. They don't know. *Nobody* knows."

"So what, everybody's leaving?" Mikosh asked, strapping himself into the transport. Better Mikosh stepped onto the side of the single-person conveyance and nodded appreciatively at Mikosh's efforts to secure himself. Then he pointed down the line toward Row Three. Mikosh gave a last look at the unfinished row where he'd been blown loose like a daisy in a rainstorm. Something pale and white flickered up out of the dust. Better Mikosh chuckled.

"I'm sure if you want to see it in full, you can just wait a few more minutes," he whispered to Mikosh. Mikosh hit the accelerator and the transport rattled out of the station, pushing him into the seat as it rose to near full velocity.

"No, Mikosh," Velona said. "Everybody is *gone*. Everybody but you, me, and possibly Kaid. There's a chance that the pulse will rip the harvesting deck to shreds when it hits; that seal isn't rated for that sort of barrage. And there's the chance the local star will throw something larger into us as well." She sighed.

"I didn't want you to panic while you were blind and suffocating out there in the rows, Mikosh, but this is fairly serious," she said. "There are enough lifeboats on station for six times the amount of people we jettisoned after that impact, but those are all getting picked up by rescue vehicles in the next hour or so. They might always come back for us, sure, but I'd rather be on them and gone than floating in space with no shielding during an asteroid storm."

"Me too," better Mikosh whispered in Mikosh's ear.

"If you can't find Kaid," she added in a low voice. "Then you can't find him. If you *did* see something out there by that sled, you don't have the time to go inspect it, and you *certainly* don't have the time to drag a half-insane man back to the central lift on a single person transport."

"You hadn't even thought of that, huh?" better Mikosh asked.

He hadn't.

Mikosh lost his mind completely as they passed through one of the final lift shelters before arriving at Row Three. Lift shelters were temporary barriers that rose from the work decks near the central column so nobody accidentally strayed in front of a magnetic rail car shuttling along at one hundred kilometers per hour. They slipped out of recesses in the decking, curving at light angles to hang over the tracks. The sides of them were painted in brilliant orange and white stripes.

When Mikosh passed this last set of rising barriers, his pupils widened until nothing was left of his irises. His mind painted pictures for him to make sense of the universe he could see, but nothing that could ground him back into reality.

He was falling face-first through a copse of trees

from a mountain on some planet from humanity's remote past. He was sitting in the musty guts of a wooden boxcar, riding the rails on an ancient, primitive train. He had traveled beyond space and time to the final moments of this universe, where a great dark thing lay rotting in the light of the last dying star.

Then he was himself again, but drained. He slumped back in the seat of the transport, head rattling painfully against the plastic rear wall. He made an accounting of himself and sat up, coughing into his fist.

"That explains why people are buying this shit," he said after a while. Actually, he just thought it. Better Mikosh said it from where he stood a few feet away on the Row Three work deck. He pointed to the ground and said, "Look at this."

Something tacky and black had been smeared across the work deck, clumping and clotting around the little diamond grip plates and catching the settling dust. Mikosh coughed and bent over the stain, reaching down to dab his fingers into it. He hoped it was hydraulic fluid, but of course it wasn't. Despite being nearly dry and gummy with dust, the coppery stink of blood still filled the air.

Mikosh looked around at the row behind him. Aside from the great black sheet of metal covering the bay window, the area looked no worse for wear than the rest of the rows. There was a sort of cup-shaped depression in the center of the row, but the catalyst had fallen and covered whatever damage might lay beneath. He turned his attention back to the stain.

It was impossibly wide, he thought. Too wide and too oddly shaped to have come from a human being. If — for some insane reason — he were to lie down on the dun-colored mess, he wouldn't be able to reach beyond any two sides of it with his fingers all the way outstretched. The stain was also shaped like a fan, and almost perfectly uniform in its covering of the deck.

Mikosh looked closer and saw a much thinner trail leading back into the rows. His eyes flicked from the stain to the row and back again, wondering what to do and thinking of the odd fluttering shape he thought he'd seen out there in the dust. Then Better Mikosh tapped him on the shoulder and pointed at the ground by their feet.

Better Mikosh spit onto the platform, a giant, disgusting glob of blackened phlegm much the same as Mikosh had been coughing up in the eye wash station. Mikosh watched him smash his foot down onto the gob, then slide his foot back and forth over the ground, scraping the liquid from side to side. Then he swept his foot straight back toward the seedbeds. The shape the spit had left on the deck was almost exactly the same as the greater bloodstain beside it.

"Yes, I suppose so," Mikosh said under his breath, wiping his mouth and fitting his mask back into place. He looked at his hand and saw the black smudging his glove. Better Mikosh had disappeared. Mikosh looked at the bottom of his foot and saw it was wet from where he'd swiped it back and forth over the decking. "Medical. Perhaps he made it to Medical."

From where he was standing, it was a short drive back to the assignment desk and the medical bay beside it. During normal operations, Medical would be staffed with a doctor and at least a couple nurses, standing by to assist in case of an accident. This was the skeleton shift, of course, so Medical would be empty, but the automated health systems would be functional. If Kaid was injured, he probably went to

Medical for treatment.

Mikosh gave the ugly smear on the work deck one last look and then left, ignoring the nagging sensation of being followed.

￫

The transport took Mikosh to the Administration deck and he almost collapsed when he saw Kaid's transport docked in station. He jogged over to it, feeling his pulse thump in his head as he did so. The transport was empty save for a faint, roughly hand-shaped smear of blood on the sidewall. Mikosh ran a finger over it and saw it was dry as paint. A few curlicues of fluff had dried in place on it.

He hobbled toward Medical as quickly as possible, hailing Velona on the transmitter embedded in his rebreather.

"Hey," he said. "Uh, I think Kaid is badly injured, but he might be walking around. I'm heading for Medical to check on him."

"Okay," Velona said. Her voice echoed at him, both her and another her talking at the same time. He wondered absentmindedly if the other her had the same blue eyes, blue eyes like the great blue eye hanging in space outside the station. The pale blue star whose light he could see bathing all of the station interior save where the black sheet covered the window over Row Three. "What did you find that makes you think he's still alive?"

"Blood," Mikosh said. "There was … a lot of it near where Kaid had been working, but up on the work deck. And it was … I don't know, smeared around."

"Smeared?" Velona asked.

"Yeah," Mikosh said. "Also, his transport's back at the Administration deck. That makes me think he tried to get to Medical. There's blood on that too."

"His transport's back at Administration?" Velona asked. He could hear her fiddling around with something at her desk. "Are you sure? My readout up here says his transport is still at Row Two."

Mikosh stopped and looked back at the transports all tucked in next to each other in station. From this distance, he couldn't tell for sure that the transport he'd thought he'd seen was there, but he was sure he'd seen it.

Then again, he was sure he'd seen a lot of things.

"Yeah," he said, turning and heading for Medical. "I'm sure."

"Okay," Velona said. He could tell from her voice that she was taking it on faith that he wasn't just seeing things. "The impact could have damaged the transport or the track's feedback system somehow." She paused. "Anything's possible."

"Yeah," Mikosh said. "I guess so."

The lights in Medical, like in the rest of the station, were automatic and motion-sensing. They flicked on in the entrance when he walked inside, fluttering to life and bathing the waiting room in light that seemed garishly yellow compared to the pale blue of the local star. The door snapped shut behind him and he heard the sound of the air scrubbers kicking on, a dull snap followed by a great rush of air.

If a speck of dust remained in the place, he couldn't find it. The only mar on the antiseptic white of the waiting room was another of the almost hand-shaped blood stains on the wall beside the door to the examination rooms. In here, the rust-brown looked almost painted on, impossibly dark. Mikosh could see every little dip and dash where the fabric of a wet glove had smeared the doorframe.

The door opened as he approached with a silent rush of air, the white steel-and-plastic slab flitting away into a recess built into the wall. The hallway led right and left, the sign arrows in front of him suggesting right was for DOCTORS and left was for ALL OTHER PERSONNEL. He turned left and found another bloodstain, this one far smaller than the others, marring the wall where the hallway bent into another corridor. This stain glowed brilliant red for just a moment, and then spread across the wall, filling the hallway with ten thousand squirming centipedes. Mikosh shuddered and swallowed, blinking at the sweat trying to slip into his eye.

The vision faded just as the crawling things started to work their way up Mikosh's feet. Despite himself, he could still feel imaginary bugs picking their way up his legs, getting stuck in his leg hair. He shuddered.

The bloodstain remained, though it was now dull and brown and unmoving.

Mikosh followed the corridor to a changing room beside what he knew was the auto-doc hangar. The auto-docs were large steel and glass tubes that filled with suspension fluid. They could diagnose and treat a host of problems, but their primary use was to float workers with critical injuries so they could be taken off station to a more comprehensive hospital.

Mikosh had been in one on a different station years back to get his appendix taken out, a fairly simple procedure that had left him unconscious in suspension for about a day while he recuperated. He'd popped out of the thing with a fresh scar and ready to work like nothing had even happened. If Kaid was hurt, he would have known to come here for treatment.

All Mikosh would have to do is pull the red emergency tab on the back of the machine to send it up to the escape pods automatically. He had to find which pod Kaid was in first, of course, but there were only twenty or so auto-docs in the hangar and Kaid would be the only person in one. There was even a chance his pod had been jettisoned already, but sometimes you had to hit the emergency tab physically to get the things to work. At least according to the orientation videos Mikosh had watched about thirty million times.

And you couldn't do it yourself.

Mikosh found Kaid's uniform in the locker room and had to hold a hand over his mouth to keep from puking. It was the only thing left in the room that had any sort of color, and that color was bad. Brown and red stains covered every inch of the fabric, and the fabric itself was torn and ripped from wrist to toe. Mikosh thought of his own suit's hardening factor and wondered what kind of forces Kaid's body had been subjected to. He turned and found Better Mikosh standing just inside the hangar entrance, his hand on the doorframe.

"Why's the light on already?" he asked. Mikosh stepped past him and looked into the room. From where he was standing, he could see little more than the odd tubes and boxes that fed the rows of cylinders lining the two elevated mesh walkways. Each of the cylinders, the auto-docs, were emblazoned with a number near the top. From where he stood, he could see the very tops of all of them save one, number sixteen, which was missing from the rows.

"It's because something is moving in here," Better Mikosh whispered in Mikosh's ear, undeterred. Mikosh looked at him, and the imaginary man pointed up at the ceiling. Both their eyes followed his finger up to where something was swirling in faint black patterns on the wall. A shadow. Mikosh turned in place to get a better look at it, not sure what he was seeing.

It waved like seaweed in a current, a gentle swaying interrupted by the occasional flick of one of the tendrils left or right. It reminded him of an insect feeling its way along by its antenna. Without warning, he coughed, barely catching the noise in the crook of his arm. Better Mikosh glared at him.

"Are you kidding?" he asked. The fronds of the shadow froze in place. Mikosh heard movement in the machinery at the center of the room. He peeked around the side of it to the rightmost walkway, which fed units eleven through twenty. A naked human leg took an unsteady step onto the walkway. Mikosh swallowed.

The skin color matched Kaid's, that same deep brown, but the proportions were all wrong. The thigh and calf were long and oddly bent. The foot, too, was exceptionally long, and fitted with toes that gripped the mesh like fingers. The hair on the leg waved and writhed like amoebic cilia. A hand came into view and Mikosh cursed under his breath. It wasn't human. It couldn't be. It was all, *all* wrong.

He looked around in a panic and then made a mad dash for the closest pod on the side opposite where the thing was emerging. His "mad dash" amounted to little more than awkwardly tiptoeing the distance to the cylinder before gingerly opening the door and stepping inside. Better Mikosh stood just outside the closing door, giving Mikosh a worried look and holding a finger to his lips.

"Mikosh, what's going on?" Velona asked. "Did you find Kaid?"

"I found … something," Mikosh said. "I think I'm seeing things." He heard a magnetic snap and looked around to see the little display beside the door flickering to life. He felt warmth creeping up his ankles and saw the cylinder had started to fill. "Oh shit."

"What?" Velona asked, clearly worried.

"I just locked myself in an auto-doc and now it's filling up," Mikosh said. A mouthpiece similar to his rebreather slid down from overhead and Mikosh looked down at the fluid quickly rising over his knees.

"Why?" Velona asked, nearly shouted.

"I think something's wrong with Kaid, he looked … weird," Mikosh said. "I've … I've got to go. I need to put the other mask on."

"Damnit … okay," Velona said. "But listen, the absolute *second* you get out of there you need to hightail it to the escape pods. I … Don't worry about how much time you have left, just assume it's basically none, okay? If you don't hear from me … it's because I've already left Administration for the pods. I'll wait for you as long as I can, but …" Mikosh ripped his rebreather off and put the auto-doc mask in place.

The water passed over his head and his eyes. The auto-doc's mask had a painfully awkward tube that pushed his tongue down against the bottom of his mouth and scratched the back of his throat. He could feel it pumping air in and out of his lungs as though the organs were just an afterthought. A voice piped up in his ear.

"Worker Mikosh," the auto-doc said. He could barely see out of the cylinder, little more than form and shadow, but something *was* moving outside the tank.

Getting closer.

"Readings from your breath alone show an almost impossibly high concentration of catalyst contamination in your bloodstream," the auto-doc said. Mikosh couldn't respond, as if it would make a difference. "Imaging shows a great deal of corneal abrasions and catalyst particulate in your eyes. Processing. Are you experiencing hallucinations? Please nod your head." Mikosh nodded.

The thing was just outside of the cylinder now, its odd body moving in ways that made Mikosh sick to think about. It seemed alien, but it could also just be the catalyst in his system. He thought of Better Mikosh, a hallucination so solid that Mikosh thought perhaps he may have always existed. It was absurd. The shape outside his cylinder was still human enough to be Kaid.

It was possible. Anything was possible.

"A mixture of atropine and antipsychotics should alleviate the worst symptoms of the catalyst exposure," the auto-doc continued. "But the particulate concentrations in your lungs and eyes need to be removed first. Please stand by for administration of a pre-surgery paralytic and anesthetic."

Before Mikosh could protest, the machinery connected to his mouth hummed and filled his lungs with just what the auto-doc said it would. He felt his chest go numb from the inside, a terrible sensation that made him want to claw open his own chest cavity. It itched. It burned. And the thing outside the cylinder was now standing just inches away, so that Mikosh could make out the faintest outlines of human features in the face.

There was an expression there. Was it concern? Was the face smiling? He couldn't tell; all he could think of was the hand he'd seen wrapping itself around the safety railing beside the auto-docs' machinery bay. A thing nearly as long as the forearm it was connected to, with great divides along the carpals so that every finger met only at the wrist. And each of those fingers flicked back and forth along double-hinged joints, curling backward, knuckle-first around the railing.

"There will be some discomfort," the auto-doc said. "Your lungs are being filled with oxygenated suspension liquid and pressurized to allow the surgical instruments room to work." The sensation was immediate; Mikosh was dying. He was being forcibly drowned by this machine while the shadow outside the cylinder watched him die. He could feel his deadened muscles spasm lightly despite the paralytic, but that was it. He was trying to scream, to gag, to rip the thing out of his mouth and kick his way out of the cylinder, but he could do nothing.

Then he could feel the surgical instruments in his mouth and windpipe. He could feel them moving into his lungs like living dolls' hair, scraping and flicking against every imperfection in his brachial tube. Then they were in his lungs, and he could feel nothing, but he knew they were in there.

His mind showed him what they were doing. How they were tearing and ripping little slivers of flesh away from the lining of his lungs. He saw, truly, deeply *saw*, blood pooling in the hollows of his air sacs. He saw the things burrowing deeper into his body, pushing until they were scissoring through his flesh and into the suspension fluid in front of his face.

Then he saw the dolls' hair surgical instruments floating closer and closer to his eyes. They twitched and course-corrected with the same direct, insectile movements of the thing he'd seen outside the cylinder. He wanted to move his eyes, but they too were numb now, frozen in place. The little hairs began to brush against his cornea, all but blinding him.

But he could see the thing outside the glass, the shape of it distorted by the liquid.

It pressed its face against the cylinder and he saw its eye flatten over the glass. It was broad and milky yellow, fat as the palm of his hand. It seemed distended from the skull that bore it, reaching out of the bone and flesh on a stalk like a snail's eye.

Or a crab's.

Then it was gone, and so were the surgical instruments. They flitted away like a dream. If Mikosh was capable of holding his breath — and he sure as shit would have been holding it through all of that — he would have exhaled in relief. As it was, he felt a series of pricks in his neck, and the sense of feeling returned to his body.

"The procedure is a success," the auto-doc said, its voice anything but cheerful. "All foreign bodies have been removed from Worker Mikosh with a surety rating of ninety-nine point nine percent. This unit would like to remind Worker Mikosh that surety ratings can never equal one hundred percent due to the liability constraints of the Blackwell Corporation's Automated Diagnosis, Observation, and Correction System." Mikosh felt another prick in his neck. The world brightened instantly.

The thing outside the glass was gone.

"The catalyst counter-serum has been administered," the auto-doc explained. "Worker Mikosh should be advised that his catalyst intoxication has been reported to his superiors, and any relevant incident reports regarding the incurring incident should be filed to avoid penalties. Worker Mikosh's wages have been garnished at seventy-two percent to compensate the Blackwell Corporation for the medical treatment received, barring an accident forgiveness rebate."

The cylinder drained, dumping Mikosh against the back wall. He ripped the mask off and expected to begin coughing immediately, but his lungs felt fine. For some reason, he almost felt cheated. The door of the cylinder popped open, but the auto-doc kept talking.

"The catalyst counter-serum is only meant to reduce the most drastic symptoms of intoxication and works at different rates depending on the physiology of the patient," it said. "Please exercise caution for the next several hours, and do not operate heavy equipment, power tools, or any non-automated conveyance until cleared by a supervisor." Something in the housing clicked.

"Thank you," it said. "And have a nice day."

Mikosh stumbled out of the cylinder and immediately looked around for whatever he'd seen, what he'd taken to calling the Kaid-thing in his head. His eyes felt scalded clean. He had to squint to see in the artificial light, stumbling his way out of Medical and strapping his rebreather back on as he did so. The suspension fluid evaporated quickly outside of the auto-docs, leaving him dry but terribly cold.

"Velona," he said, hoping she could hear him. He pawed around in the reception desk at Medical and found a pack of the cheap dust goggles issued to the non-work staff. His real goggles, lost in the rows and damned to be disintegrated by the local star when the radiation pulse hit, were heavy-duty and padded and comfortable.

These cheap things fucking sucked, but it was better than getting more dust in his eyes. He strapped them on and stepped outside, feeling much better than he did when he'd woken up coughing a lung out in the rows just half an hour earlier. The rough plastic edges bit into the skin over his cheekbones.

"Velona," he said again. She responded, but her voice was garbled. Completely unintelligible. Maybe she was telling him to hurry up. Probably, yeah.

He stopped just short of the Administration deck elevator, the one he'd taken down here to start the day just an hour ago. It seemed longer than that. But it wasn't the memory of the trip down that stopped him in place.

Kaid was there. Standing right in front of the elevator with his back to Mikosh. Mikosh saw the elevator lights were ticking down one by one as the platform itself got ready to arrive in station. It was coming all the way from Admin, which meant there were several minutes left in the trip.

"Hello, Mikosh," Kaid said, not turning around. He wasn't wearing a rebreather, but he had put on his ruined work uniform. It hung from his body in tatters, badly stained and barely concealing any of his skin. The skin itself looked fine. So did his hands and feet, for that matter. He wasn't wearing shoes. "I've wanted to speak with you."

"Okay," Mikosh said. "Uh, where's your rebreather? Are you, uh, are you okay?"

"I'm fine," Kaid said. "You made a comment to me earlier that I wanted to confront you about. That's what I remember. You said something about the catalyst and it upset me." His head turned and Mikosh saw the man was looking down at his hand.

"You sound funny, Kaid," Mikosh said, looking around. There was nothing but the empty Administration deck and the closest rows, numbers one and forty nine. He could see something moving around in Row One. It was unmistakable.

"Something's not right here," Better Mikosh said.

"I know something's not right," Mikosh responded, trying to find Better Mikosh. But the other blood-red-haired version of him wasn't there. He was surprised how lonely it made him feel.

"Who are you talking to that's not me?" Kaid asked. He started walking toward Mikosh without turning around. Mikosh looked down at Kaid's feet and saw they had shrunk to ball-ended stubs. Even as he watched, Kaid's tarsals and metatarsals pushed out of the gummy flesh and began click-clacking over the floor. The man's gait was made all the more awkward by the fact that his knees were still facing the complete wrong direction.

Little wires of flesh crept out along the exposed bones, followed by thicker cords of muscle and then an envelope of flesh. The finished feet looked like a clumsy impression of the real thing.

"Like if the only person you'd ever seen up close had been completely crushed before you got a good look at him," Better Mikosh whispered, though he still wasn't anywhere to be seen. Kaid's knees snapped through their hinges so that he was almost walking the right way. The sound of the joints readjusting made Mikosh queasy. He took several steps back.

"I am upsetting you, Mikosh," Kaid said. One of his arms, still facing backward, clicked and popped and split up to the elbow. "But not as much as you upset me. I remember needing that 'good connect' so I could pay off some loans. Paying off loans is very important, Mikosh." Kaid reached for him. "If I make you a silent person you won't make trouble for me anymore. And neither of us will be upset."

Mikosh turned and ran for the transport station, making it a few dozen meters before he saw something rolling up and out of Row One. Perhaps a hundred viscous yellow eyeballs dotted the appendage it threw up onto the platform. The arm itself was the size of a child's bed, if you cut it in half and stretched it out lengthwise. Mikosh skidded to a stop and turned to see Kaid had fallen over onto all fours.

"This is a clumsy way to move around, but I'm not doing it right," Kaid said, his neck turning at an impossible angle to give him a better view of Mikosh. The platform rumbled underfoot as whatever it was crawled out of the row. Mikosh took off running past Kaid, watching as the man's eyes, sockets and all, cracked the plane of his face to rest on Mikosh. They were dull, magnetic yellow.

Mikosh didn't know what he was doing; he was just running. Panic suffused every part of him, more than he'd ever felt in his life. It was like electrical currents were pushing his muscles along independent of what his waking mind wanted. He could hear the Kaid-thing clumping along on all fours behind him. It spoke without sounding winded, despite moving at a full clip.

"Where are you going, Mikosh?" it asked. "I have a way to fix this that benefits both of us. Are you okay? Are you seeing things? Did you breathe in the catalyst?" It was running alongside him now, the limbs propelling it along the deck looking only remotely human. The feet it had grown out of Kaid's hands looked like deer hooves.

"This is really quite ridiculous," it said. It swiped Mikosh's foot out from underneath him just short of the edge of the seedbed and Mikosh took his second nasty tumble into the fluffy grey catalyst. He disappeared beneath it and everything was silent again, that deep, almost unfathomable quiet. He barely felt the thud of the thing jumping in along with him.

Mikosh stayed low and crawled through the fluff, kicking up a cloud of dust overhead. The greater cloud from earlier had all but died down, though the orange fog still lingered at about hip height in the seedbeds. He figured he could duck around the thing if he stayed quiet and then head back for the elevator. Deep blue light shined out at him through the catalyst and he froze.

"I do not need to see you to find you, Mikosh," the Kaid-thing said. Something struck Mikosh violently from behind and he had to make a series of clumsy pirouettes in order to not come into contact with pre-radiation crystal. He'd thought it'd looked blue a second earlier, but he realized it was actually a fairly deep purple.

Indigo, he thought. Then something hit him again and he screamed. The impact was like a whiplash that managed to cut through every bit of protection his suit offered. He turned to where the attack had come from and saw the Kaid-thing standing in the fluff. He could see the flesh of its legs through the tattered work uniform. The thing's thighs looked tattered themselves, a series of springy ribbons haphazardly knitted together to keep it standing. The hands were splitting along the metacarpal lines again as well, snapping back and forth over the worn hinge joints.

"I will finish this and then go be with the people," the Kaid-thing said. "It has been a long time and I am sick of being a lonely thing. It is lonely here. I hate it." It raised its arm over its head and brought it down like a whip over the arm Mikosh was shielding himself with. The pain was incredible. Mikosh felt the suit harden to the consistency of a steel cast, but there were still dents in it. He thought his arm might be broken. The Kaid-thing wrapped the odd phalanges around Mikosh's forearm.

"This is a novel creation," it said. "Extra skin. Hard, but pliant. Everytime I meet the people again they have new tools." The Kaid-thing had started talking out of the base of its neck, the vertebrae parting to make way for a clumsy speech organ. Mikosh's head swam — from confusion as much as pain — as an entire face formed in the hair on the back of Kaid's head. The milky yellow eyes found him and blinked.

"I am beyond tools," it said, clenching its fingers until Mikosh could feel the bones in his arm clicking and grinding against each other. They were about to shatter. It was like being in the clutch of a big jungle snake. He screamed and dug his free hand into the catalyst. The Kaid-thing was watching the damage it was wreaking on Mikosh and not paying attention to the man himself until it was too late. "What is this?"

Mikosh clenched his eyes shut and screamed and shoveled a handful of the catalyst and egg-sized pre-radiation crystal into the Kaid-thing's face.

It put its hand up, for what little good it did the thing. The crystal reacted instantly, creating a splitting white void that turned the tinting in Mikosh's cheap goggles flat black. Still, he could see the reaction point growing, could feel the gentle drag as it ate its way into existence.

Mikosh had pulled his hand back at the last second, and the slow-burning reaction ate the wad of catalyst in his palm instead of the palm itself. The thing wasn't so lucky; the reaction point had caught its physical mass at that exact area in space. It released Kaid's arm and inspected the white light eating away at its body with an expression Mikosh couldn't for the life of him understand. But its body language suggested little more than a passive fascination with what was happening.

"This is me," it said over the rip of air being sucked violently into the reaction point. All Mikosh could see of it was the distended shadow of its head as it was sucked in up to its shoulder. "The people have made a tool of me." Its grip tightened and Mikosh screamed, clawing at the floor beneath him to get further away from the reaction point. "A clever tool. What do you use it for?" Its head had been sucked in completely. Mikosh couldn't understand how it was still talking.

"I am beyond tools," it said. "Will you join me

in the void beyond this tear?" It tugged at Mikosh and the man did everything in his power to get away from it, from the steadily growing reaction point. He screamed and kicked like a child.

Then it was over. The reaction point flickered like an old light bulb and vanished into itself. The thing's phalanges released his arm, allowing a new and fresh pain to flood into Mikosh. Its grip had served as a sort of tourniquet, cutting off the blood flow to the clearly broken arm and, thus, all the pain he was now feeling.

What was left of the Kaid-thing — a disconnected arm, a structure that might have been a badly chewed human hip bone, and Kaid's ruined legs — fell into the seedbed with a poof of dust. Mikosh got to his feet and clambered out of the seedbed as fast as possible, honestly expecting the thing to come back to life.

"The thing?" Better Mikosh asked, jogging alongside Mikosh now, a big, sad grin on his face. "Are you sure that was a *thing?*" Mikosh looked past the assignment desk, where something large was crawling out of the rows. It seemed intent on some other purpose, though its baleful yellow eyes passed curiously over Mikosh. Some of them, at least.

"*That's* supposed to be real?" Better Mikosh asked. "Why isn't *it* coming after you like your supposed Kaid-thing?"

"I don't know," Mikosh said, pressing the call button on the elevator. The doors opened immediately.

"What *I* think, is that you're still high as shit and this is all you dealing with the trauma of the accident," Better Mikosh said, following him onto the elevator. He really *was* Better Mikosh. Regular Mikosh only just noticed the man was also a good two inches taller than him, in addition to being well-spoken and handsome.

"What does that even mean?"

"That means you just murdered your coworker after he tried to murder you," Better Mikosh said. "You had to go and throw that line about the catalyst in his face, huh?" The imaginary, superior Mikosh crossed his arms behind his head and smiled. "The incident jarred you, hurt him, and maybe he got a good old sniff of the catalyst too. So he got it in his mind to take you out real quick."

"If you think about it, it's a perfect crime," Velona said in Mikosh's ear. He rubbed the spot over the transmitter on his rebreather. Now that he was inside the air-scrubbed elevator, he didn't need it anymore. He took it off and dropped it on the floor, rubbing his jaw. The goggles came off too.

"All that confusion, some asteroid crashing into the station and causing this huge industrial accident," Velona continued. Her voice was clear as a bell despite the transmitter being on the floor of the elevator. Outside the window, the local star was growing brighter. The clusters of asteroids in the belt near the station had started to move with an increase in magnetic activity, shuffling loose of their rotting orbits and casting odd shadows in the stellar dust around them.

"You were hurt and couldn't get out in time," Velona said. "It's not like the Blackwell Corporation is going to investigate very hard."

"What about this?" Mikosh said, holding up the badly damaged left arm of his suit. The material was frozen in place. The pain of the injury was all but making him sick. He was probably twice as pale as usual.

"Didn't you hurt it when you got thrown by the

impact?" Better Mikosh offered.

"Auto-docs can't set bones without a doctor present," Velona said.

"What about the monster? That thing crawling up out of the rows?" Mikosh tried to see the thing in question out the windows, but the elevator was already too high to get an angle. A second later, the windows switched to flat black as the elevator entered the tube that fed the uppermost parts of the station.

"Just you trying to make sense of the incident, that big explosion and all that," Velona said. "It's not uncommon to use coping mechanisms like that in cases of trauma. You probably have post-traumatic stress disorder from the accident already; it's not like it takes time to set in."

The elevator arrived at the floor above Admin, where the station's lifeboats sat recessed in black cylinders with bright orange caution signs ringing them. Mikosh took a deep breath when he stepped out of the elevator and saw the light from one of the dark pods shining into the spherical docking room. Velona was still waiting for him, which meant there was time still for the evacuation. He set his hand on the guardrail and paused, noticing something odd.

He looked at the otherwise clean palm of his glove and saw it was now covered with dark, shining red. The color was almost black. The smell was unmistakable. Tacky blood glistened where Mikosh had smeared it over the guardrail.

"It could be yours," Better Mikosh said, walking alongside him toward the glowing white light spilling from the escape pod. "Or even Kaid's. You're not right in the head, after all. That atropine might not have really started kicking in." He chuckled. "Then again, maybe somebody was bleeding up here too. Bleeding bad."

Mikosh looked inside the pod and saw a woman sitting on the ring of upholstered white seats. They looked nice, but were also fairly formidable restraints, fitted with four-point harnesses and all sorts of other amenities. The woman was already wearing the beetle-black full-body suit and helmet that came standard in the evacuation pods. If he had longer, Mikosh would have put one on as well.

She wiggled her fingers at him.

Hello.

But she didn't say anything, instead tapping the front of the helmet where her mouth would be and shrugging. He wouldn't be able to hear her without putting on a helmet too, but there would be time for that soon. Probably. Maybe.

The door shut behind him and he took his seat as the pod began sliding slowly out of the blast hatch and into the vacuum of space. Disk-shaped windows over all the seats allowed him a view of the stars, and the twinkling specks of the other pods blipping out distress calls while they waited for the rescue boats.

Better Mikosh had taken a seat next to the woman. Velona. It was Velona.

"Of course it's me, silly," she said in his ear. "Who else would it be?" But it wasn't her, of course; that voice and Better Mikosh weren't real. They were just the fading aftereffects of a bad dose of catalyst. Maybe even some head trauma.

"You know, I was saying all that in the elevator and you seemed pretty quick to dismiss me," Better Mikosh said, smiling at Mikosh and running a finger down the side of the woman's helmet. Mikosh could see the blurry shape of himself reflected in the gently curving dark of the plastic. He took a deep breath and looked around the lifeboat, eyes lingering on the bright red handle that would blow the hatch and jettison the oxygen and everything else. IN CASE OF FIRE, the sign above it read.

"Nobody wants to believe they're crazy, but sometimes safe *is* better than sorry, isn't it?" Better Mikosh said. The pod was rotating slowly, causing the distant stars to slip past the windows. The woman — Velona, of course it was Velona — stretched her arms over her head and then raised her fingers to the clasps that would allow the helmet to depressurize and detach.

"There's no real reason to take that off," Better Mikosh said, looking Mikosh dead in the eyes. His smile was calm and collected, slightly mischievous.

"I'm not going to sit in this capsule for potentially hours and not talk to you," Velona said in his ear. "It's so weird talking to the black of people's masks when you're stuck in these things. It's … impersonal."

"So, Mikosh, which of us is right, you think?" Better Mikosh asked.

She pushed the clasps loose and the helmet popped upward slightly as it depressurized. The hiss was jarring. The great blue orb of the local star slid perfectly into the center of the window behind her head, bathing Mikosh in its pale light.

Her hands pushed upward on the helmet, allowing a spill of dark hair to fall loose onto her shoulders. Mikosh felt his heart roaring in his chest, thinking of the red lever set into the wall of the escape pod, and wondering if he'd see blue eyes.

THE END

The Three Flights of Mated Jefferson

It was an oddly cool June afternoon when Mateo Jefferson made his first long run for the fences. The fences, of course, were of little concern to him, being nothing more than stout, four-foot posts and the three seemingly endless trails of rusted wire that began where the brickwork left off past the front gate, continuing out of sight behind the hills heading toward the coal mine. Mateo was far more concerned about Mr. Chifford Lewer's Bluetick Coonhound, Rex, whom the lot of us could already see closing the distance with little effort.

"There he go," said Arnold Capley, kicking at the anklets of the leg irons he'd been put in as punishment a few days earlier. The chain rattled and caught my attention and I saw the chafing on his scrawny, dark ankles. His skin was black enough that the raw, red flesh was more garish than the marks on my own ankles.

We all watched the boy — a young, legally ageless teenager like the rest of us — darting across the freshly sprouted corn field. His bare feet kicked up curds of dirt shoulder-high behind him. He was a member of Detachment G — the work party named for the hall he lived in at the asylum — and was so far down the line from Capley and myself he seemed like little more than a gnat scurrying over a filthy brown tablecloth.

"Boy gets to that fence he's free," Capley said, putting his shovel down into the dirt and resting his chin atop the worn and cracked shaft. His eyes were wide enough you could see the whites all around. "That Bluetick can't jump. Won't jump. I tell you, that boy gets to the fence he's free as a damn bird."

I imagine that, for Mateo, the moment was short and terribly personal. If I were him, my focus would have been laser-tight on that fence. I could almost feel the cold press of the earth the way he might be feeling it, the tightness of the skin between his toes as they dug into the ground to push him. Even the occasional sharp poke of sticks and rocks in the mud, I could feel that too. In my head at least.

Maybe we all could.

I think all of us wanted to cheer him on some, raise our broken farm tools into the air and shake them and scream. But Mr. Chifford Lewer threw back a long, ugly look at us from the saddle of his horse and we bent ourselves back to sod busting. Like most of the others, I worked slowly and peeked back behind me, cheering silently for Mateo to make it to that fence. To jump the ugly, rusted wire and make for the river, where he could hop in the water and lose

Rex and this place in a heartbeat.

They'd look for him, but not hard. He could hop a freight train in town and ride it the hell out of this valley, away from Weston, West Virginia, and this cursed place.

It was a damn shame Rex caught him. The dog wasn't cruel — unless Mr. Chifford Lewer commanded he be — but he had a firm bite that would only tighten if you didn't give in right off the bat. Capley's arms had a series of purple-white scars that testified to both the dog's danger and patience.

The arm was wounded, but still there, after all, when a dog that size could easily have made it not be.

Rex caught Mateo twenty strides shy of the wire, tackling him like I'd seen a tiger attack a hunk of dead turkey on a string at the Cincinnati Zoo one time. That flop-eared dog hopped into the air and curled his front paws over Mateo's neck and shoulders, dropping the boy into the mud and sliding him a good five feet. Like I said, I was far away, but I could still hear Mateo cursing that dog until Mr. Chifford Lewer jogged his horse over to break up the tangle.

"Hell, I thought he might'a had it," Capley said to himself, stretching his chest so hard I heard his sternum pop. The noise drew my attention and for a second too long, I suppose, my gaze lingered on the sinewy outlines of Capley's naked upper body. He noticed the trespass in a second and all sense of calm fled him.

"Dick-suckin' motherfucker," he screamed at me. "Fuck you. Fuck you looking at me. Don't you fuckin' look at me. Don't you fuckin' look at me." He lost his composure in a second and started pacing, breathing hard through his teeth and out through his nose. He took up the shovel in both hands and, though he was terribly scrawny, started twisting the shaft. The dry wood squealed.

At the far end of the field, Mateo lay on his stomach with his legs up in the air, Rex playing up a mean growl while Mr. Chifford Lewer clapped irons on Mateo. I'd have liked to watch; it was the only interesting thing that had happened in weeks or maybe months. A diversion of any kind was welcome in this place.

"Cocksuckin' boy-fucker, I'll fuckin' kill you," Capley hissed now, poking the air in front of me with his shovel. His eyes rolled up and down in his skull so that they almost flickered, his brown irises turned into a swirl of color by the sheer speed of movement. White and brown and white and brown and white. It seemed impossible that he could focus on me, much less hit me with the shovel, but he managed it all the same, popping loose one of my shirt's three remaining buttons and leaving an ugly scratch on my stomach. So I hit him with my own shovel.

Hard.

His eyes finished their mad elevations and settled on "up" as a final destination, the weight of their stopping enough to make Capley's suddenly stiff body fall flatly backward like a plank. I looked over at Mr. Chifford Lewis, now carting Mateo onto his feet and tying him to the saddle of the horse, and then down to Capley.

I could feel it then, plying at the edges of my brain, treating my self control like bark to be peeled off the heart wood of my sanity. Painful, then pleasurable, I found it swallowing me up before I had a second to think. To consider otherwise.

I stood over Capley and rested the sharp, spade-end of my shovel on his throat. I put my foot on the little outcropping of rusted iron and prepared to drive the thing home. Mr. Chifford Lewer and Rex were far away, too far to intercede.

I could smell, for just a second, the stream behind my former parents' home in Blunt. I was almost there again, fresh water and snot streaming from my nose and the sharp, coppery taste of blood. The *feel* of bleeding. The fiery pain of welts raising all across my face from the beating I'd received.

Then I really was getting hit. I saw my shovel tumble away past Capley's head as my torso bent clean in half sideways. At least, that's what it felt like. Then I was skidding through the rocky dirt on my shoulder, and somebody was punching me.

I found the sweet, upturned face of Arnold Bean curled into a frown. His fists rained down on my face as he cried, screaming something like, "nope, nope, nope." Then he got a particularly good one in and my jaw snapped sideways, knocking me flat unconscious.

I woke to Arnold sitting beside my bed, caressing my hair with his stubby fingers and gently sobbing. He had an idiot's face, which, if you haven't met one, is a face devoid of guile. His was a child's pure and undiluted sorrow, expressed to the absolute degree by a frown I found almost comical.

"Couldn't let you do it," he told me. "They'll give you the rope." His head nodded in time with his spoken thoughts. "I wish you hadn't made me hurt you, Ezra. I wish you hadn't. I can't get it out of my head now. I hurt you so bad."

"No," I said, trying to sit up and feeling the full

weight of the beating Arnold had handed me. I hissed and gave up on it, settling instead on pulling his hand off my hair and caressing the back of his massive, doughy palm. "I did it to myself. You did a good thing, Arnold. You stopped me before I did a bad thing."

"I didn't like to do it," Arnold said. "It didn't feel like a good thing." He put his hands under my arms and hauled me to a sitting position, moving me with such ease I may as well have been stuffed with straw.

"That's how you know you're a good boy," I told him, grabbing his shoulder. I smiled, noticing I'd lost a tooth for Arnold's troubles, but one of the kind in the back of my mouth, where it wouldn't make me ugly. "If you hurt people and you like it, then you're being bad."

"Like you like it?" he asked.

"Yes," I said, after some hesitation. "I'm bad, but you're not. You're just doing your best." He nodded sagely, his eyes focused on something between our faces now. He stood without saying another thing to me, still nodding and walking to his bed.

Director Prescott entered our hall — the open bay of one hundred some-odd beds we slept in — a short while after Arnold left my bedside. Nurse Marco, a man of considerable proportions despite his occupation, followed closely behind with a stack of bedding cradled in his arms. Mateo Jefferson came next — fresh chains scraping the concrete floor — and Mr. Chifford Lewer brought up the caboose.

The procession stopped at the foot of my bunk, and Nurse Marco dropped the bedding on the top rack. These were all two-person bunks, by the way, squeaking, rattling, shaking things that would wake you up in the middle of the night because you turned over too fast and set the old metal squealing like an alarm.

"On your feet for the director, Mr. Ezra Finkle," Mr. Chifford Lewer told me in a gruff voice. I smiled at him and shrugged.

"I'm feeling a little—" I tried to say, "under the weather," but I didn't manage to finish. He pulled me off my rack and to my feet. I could feel my bruised and loosened brain tumbling around in my skull, and it took some concentration to keep myself from vomiting. He balanced me precariously against the bunk's footside support pole, holding me in place with his free arm.

"Mr. Finkle," Director Prescott said, smoothing his moustache with his thumb and forefinger. He did this by pressing the two fingers together just under his nose, and then spreading them to the edges of his lips. "I understand you were assaulted by young Arnold after yourself badly injuring Mr. Capley."

"I suppose, sir," I said, curling my arm around the post to keep from falling.

"You're in something of a stupor, I gather?" Director Prescott said with a coy smile, running his fingers down my cheek to my chin and lifting it to get a better look at my face. At the time, I suppose the man was in his mid- to late-40s. Full grown and then some, at least. I was fourteen at the time, and yet to grow into manhood by any measure. He chuckled and let go of me.

"Your eyes seem fine," he said. "If you notice any localized numbness or you can't use the restroom yourself, or you find you can't hold it until you get to the restroom, then be sure to notify the staff immediately."

"Yes, sir," I said. Nurse Marco looked me up and down. He looked like a drawing of a military man you might see in a drugstore magazine. He had almost no waist to speak of, but his shoulders spread crane-like out from his torso so that his thick, ropy arms seemed to dangle a great distance from his hips. His head was flat and ugly, eyes hidden in the shadow of his thick forehead ridge. Though, when they caught the light just right, you could see something twinkling in there.

"This is Mateo Jefferson, Mr. Finkle," Director Prescott continued. Mateo kept his eyes on the ground, head hung low over the bundle of personal effects in his arms. "He is to be your new bunkmate."

"Okay," I said.

"What was that?" Nurse Marco all but yelled. His voice wasn't as deep as it ought to have been, but somehow whiny and cracked. Almost feminine, despite the size and masculine shape of him. It took me aback, but I was too punch-drunk to make much of a reaction.

"Yes, sir," I said, correcting myself. "Where will Capley sleep?"

"He's been moved out to the colored hospital in Point Pleasant, Lakin whatever," Mr. Chifford Lewer said, crossing his arms. "Where he might be for the next couple of years, or days, depending on how things go." He narrowed his eyes. "And if it's the next couple of days, Mr. Ezra Finkle, you'll be heading to the Glory carriage gate sooner'n even I ever expected."

"Thank you, Mr. Lewer," Director Prescott said, somewhat sternly. Lewer rankled at the mention of only his last name, but moved away from me and back behind Prescott, who smoothed his moustache again and pushed Mateo toward me.

"Take good care of Jefferson," Director Prescott

said, turning away and leaving the hall with a trade-mark sort of abruptness. Nurse Marco gave Mateo one last, long look and then followed, but Mr. Chifford Lewer stayed behind to lean in and whisper to me. Fairly loudly, I should add.

"If you want to do this darky here? Then you man up and do him on the grounds, you little freak," he hissed. "We don't need no state inspectors comin' 'round asking questions, and I sure as shit don't need to be hauling half-dead coloreds into town and talking to their kind, givin' 'em money to get hauled out over the hills." He worked his tongue in his lip, checking for a lump of chewing tobacco that wasn't there. "You understand me?"

"Yes, sir, Mr. Chifford Lewer," I said. He nodded, glared one last, long time at Mateo, and then left. The entire hall breathed a sigh of relief when he'd gone. I fell to my knees and hacked up a stream of yellow bile. Arnold came over in a huff and tried to clean it up with his blanket. The other kids went about their business, talking and trading cigarettes and doing whatever.

They didn't bother with me, and I didn't bother with them — the others that is — generally speaking. So don't get excited like I might be telling you about them and our exploits like they're some big cast of characters. People kept to themselves at T-A, myself especially. Well, people kept *away* from me. So I didn't bother learning any names and, I guess, that means you won't learn them either.

I pushed Arnold away before he could get my sick on his blanket, holding the glass shards of my skull together and all but shouting at him until he left. Where the lot of us mad children were in our teens and younger, Arnold was something in the ballpark of about thirty at the time. He didn't know his own age in truth, and wouldn't be able to act that age regardless, so he was one of us. And, of all of us, he was the only one who seemed to know everybody and whom everybody liked. So, in that way, he gets to be a part of this story and you get to learn his name.

Mateo took some time setting his stuff out on his mattress and then carefully putting the few items he owned away in the footlocker at the end of his rack. In that time, I bartered some cigarettes for old toe rags and towels and the like, using that to clean up what I'd left on the tile before it stained and set to stinking. Then I all but fell into my bed, curling up on myself and hoping to sleep.

"Hey you," Mateo said, waking me up perhaps an hour later. The lights in G Hall, situated on the top of the asylum's three floors, were doused for curfew, but the night itself had yet to fruit in full. As it stood, the last orange traces of light from an otherwise miserable day played over Mateo's soft and oddly beautiful features.

I had never seen a mixed person in my life, or, if I had, had no inkling of what I'd been looking at and had skipped my eyes over them the way my eyes skipped over most living people. But up close, he was something to behold. His skin was like the aged, stained wood of a fine writing desk — the grain sanded flawlessly smooth — and I thank God I wasn't in any state to move or I might have touched him to just slake the thirst of how looking at him made me feel.

"What?" I asked instead, curling up on myself.

"You hate negroes?" he asked me, more like stated outright than asked.

"Doesn't everybody?" I fired back, feeling another wave of nausea when the pressure of simply speaking filled my head near to bursting.

"Lewer said you hit that boy, Capley, with a shovel because he's Black and you don't like black skin," Mateo said. He took a breath like to say something else, but then stopped. I realized he was sitting on the ground beside my rack. He looked oddly comfortable, despite the line of questioning he was running through — more like he was running through a survey than asking if I was a violent racist planning on hurting him in some fashion. I sighed.

"If he, or any of his creatures around here, *hear* that you called him anything but Mr. Chifford Lewer, he's going to take it out on you and then some," I said. I turned onto my back and held my hands over my eyes so that I could talk. I have no idea why that helped, but it did. "You haven't been here long, have you?"

"Four months," Mateo said, standing and leaning against the rack so he could see my face. I looked at him through the spaces between my fingers. He really was beautiful, almost terribly so, and I closed my fingers again to speak to him. God only knew what I might do if I started to feel for him — for *anybody* — in that way.

"Do you know why you're in Hall G now?" I asked.

"No," he said.

"So they can send you down to the state penitentiary in Glory when you turn eighteen," I told him. "You tried to run, so you're a criminal now, and they've got you by the short hairs. Whatever you were in for, now you're criminally insane and facing a lifetime behind bars. Or here, if you actually lose it before then."

"You're lying," he said. I actually moved my hands down to roll my eyes at him, and then quickly returned them. Even weak sunlight felt like railroad spikes in my brain. "I … I'm not even crazy. They put me here over some … some goddamn nonsense."

"Probably," I said. "What for?"

"My mother is … *was* … a white woman," he said. "Papa died with all them others when Monongah blew way back when." He sniffed, but when I peeked at him, his face was as stoic as ever. "I wasn't more'n two or so, and Mama washed clothes and did some work in bars up until the consumption caught her two years ago. Then that was it and I was on my own."

"Long story," I said. He glared at me and I smiled at him. Oddly enough, that made him laugh. I took a breath and looked away, telling myself something. Something.

"She passed and I was on my own, trying to get work and passing myself off as older'n I was," he said. "Tried to get some assistance and shit, but people got wind of who my mom was and our family history. They … they said I was trying to pass myself as white, and that was a condition. Caucasoid Delusion, they called it, and I got brought up to a judge and here I am."

I laughed. He frowned.

"That's … that's a good one," I said. I took a deep breath and moved my hands off my eyes so he could see I was serious. "There's only two people in this place, alright? Those who are, and those who damn sure ought to be. I guess you're just the first kind, which is fine." I sighed. "That boy I hit, Capley?"

Mateo nodded.

"He's the kind ought to be in here, understand?" I asked. Mateo gave me a grim look. "You never met him, but he talks to God like they're best friends, and he quotes parts of the Bible haven't been written yet, because he hasn't written 'em. Understand?" Mateo looked at me for a long time, and then nodded. "They put me in his bunk when I got here 'cause they thought he'd do me. You understand what I mean by that?"

Mateo nodded again.

"That was a couple years back, but we got along well enough until today," I said, looking at him squarely. "Do you know why?"

"You gonna tell me, though, right?" he said.

"Because some people *ought* to be in here," I said, looking at him a while longer and then covering my eyes. "Of the two of us sharing this rack here on out? There's one that won't ever be leaving this place on good terms."

"They can't keep me here," Mateo said sternly.

"I wasn't talking about you," I said.

And that was it between us for a few days.

~

I woke in the dead of night, feeling something like a rock laying on my chest. My brain, still swimming from Arnold's beating, told me it was a cat. A fat, black thing with shimmering green-yellow eyes, just waiting for me to finally stop breathing. I tried to force my chest into action, but it wouldn't go. Neither would my arms or legs, I realized in a panic.

Moonlight smeared the hall in striped and triangular patterns of old gold and cerulean. My eyes alone were free to move, to see this.

The cat grew heavier. I could feel my chest caving under the weight of it, my ribs cracking like plaster and my lungs being crushed into jelly. I was dying without actually dying. I tried to calm down and listen.

I could hear the soft snoring of the others in the hall, the gentle shift of somnambulant limbs adjusting beneath the coarse military blankets. Yet there was something else, something both above and below those comforting sounds of young boys sleeping. An unsteady ticking, an odd clicking, a strange clacking, all together and reminding me in an instant of a cold sheet-metal steampipe adjusting to the sudden heat of a furnace refilled with coal.

And like coal, there was an aroma of dust. A light and fragrant scent that fell at once thick and cottony into the throat, gathering and gathering and gathering, choking and dry and filling my eyes with tears that couldn't fall, for they were growing thick, thick, thicker too in this odd haze. I could see it then, floating in like a cloud of ash rising over a burning building to fall over the surrounding neighborhood.

And that clicking, clattering, snapping noise grew. Its rhythm intensified until I could hear nothing else. Until I could feel the odd staccatos harmonizing with the springs of my bedframe and my mind made sudden sense of them. This was movement, my brain told me, like of some great insect.

And as though that thought brought the thing to life, I could see the shapes of its body played out on the ceiling past the bottom of the rack above me,

Capley's old bed — now Mateo's. I saw limbs moving like a great army of living scissors, swishing and slipping past each other as they propelled some *thing*, some living *thing*, through our hall and toward me. Toward us. Toward my immobile form.

I could not see it in truth. The moonlight lay behind it, so all I saw was the thin and insectile limbs, interspersed with and almost impossible to separate from the shadows they cast.

Still my breath would not come to me, my lungs would not respond. If I hadn't led the life I had until that exact point, I might have pissed myself with fear. Perhaps, even, I would have if not for the strange paralysis that befell me.

I waited for pain. I waited for death.

I heard, instead, a noise which made me lust for both.

Slow movement played out over the ceiling, and Mateo tried to cry out in his sleep. I heard his voice, familiar though I had spoken to him only the once, making the simplest of beggaries. Mercy, please stop, and all manner of other shameful things that I won't, will never, repeat.

I could not move to brush away the hot tears running over my own cheeks.

Then I heard some sound, a shuddering, sucking noise for which I possess no earthly metaphor. I have heard that before a great explosion there is a draining of air from the atmosphere itself. A vacuum is created that spares nothing, which drags into itself all possible things before that last and violent expulsion.

If this thing I heard was not that noise's brother, then it has no family on this earth.

Or in this universe.

I clenched my eyes shut — I was so horrified —

and then all was finished. I could suddenly breathe, and did so, blindly sucking in breath after breath until I was sitting up over my knees and coughing and wheezing through a haze of tears.

The entire hall filled with the sounds of these soft, terrified coughs, and so I knew I was not the only one who experienced this … this horror. But when I would ask the others — gently, discretely — if they'd experienced anything similar in the days and weeks to come, they would demure or grow irate or ignore me entirely.

All save one boy, whose soft crying covered the entire hall like a cheap and insufficient blanket that night, leaving the lot of us cold and short of sleep.

The hall felt different the following day. By design, G Hall was filled with the most rambunctious of the kids given over to the asylum by the state, but you wouldn't be able to tell that looking at the sorry creatures moping around in the blue-grey light that morning. It felt, in fact, like we were all still asleep somehow, or that the sun had never quite risen. Despite the sunlight touching our faces, the world remained dark.

Not until breakfast in the cafeteria did some of the vigor come back to the mad boys of G Hall. I know for a fact, for certain now, though I had a strong inkling then, that whatever had transpired that last night had fouled the hall somehow, and the lot of us along with it. I had nobody worthwhile to share this information with, however, as the rest of the boys gave me a wide berth in both the cafeteria and in life.

All save sweet, stupid Arnold, who plopped down on the bench across from me and dug into his … I think it was porridge … with the steady gracelessness of a half-starved hog. I watched him for a while and saw nothing amiss with him, though he passed me an oddly guilty look I couldn't quite place.

"How are you this morning, Arnold?" I asked. He shook his head and kept to his meal. That would be it for that, then, but his reticence told me all I needed to know.

Mateo limped into view a moment later, dark eyes focused on the floor as he tried to find somewhere to sit without giving away his intentions to do so. I tried to remember if he'd had that limp the night before, when he'd made up his rack above mine, and decided he most definitely hadn't.

I called him over, not bothering to put on a show of false friendship. He saw the invitation and scanned the cafeteria again before settling on joining us. He sat and went to work on his breakfast in much the same manner as Arnold, not bothering to say a single word to me.

"Something strange happened last night," I said, eating my own meal slowly. Mateo stopped, turned his eyes to look at my tray, and then went back to his food. I let the silence linger until he felt he had to answer.

"So," he whispered.

"That was you crying," I said. "I know it was."

I don't know what sort of reaction I expected. I had *hoped* for some outpouring that might explain whatever happened last night. If anything, he was on the top rack and, therefore, able to see a great deal more of the hall than I could.

I can't even tell you why I cared. I *don't* generally care about things. Not anymore.

That ended when they sentenced me to the asylum.

What Mateo *did* do was glare at me, slurp down the remainder of his bowl, and then slam the cheap, thin-walled tin onto his tray before storming off.

I watched him go, dipping my spoon down for another bite of my own food. I hit nothing but the flat surface of my tray. I looked and saw Arnold slurping down the lion's share of my breakfast.

"Goddamn you," I said, flicking my spoon off his forehead. This didn't faze him one bit. I pushed my tray at him and stood to leave. "You clean it up then."

The following days and nights were as normal as one could expect in the asylum. The hall retained that sticky, unclean feeling, but there were no more odd events in the dark. Still, I often heard Mateo startling himself awake in his sleep. His fits would shake the bed and set it to creaking.

I kept on him about whatever it was that had happened that night. There was no real reason for this other than being in the asylum is almost no different than being in prison, and I had nothing else to occupy myself. Our days consisted of little more than being moved from place to place — hall, showers, cafeteria, work — and any break in the monotony was welcome.

But, I can hear you asking, didn't we receive some sort of treatment too? No.

Flatly. No.

And there was no suggestion we would ever receive any.

This was a place where they put young things nobody wanted to deal with, and once we were here, there was no profit in ever seeing us released. Thus, the work detail.

It was on work detail that I finally got Mateo to speak to me. The nasty wounds on his arms, left by Rex's teeth, had healed only for his ankles to be chafed raw by his new leg chains. He'd never had to wear them before, but after a few weeks, he'd gotten the hang of it.

"It's something like, I don't know what," he said suddenly, face dark and fixed on the dirt. His shovel nudged the earth, but didn't break it. I kept working, letting him find his tongue at his own pace. "It comes at night sometimes. Most nights, really, when you live in A Hall." He shuddered. "Kids called it the Ticky-Topper, on account of it gets on you like a tick." He paused. "And how when, once it gets a taste for you, it doesn't want to let go." He said nothing for a long time.

"Is that why you ran?" I asked. He nodded. "You know, I've been in here a long, long time and I never heard about anything like that." His eyes found mine, suddenly sharp and somehow darker. His knuckles turned white on the shaft of the shovel.

"Yeah, well I heard about you," he hissed. "I don't need you telling me what you know and don't know." It was my turn to get angry.

"What have you heard about me?" I asked, voice steady and clear. "Tell me."

"I heard you killed a boy in Blunt," he said, raising his chin. I could tell he was glad to finally have some power, that this little show was his way of holding onto something that could make him feel less helpless. A common, forgivable sin in that place. "I heard why too. I heard that you're a—" I tapped the raw flesh over his ankle bone with the sharp edge of the shovel. Not much, but enough to let him know to be quiet.

"If you finish that sentence," I said. "If you *ever* say that word you've got sitting on the edge of your tongue right now, I will open you like an old coat." He glared at me, but he didn't say a thing. "Capley got the same warning; he just didn't take it."

We went back to working and didn't say anything to each other for a few days.

In the meantime, it came again.

It didn't herald its own coming like the last time, this Ticky-Topper. I woke to the screeching of steel as the rack bucked me gently up and down over my mattress. I again felt that odd, terrible pressure on my chest. Raw, animal panic rose in me as I tried to get my lungs moving at my brain's command. The sheer amount of energy I was trying to use should have shot me face first into the bottom of the rack overtop me, hard enough maybe to brain me unconscious, but I didn't budge an inch.

I could have given myself a heart attack as I desperately tried to move my body, listening to the horrible sounds coming from above me. Instead, the colder, uglier parts of my mind, the ones that had led me to this place, took over and chilled my frayed nerves.

I realized then that I wasn't suffocating, but that my lungs were simply moving slowly. Taking the shallow breaths of someone in a deep sleep.

I'm asleep then, I thought to myself. *Or, at least, my body is asleep and my brain is awake.* Above me, I could hear the sounds of two throats breathing. One of them sounded pained and muffled. The other was louder and making a sort of noise I had no reference for. Though, perhaps, I did.

I focused on trying to wake myself up, thinking of my body in pieces. Once I relaxed, it all seemed to fall into place. I could feel the tips of my fingers, could even move them just a bit. My toes came next, and then I was rotating my ankles and wrists. I felt *it* now, that same sticky, unclean feeling that lay over the hall after this creature's last midnight visit. This invisible stuff was touching all parts of my body, but losing its hold as I worked the life back into my limbs.

I was moving my arms like snakes — only barely cognizant of the noises above me — when I regained control of my lungs. I took a long, sucking, whining breath that filled the entirety of my chest and made my head swim from all the fresh air. It was only a half second later I realized just how *loud* I had been.

The Ticky-Topper stopped moving, and I could hear its wet, raspy breathing above a more familiar sound. Mateo crying. Sobbing, really, and I could tell his face was pressed deeply into something thick and cottony.

I lay perfectly still at perhaps the last possible second before the thing, this Ticky-Topper, ducked down to look at me. I was not prepared for what I saw, and thank God my body was still half-paralyzed, or I might have been so badly startled I would have given myself away. As it stood, I made myself utterly motionless, closing my eyes to mere slits and peeking at it through my eyelashes.

I shouldn't have been able to see much of anything. Unlike that first night, the moon wasn't full and bright. Instead, I saw the glow of the thing's eyes. They burned with cold, orange light, like the embers of a coal fire through smoked glass. Sickly numbness spread over my body as the light of its unearthly vision fell onto my skin, a cousin to the paralysis that had taken me in my sleep.

I dared a glance at the thing as the pool of orange light trailed down my body toward my feet. There was little illumination to see by, as I mentioned, but I could make out some of its features. Enough, at least, to tell this creature was by degrees *based* on a human being. But the proportions of its nose, its mouth, its eyes, they were all wrong. And, to top it off, the positions of the thing's mouth and nose had been switched, so that its mouth gaped open in the center of its head. It moved on a jaw that seemed to be hinged at the back of its skull, and, though I could see little else of that odd apparatus, I could see the teeth. And there were many.

It finished its inspection of me and returned to the top bunk. There were two hard shakes of the bed, and Mateo cried out, his mouth seemingly no longer blocked by whatever had covered it. Then there was an odd thumping and clicking as the thing made its way across the ceiling and out of the hall.

I waited until I was sure it was gone, and then resumed my attempts to get my body back under control. It was slow going, but soon enough I was sitting on the side of my bed and taking long, controlled breaths.

Following this, I stood to make an inspection of

Mateo, wanting to see what the creature had done to him. Hoping, I suppose, that somebody else had experienced this in earnest and I hadn't actually lost my mind.

The boy was curled up on his side, face buried between his knees under the badly twisted bed sheets. Sweat stippled his forehead and soaked the flat, shapeless pillow he'd been given.

I don't know what I did that caused him to look at me, but look he did. His eyes were wide and fearful. Hurt shone in them in a way I'd never seen.

"Are you okay?" I asked, not knowing what else to say.

He hugged me then, his arms wrapping around my shoulders and pulling me close in an instant. It almost knocked the breath out of me.

It was so easy then, in that place, to forget we were children. I had forgotten a long time before that, and the sudden memory of just how young and fragile we were struck me in the heart like a knife. I wrapped my arms around the boy and crushed him against my chest, thinking of the smell of a river in spring. Dreaming in an instant of cool water rushing over my arms and sucking what little heat the sun had given me free of the flesh.

Mateo ran again the next day.

I had slept after all that — I don't know how — and woke to the disjointed sort of screaming one only ever hears in a mental institution.

Like I've said, there are two sorts that came to that

place: Those who were there, and those who *ought* to be there. Of the *ought to be* sort, there were mostly kind and indifferent souls tainted with some malady beyond the comprehension of modern medicine. They saw demons and carried dozens of mad voices in their heads. Some of them were born crooked, in body or mind, and so were trapped in a diminished sort of life where they could barely understand this world, much less live in it.

These latter few, like poor Arnold, didn't take well to stress. Their minds were like houses of cards, awaiting whatever gentle breeze might blow them to pieces. It didn't help that they associated their own outbursts with the inevitable pain of the orderlies' rough and violent suppressions. Memories which only seemed to surface in times like these, and served only to make them more distraught.

I learned to read these moods soon after my incarceration in this place. Like a flock of birds escaping a raptor, you could find patterns in the frenetic movement that would lead you to the cause. Most all of the time it was one of the more ill-treated patients suffering a terrible fit or, if they were new, having one of the customary panic attacks that came when they realized their parents were not — were *never* — coming to pick them up from this place.

This time, it was the second flight of Mateo Jefferson that had caused the commotion. Specifically, it was one of the ward bosses, an orderly named Covington, smacking a truncheon around on the bed frames and screaming for order and quiet while checking under the bottom racks for someone. It took me only a second to realize Mateo had gone, though I thought it strange he was looking here for him. It was like somebody knew he'd fled without seeing it happen.

I saw Arnold sitting between the metal bottoms of his rack on the opposite side of the hall, hands covering his ears while he wept into his lap. I decided I'd had enough of this spectacle and slipped Mateo's pillowcase free of the pillow, crouching and making my way through the thick press of bodies trying to get away from Covington's insane noisemaking. Up close, the sound of the ringing metal seriously hurt my ears, and I could only imagine how badly it bothered the others.

It stopped when I flipped the bedsheet over his head and strangled him unconscious, digging my knees into his back and bracing for the impact of him falling to the floor. That was how they always tried to dislodge you, by falling on top of you like that would somehow break your resolve.

I released him a few seconds after he stopped struggling and then picked his truncheon off the ground, giving him a smart whack on the side of the head with it. I had pulled my punch to avoid killing him, and I was dismayed when I saw him shuffling and snorting back to consciousness. I delivered another *considerably* sturdier blow and was preparing a third when I heard the telltale trundle of Arnold — my sweet, sweet guardian angel — coming up behind me.

I wheeled around on him and pointed the truncheon at his face. The others had grown silent and now watched me or went about their own insane business, muttering to the walls and the like. Arnold gave me a glare that was equally hilarious and horrifying. He had little control over his facial gestures.

"You'll get the rope," he said. "Then that's it. The rope and that's it."

"I'm just helping him get to sleep," I said, giving Arnold a smile that did little to assuage his protective anger. Covington made a noise and then began muttering some ugly little threats under his breath. I turned to see him pushing himself to his feet and smacked him again on the back of the head without hesitation. This strike was loud enough that one of the other patients yelped and began to cry.

I turned just in time to point the truncheon at the space between Arnold's lip and nose. His eyes crossed to look at the thick, black hunk of wood.

"Sleeping," I told him. "You haven't broken any promises." I stepped aside and put my hand by Covington's mouth. The wetness of his breathing sickened me, but I smiled at Arnold and gestured for him to do the same. He did, laughing when he felt Covington's weak, but steady, breath.

"It tickles," Arnold said.

"Yes," I told him, smiling. "Yes, it does." I clapped him on the shoulder and then left for the stairs. I wiped my fingerprints off Covington's truncheon and dropped it down the laundry chute, taking the stairs two at a time until I made it to the common area by the front door. I could hear Rex's happy barking already.

The nurses who typically manned the front entrance were already outside, cracking their knuckles in preparation for beating on Mateo. Mateo himself had new, bloody marks on his forearms and an ugly gash on the side of his face. His hands were bound with manacles and those were bound to Mr. Chifford Lewer's horse.

The beating commenced and I watched from the shadows of the front door. You might like me to say I did something heroic to intercede, but I didn't. I honestly didn't even consider such an inappropriate action. Even when Mateo's sad eyes — well, his sad *eye,* the other was closed shut with swelling — found me in the doorway, I didn't feel any urge to budge.

I only barely noticed anyway; my attention was on Director Prescott and the few orderlies not joining in on the beating. They chatted idly, pointing here and there around the grounds, no doubt congratulating themselves on the capture. All save one of them, who stood between the violence and plaudits, watching Mateo's beating with much the same dispassion as myself, though there was something else there as well. A touch of regret, like he was watching a freshly bloomed flower being crushed under the heel of a boot.

Then Director Prescott got his attention and made something of a show of shaking his hand and clapping him on the back.

Job well done, that look said. More than the man with the dog that had brought the boy back, more than the disciplinarians kicking the last of Mateo's sense out of his head, and more than the other nurses who had searched the wards. *You, in particular. Good job you.*

Good job, Nurse Marco.

I watched a second longer and then returned to Hall G. Covington had apparently woken and left in that time. Perhaps he was too embarrassed to raise the alarm about his assault, or perhaps the alarm never *was* raised. I thought about asking Arnold what had happened with the man after I'd left, but that sweet boy was sitting beside the window and singing one of his nonsense songs to the birds that liked to rest outside the bars. So I left him alone and went back to sleep.

I decided that afternoon, while feeding Mateo his porridge in bed, that I no longer wanted him in this place. It depressed me. I hated it. The self-satisfied looks the other nurses passed each other when I had to wheel him down to the baths or to his therapy sessions made me sick. I say therapy sessions, but in fact Mateo's beating had been severe enough the duty physician demanded to see him at least weekly to ensure he wasn't — or wouldn't become — permanently disabled.

Moreover, this boy had thrown my simple understanding of my new universe completely off track. There were people who were here, and people who *ought* to be here, but now I had to contend with a third option. People who should never have been brought to this place. Creatures for whom this miserable stack of brick and mortar meant nothing but harm, and an absolute harm at that. A wounding that would strike not just them, but also the world, for it would never enjoy the bounty of their presence in it. And I would not allow that beauty to be deprived.

The simplest part of this plan was ensuring his broken leg healed properly, and that he retained the vision in his swollen eye. The cuts the beating had left him I thought would ruin his flesh forever, disfigure him immeasurably. But as the months passed, as fall turned to winter and then to spring, the wounds closed and the scars they left were fairly insignificant.

The nastiest of them was a flat, brown-grey line that crossed his left eye from forehead to cheek. It served only to make him look more roguish, giving his young and beautiful features a decidedly grown-up tilt.

I should remark that, though I'm fairly generous in my compliments to Mateo, I never felt anything like a romantic attraction to him. I loved him, I can tell you that easily, though why I loved him I have some difficulty putting to words. In any case, it should simply be said that we became friends as I nursed him back to health.

And so, we talked a great deal as well. He mostly told stories about his mother and their lives in Morgantown before she died. She was a nice woman, and did her damndest to get him the education she said "he deserved," though he told me he couldn't make heads or tails of what she meant by that. I asked him who sent him here, which of his relatives, and he looked at me with wide eyes.

"Said he was my uncle," he said. "A man named Gulliver." I laughed.

"Was it Gulliver Loeb?" I asked with a chuckle. I had asked as a joke because it was the only name I knew with "Gulliver" in it, though it was frankly impossible. Mateo glared and sat up in his bed, a move that pained him but that he could manage all the same.

"How the hell do you know that name?" he asked. I laughed harder, patting him sympathetically on the leg.

"Are you serious about this?" I asked. He gave me a dark nod. I shrugged and shook my head. "He had some business dealings with my father once upon a time. Dad didn't like him much, but if you're related to him, then your mother wasn't exaggerating with that talk about the 'education you deserved.'"

"He's rich?" Mateo asked, lying back on the pillow.

"His father's rich," I said. "That'd be your grandfather, I suppose. Assuming you're not mistaking who you spoke to, and that I'm not making a mistake either." I sighed. "Maybe you'll get to find out when you're out of here."

"Sure," he said, glumly. "Then. Maybe." Without looking at me, he asked. "Why are you here? You got unknown family let you down too?" I smiled, fixing the simple cotton and wood splint I'd been working on into place. He hissed when it tightened.

"My family did the best they could for me," I said, softly. "I bear them no ill will for putting me here. By all considerations, it's better than what might have been visited on me for what I've done."

"God, you talk weird," he said. I flicked his mending arm and he laughed.

"I fell in love with somebody and they …" I sighed. "*He. He* betrayed me."

"He?" Mateo asked, a touch of concern in his voice. I don't know what I expected from him, but I wasn't offended.

"Yes," I said. "*He.*" I didn't know where to go from there. I considered trying to comfort Mateo, to convince him I wasn't some slinking predator, but I didn't have the strength to perform that song and dance. I finished and lied down in my rack, looking up at the dark underneath where Mateo lay. There was a long silence.

"What did you do to him, that … that boy?" he finally asked. The softest notes of friendship lingered in his voice and I might have cried for hearing them.

"I killed him," I said flatly. "And then someone else, as well." I tested every current of air flowing in that dark hall — that forgotten repository of the mad and dangerous — for any hint of how he'd taken that news. But I could gather nothing. No note of concern, of fear, of surprise, of anything. After a time, breaking with character, I spoke first.

"You're not going to die in here, Mateo," I said softly. "I won't allow it."

"Sometimes I want to, Ezra," he replied almost immediately. "Once I'm fixed up again I know it's gonna come back. The Ticky-Topper. It likes the pretty ones, that's … what it told me." I could hear him sobbing.

Despite myself, I could feel my teeth grinding, and I could smell the soft sweetness of that springtime river in the hills down in Blunt. I could hear them laughing at me again, and I could feel the rock in my hand, clenched so tightly the sharp corners of it cut painfully into the skin of my fingers. And above all that, I could hear *Her* laughing, that tall, spindly creature I'd found in the woods.

The woman-thing that had made such odd plans and predictions for me, asking not a dime or drop of blood in payment.

The Ash Tree. Bellow Legs.

Angie Friday.

The Witchum Woman.

My thoughts turned to that terrifying, spindly creature as I shuffled away from the chain gang the next day. It was the other halls they expected to do the intelligent work, planting and digging furrows in nice, parallel lines. Us in G Hall were given hard earth and shovels to tool around with while the more important work was done down at the further ends of the field. These vital tasks required oversight as well, because the food we grew here was all that sustained us during the year.

As such, it gave me a good deal of time to make my way to the equipment shed.

I thought of Her as I walked, that twisted creature I found in the woods behind my house one day. There had been a squirrel trapped in the cup where two roots joined at the bottom of an oak tree. It was injured to some degree, or sick, I couldn't really tell. I had cornered it with the pointy end of a stick I had sharpened on a rough chunk of old brick I found by the coal shed.

Ours was a nice, large house. Father had made his money organizing the timber trade in the region, selling shoring and support columns to the mines and rail ties to the railroad companies. He also sold and traded whole forests of ash and pine and supplied most of middle West Virginia with the poles they used to hang the power lines across the state. Then the phone lines after that and whatever else men might hang off poles and cross-braces and girders.

I was queer by any standard, and the other children despised me for that and for my father's wealth. As there were no other children in Blunt then that were both odd and rich enough for me to associate with, I began spending long periods alone in the woods. It didn't help that Father liked to speak with his fists and abhorred what my mother referred to as my "soft ways."

But I didn't feel soft. I felt sharp, and ugly, like this stick I was pointing at the little squirrel. I could see its heart railing in its chest, its fur standing on end as its beleaguered lungs beat out the sides of its body. I realized I wanted to kill this thing, just because I could. And that if I did, it would be a little like flipping off a switch to a part of my heart I no longer needed. Not really. Because it was the part for people, and I had no use for them and they no use for me.

Then She spoke.

"You, boy," she said. The suddenness of the voice, and its position directly above me, frightened me enough that I almost dropped the stick. Almost. I gathered myself and looked up until I saw her, a stretched and dangling thing. Her body was like rotten sailcloth that had gotten tangled in the limbs of the tree. What skin I could see — most of her was covered in this black fabric, silk and old leather — was corpse pale and withered like an old woman's.

Her face, above all things, most horrified me. Her jaw flapped when she spoke, as though the bones there were either gone or badly broken, and the entire orifice hung open to enormous proportions. Jagged yellow teeth lined the rims of that gullet, though they looked mostly normal when she smiled and spoke, two things she was doing right then.

"The squirrel asked me to kill you for bothering it so," she said. "But he has little to offer in trade. The lives of squirrels mean little to me, but he knew my name and called me all the same." Her limbs made themselves seen and she slipped through the back branches to wrap herself around the trunk. Her head hung at a slight angle as she spoke to me, her mouth working like a badly strung puppet.

"You know me," she said before I could ask. "Say my name, boy."

"You are the Ash Tree," I said without thinking. "You are Angie Friday, and Bellow Legs." I paused.

"You are Molly Longmouth and Tall Jenny. You are the Widzchum. The Witchum Woman." I stepped away from the tree and the squirrel fled. Angie Friday's face followed the poor thing and I knew she was watching it, even though I couldn't see her eyes. Those were hidden behind dark circles of smoked glass.

"Yes," Molly Longmouth said. Her words were a thousand snakes singing in concert. I fell to my knees, not knowing what to do.

"How do I know all that?" I asked her. She slipped from behind the tree and squatted before me. Her legs were clad in the striped woolen fabric my father wore to work, but also in something else I couldn't wrap my mind around. Something approximating clothing, but in truth was little more than her own natural covering.

A bear's fur. A snake's scales.

"You were born at an odd time, in the heart of my territory," Bellow Legs said. Even kneeling, she towered over me. Her fingers, long and many-jointed, touched my chin. "All the things here belong to me in some fashion, not in the way your father owns the pebbles and stones in that river behind your house. I *own* nothing in these lands, but all *belongs* to me." She smiled, the sides of her mouth curved all the way up to rest beside her eyes, over her cheekbones.

"Are you going to kill me? Eat me?" I asked.

"No," Tall Jenny said, her fingers snaking behind my head. "You are worth more than a meal to me, sweet boy. Of all you own or will ever own, nothing is more valuable to me than the life that you might live." I saw then the milky madness of the eyes behind the smoked glass and my stomach turned. "I would make a deal with thee. Interested?"

"Yes," I said. The answer was true, the Ash Tree

had pulled it out of my deepest heart with little consideration to whatever guile I might possess. It would have been like arguing with my own dreams.

"You will make only one valuable choice in your life," the Witchum Woman said. Her eyes were again hidden. "To fight, to kill, to take, or to simply exist peacefully. If you choose the latter, then you choose the latter. I will take no umbrage. But if you choose the former, you loveless thing, I will ensure you enjoy the taste of love before you die. I will keep you breathing until you fully know that pleasure as a man."

"And all I have to do is fight?" I asked.

"A man who learns to live in violence will never learn another way, even if he lives a thousand years, violence and all her red sons will be ever at his heels and toes," she said, her voice grim. "Do you accept?"

"Yes," I told her, and it was done. The nails of her hand flicked down across my chest and her mark bled slowly, gently through my tattered shirt.

The Hand of Sticks.

Then she was gone. At least, as gone as the Widzchum can ever be gone from the dark and rolling hills of Appalachia.

I touched my chest as I smashed open the lock on the utility shed at the far end of the fields. The building itself was stout brick, but the door was old and partially rotted from poor maintenance. Faded scars remained where she had marked me, so fine and thin against my already pale flesh that only the brightest sunlight might reveal them, but still they were there. Not a constant companion, but rather an occasional, itching reminder. A mostly faded memory that seemed most times more of a passing dream than a living reality.

It itched now, the way nasty things do when they

heal. I scratched at it gently as I broke the weathered hinge-lock and opened the door. Scattered light filled the brick building, pouring more often through cracks and missing mortar than through the door I had opened, though the lion's share came from a metal and glass refraction box set in an alcove on the ridge of the gabled roof. It was simple, dented tin set at angles, and the light it passed inward from the sun lay looped and whorled on the walls, making a series of disks and oddly misaligned circles.

I found what I was looking for at the back of the shed: a pile of blackened rags kept for polishing various bits of metal around the asylum. I thought I even recognized a couple I might have used myself to shine up the handrails in the stairs or the tack on Mr. Chifford Lewer's horse. The rags were kept in a simple slat-sided milk crate with some red paint around the rim, a marking I suppose meant danger. It could also have been the official colors of the dairy farm as well, who knows?

I took a handful of rags and set one of them on the ground. Then I painstakingly rang out each one until the one on the floor had grown damp with used kerosene. I kept near the door during this for fear of knocking myself cold from the fumes, but in the end I had what I'd come for, and not a second too soon.

I could hear Mr. Chifford Lewer humming a song as he made his way to the shed. I heard him grumble as he found the damaged lock, muttering something about "the goddamned kids in this place" and then finding a seat on the stack of crates just inside the doorway. I knew he would be here because I'd seen him come this way a hundred times, and it wasn't any great secret how Mr. Chifford Lewer spent his free time. From my position, just behind him and a few feet back, I could hear him muttering the words to his newest poem under his breath and the faint scratch of his stubby coal pencil tracing letters onto the paper.

"Sweet and tawny beast of the field,"

He mumbled.

"How I wish I could run like you,

To be a horse among the daisies,

Living my life freely and true."

He mumbled something like "that's nice" and might have continued for some time if I hadn't wrapped the kerosene-soaked rag over his mouth and nose. I almost expected it wouldn't work, that his constitution would overpower the oily gas or that the kerosene itself wouldn't work as I'd predicted. I didn't, you see, truly know what to expect. Only by my own uncomfortable interactions with the stuff did I come up with this plan, figuring that if a small amount of it dizzied me — I'd accidentally inhaled a whiff straight off a rag while working — a large amount would for sure have some greater effect on Mr. Chifford Lewer.

What happened was that he screamed once, not a high scream of fear, but the guttural *yawp*. A battle cry that shook me to my core and might have made me let up, if I were a less focused individual. As it was, that scream of his was the last human sound he ever made. I think what had happened was that the kerosene burned his eyes, which caused the scream, but the scream emptied his lungs and so that necessitated a refilling. But what he got instead of clean air was almost pure kerosene fumes.

He coughed and sucked in more in short, panicky breaths. His body rose, easily pulling me off my feet, and then slumped forward onto the ground. My hand protected his face from the impact because of how I was holding him, and was badly scraped on the gravel floor.

I extricated myself with some difficulty and then searched his pockets, hunting for his lighter. I had originally planned to burn him and the shed to the ground, but as I moved him to get a better position to rifle through his jacket, I saw his face. The man was stone dead, no mistaking it. His face had gone a terrible, pale shade of green and there was foam around his mouth. His eyes were open and looking at me.

I thought for a second and then simply placed the kerosene rag in his hand and left the shed, giving a quick look around before stepping into the open. Moira, Mr. Chifford Lewer's horse, was stamping and moaning beside the shed. I knew in an instant she understood he had died, and that she wanted to go to him, *would* go to him, if the fumes from the kerosene weren't so strong.

She passed her baleful eyes over me one last time. Then she walked to the front door of the shed, lying down and quietly looking at her dead friend as I made my way back to the work line.

⚓

I washed myself with wet dirt on the work line,

though only Mateo was close enough to me to smell the lingering kerosene. He'd watched me trundle back into place, chains clinking on the long walk across the yard, eyes wide and trying to find whatever supervisor he believed would strike down from the hills on a horse and club me to death in full view of God and all Creation. It never happened, of course, because the guard staff at the asylum was laughably small on even the best of days.

In fact, with Mr. Chifford Lewer now dead, the outdoor guard had shrunk to about ten in total, with most of those men on different shifts and spread out along the walls on the front of the camp. There was no reason to guard the back of the camp, as it opened onto little more than mountains and the West Virginia wilderness, in which even a sane person would have trouble surviving, much less the mental invalids that made up most of the patient population.

Did that mean people didn't run that way? No, but they always came back dead or alive within a week or so, either wandering in of their own accord or transported by some farmer or woodsman who found them.

But if they ran toward town, the only thing that could stop them was bad luck or Rex, and Rex was nothing more than a sweetheart without Mr. Chifford Lewer's command. And she would never get those commands again.

It wasn't until supper that we were escorted into our rooms and word of what had happened to Mr.

Chifford Lewer spread through camp. Because there was little information, and because what *did* make its way to us in the halls was overly vague, I figured they must have ruled his death a suicide — by misadventure if nothing else.

I imagined Director Prescott finding Mr. Chifford Lewer's book of horse poems and trying to make sense of that. We, and I suppose Director Prescott as well, given the rumors, had thought Mr. Chifford Lewer was going to the shed to masturbate or indulge in some on-the-job drinking. The poetry, I admit, had surprised me.

Mateo pressed me for information, but I rebuffed him, changing the subject quickly.

"I want to sleep in your rack from now on," I told him, giving him a flat look. His eyes became worried and he almost started to stammer. "By myself, you idiot." The boy's almost instantaneous relief irritated me, but only slightly.

"Why?" he asked.

"Because you're getting pretty again," I said, giving him a mean smile and then tossing his pillow into his chest. He took a wide-eyed gulp of air, holding his pillow tighter, and then shook his head and sat on my bed. He passed my pillow up to me and that was that.

It took five or so nights more than I expected for the sinking, sticking, suffocating feeling to wake me. Again my chest felt as though a boulder had been laid atop it, and my arms and legs, though full of feeling, were not my own. Moonlight, bright as that first night, shone into the hall and colored the ceiling a cold shade of blue. Even as my eyes took this in, I saw the first odd shadows moving crossways over the beds.

I made myself calm, moving my fingers free, and my arms, and my legs, but I wasn't doing this quick enough. Unlike the previous visits, this time the thing, the Ticky-Topper, wasn't wasting any time making an entrance. A dull thought surfaced in my mind that maybe it was sick of waiting for Mateo to finish healing.

I could see its limbs this time — the moon was bright enough for that — and I really wish I hadn't. Despite the peculiarities of my disposition, the detachment, my penchant for thoughtless cruelty, despite *all* that, the sheer alienness of it sent my heart to racing. It moved on dozens of irregular arms, all of them swooping and clicking and tapping their ways into the cracks and crevices in the ceiling. Some rested as well on the metal headboards of the racks or the sills and steel furniture of the hall's large windows. None of these perches made so much as a whisper while carrying the thing's weight, most likely because it was so well spread out amongst them. Inside these dozens of ropey arms, at the near center of the mass, was the body of the creature, and the dull orange glow of its eyes passing over the faces of the mad and crippled boys beneath it.

The body made no error in its steady, silent floating. It seemed perfectly suspended amongst the mass of quivering, shifting limbs. Those flicked and flittered to this perch or that, or, failing to find quickly what they were looking for, would instead creep along whatever surface on their odd, three-toed feet, hunting for something to grab. It made me ill to look at, and still I hadn't freed myself of the suffocating, paralyzing feeling this thing's presence induced.

And then it was overtop me.

It touched me before it looked at me, one of its nubby feet sliding under my covers and down my chest. Lower, over my stomach. Lower still. It found what it was looking for and crushed them, a slow, rolling feeling that nearly made me vomit. I whimpered despite myself, and the thing chuckled in my ear. Its breath found me, a wet and sickening breeze that I could feel leaving condensation on my ear.

"Do you like that?" it asked, knowing full well I didn't.

I wasn't in that bed though, but rather the river behind my father's house. My shoes were on the riverbank by some of the other boys, the ones who had been hiding in the bushes before all of this started. And he was standing in front of me — not this creeping thing of nightmares in the asylum — but something far worse.

Something real.

His name was Benjamin, and he was beautiful. Not like Mateo, not that wild and raw sort of beauty, but the man-made and cultivated sort. The sort where every hair is in place and every line and curve seem to have been penned by God as some sort of temptation. That sort of beauty.

I'd made a game for myself of getting closer to him, sure at the start there was no hope of ever getting what I wanted out of it. I knew, my father *ensured* I knew, that my particular desires belonged in no polite society on God's green earth. But what value had that simple stone against the greater temple of a young man's longing?

Nothing. Nothing at all.

And so I was surprised when Benjamin found me out and invited me to the river behind my house for a meeting. He lived just up the street, he said, and so this was the best way for us to rendezvous in secret.

The water in the stream was cool when it should have been cold, and we'd taken our shoes off to stand in the muck there. He had drawn me close, with words at least, and I had gone to him with my heart raging in my chest. I had eyes for nothing but blond hair and blue eyes, and all the rest of Creation be damned.

Then he had smacked me full in the mouth with a wad of stinking river mud, and the boys had leapt out of the bushes to laugh at me. I fell to my knees and saw my own reflection in the slow-moving water of the river. It was a stream, really, but they called it a river. I called it a river.

And in that river I saw a face with no face, just two bright white specks of eyes floating in darkness.

I washed myself clean and grabbed a rock. I stood and struck Benjamin in the side of the head with it, surprising myself when he didn't so much as move. He looked at me, but there was nothing in his eyes. Blood began to pour from the gash I'd left in his head, and he fell, slowly sinking beneath the smoothly flowing water.

A boy pushed me from behind and screamed at me and I leapt on him. I forgot the rock and pushed this nameless face down, down into the dark and the cold. His arms flailed around and his hands slapped my face, tried to claw at my eyes.

I don't remember a thing about how he looked, although they showed a picture of him at my trial. His name was Michael Green and he was about a year older than me, one of Benjamin's closest friends. The one Benjamin might actually have been in love with, if he was that sort.

I drowned him while the other boys screamed on the shore, screamed for help that came far too late. My own father, in fact, thinking he was coming to save me.

I felt now like that boy might have felt then, trapped beneath cold and suffocating pressure. I *was* him, lying on my rack so many years later, looking up into my own face as I hurt myself, orange eyes glowing and my own large and misplaced mouth splitting open to reveal a long and thickly pebbled tongue.

"Did you both think you were clever?" the orange eyes asked, and then I was back again in the asylum. My chest itched. *Burned.* "Switching beds?" Its voice was syrupy and thick, disgusting, like a man drowning in a honey pot. Its orange eyes turned up gleefully at the bottom of its face, or perhaps the top of it. "Now you are mine too, and I will call on you whenever I feel like. Both of you sweet, soft things. You can't hide from me, understand?" He squeezed me and I yelped, forcing myself not to react too soon to this intrusion. To the disgusting feeling of him on me.

He moved his hand underneath me, I need not describe where, and prepared to defile me absolutely. The orange glow of him passed down further, further, off my face and closer to where he intended to hurt me. In that brief second, I slipped my fingers up the sleeve of my nightshirt and inched free my most valuable piece of contraband. I took a deep breath and prepared myself.

"Are you ready for me?" the Ticky-Topper sneered.

"I was ready before you walked in the room," I said. Its eyes widened and turned toward me, clearly not expecting much more than an inarticulate whine.

I buried the makeshift knife, a broken slice of shovel head I'd sharpened in secret over the past few years and bound up with strips of old shirt, into the thing's left eye. It howled and the puke-orange eye spilled onto my sheets, still glowing.

I maintained a good grip on its head — there was some hair I could grab — and I stabbed at it as much as I could. I missed several times, but when I struck home I could feel the thing lurching and twisting in pain. Its arms were individually quite weak, each of them like a subdivision of an adult arm. They swung for me and eventually knocked me back onto the rack, causing my weapon to slip from my hand.

I expected a counterattack, but it didn't come. Instead, I saw the shape of the thing cross two racks and then stumble and fall to the floor. I set myself to regaining control of my waist and hips as it dragged itself toward the communal bathrooms and stairs at the end of the hall. It had made it through the doorway as I rounded off the rack and onto my feet.

"Ezra," Mateo whispered as I landed. Apparently the thing's odd magic had lost its hold on the room. I could hear the others waking as well. I gripped Mateo's hand and then set off for the thing, finding it just a few feet beyond the door.

What I saw happening to it nearly stopped me in my tracks, but only just nearly.

The dozens of limbs on the left side of it were still trying to pull it along, but those on the right side were clicking and popping and snapping together, weaving into each other like lengths of cord making a rope. Suddenly, I was looking at the fully formed arm of a human being, white and thickly muscled, but covered as well in dozens of cuts that started and stopped abruptly as though they had begun in one place and ended in another, with no connection to be found between them.

It turned and I saw its misshapen head performing the same magic act, cracking sideways and then closing so that the mouth and nose and eyes aligned the way you'd see on any human face. The remaining eye still glowed dull orange, but it had shrunk to the size of a normal, adult eye. And so I could recognize the owner.

It was Nurse Marco, of the ward that Mateo had transferred out of. The revelation was meaningless to me. This was all coincidental to what I had planned.

His shirt lay unbuttoned on his chest and would have fallen completely away had it not been pinned in place by my knife. When I pulled the blade free, a torrent of blood came with it. Marco made some sort of plea I could only barely hear, much less pay attention to. My eyes were fixed on the pale symbol carved into his chest.

The Hand of Sticks, I thought, bending down to touch it. It was the same shape and relative size as mine, though rougher and clearly self administered. A curious addition to an already curious night. My own shirt had been ripped to pieces during the earlier fray — it was a very cheap and flimsy material — and he could see that same mark on my chest. His eyes were wide and confused.

He tried to ask me a question, but I started slitting his throat, and that threw him off some. He slapped at me with the rapidly weaving threads of his left arm and even his leg, trying to keep me from finishing the job. The hunk of sharpened shovel steel made a fair puncture, but was terrible for cutting. It took me several minutes to finish sawing down to his bone, and at that point I surrendered the effort. All the while, his now human hands made feeble attempts to push me away, rubbing over my face and neck and chest.

Finally finished, I stood, breathing heavily and letting the din of the hall fill my ears. It had been there all along, but the moment between Marco and me had been so intimate, so intense, I had gone temporarily deaf. "Ezra," Mateo said. He was standing behind me.

"Those who are here fall into two camps," I said to him, tossing away the all but ruined steel. I put my hands on his shoulders and smiled. "Those who are simply here …" His eyes were horrified beyond anything I'd ever seen. I inwardly hoped he could forgive me for what I'd exposed him to one day, and pulling him close, laid a single, bloody kiss on his forehead.

"And those that ought to be," I told him, letting him go and stepping back, leaving my bloody handprints on his neck and shoulders. "It's time for you to go, Mateo. I'm going to go downstairs. You wait a bit, and then make a run for the front gate. Hop a train to anywhere and figure things out for yourself, okay?" He nodded.

"Thank—" he tried to say, but I shook my head.

"Don't thank me," I told him. "Somebody like you, it might make you sick someday to remember how you thanked me for this." I sighed, tilting my head and smiling at him one last time. "Thank *you*, Mateo. And goodbye."

I walked downstairs and into the main hall where some of the night shift were already congregating, asking each other where all that noise was coming from and what they should do about it. One by one, their eyes fell on me and they went silent. I raised my arms out to my sides, letting them get a good look at me. Disheveled, bloody, and with my eyes closed and face toward the sky, they fell on me.

The beating felt like nothing, nothing at all, though I suspected it might kill me. And, if it didn't, perhaps the rope in the gatehouse at the West Virginia State Penitentiary in Glory finally would. Poor, sweet Arnold was upstairs and unable to remind me of that at the moment.

But it didn't matter. As I lay on the ground, arms still out to my side and with two full grown men standing on each, I raised my eyes again and saw Mateo Jefferson standing in the back hallway, wings wide and ready for flight. I smiled at him, despite my broken teeth and closing eyes, and he nodded at me.

Then he was gone, and all the world was darkness and pain. But in the black center of my worthless heart lay the face of Mateo Jefferson, and I accepted that the strange and awful creature's deal had come true.

The Witchum Woman had paid in full, and before the end, in that deepening numbness, I had known love.

Love, sweet love.

THE END

CARRIER

He felt a moment of clarity in the fog, a woman's eyes catching his across the visual din of the bar. It was accidental, brief, but the effect was like teeth catching in a slipped bike chain. His mind hitched, spun, and dragged him up from the alcohol mists and back into the bar. His drink was gone. The seat beside him was empty. "Carl?" he asked, looking around. His brain tried to put the scene together, to get him back on track. There was a receipt on the bar, which he picked up and looked over. About twenty drinks split between the two of them and a stack of small bills on the paper for the tip. "Ah, fuck."

"Your friend left," the bartender said, gathering up the cash. Ollie swiveled to see the guy, trying to focus with one eye. The bartender was many. He handed Ollie a drink. "He closed out *for* you; you're cut off after this one. It's from her down on the end." He pointed and Ollie followed the finger to where the girl had been, the one that had looked at him. Her eyes had been…

Ollie took a sip of the drink — a fruity, colored thing not at all his speed — and shook his head. He put it down on the bar and raised a hand.

"I think I've had too much," Ollie said. There was more clarity in the world now, but only just a bit. "I need to get home."

"Whatever," the bartender said, pulling the drink off the bar and dumping it in the sink. Ollie listened to it swirl away and then stumbled off the bar stool. The crowd had dwindled some since he'd gotten there, but it was still thick enough he had to fight his way out the door. Ollie wasn't a big guy. Crowds were a pain.

Cigarette smoke colored the air dull grey outside the door, clinging longer than usual to the chill, motionless October air. He lit a cigarette of his own — an almost tasteless Marlboro Ultra Light — and leaned against the exterior bricks of the bar. Cold prickled his skin, dragging him further up out of the boozy stupor he'd been in just a second ago. The houses on the opposite side of the street were festooned in orange and black decorations, pumpkins and black cats and the like.

He finished the cigarette on the walk, turning his coat up against the wind and looking behind him more than a few times when he thought he heard something. It always turned out to be leaves, but that didn't much take the edge off. He still lived near campus, despite having graduated nearly four years ago, and muggings were on the rise now that it got dark early.

Then he turned around and did see something that nearly made him jump out of his skin. A woman, or maybe a short man, was standing in the middle of the road in some ridiculous Halloween costume. A black cape with a high-peaked collar that completely obscured the figure beneath. The sight was startling enough it froze him in place for just a second. Then he was looking around in the bushes near him for kids with a camera. The news was full of stories of teenagers hurting themselves and others trying to copy the pranks from that Jackass show on MTV.

"Real fuckin' funny, asshole," he yelled at the person. They stood beneath a street light not really in the center of the street, but sort of off to the side where a car might usually be parked. There was some movement as the cloaked person raised their hands over their head, pushing the fabric of the cape upward and making a black splotch of a silhouette against the streetlight.

"Fuck *you*," Ollie whispered under his breath, turning and shoving his hands in his pockets. The night was colder than he expected, almost bitter. Cutting. He should have bit the bullet and taken a taxi or something. Walking faster, he could feel the wind cut deeper into his skin. He wanted to walk backwards, but he was worried about looking weird in front of the kids that may or may not be hiding in the bushes with cameras and laughing at him.

He looked up and froze, not really noticing the wind anymore. There was another person in the same stupid cloak ahead of him now, again beneath a streetlamp. He looked around and found a fairly well-lit alley that cut through to the street he lived on, Lawrence Avenue. The alleyway was still several blocks up from his house, but it'd put a solid wall of buildings between him and this crew of assholes.

The person in the cloak raised their hands up again and he shook his head, ducking into the alley without a second thought and starting into a light jog. He tucked his chin and cheeks into the neck of his hoodie to warm himself, trying to ignore the hairs standing on the back of his neck.

If those kids want to shoot me running away like a chickenshit, then fine, he thought to himself. He heard a scratching in the alley behind him, turning to see the cloaked person standing just a few yards away beneath a motion-control light that had clicked on when he'd passed a second ago. It raised its hands slowly, or, not its hands but something else. This close, the black fabric looked thicker, far more substantial, and darker than simple cloth. Something more like leather.

Something slightly wet.

The light clicked off.

Ollie turned and ran, hearing and sort of seeing the light click back on behind him. Then there was a noise unlike anything he'd ever heard, the rasp of something powerful sliding quickly along the ground. A rush of air accompanied it, blowing up a gust of leaves that crashed into Ollie's face. It brushed his leg as well, nearly knocking him off his feet. He caught his balance, lost it, and then tripped over a stack of flattened cardboard boxes. He landed on his knees, hissing when the rough concrete shredded through his jeans and into his skin.

Then he saw it, laying formless over the cracks and pebbles like a puddle of half-dried sealing tar. It was black, deeply black like silk or space or something else. He couldn't make sense of it. It rose from a pile of leathery, wet flesh too loose and formless for anything with bones. Rose and pushed and pulsed until it was standing, tall and almost maddeningly two dimensional before him.

It assumed the shape he'd seen, looking like a person inside a cloak. And he *could* see something vaguely human in the shapes before him. The contours of an eyeless skull, the lines of fingers. Other shapes and shadows that were both familiar and then maddeningly, horrifyingly, impossibly wrong a moment later.

Ollie pushed himself to his feet, wincing when he felt how badly he'd skinned his knees. He raised his hands, not knowing what he was seeing, not knowing how to defend himself from this strangeness. It was still growing and stretching even higher over a thin bit of framework that might be hands. A last, foolish part of him was still holding out hope that a group of industrious teens were about to jump out of the bushes and laugh.

"Please," he said, not knowing what else to say.

The thing burst open, tearing top to bottom and casting its wavering flesh to the entire width of the alley. Ollie saw wet viscera shining like the pearlescent interior of a seashell. Light caught and danced in the thin scrim of mucous along this membrane and then exploded in rolling brilliance into Ollie's eyes. Pulse after pulse of magnetic rainbow illumination, tearing into his mind, into his thoughts.

He turned and vomited and stumbled away from the lightshow, trying to crawl on his hands and knees. Something like a hand dragged him back by his ankle. He screamed and kicked at it, feeling a give and hearing something almost like a scream. He looked to aim another kick, to finally free himself, and caught another full dose of the light in his eyes.

This time he felt it filling his mind, pushing all the furniture up against the walls to clear space for something more. He tried to backpedal away, managing only to push himself onto the pile of cardboard. Then the thing fell on him, engulfing him in this electric light show. He tried to push it away, tried to claw at the translucent material flickering all around him. Deadening him.

He saw something like a face in that madness, again the smooth and almost human shapes of cheekbones and eye sockets. This thing was only inches from him, as much there as not. An illusion in a mad rainbow.

It stabbed him.

Ollie screamed, clutching at the barb now buried in the right side of his abdomen, feeling the slick hardness of it as his own blood seeped up around the wound. Then a cold burst of ecstatic confusion rushed into his system, washing over his brain and crushing what was left of his consciousness. The stinger pushed deeper inside his abdomen. Pain pulled Ollie out of his stupor and another surge of chemical euphoria pushed him back down, held him under like a riptide.

Then the numbness was complete, and he could do nothing but push into the rubbery flesh around him, trying in vain to scrape through it with his stubby fingernails. He felt his eyes rolling back into his head.

He was dying, he thought, letting the numbness take him now, letting go entirely. The worst part was he liked the feeling of it. In a sick, nonsensical way, he liked it.

He liked it.

Ollie woke in the pile of flattened boxes the next morning, his breath a light fog over his eyes. Pain in the right side of his torso dragged him out of a cottony deep sleep. He touched the wound he found gingerly, wondering how he could still be alive, and then lay back on the boxes. Maybe he was dying, and it just hadn't quite taken yet. He looked at his hand and saw a mix of tacky blood — his — and some indefinable goo. A clearish sort of mucous he wiped away on the boxes.

He didn't have the courage to look at the wound yet, but it felt bad. Bad not just because it was fairly large, the size of his thumb at least, but bad because it was already closed over. Bad because his guts weren't spilled out of his abdomen and laying out in the street. Bad because there was something hard and tight beneath the surface of his skin, and he could feel it moving, if only a little.

"Why?" he asked the sky, and the sky said nothing.

Eventually, Ollie pushed himself to his feet. Nothing remained of the shrouded, flickering thing that had attacked him save the blood on his shirt and the boxes. The boxes, he noticed, had been shredded to pieces here and there and packed in tightly around him like a sort of nest. If he'd laid there unconscious without it, he might have succumbed to the cold. But he hadn't.

Ollie looked at the outline of himself on the cardboard and then fell to his knees and puked. The color was all wrong, brown and red, flecked with chunks of something black. The sight of it made him puke again and again until there was nothing left, leaving him to collapse, shuddering, against the wall.

Ollie decided against just giving into hypothermia and started walking toward his house down the block. He clutched his arms above his elbows, trying and failing to return some lost warmth that now seemed forever gone. He tried not to let people see his face, either, though he didn't know why. Maybe, he thought, they'd have seen him sleeping in the alley. Maybe, he thought, they knew what had happened.

Maybe, he thought, they'd laugh at him.

Surely, he knew, they wouldn't understand.

Ollie stopped in front of the stately old brick building where he rented one of the upstairs apartments with his girlfriend, Allie. She would be worried about him, and probably more than a bit pissed off. He was supposed to be home probably two hours before … well, before what had happened, happened. Now it was mid-afternoon on a Wednesday. He swallowed.

He nearly jumped out of his skin when a jogger he hadn't noticed brushed by him, already yards away by the time Ollie could turn and look. The man was wearing sweatpants and an oversized hoodie with the arms cut off, but the shape of him as he ran off down the street was enough like the thing to make Ollie feel unsettled. He looked up where his apartment was — where Allie might be right now furiously watching some trashy reality TV show and waiting for him — and thought better of it. He turned and walked down

     CARRIER

the street to find something to eat.

*

Ollie finally settled on a down-home style fried chicken diner about ten blocks from where he lived. He'd been there with friends one time while they were drunk. They'd all hated the food and Allie never talked about the place, which made it perfect in his mind. He wouldn't run into anybody he knew, and nobody would remember him.

He barely made it inside. Pain from the wound had grown to unbearable levels as he walked, rising from a dull ache to a constant stabbing that made him grit his teeth. He was thankful, at least, that he'd worn a dark concert t-shirt the night before, because the blood didn't stand out against the black fabric. Thankfully, as well, the thing hadn't stabbed through his hoodie, so he zipped it up tightly.

"Good morning, hun," the waitress said, only partially paying attention to him. She was a hefty, middle-aged woman wearing jeans and a tight black t-shirt. He kept his head down and ordered, having to repeat himself when the woman said she couldn't hear him, "For all his mumbling." He apologized and walked through his order again, hating the sound of his voice and wondering if people were looking at him. When the lady was gone, he glanced around and saw the restaurant was mostly empty, and the few customers had their own business to mind.

The order was coffee, chicken, and waffles. Normally a meal that size would have him requesting a to-go box by the end. Instead, he found himself asking for seconds, though he got milk instead of coffee on the second go. All the eating made him feel better, a little giddy even, though he still didn't like the thought of people seeing him.

"Baby, are you okay?" the waitress asked him when she brought his check over. He pulled out his wallet quickly to show her he had money, thinking that was what she was about to ask him. He looked like shit, he knew — he had to — but he'd hoped he didn't look like some dine-and-dash junkie.

"I'm fine," Ollie mumbled, hesitating for a bit. "Sorry if I don't look it."

"Sorry?" the woman asked. "You didn't do anything wrong. And you can put most of that cash back, hun, the bill was only ten bucks." Ollie looked down at the cash he'd thrown on the table. Nearly fifty dollars, all the cash he had left after a long night of drinking. His mind wandered to Carl and where his friend might have gone the night before. Something caught in his chest and he almost hiccupped, then he realized he was sobbing.

"Hun, do you need help?" the woman asked softly. He looked up and saw the concern on her face. She wore simple, wire-frame glasses with a neck chain that made her look comically older.

"I'm fine," Ollie said, tucking some of the money back into his wallet. He looked at the empty plate on the table. "Just … just a little sick I think."

"You sure?" she asked, and this time she touched his shoulder with the barest tips of her fingers. The reaction was like a lightning bolt, coursing all the way through him. He stood sharply and backed up against the wall, taking a deep breath. The few other patrons looked over at them now, mostly just curious. Ollie couldn't take his eyes off his shoes. There was a spot of dried blood on the right rubber toe cap. So small probably only he could see it.

Because he knew where to look.

"I'm sorry," the woman said. "I didn't mean…"

"It's okay," Ollie said, pushing past without touching her. "It's fine."

✤

He walked — not really knowing where to go — finally deciding on a corner gas station where he knew there was a single-person bathroom with a door that locked.

He felt like a criminal, keeping his head down and his hood slightly up, though the attendants paid him no mind. The dozen or so customers in the place were all lined up at the counter. Ollie glanced at each of them individually, not knowing why, just understanding that he needed to.

He had to wait the better part of five minutes for his turn in the bathroom. A legitimate heroin addict took the stall before him, and Ollie waited out the soft sounds of the man getting his fix. Little drips of water and the flick of a lighter's flint wheel. Tapping. A sigh. Eventually, the man stumbled out, and Ollie flitted in and locked the door behind him.

The air smelled like whatever the previous occupant had shot up with, alongside the usual stink of piss and pine-scented air freshener. Ollie took off his hoodie and hung it over the horizontal hand bar beside the toilet before looking himself over in the mirror. It wasn't good. It was, in fact, quite awful.

There were bruises on his face he didn't remember getting, as well as a heavy purple mark on his neck that looked like some sort of bite. One where teeth hadn't broken skin. Smears of blood covered his face and chest, though they had dried to the color of dirt and mostly faded. His skin was grey with exhaustion. He looked older than his mid-20s for sure.

The band T-shirt was ruined. A loose, ragged hole in the fabric hung like a broken jaw. The skin beneath was so blackly bruised it almost didn't seem like the shirt had a hole in it, or maybe that he was wearing an undershirt. He pulled the clothing off, wincing and bending his torso to keep from irritating the wound.

The hole was hideous, though not as bad as he'd expected. Not as bad as it should be, at least. The puncture looked puckered shut, like an asshole that'd been super-glued closed. Blood smeared the skin down to and past his hips, and had soaked his jeans in a rust-red crescent that spread all the way to the top of his right pocket. The denim was crusty to the touch.

Worst of all was the area around the puncture wound. It was swollen and bruised fully black in a circle bigger than his hand. A hard bit the size of a softball sat beneath raised flesh, and more bruising spread sideways across his stomach and hips in slender, horizontal splotches of light purple. They looked almost like clouds at sundown.

He touched the opening gingerly, using just the tip of his right forefinger. The reaction was immediate, intense pain and a sudden feeling of dizziness that threatened to drop him to the floor. Then, worse — much worse — he could feel *it*. Something *inside* him. It twisted inside the softball sized mass in his stomach, clenching and unclenching itself. Wriggling.

The sensation was too much. Ollie dove for the toilet and prepared to puke up the massive breakfast he'd just eaten. He only managed to dry-heave there for a long time, stomach bucking until tears came to his eyes, producing nothing more than a stream of hot bile.

There was nothing left in there. Not a goddamn thing.

Allie was waiting inside the archway to the kitchen when he finally stepped through the front door of their apartment. Her arms were crossed, and her hair floated in a messy ball over the soft folds of a thin, pink sweatshirt.

"Where were you?" she asked, voice softer than her eyes. He looked around the room, not knowing what to say. "I called Carl. He said he hadn't seen you since last night." Ollie cleared his throat, said nothing, and then walked into the kitchen.

"Are you serious?" she asked. She never raised her voice — at her loudest it was as still and scratchy as a fresh needle on an old record. He grabbed a drink of water at the sink and finished it in a gulp. Then another. Another. She followed him to the sink, pushing him lightly on the shoulder. Her eyes were more serious now, and he could see the bags underneath them.

"Something happened," he muttered, looking into the sink. Dots of water lay still on the aluminum catch basin, throwing back his distorted reflection. Only the barest swatches of color. His shirt. His hair. His skin. Idly, he thought these things would be how they identified him in the alley if things had turned out differently. He would have been Male, Brown Haired, Fair-Skinned, until the police dug out his wallet.

"What?" she asked. He could tell by her tone she already had an entire story in her head, start to finish. Something she'd been working on between episodes of Pimp my Ride and Charm School. "Who is she?"

"I don't know," Ollie said, surprising himself with the answer. It felt simultaneously correct and was also not at all what he'd wanted to say. He tried correcting himself, but Allie was already pushing him, tears spilling onto her cheeks.

"You motherfucker," she all but whispered.

"It's not like that," he said, grabbing the counter to keep from falling. Allie was actually something of an athlete back in high school, and still retained most of the muscle and all of the assertiveness. She worked shit hours as a paralegal at the same law firm where he was a janitor. It was how they met.

"Who *is* she?" Allie said, pushing him again. He was crying now too, feeling sick and hot-skinned. Slick. He grabbed her arms, trying to hold her back, trying to say what had happened.

"It's not *like* that, Allie," he said. She jerked free of his grasp and pushed him again, but low in the belly this time. The pressure on the thing in his abdomen created a riptide of pain that buckled his knees and dropped him to the floor. His vision went grey for a moment. When he came to, he realized he was lying on his side on the ground, curled up around the nasty little lump and howling with pain. Allie was standing over him, eyes the same shade of horrified you give to a homeless person screaming at God in a pet store window.

"I can't breathe," Ollie said. It was mostly true.

The breaths came in gasps. Short, little puffs that he couldn't quite keep down. Allie held her hands out overtop him, her fingers wriggling the way they did when she was trying to think fast.

"Are you … are you fucking with me, Ollie?" she asked.

"No," he said between breaths. He tried to get off the floor, but only succeeded in rolling onto his knees. His forehead stayed plastered to the kitchen linoleum. He could feel the voids between the material and the decking beneath, sticking and unsticking on ancient glue every time he moved his head. The surface smelled like feet and water, with a lingering scent of some lemon cleaning agent.

He gagged.

"Jesus Christ, Ollie," she said. He could see she had the phone in her hand. "I'm calling for an ambulance."

"No," he whispered, but she didn't hear him. He could barely unclench his jaw to speak. He fell onto his side again, and when that sent another shockwave of pain through his body, he rolled onto his back. He could see Allie worriedly pacing the kitchen as he lay — dying maybe — on the linoleum. He could feel specks of dirt sticking to his cheek and thought absently that they really needed to sweep in there.

"They're on their way," she said, hanging up the phone. "Is this where it hurts?" She placed a hand over the sweaty fist he'd made over the wound and he nodded. "Please let me see, Ollie."

"Attacked," he said, barely holding onto his senses. "… in an alley by the bar …" He felt the strength flooding out of his muscles then, out of his mind. It was like his sense of self was a tide that had just then receded from the sands of reality, leaving only a sort of fog. The smell of memory. Dead things and their empty homes. Shells. Billions of them. Smashed into the sand until the sand they became.

Listless. Lost. Floating at the edge of eternity in a ball of black cloth. The stars passing in gentle circles around him. The cold of space not really cold, but an absence of heat and presence so deep it stole the heat of the soul. Leaving him dead and floating in that sea of blackened death. Searching for a shell.

Searching for the shore.

"Oh my God," she said. The sound of her voice pulled him out of the dream like a string had been threaded into his empty eyesockets. Then he could see again. The kitchen ceiling was covered in terrible, yellowed wallpaper that was the exact same pattern as the linoleum. The previous tenants had smoked, he remembered. He couldn't move his arms or legs, though he desperately needed to. The pain was unbearable, and somehow not being able to curl up around it made it worse.

"Ollie, what happened?" Allie asked. Her face was a swimming mass of light and dark, utterly without contrast, just shadows and highlights and the blurred borders between those areas. Her voice sounded like a tin drum being smashed with old circular saw blades and wooden mallets. Coming in. Coming in. Coming in.

The image of his girlfriend resolved itself, and he could see the horror on her perfectly normal, perfectly human face. His hand moved now too, though only with great effort, as though his brain were screaming to get the signal to reach.

"It got me … in the alley," he said. "I don't want to talk to the police."

"The police?" she said, her face screwing up in

confusion. "What do you mean, 'It'? You said you were with some girl."

"Was I?" Ollie said. He breathed still in small, short bursts. Little gasps of air that felt like they were passing through cotton. "It was beautiful. Like fireworks. It hurt me."

He wakes up a couple times in the back of the ambulance, and then on an operating table. The room around him is empty and his clothes are gone. There is a great disk of light floating over him, the surgical lighting apparatus. Beyond this petty internal sun is the faded grey chalk paleness of the ceiling, which he can see is made of white, plastic panels. Dimples along these panels cast conical shadows, all of which point toward the light floating over him.

He sits up and looks down his chest to where a simple piece of white paper covers his genitals. The sparse hair on his chest and stomach have been shaved bare, leaving only dots of stubble. A series of black dotted lines and nonsensical symbols are drawn on the flesh over the lump the thing had left inside him. They encircle and criss-cross, terminating at the puckered entry wound.

He can see it moving inside, writhing, tiny little claws nicking the surface of his skin. Pressing until the flesh is pushed to a high thin point.

Then the skin splits and slips down over the claws, leaving blood to trickle away from the wound at a steady pace. One claw, two claws, five, eight, ten. His stomach is growing a mouth of nasty little viper fangs. The pain is enormous. Then there are eighty, ninety of these little claws, all arranged in a circle that shifts suddenly, tearing a great disk of his flesh loose. And then the claws are moving out onto him, and the thing that pushes itself free is draped in his intestines, chewing the half-digested shit out of his bowels and letting it drip over the white paper covering his groin. Its eyes are like the spaces between stars. It moans and looks at him.

He screams.

⚓

"Son, settle *down*," the doctor said. Ollie can only barely see him; he is still half in the dream. Orderlies and men in other uniforms are holding him down against the bed. There is something vaguely military about everything, even the cotton of his new clothes is heavy, stiff, and uncomfortable. The doctor grabs him by the chin and makes their eyes connect. "Calm down, Olliver."

He does this time, taking a great many breaths and blinking and looking around his new surroundings. He is in a single-occupant hospital room, the kind he watched his Uncle Matthew die in when he was six. There was a table, a few chairs, and the complicated plastic bed where they'd laid him. An oblong curtain rod hung over and around him, but had been pulled back behind the headboard. The men surrounding him had the grim, professionally bored expressions he associated with cops and other professional trigger-pullers.

"There we go," the doctor said. "How are we feeling? A touch confused, I wager?"

"Yes," Ollie said. "Where's Allie? Where am I?"

"The hospital, of course," the doctor said.

"What hospital?" Ollie asked.

"Your friend, unfortunately, couldn't come along with you," the doctor said. "I understand you're in a relationship, but, unfortunately, you aren't married, so she's not allowed to visit. Just yet, at least."

"Who are you?" Ollie asked.

"Doctor Jeffrey Crabbe," he said, holding out a hand. Ollie shook it, noting the rubber medical gloves. He could see the man's knuckle hair coiled beneath the translucent white like snakes. "I'm the head of a, well, a special cases department here at the hospital. I've been tasked with overseeing your … situation … after it was transferred to us by your local doctor."

"Local?" Ollie asked. He touched the ball in his stomach. It had grown. "I thought you'd taken it out of me. I remember an operating table."

Doctor Crabbe raised an eyebrow, looking at some of the other men in the room as if to confer with them. The lot of them remained silent and placid, almost frozen in place. They'd let go of his limbs now that he'd stopped thrashing, but remained close.

"You *were* on an operating table earlier this week, yes," Doctor Crabbe said.

"This week?" Ollie asked.

"*Fortunately,* operations were … *stalled* when the doctors at your local ER noticed the … *ahem* … *uniqueness* of the surgery they were about to undertake," Doctor Crabbe continued. "Your little passenger down there, son, is incredibly valuable."

"Passenger?" Ollie asked.

"Yes," Doctor Crabbe said. He made a shooing

motion and the orderlies cleared the way for him. A female nurse wearing gloves and a surgical mask dragged up a heavy-looking machine cart made of the white plastic ubiquitous to hospital equipment. She flicked a series of switches and the thing slowly came to life, sounding like an asthmatic office printer.

Then she pulled up Ollie's shirt and squirted a cold gob of gel on his stomach. He hissed, but she didn't seem to notice. She, instead, rubbed something that looked like a combination electric razor and computer mouse over the ball in his stomach. It was terribly uncomfortable, and he found himself bracing for an onset of the painful shockwaves he'd experienced when Allie had pushed him.

Allie. He needed Allie here right now; she was all he had. His parents were trash, junkie fuck-ups who split their time between the highway underpasses downtown and single-wide trailers out past the 264 loop. All he'd had was his uncle and his aunt, and he'd lost them both by the time he was in his late teens. Just in time for him to not wind up in some fucked up group home, but that was the best he could say for himself. But he'd had Allie through most of that.

He wanted her here.

"There we go," Doctor Crabbe said, moving the nurse aside. She stumbled out of the way, but kept the weird mouse-razor thing in place. Ollie nearly puked when Doctor Crabbe turned the monitor in his direction and pointed to the swirling black and white figures on the screen. "Do you see here and … here?"

"No," Ollie said, his voice low and horrified. The shapes were terribly apparent, curled up into a ball beside each other. Even though they weren't really human shaped, he could see what they were perfectly. Beyond and about them, something like a tight sac rested against the ghosts of his intestines.

"Ok, well, what you're seeing is…"

"No!" Ollie yelled, reaching down and slapping the ultrasound device out of the nurse's hand. She yelped, jelly splattering across the front of her scrubs and the plastic handheld device clattering along the floor at the lengths of its wire tether. Even Doctor Crabbe looked taken aback.

"Now, son, I know this must be fairly extraordinary news," he started, raising a hand. The heavies around the table — the large male orderlies and the men with the unfamiliar uniforms — took a step forward, but Doctor Crabbe stilled them with a snap of his fingers. "I know this must be fairly extraordinary news, *but*, it is very much a good thing. Both for you and for this country."

"What the fuck are you talking about?" Ollie all but yelled. "It's *inside* of me. I don't want it there. I don't even want to see pictures of it."

"Mr. Combs," the doctor said, but Ollie continued.

"Why are we *still talking?*" he gasped. He could feel the things inside him shifting. He knew there were *things* now. Plural. He wanted to fucking die, but more than that, he wanted them gone. "Cut them the *fuck* out of me." There was a jolt of pain, and he realized it was the creatures reacting to his agitation. The thought made him sick, as though he could feel any more ill than he already did at the moment.

"I'm sorry, son, but we can't do that," Doctor Crabbe said, folding his hands. The nurse had retrieved the ultrasound device and was now cleaning it with a blue paper towel. When she squirted more of the nasty petroleum jelly on Ollie's stomach, he could sense outright animosity in the sheer amount she used.

"This is … in short, a *miracle,*" Doctor Crabbe said. Ollie just looked at him. "*The* miracle, in fact, of *life.*" Ollie shook his head in disbelief. The doctor continued without pause, pointing at the eel-like forms squishing over one another in the display. They were fairly immobile, on second view, and Ollie realized what he was seeing was a heartbeat.

"These creatures have *no* analogue on Earth, Mr. Combs," Doctor Crabbe said. Ollie could see some glee in the man's eye. "This is an entirely alien species to this world, never before seen. And — it should be said — I understand your discomfort and unease at hosting these life forms—"

"You understand?" Ollie almost shouted. The heavies moved closer without Doctor Crabbe's order, flooding the space around the hospital bed like so many Nazgul. "There is something fucking *growing* in me and I *want it gone.* What the fuck is the hang—" He'd grown too agitated and the pain surged, shocking the rest of the words out of his throat. The heavies exchanged glances, wordlessly wondering whether this deserved some intervention on their part. Crabbe opened his mouth to say something, but the nurse hurriedly tugged on his sleeve, pointing to the monitor. He turned to it and they conversed in hushed voices, hitting buttons on the machine until it spat out a yard of information on what looked like drugstore receipt paper.

"*Miraculous,*" Doctor Crabbe said, turning back to Ollie. He took a breath and continued talking. "I don't use that word often, you know, I'm a man of science. It's rare to come across a true miracle, and I consider life one of those. Babies are sacred, you understand. Blameless creatures. Innocents. And there is no greater sin in the eyes of God than to hurt an innocent.

"These creatures are no less innocent than any baby, son, you must understand that. I understand your … conception of them must have been fairly traumatic. Your, erm, *live-in girlfriend* told the paramedics that picked you up that you'd been attacked. Her understanding was that your injury was a badly infected stab wound.

"The truth is, you were struck with something akin to an ovipositor, a mating tube that forcibly pushes the larva of one species into a birth host. Either a creature of that species, or another. It's not without analogue on earth. In fact, there are several forms of parasite, wasps in particular, that breed with this method."

"Parasites," Ollie said. He was getting sick. So desperately now that he wanted to just live over a toilet and puke out his guts until he died. He was still waiting to wake up, to be honest. This might only be a second layer of dreams. A deeper sheet of nightmare laid over him while he slept away a fever in some better place.

"Oh, don't think of these creatures that way," Doctor Crabbe said, pointing again to the screen. "They are certainly parasitic in their reproduction method, but the setup of their prenatal environment inside … *you* … is quite remarkable. They have their own amniotic sacs that have attached to the fascia inside your torso. These umbilical structures here and here are siphoning nutrients and, incredibly, excreting waste materials directly into your kidneys. You will have to drink a lot of water."

Without looking at Ollie, the doctor stood before the display, shaking his head.

"What I'm trying to get at is that these unborn

children won't hurt you," the doctor said. "There will be some fairly extraordinary discomforts, of course, but no permanent or even lasting injuries, I believe. We'll monitor the gestation like any other atypical pregnancy, just in case they start having an undue effect on your internal organs." Ollie just looked at the man, not knowing what to say.

"I want it out," he said. "I don't care about … *anything* you just said. Fuck miracles. I want them out."

"Them, meaning the babies," Doctor Crabbe said. His eyes were low and insistent, meaning he wanted Ollie to use that terminology going forward.

"The fucking parasites," Ollie corrected him, glaring. "I want them gone." He sniffed, not realizing he was on the verge of tears. He wasn't given to crying, but the situation was insane.

"I know this is hard for you, but—"

"The thing fucking raped me," Ollie hissed. He was crying now, really crying. He hadn't expected himself to say that out loud, but he did. His entire body was shaking. He also didn't expect one of the heavies near the foot of the bed to chuckle. The entire room looked at the man, including Doctor Crabbe, and he left without saying a word. But nobody ever apologized on his behalf.

"It did," Ollie said, quiet now, almost so nobody could hear him. "That's what happened. That's what this is." The nurse beside the ultrasound machine coughed, placed the handheld device back in its cradle without cleaning it, and left the room as well. Doctor Crabbe watched her go with a look of dissatisfaction on his face that he eventually turned on Ollie. He tried to put a reassuring hand on Ollie's shoulder, but Ollie shuddered and slapped him away.

The doctor looked at his hand briefly and then returned it to his side.

"What happened to you is regrettable, unforgivable even," the doctor said. "But — and I don't say this lightly — you cannot take revenge on your ... on what did this to you ... by killing its children. That's terribly unfair, don't you think?" Ollie opened his mouth to say something, but didn't know how to respond.

"Let me show you something," Doctor Crabbe said, taking the greasy ultrasound handheld out of its cradle. The unclean thing had garnered a lump of grime and fuzz on its head that Ollie could feel scraping against his skin. The doctor pointed to a pulsing white speck on the screen. "That, right there? That's a heartbeat," Doctor Crabbe said.

"Okay," Ollie said, turning his head away. The doctor nodded to one of the heavies, who pushed Ollie's face back toward the screen. Ollie's eyes burned with humiliation.

"This here is the second heartbeat," the doctor said. Then his finger traveled from place to place. "Right here is a surprisingly developed skull, for this period of gestation, and here and here you can see the eyes. More interestingly, you can see the density of the brain tissue here and here. Do you understand what that might mean?" Doctor Crabbe gave Ollie a serious look, but Ollie just turned his head, trying to push his face into his pillow. He couldn't turn his torso without feeling like his guts were about to burst.

"It means these creatures, these *babies,* could be as sapient as you or I," the doctor said. "They are capable of thought."

"You don't know that," Ollie whispered.

"Of experiencing and *understanding* pain," Doctor Crabbe continued.

"You don't know that," Ollie said louder this time.

"Of feeling, and dreaming, just like you," the doctor finished.

"You *don't know that!*" Ollie shouted. He sat up to get as close to the doctor's face as he could, but the sudden movement kicked the spasms into high gear. Pain flooded his body, straightening and then arching his spine, forcing him to bury the top of his head in his pillow. Doctor Crabbe looked down on him pitiably.

"I understand your pain," he said. "And the emotional trauma this is causing you, but we will not allow you to hurt these … little miracles you are carrying." The orderlies rushed to straighten Ollie out, one of them somehow managing to jam a tongue depressor between his teeth. He felt it splinter. "We've had discussions with some officials who oversee this sort of thing, and they're of the mind that Roe v. Wade doesn't apply in your situation in any case, because you're not a woman."

The tongue depressor snapped and Ollie felt splinters rolling between his teeth and into the spaces between his gums and tongue. The tongue itself was mostly out of the way save for a part that had gotten caught between his left incisor and the tongue depressor. Bloody spit filled his mouth, choking him.

"Simply put, you have no right to terminate these babies just because they're inside you, son," Doctor Crabbe said. "The good news is — even though we don't technically have to — we *are* going to provide free treatment to you for the duration of this gestation. In return we'll oversee your daily life to ensure you're doing what's best for the children. You can't be drinking, smoking, anything like that."

Ollie would have told him to go fuck himself, but

the ongoing seizure and the tongue depressor made that entirely too difficult. He tried, instead, to hate the doctor to death with his stare alone. It accomplished nothing.

"Let me know when this passes, and we'll get him cleaned up, dressed, and on his way home," Doctor Crabbe said to the closest orderly, whom he slapped on the back before taking one last look at the ultrasound readout and leaving. By the time the door was closed behind him, Ollie was unconscious.

Ollie was leaning against a wall at the law firm where he worked — sweating, crying, and cleaning a puddle of his own yellowed vomit — when he was fired.

The bosses had known something was wrong with him for a while. Allie had covered for him when she could, but cheap excuses quite literally weren't worth much. It had been a few months since the attack in the alley and the horrifying stay in the hospital. He'd been back *there* a few times, even though it wasn't a place he could find on his own, much less visit. He'd been spirited away into an unmarked ambulance at University Hospital right in front of Allie and then dropped off back at their apartment a week later. She still sort of thought the wound had something to do with a knife attack. He didn't have the heart to tell her what had really happened.

In all honesty, he didn't know how she'd look at him when, *if*, he ever told her. The thought of that scared him the most. That she'd think of him as damaged — or used up somehow — if he told her the worst of it. That for a second toward the end, he'd actually liked it for some reason. That he'd surrendered to it.

If he told her that, she wouldn't love him anymore. And if she didn't love him, then nobody on earth did. Especially not himself.

So the firing, while not terribly unexpected, was still a kick in the gut.

"You've gotta go," Guillermo, the head janitor of a staff of three, told him. Ollie looked from the pile of mess on the floor and then to Guillermo.

"You clean it then," he said, tossing the mop at Guillermo. He tried to take a step and almost fell to the floor. The familiar pain of the things flared up, nearly dropping him to his knees and sending a wave of nausea through his body. Guillermo caught him and the mop, one in each arm, and deposited both against the wall.

"The fuck is wrong with you, man?" Guillermo asked. He was middle-aged, his eyes and uniform the same shade of brown. "You were a good worker and then, what, you start doing drugs or something? You drinking? Falling around all over the office, pale as a ghost. The fuck, man?"

"I'm not some fucking junkie," Ollie said, feeling sweat breaking out on his face. "I'm sick, is all." He almost gestured to the massive lump on his torso. The things had swollen him up like an honest-to-god pregnant woman while stripping away whatever muscle and fat they could take — it seemed — without killing him. His baggy janitor's uniform made it look like he'd grown an ugly beer belly.

"Sick," Guillermo repeated. "Dying. You're fucking dying. Look at you." Ollie didn't have to see a mirror to know what Guillermo meant. He had no fat left on his skullish and sunken face, eyes bugged out and dark beneath stringy hair.

"So you fire me, huh?" Ollie said.

"It's policy, man," Guillermo said. "You're sick? Fine, but you're out of sick days. Used them up, and now you're coming to work and puking on shit. Slumping around. Barely getting anything done. What am I supposed to do, have everybody chip in on *your* work until you get better someday?"

"I will get better," Ollie said. "Soon."

"Soon," Guillermo said. "Well I need *that* mopped up soon." He pointed to the puddle of puke on the ground. "And I don't think your version of 'soon' is going to be any quicker than me just hiring a new guy, huh?"

"Guess not," Ollie said, turning to leave. Guillermo sighed.

"Hey, fuck, at least let me help you to the door," he said, grabbing Ollie under his arm. Ollie shrugged him off, nearly falling to the floor.

"Get the fuck off me," he whispered. He could hear Guillermo muttering to himself and the sounds of a mop being splashed around as he left through the front door.

Ollie waited at home for Allie, but she never showed. He fumbled around the apartment, not quite knowing what to do while he waited. He did the dishes, swept, and mopped, all the while looking at the door and straining his ears for the sounds of her feet on the stairs outside.

At around one in the morning, he fell asleep, worried now and sitting by the phone, waiting for it to ring. Waiting. Waiting. Waiting.

He floated in darkness, feeling for warmth with his face. Not the sterile, itching warmth of the buffeting solar winds, but the deep electric warmth of people. Of life and love and thought. The magnetic ripple of thought pervading the space between spaces, filling the static-laced voids with the spore of creation.

And he finds it, feels it, floats toward and toward and toward it. He travels at speeds beyond sense or understanding, feeling all the while that he is not moving at all. Then he is there, living in the lush warmth of extant thought and feeling. Empathy and antipathy drip from every hard surface around him. He twists his skin until he is one of them, the ones that live here in this place teeming with life. It has been so long he doesn't know how to conduct himself anymore. The light of these creatures is so bright he is blinded back to darkness.

But he finds one and lets it into himself, using its information to fill the appropriate spaces and then relishing in the feeling of creation. New life. Eggs whipping themselves together inside long dormant organs, now growing, now pulsing with their own thought and desire. They are only partial forms, however, and must be made whole. Must share incubation and DNA, must let another's empathy and antipathy shower them, mold them, soak them, fill them, create them.

She finds him in one of the places where breeding pairs are formed, a synthetic cavern riddled with chemical scents. The reeking odors of fermentation and distilled chemical spirits, of water-wet matter and organic cooling secretions, of mating hormones and fear hormones and the chemical markers of good mates and healthy mates and willing mates.

She finds him amongst all this and pursues, knowing he's the one the way anything that hunts meat knows the smell of blood and pursues it. She is fragile, of course. Stellar bodies are not made for the harsh gravitational wells of planets — despite their need for them to procreate — and so she is careful. He could kill her with a hard swipe of his crude internal skeleton. He could use his powerful, primitive muscles to push those hard calcium edges straight through her skin, spilling her insides and her children into the bacteria- and virus-laden atmosphere.

So she is careful. She follows at a distance, moving slowly, waiting until the appropriate moment to show him her glory. To have him bear witness to the knowledge of the stars. The raw information bathes his optical receptors, which understand but cannot piece together the code. His mind slips and slides and is almost entirely gone. She does not want to hurt him, but she must.

The mating tubule is thrust into his abdomen and, for a second, he almost breaks free of the mental fugue and tears her apart. His limbs flail, and she can feel the terrible bruising inside of her, the tearing of essential systems and the flush of important fluids from one place to another. She gives him peace, along with her eggs, a secretion to send his simple endorphin distributors into overdrive.

It works. He sleeps, and she finishes despite how wounded she is. The ground beneath her is about to rotate back into the light of the local star, but not soon enough for the radiation to warm the atmosphere sufficiently for her mate to survive. Her shape becomes like his shape and she makes a nest for him out of the cellulose panels beneath him.

Once this nest is finished, her own primitive instincts draw her away from him and she unfurls, allowing the planetary winds to whisk her up and up and, as she grows, the polar magnetic winds, and further from that, the steady and insistent winds of the local star, until she is loose and floating again in the black cocoon of eternity, tucked into the darkest space behind the planet's only moon.

She sleeps deeply and dreams of the enveloping warmth of mental energy on the planet, curling tightly over the terrible damage he's done to her and allowing it to heal as she rests.

⊣

Ollie kicked awake to the sounds of feet coming up the staircase, trembling badly and trying to shake away the dream, the nightmare he'd had about the creature from the stars. It faded quickly though — like any dream — and he took stock of himself. He was sitting on their couch, a ratty blanket tangled in his hands and tucked up underneath his chin. His mouth was dry and tasted like shit. The door opened.

Allie stepped through — her eyes betraying the deep misery of a terrible hangover — and looked at Ollie. She held the door open, staring at him with one foot still outside.

"Oh," was all she said.

"Where were you?" he asked. She sighed and shut the door, locking it and then placing a hand high on the wood. She let it slide down slowly, the rasp of her fingers the only lonely sound in the room.

"Out," she said, now looking at him. "I went drinking with co-workers last night."

"You know they fired me?" Ollie asked.

"Yeah, that's …" Allie sighed. "That's why I went out with them." He didn't know what to say, so he didn't say anything. Eventually, she spoke. "I had sex with Carl and, I, um." She put her fingers to her forehead. She broke into tears and Ollie could tell she was crying in spite of herself. "And I don't … *know* … if I care that you care."

"Jesus," Ollie said, standing up and folding the blanket. It was hard to do, given the massive lump on his side. He had to stand crooked to support the weight. "Why?"

"Because …" she took a deep breath, shrugged, and slapped her thighs. "Because I'm pissed at you. And myself. And you don't … fucking … touch me anymore, or look at me anymore, or let me touch you, or look at you, or talk to me and it's really … Ollie, it's really, really fucking hard for me to live like that." She laughed, sobbing all the while. "I know something happened to you that night, and I'm sorry for that, but it's killing you, and watching that happen is killing me." She shrugged and slumped back against the door, sliding down until her face was buried in her knees.

"Can you move?" Ollie asked. He'd slipped on his sneakers and a new, gigantic jacket he'd bought to keep the mound of parasitic flesh covered when he went out. Allie looked up at him with a curious expression on her face. Then she moved out of his way and he left, not bothering to slam the door behind him.

He walked to the alley where it had all happened, all but limping for the pain of carrying the things with him. He could feel them reacting to Allie's betrayal, and the feeling it gave him wasn't pain, but an almost hallucinatory level of vertigo. It might have dropped him to the ground, but his determination to get away from that apartment was the strongest thing he'd felt in months.

He wasn't even mad at Allie. He wanted to be, but feeling was an effort, and she suddenly wasn't worth that effort anymore. It probably wasn't all her fault, the way she felt at least. Fucking Carl was, for sure, something she did completely of her own volition, but he hadn't been the best to her since the attack. It was just that the feelings were his and he didn't want to share them. They'd feel too real then, and that's the last thing he wanted.

Then he was in the middle of the alley again, which made things more real than any simple admission might have. The cardboard was still in the same place, though the makeshift nest was gone. All the cardboard from that night — in fact — was gone. The spot there was probably just a routine dumping ground for the same sort of boxes. Still, he went over and laid on it, looking up at the sky.

He thought he might feel something. Feeling anything but pain had been impossible for months now. It was much the same right then, as he looked up at the pale thumbnail of moon resting in the blue sky. It was the sort of sky where the clouds are so white you don't notice the sky's gone pale until suddenly there's no blue left — the kind of sky that makes cold weather feel all the more crisp.

He laid there until he heard feet crunching over stray chunks of sidewalk salt nearby, and then — feeling embarrassed — stood and waddled back home.

Allie was gone. Oddly, the most upsetting thing was how little the absence felt like an absence, like she'd been gone all along and the earlier interaction was nothing more than a blip. Or an afterthought.

Only the bedroom held any sign of her passing, the typical post-hurricane feel of quickly emptied closets. A few of his things — and a few of hers — lay strewn on the floor. He wondered if the mess was supposed to be a slight, or if she was just too busy to pick everything up. A folded piece of paper lay on the bed, the gentle curves of Allie's writing indenting the paper in blue. He picked it up and walked through the apartment to the trashcan, slipping it through the side of the flip-top lid without ever opening the thing.

He returned to the bedroom and cleaned up what Allie had left. The numbness was almost deadening, so that his fingers felt soft and full of sand when he used them. The last article on the floor was a lone wire hanger, the kind with a cardboard tube along the lower crossbar, probably leftover from some long-forgotten trip to the cleaners. Ollie picked it up and went to the kitchen.

It took him a few minutes to find their meager tool kit, and a few seconds more to unfurl the neck of the hanger. The work was harder than he expected — his limbs were exhausted. He could barely even keep his eyes open, really. The thing made a satisfying pop when it came apart, having been under far more tension than he expected. A few more tweaks and the curves had become awkward bends in a mostly straight and double-barbed skewer. Turning it over in his hands, it reminded Ollie of the pronged metal sticks his aunt and uncle used to bring along on camping trips to roast marshmallows. This was more twisted, uglier, and skinnier, but the resemblance remained.

He undressed in the bathroom, taking off the big jacket, the two hoodies underneath that, the two shirts beneath those, and the undershirt that was the last layer in contact with his skin. He grimaced at the sight of himself the way he always did when he was faced with a mirror these days. The parasitic node was grotesquely swollen, lopsided, and bruised black near the entry wound. It faded to an ugly maroon red ring around its base. The wound itself was a puckered, hideous mess. An asshole set in the side of his stomach.

His belly button twisted up toward the right, pulled sideways and thinned some by the stretched skin. The stretching had left vicious, grey-red marks all across the massive welt. They looked like scores upon scores of lacerations made with a crude and ill-used knife and all somehow sticking to the same vertical patterning despite their chaotic placement. He pressed his fingers to the outside of the hole, wincing and bracing himself at the dizzying onslaught of pain.

He pressed harder, still using only his fingers, watching as a thin stream of clotted blood and yellowish slime beaded, fattened, and dripped into the sink. He was so sick from the hurt of it he had to lean his head against the mirror. Ollie watched as more beads of the stuff landed on the white ceramic, enough now to gather into a little pool that broke its own meniscus and slid quietly to the drain.

The smell of it was terrible — not just infection, but something else entirely. A smell wholly alien to his body, to the human organism even, that came across as a mix of ammonia and menthol. Below that lingered the smell of blood and the sticky-sweet scent of sickness. Terrible sickness. Terminal sickness. It had to come out. The things had to come out.

He'd tried before — falling, drinking — but nothing affected the things inside his gut. The drinking maybe, but by the eighth shot a gloved hand had landed on his shoulder and he'd been escorted out of the bar. There followed another trip to the hospital, this time in a blacked-out SUV where he couldn't see through the windows.

The men around him had those same terribly bored expressions, as though anything shy of bloody violence wasn't worth their time. They wore civilian clothing, but it all seemed like a uniform anyway, all the shirts tucked in and tight and collared. Every belt loop had a belt in it, and the jeans looked almost starched. He noticed that even their shoes weren't really shoes, but brown, soft-soled combat boots.

They all had tattoos as well, some more than others. One man had a hand coming out of his shirt to wrap around his throat, missing ink on the knuckles forming the shapes of moons and stars. The driver — the only man not wearing full sleeves — had a complicated geometrical pattern that covered his forearm. But all of them seemed to have at least one tattoo of a feather. Crossing a thumb, on the back of a hand, one of them had it on his neck and another on his face, so small it almost looked like a birthmark.

Then Ollie'd been taken out of the car and led to Doctor Crabbe's office, keeping his head down as the men all but dragged him. They never talked unless they had to, and they had little of interest to say. Right then, it was the man with the feather tattoo on his neck that said, "Sit here and wait."

He'd done what they'd said, shifting uncomfortably until he got the heavy, disgusting ball in his gut to settle in a way that it didn't rest on his permanently aching hips. Eventually, he was just lying across the hard plastic chairs, scooting his legs back and forth until the curve of the seat held his knees in a way that didn't make him want to cut his own legs off.

It had been at the exact moment when he got comfortable that Doctor Crabbe called for him, pointing to a similarly uncomfortable chair inside the office. There had been little in the way of small talk, just a lecture on the dangers of drinking alcohol while carrying a life around in your stomach. The doctor also shared the results of the last battery of tests with Ollie, continuing on even when Ollie protested that he didn't care to hear any of that and just wanted to go home.

"Everything is progressing like a normal pregnancy," Doctor Crabbe had said. "Save, of course, for the oddness of the situation, the children are developing nicely."

"Can you not use that word," Ollie had said, not looking at the papers Doctor Crabbe had dropped onto the table. Crabbe sighed.

"Your *gestation* should be at a close soon," the doctor had said. "But fetal health is paramount, especially in the last … well, *trimester* isn't the correct word, but you get the picture." Doctor Crabbe crossed his arms. "I know this isn't something you might like to hear, but you should be grateful for how short this is. I've overseen numerous pregnancies in my career and human babies are heavier and more demanding than

                    CARRIER

what you're carrying. Your hormone levels are normal, you don't have any risk of the myriad of complications that come with a typical pregnancy. My God, even the term is only five months compared to nine. You should really be thankful you're so lucky this is easy for you. A lot of women have it much harder."

"Can I leave?" Ollie had asked, and the doctor had let him go after a touch more lecturing and some unwelcome — possibly unnecessary — body inspections. But he had let him go, and the same group of silent, irritatingly boring men had dropped Ollie back at his apartment. Allie had been there then, though she wasn't here now. Now he was alone.

He took off his jeans and shoes and socks, stripping down to his underwear and sitting on the edge of the bathtub. He took the wire hanger and prodded at the weeping hole in his stomach. The pain was greater by far than he'd experienced just touching the region. He pressed harder and felt something give, unleashing a torrent of bloody yellow horror out of his belly and onto his legs and underwear. The smell was beyond belief.

He pressed harder and felt himself swoon, waking up in the bathtub a few seconds later. He'd slumped down into the basin, his legs collapsing against the wall by the faucet in a way that had cut off his circulation. For a long, panicked moment, he struggled to untangle them, being thwarted all the while by the odd shape of his belly, the slipperiness of the gore-slicked tub, and the fact that his legs wouldn't respond in the least. The thought of losing his legs over something so stupid caused a burst of panicky adrenaline that let him push himself onto the rim of the tub. He sat there, feeling his legs burning as the feeling returned and looking into the basin.

His shadow moved away from a pool of red-yellow horror that made him turn and vomit onto the bathroom floor. Bits of hard, crystalline black chunks — some worn soft on their edges — were being carried along in the stream of goo toward the drain. This stuff was coating his arms, his legs, and his back too, as well as most of his belly.

He held his breath and turned on the shower, not bothering to pull the curtain. If water got into the downstairs neighbor's apartment, then fuck them. He had worse things to worry about.

The water cut through the grime better than he thought it might, turning the basin into a bubbling soup. He managed to stand and clean himself without falling, though a terrible vertigo had set in. He was half afraid to collapse and brain himself to death in the shower, half eager to just have it all done with. He pulled off his stained and ruined underwear and threw them into a pile beside the sink.

Then he caught a glimpse of himself in the mirror. Despite the horrific amount of material he'd gotten out of his body, the lump hadn't shrunk. Maybe a bit, but not much, not that he could tell, at least, from looking. He could see himself now, all the more pitiful for his wet hair, ketchup and mustard stained legs, and the sad sight of his penis beneath the mass of bruised flesh. Beneath the parasites.

He gritted his teeth and knelt in the shower, finding the twisted and double-barbed coat hanger catching water near the head of the tub. He picked it up and put it into place over the hole in his stomach. He would be rid of them, he thought, holding the thing tight with both hands. He would be rid of them.

Ollie fell forward, letting all of his weight drive the twisted wire into the hole in his stomach. Pain became a growing white light, suffusing the sound of the water pouring and pooling around him. Dissolving his thoughts and letting them evaporate, to rise and rise and rise.

She shudders out of her healing sleep and flutters fully open in the shadow of the moon when she feels it. Death. The host. Death. Pain. The host. Pain. The children.

The empathic magnetism of the event is too great to bear and the frail matrices of her consciousness buckle beneath the strain, but hold. Then she is flying, dropping, accelerating in a mad dance through the rolling waves of the planet's magnetic field, curving herself to catch the bounding solar radiation falling like rain from the surface of the moon. She becomes thin, thin as a razor, before she strikes the atmosphere and so slips between the resisting air currents, letting them catch here and there to make small alterations in her flight path. Letting the winds carry her further still, whipping her across the surface of the planet toward the ugly miasma of pain and hurt that even now is beating at her fragile psyche.

Then she is inside the cloud of psychic pain and loss. It echoes out like a scream, a storm, and she is hurtling herself toward the heart of it, burning reserves of solar radiation to push herself further, risking the possibility of implosion or even combustion as she opens herself to the electromagnetic chaos over the ground. It pushes her faster, faster, faster.

Then she is inside the building. The place feels alive with the echoes of birth and death, of sickness and recovery, but the undercurrent and overcurrent of the place is pain. Rivers of agony. Eddies of torment. A thousand forms of suffering to which she has never been privy. She shapes herself like them and walks the corridors, leaning forward as though she is walking against a great gale.

Then she finds it, the center of the storm. He is there, the host, but he is empty now and mostly unconscious. Tubes feed his own blood in and out of him, along with noxious gases she knows keep him still. There are others, as well, large members of the species who ring the host and are now turning to look at her. They use the air to vibrate their thoughts at her, but she can feel only the presence of her children, born too soon, in the space behind the things.

She splits and lifts herself high, feeling the panic, the growing aerial vibrations as the creatures see her true self. Then she is giving them the light, the truth, overloading their primitive minds with the deepest knowledge of the universe. One comes close enough to touch her, his fingers brushing down the sleek inner edge of her body, and she must steel herself against the pain this causes her. But her only concern is her children, so she does not relent until the lot of them are mad and blind, thrashing on the ground.

She finds her children in a clear container, laid on sheets of woven fiber. Only one is alive. The other is dead, punctured through the heart and head, its tiny organs on display through ruptures in its frail skin.

She turns on the host, it is his fault. She can feel his intent through her children — the malice, the raw need to be rid of them. She turns to him and opens herself, seeing the gases haven't completely stolen his consciousness. She will blind him, she will tear away his sanity for what he's done to her. But she hesitates.

She can feel it, growing as he sees her. Not the great and terrible cloud of misery that was her dying and now dead child, but a small and sharp thing. Rage. Hate. A pure, distilled need for violence against her so powerful, the images of her in his mind replace her own thoughts. He is ripping into her. Tearing her. Ignoring her lights and the overwhelming power of her knowledge.

She staggers back and picks up the children, the living and the dead, and flees.

Ollie woke some hours later, gasping, skull pounding like he'd been slammed over the head with a hammer. Something was suffocating him. He pushed at it and found the flexible plastic of a hospital gas mask resting over his nose and chin. Then it was gone and he was breathing pure, cool air again. It tasted almost sweet, despite the ammonia and antiseptic hospital smell of the room.

He was naked, of course, save for a stained paper hospital gown. He touched the side of his body where the things had been, the parasites, and found it flat. There was nothing there now, save for some baggy flesh and a series of fat, black sutures. He lay back on the hospital bed and wept.

Eventually, he got out of bed and saw what had happened to the men that had brought him here. He'd only been partially conscious — maybe not even that — when they'd dragged him from the bloody pool in his bathtub. He'd had a full seven inches of the wire hanger buried inside his gut, suffering a pain so vicious he'd been laughing and screaming like a lunatic.

He might have been doing that before they even got there, which would explain how they even got the call. Though why they'd come instead of the regular police was a mystery he might never find a solution to.

Neither those men nor Doctor Crabbe could ever tell him. The lot of them were laying spread out on the floor — either face down or on their backs — humming and chanting through chapped lips at the floor or ceiling. The eyes he could see were black, sunken, and cracked. Their faces were all red, like they had a bad sunburn, and most of them were missing eyebrows.

Naked and unsteady, Ollie wandered man to man, gathering their wallets, car keys, and anything else of value laying on the hospital bed. The bed itself was badly stained with blood and more of the nasty yellow stuff. Most of them had guns, which he didn't bother with. Altogether, their wallets had a combined $2,300 and change.

He stripped Crabbe to his underwear. The doctor was the only man in the room small enough that his clothes could fit Ollie. The other men were giants. The doctor never stopped gibbering as Ollie undressed him. The sounds coming from his mouth were unlike anything Ollie had ever heard a human make.

When he was finished — looking almost like a silver-screen tramp in the doctor's oversized corduroy pants and jacket — he looked at the plastic baby bed placed in the center of the room. He remembered the thing coming back for them.

My children, her thoughts echoed. He had *felt* her, now and before, he knew. Those dreams had been more than simple nightmares.

He looked at the stains in the baby bed, all that remained of the things that had been inside him, and walked away without looking back.

Time passed, and things moved on. For a while he was back together with Allie, who now refused to be called anything but Allison. He stuck with Ollie, though she tried to call him Oliver. The times were okay, but every day felt like a bandage crusted over a mostly healed wound. He told her most all of what had happened sometime before the end, and then they went their separate ways.

The last thing she ever said to him was, "I wish you had told me about it."

He'd wanted to tell her, "It wasn't any of your business. It shouldn't have been anybody's but mine."

What he did say was, "Sorry," and they shook hands.

Years passed. And jobs. And girlfriends. Then one boyfriend. Then a long, lonely period where he worked in the hours between sundown and sunrise, eating dinner when most people were rubbing the sleep from their eyes.

For better or worse, he'd decided that other people weren't worth it. He'd just slug out life on his own until there wasn't any more to go. The government could deal with whatever they found in his squat, one-bedroom apartment near campus when the time finally came. At least, that's how he felt.

It was in the bloody dawn sunlight — outside a diner in a busy part of downtown — when he saw them in the crowd. A woman and child, holding hands across five lanes of Main Street, standing by the bus stop that would take him home. They were hard to see amongst the people crowding around them. They could have been anybody on earth, though their hair was slightly too white to be blonde, and their eyes a touch too red to be brown.

It was the eyes of the woman that caught his attention, cutting through the fog of his life like a bit of cold water in an otherwise warm pond. They looked at each other for a long time, the little girl staring hard at him and then the crowds and then nothing at all, the way children do. The street cleared and the walk sign flicked to white and then the crowds were moving around him — toward that woman and her child.

He thought about crossing the street with everybody else, but instead turned his head, spat on the concrete, and left in another direction, content to find his own way home.

THE END

　　　CARRIER

Welcome to the End, Friend

The work of the world is the work of the world's workers, and I among them enjoyed the wonderful support of many fine people who together helped me make this work possible.

Thank you first off and more than most, to Sam, my wife and editor. The thin picket fence that keeps well-reined the most errant horses of my imagination while never blocking the beauty of the sky.

Thank you to Yui Breedlove, whose wonderful paintings have become the visual shorthand for both the podcast and this collection. Also, to her daughter Scarlet, born between the airing of the final episode of season four and the crafting of this collection. If she ever finds her way to these thank-yous, then happy birthday little one, and well met.

Thank you also to Jack Luna, of the Dark Topic Podcast, who helped me out a great deal when I had basically no listeners and was just starting out. I swear to God I'll make it to Manitoba someday, man.

And thanks, of course, to my supporters on Patreon and the hundreds of fans who've taken time out of their day to write me and share the podcast and otherwise show their support.

You all mean the world to me and I can't thank you enough.

In parting, a prayer and a warning:

Keep the sun on your face, Child of the Earth. And make sure your shadow stays lonely.

–August 2021, Louisville, Kentucky

READY FOR MORE?

CHECK OUT THE PODCAST THAT STARTED IT ALL:

The Westside Fairytales

WESTSIDEFAIRYTALES.COM

Tyler Bell lives in Louisville with his wife, Sam, their rabbits, Rosie, Marcel, and Warren G (Sweetcheeks), and their dog, Buck. Originally from Cincinnati, he served as an 0331 in the United States Marine Corps during Operation Iraqi Freedom and worked as a journalist at newspapers throughout the country, including West Virginia, before switching full-time to fiction. His podcast, The Westside Fairytales, boasts millions of listens from people all over the world.